You made me lo-ve you! wailed the gramophone as Tony circled the polished floor of the drawing room in Mike's arms. He had recklessly thrown the rugs and furniture to one side and with flushed cheeks and glowing eyes looked as if he were enjoying himself. Now, his chin resting on her curly head, he softly sang the words of the song:

You made me love you . . .
I didn't want to do it –
I didn't want to do-o it –

Her warm pliant body close to his brought him a sort of peaceful comfort. For a short time he was alone in a glass bowl with her, cut off from the others in the room, two fish swimming round and round indifferent to the noise outside the glass . . .

By the same author

Shadows on the Ice

ZENA MEYLER

Flower of the Forest

This edition published 1995 for
Parrallel Books
Units 13–17 Avonbridge Industrial Estate
Atlantic Road
Avonmouth, Bristol BS11 9QD
by Diamond Books
77–85 Fulham Palace Road
Hammersmith, London W6 8JB

Published by Diamond Books 1993
First published by Grafton 1988

ISBN 0 261 66700 9

Printed in Great Britain

The author would like to thank the following for permission
to quote from the sources indicated:
Barrie Pitt for *1918 – The Last Act;* Hutchinson Publishing
Group Ltd for *Lady Cynthia Asquith – Diaries 1915–18*
G. T Sassoon for *The Troops* by Siegfried Sassoon

For David Hamersley
May his generation never know war

Part One

It is doubtful whether many were deceived:
only the young, the prisoners of hope.

Barrie Pitt: 1918 – The Last Act

CHAPTER ONE

The Pagets

It was amazing how fond she had become of the place. Polly Paget, after only two terms at Girton College, could look out of the window of her sitting-room and feel real regret at what she was about to do. It wasn't as if the buildings were beautiful, as most of the men's colleges in Cambridge were. Some people thought Girton's bright red brick, its masses of chimneys, its Gothic arches and turret staircases hideous. And it was still too like a girl's school with its petty rules, or so its inhabitants thought. With chaperons and locked doors, Girton guarded its young ladies as zealously as if they were still in the Victorian age – and this at a time when girls were in possession of more freedom than ever before.

That was why Polly had decided to go down for the duration. She couldn't stand being kept out of the hurly-burly of real life – the war – any longer. Her subject, medieval history, was as remote from the battles on the western front as it could possibly be and she no longer had the heart to pursue it.

She glanced at the little clock on the mantelpiece: nearly three o'clock and time for her interview with Miss Conway. With a sinking feeling in the pit of her stomach, she ran down the stairs to her tutor's rooms and tapped on the door.

'Come in!' Miss Conway looked up, her cold grey eyes searching her pupil's face. 'Now, Miss Paget, what did you want to see me about? This is the last day of term and I have a great deal to do.' She was smoking a black Russian cigarette as usual. In its amber holder it was only half smoked and she laid it carefully across an ashtray as a signal to her pupil that the interview would not be a long one. A thin curl of grey smoke wafted delicately ceilingwards, filling the room with an exotic smell.

Polly swallowed and drew a long nervous breath. She was frightened of Margaret Conway, 'the cleverest woman of her generation' as someone had called her. She knew her to be cold-hearted, without imagination and something of a snob. She also had a short temper, a loud voice and liked to have her own way. Young women were often seen leaving her study in floods of tears. Fixing her large blue eyes on the cold grey ones opposite, Polly said boldly: 'I'd like to talk about my future.'

'My dear girl, isn't it a little premature? You haven't been up a year yet!'

'That's what I wish to discuss with you. I don't want to return at Michaelmas – not while the war is going on. If – if I do well in my exams and then go down to do war work, do you think the college would agree to my taking up the studentship again after the war?'

Her tutor frowned. 'It would be very unsatisfactory. We would have to award the studentship to someone else in your absence and there might not be a vacancy on your return – one could hardly take it away from someone to give it to you again. No, there's no question of holding it in abeyance for you. Go now and you lose it for good.'

There was silence while Polly chewed her underlip to hold back a rush of unwise words; she had a hot temper, too.

'I'll come down very heavily against the idea if Miss Jones consults me.'

'But Miss Jex-Blake will be the new Mistress at Michaelmas and she's already told me that Miss Burnham and Miss Roberts have asked permission to do this. She's not wholly averse to it, I believe.'

10

'They have rich fathers and are not dependent on the college for the fees,' Miss Conway pointed out tartly. 'How can you of all people afford to throw away your career in favour of war work? What has happened to you? Is the work proving too difficult?' She rustled some papers in front of her. 'Medieval history, I see. Well?'

'No, I can do the work. It just seems so irrelevant at the moment. The war has begun to take priority in my mind and now I feel strongly that I should be doing something to help.'

'You're just temporarily unsettled . . .' The tutor broke off to shout impatiently, 'Come in!' to a knock at the door.

A girl wearing a brown leather coat and khaki breeches with a saucy kepi on the back of her head came in like a whirlwind. 'Darling Miss Conway, it's me – Thelma Lacy!' She held out both hands to her former tutor. 'I'm back from Serbia for two weeks and bring you news of the Girton unit – oh, am I disturbing you?' she added belatedly and with an unrepentant smile. 'Getting a wigging, were you?' she asked Polly sympathetically.

A great change had come over Miss Conway's sharp-featured face. She lost her hard stare and began to smile. 'Miss Lacy! How delightful. How are things in Serbia?'

'Perfectly bloody,' Miss Lacy replied with cool frankness. 'The world seems to have forgotten us out there. Cholera is our worst enemy at the moment. Maud Gould died, you know.' She accepted a Russian cigarette, lit it and inhaled deeply. Then she spluttered: 'My God, what is this? Buffalo chips?'

Polly muffled her laughter in her handkerchief. Miss Lacy winked at her. 'Oh, my dear, do forgive me!' Miss Conway was contrite. It was evident that this former pupil was a favourite. 'I'm afraid my cigarettes are an acquired taste. Have a Players?'

Polly leaned forward. 'Are you with the Girton Unit in Serbia? Is there room for another helper?'

Miss Lacy had perched herself on a corner of Miss Conway's desk and was swinging her legs perkily. With the cigarette in the corner of her mouth, she said: 'I'm afraid both units are up to strength at the moment. Anyway, you're a bit young. Not twenty yet?'

Polly was dashed. 'But did you finish your three years here before you went down?'

'Not I! The war would have been over by that time. I hopped it last summer and I shan't come back until it's all over. I shall probably switch to medicine then. I thought I'd hate gore-and-guts but not a bit of it. So I've had a pow-wow with Miss Jix and she agrees that classics aren't my forte. Good old Miss Jix! I'm glad she's going to be Mistress soon.'

Polly shot a look at Miss Conway's face. What a stroke of luck that this girl had turned up! And as she listened to Thelma Lacy's account of their camp, of the recent outbreak of typhus and cholera that made their work so hazardous, she wondered what her tutor was thinking. Surely she couldn't refuse her after listening to this account?

Miss Conway was aware of Polly's eyes on her. 'Miss Paget is all ears, as you see. She is here to persuade the college authorities to grant her leave of absence after next term. As you probably know, we have already lost several people to the war. Our college secretary has left us for the duration to run the office of the Eastern General Hospital in Queen's Road. Every term there are more gaps and it's becoming very difficult to plan ahead.' She took up a paper knife and tapped it against her nails, a frown on her face. 'Very well, Miss Paget, so be it. I'll back your request. However, I don't promise they will renew your studentship when you return. I'll press for it, of course.'

'Oh, thank you!' Polly smiled delightedly. 'What a stroke of luck you turned up when you did!' she added to Thelma Lacy.

'Luck has nothing to do with it, my child. I'm in Cambridge to collect a new ambulance – you've probably contributed to it yourself. It's a beauty and I've got it outside. You're going? Best of luck in whatever job you find.'

Polly closed the door and stood in the hall smiling to herself. She felt as if she had just left her dentist without having had a tooth stopped. Filled with heady relief she ran out of the door and across the court to the gardens and the Honeysuckle Walk. Here at the bottom was a rustic summerhouse, empty for once, where she could sit and think in peace. However ugly the college was its grounds made up for it. It was only mid-March but the limes and chestnuts, the silver birches and laburnums were thick with buds and swaying in the brisk wind that came sweeping across the flat fenlands from the east. Well, she would have next term to see the gardens and glades in their full plumage, a memory to take away with her and to call her back some day. The wide East Anglian sky was a clear blue and pure white clouds scudded across it, blown by the strong breeze. Everywhere there were signs of growth, of new life pushing through the earth. At home in the North Riding the weather would be at least a month behind this and still wintry. She knew in her heart that she didn't want to leave it for good – but how could she stay when her own generation was so involved in this 'war to end all wars' as it was being called?

I must go to the war, she told herself and stood up. It wouldn't be decent to stay on in this ivory tower just because I'm a woman, when Dick has been killed and Archie so terribly wounded. I don't know how I'm going to tell the parents: Mother will be furious with me but

Father will probably say it's just as well. He's never believed in higher education for women.

Next day, in several buses and cabs, the college departed for the station. Polly travelled up to London with her best friend, Honor Thomson. Although their sets of rooms were across the corridor from each other's and they saw each other daily, they still had much to say and didn't stop talking for the whole fifty miles. The secret of their friendship was simply this: neither lent more than half an ear to the other and as both were bent on airing their own opinions and needed the other as a sounding-board, they were never tired of each other's company.

'I can't think why you don't travel straight up to Yorkshire,' Honor observed, pulling on her gloves and straightening her hat as the train ran into Liverpool Street station.

'It's a chance to see my sister. I've told you about her, haven't I? She lives with our uncle and aunt while her husband's out in France and she's having her first baby any time now. Besides, the food's so good it's worth a visit any time. Not that I like my aunt much but we're civil to each other.'

They parted at the taxi rank for Honor's people lived in North London and Polly's rich relations lived in Knightsbridge.

Number thirty-six Leander Gardens was a narrow, smart-looking house with a grey frontage, a black front door at the top of a flight of steps and a pair of tubs to match the window boxes containing spring flowers. In the gardens the chestnut trees were thick with buds and the plane trees were out in leaf, and on the corner leading out into Knightsbridge, an old man was turning a barrel organ to the tune of 'Keep the Home Fires Burning'.

The door opened at once to her knock and the reassuring figure of her uncle's butler filled the doorway. His pink face was creased in welcome.

'Well, Miss Polly, it is nice to see you again. Is this all the luggage?'

'Yes, I've left my box at the station. How is everyone, Robson?'

'In good health, miss, especially Mrs Kit. You do know Sir D'Oyly and your aunt are in Scotland? Miss Celia, too. Mrs Kit has been getting a little bored all on her own. She'll be glad to see you, Miss Polly.'

'Polly!' An ungainly figure appeared at the corner of the staircase: Mrs Kit Gromont, Alix Paget that was, was heavily pregnant and Polly squealed, 'Oh, take care, Alix!' as they ran towards each other. 'Heavens, I thought you were going to trip that time! Let me look at you: well, you can't get much bigger – or can you?'

'I've another seven weeks to go,' Alix said breathlessly. 'Awful, isn't it? I'm so glad Kit can't see me at the moment. I'm just an elephant. Oh, Robson, if lunch is ready, we'll eat at once. Just you and me, Polly,' she added over her shoulder as they went into the dining-room. 'The others are in Edinburgh with Uncle Dolly's brother – the Scottish judge.'

'I don't think Aunt Nora ought to have left you alone when you're so near your time. She is cool. I'm sure Mother didn't know or she'd have come down to look after you.'

'Would she? I'm not sure about Mother any more. She's changed since Dick was killed. It's as if she hasn't any feelings left over for the rest of us. Anyway, I've been suffocated with attention from the staff here – all the world loves a baby, you know.' Alix twinkled across the table at her younger sister, despite her bulk looking so like the Alix she had always known that Polly was comforted. They shared an affinity of looks but were not

15

alike in any striking way. Polly was small with dark auburn hair, and her large blue eyes gave the complete lie to her character. Melting and trusting, they were the eyes of a good little girl who would never argue or make a nuisance of herself. Her soft full mouth was shaped for saying pretty things in a low, ladylike manner. She looked biddable. In reality, she was intelligent and often at odds with the rest of her family.

Alix, two years older, had been the tomboy of the family. She had friendly grey eyes and a wide mouth and, like all the rector's children, was never at a loss for words. She had married Kit Gromont, her uncle's ward, last year and since then had lived in London with the Gromonts, Aunt Nora being her mother's sister.

Showing great tact, Robson served the sisters quickly and then left them to talk. After exchanging news of home, Polly asked about Kit. 'Is he to get leave soon?'

Alix's face became very still. She shook her head, looking at her plate. 'I get this nightmare . . . that he'll never see our baby.'

'Oh, Alix, that's just a passing depression, probably something to do with your condition. He's due for leave at Easter, you said in your last letter.'

'Dick never saw *his* son,' Alix said, stubbornly keeping to her point.

They were silent, both thinking of their elder brother killed at Ypres.

'Yes, but that was at the beginning of the war when the Germans were rushing through Belgium and it was up to the regular army to stop them. Kit's front has been very quiet – he told you so – '

'He says that simply to keep *me* quiet,' Alix retorted. 'Everyone says there's going to be a big push soon.'

'They said that last year. You mustn't think of the future in such gloomy terms. It's bad for the baby.'

16

'You're not in love,' Alix pointed out bleakly.

That was true and although, at that moment, Polly would have liked to deny it in order to win the argument, she couldn't. There hadn't been much time for love in her life so far and she wondered now if she would ever meet anyone she could love as Alix loved Kit: adoringly and without question.

'But you will be,' Alix confidently predicted. 'Only when you do, I hope it's someone much stronger than you are. You wouldn't be happy with someone who leant on you.'

'That's nonsense! I thoroughly dislike strong silent men with no brains and lots of prejudices. It just shows my family don't understand me at all.' Polly put down her fork with a replete sigh. How did Aunt Nora's cook conjure up such wonderful food in wartime? 'By the way, I've asked for leave of absence from Girton to do war work. Do you think Father will be very cross?'

'Hopping mad!' Alix shook her head. 'He'll never consent. You know he wants to get you off his hands so that he can finance Archie at Oxford?'

'But Archie's godfather, Mr Parsons, paid for Archie to go to Dartmouth. Won't he pay for him to go up to Oxford now that he's been wounded?'

Her twin, a midshipman on HMS *Cobra*, had lost an arm last year when his ship ran into a minefield. The navy as a career was now closed to him and he was planning to go into the church at his father's suggestion.

Alix shook her head. 'Hardly. Anyway, Father wouldn't dream of asking him, I'm sure. He considers that Gerald Parsons has done enough for Archie.'

'But with my studentship I can't be costing Father much – '

'There's still your allowance, train fares and clothes – '

'Clothes? I wear Cousin Celia's cast-offs most of the

17

time and since she's dark and tall and I'm small and redheaded, they look terrible on me. I do think it's unfair, Alix, that Father's only prepared to spend money on the boys. If I hadn't won that wretched studentship, I suppose I'd still be home helping Mother in the parish.'

'Why do you call it wretched? You ought to bless it!'

'Oh, I did but now it's turned into an albatross round my neck. If I don't go back next year, I'll have lost it probably.'

Robson came in and looked with satisfaction at Mrs Kit's plate: everything cleaned up for once. It had done her good to have her sister with her. 'I've taken the coffee up to the drawing-room, madam,' he murmured in Alix's ear. 'And Mrs Emerson says to remind you to take your rest afterwards.'

'They watch me like hawks,' Alix laughed as she allowed Polly to help her upstairs. 'Oh dear, I've eaten too much and now I'm uncomfortable!' She collapsed on to a chair and motioned Polly to pour the coffee.

'Do you ever see Imogen?'

'No. She never writes. I know she's at St Omer but that's all.'

'I suppose she doesn't have much time off when nursing. All the same, I think she should keep in touch with the parents, don't you?'

'Imogen was always a selfish little so-and-so,' Alix said with a shrug. 'Oh, I know you were devoted to her, darling, but honestly she was a blight. Always telling tales on us,' Alix added darkly, remembering certain incidents from nursery days. 'Father thought she was a little saint. They spoilt her.'

'Poor Father! Imogen was his favourite child, I suspect. Dick was Mother's and the rest of us were also-rans. That's the worst of a large family. Think of the bliss of being an only child!'

'Think of the shock when Mother produced you *and* Archie at one go! That must have spelt the death knell for our finances. No wonder Father couldn't send any of us to school and we just had Miss Emery all our lives.'

'I did get a year and a half at Whitby school or I wouldn't have got to Girton.'

'Which brings me back to the question: why throw it away?'

'I don't want to throw it away. I want them to agree to renew the studentship when I return. I'm sure Miss Jex-Blake is sympathetic and she's going to be Mistress next year. By the way, what about poor old Archie having to be a parson? I'm sure his heart's not in it. I'm fond of my twin but even I can see his limitations. He's never been particularly religious, has he? I've promised to coach him in Latin this vacation and that always ends in tears – mine,' Polly said gloomily, putting down her coffee cup and stretching.

Alix heaved herself to her feet. 'Listening to you, Poll, one wonders why we're such fools as to have children at all! I'm going to lie down. What will you do?'

'Take a walk, I think.' She wagged a mischievous finger at Alix's concerned face. 'Don't worry. I promise I won't speak to strangers and I'll be careful how I cross roads!'

Polly was up early next morning to breakfast alone. While she ran upstairs to see her sister, Robson whistled for a cab.

'Goodbye, Alix. Next time I see you you'll be a parent,' she said, kissing her sister who was breakfasting in bed.

Alix squealed as her breakfast tray tipped dangerously. 'Goodbye, Polly darling. I envy you going home to the rectory,' she added as her sister whirled downstairs again. Without Kit to support her, gusts of homesickness sometimes shook her for that safe and solid home on the moors.

With a lowering of spirits, she pushed her half-eaten breakfast to one side and indulged in tears. Kit wanted her to stay in London because it was easier to see her on brief leaves. He also believed that the medical services would be better if anything went wrong with the baby. Wiping her eyes, she thought forlornly: Oh, Kit, if only you were here! I'm frightened.

The rector himself met Polly at Whitby. The keenest of north-east winds was blowing roughly over the sea, churning the waves into a dark grey tempest. A north-easter always made the rector testy although he was normally a mild-tempered man. And dearly though he loved his family, he considered them a feckless lot; even the tardiness of the York train must be Polly's fault.

'Where have you been, child? I've been waiting quite half an hour and you know I don't like to keep Pinky standing between the shafts so long. Is that your luggage? All of it? We can't possibly take all that in the dogcart.'

Polly looked eloquently at the fat pony who despite her thick winter coat had been covered by a plaid blanket and appeared to have gone to sleep. She herself was as cold and hungry as the rector but she took care to control her hasty tongue. 'Very well, Father, I'll get them to deliver it by the carrier tomorrow.' As she went to the parcel office, she reminded herself that this didn't seem to be a good time to tell her father of her intention to find a war job. Instead she climbed up beside him and told him about Alix and the journey home as if she had no other thoughts in her head.

They made their way slowly through the little town with its fresh smells of seaweed, tarry ropes and newly-landed fish and eventually reached the moors where the wind blew as if in the rigging of a ship. At each small hill Polly was required to jump down and walk beside her father while Pinky made heavy work of dawdling up them.

'I thought Archie would have come to meet me!' she shouted above the gale as they crested the last hill and the rector lit the lamps; the dusk had suddenly become darkness.

'I made him stick at his books,' the rector said, straightening. He adjusted the lamps. 'If he's ever to get up to the House he's going to have to work at his books. The fellow's got no idea how much work he must put in. I hope you'll spare time to coach him, Polly. His Latin's pretty rusty. I have a busy week ahead of me with Easter and two funerals and so on.'

'But, Father, you know how Archie hates me to teach him! It always ends in a fight. Would you have liked it if your twin had coached you?'

The rector twisted his grey knitted scarf into a fresh knot. 'That's an irrelevant question. I've never had a twin as you must surely know.'

Polly subsided with a little groan. She ought to have remembered how literal her father was. She clambered back into the dogcart and held on to her hat, for the full force of the wind seemed to be blowing them down the hill towards home. Through watering eyes she looked at the familiar country spread before them; even in semi-darkness she knew every stick and stone of it. The rolling moor, its lines broken here and there by a tree twisted into a grotesque shape by the cruel wind. Huge primeval rocks clustered menacingly and the sound of a busy beck passing over them in a series of small waterfalls could be detected above the gale. The sweet smell of peat smoke tickled her nostrils and she knew she was nearly home. Bare and bleak and frightening though the landscape was, she loved it in her bones. Down at the bottom nestled Eskton, a little grey village where only one or two lights

21

from cottage windows still showed, and even as she spotted them they winked out. There was now a real fear of Zeppelins up here. Only last month, the L19 had been spotted floating east of Flamborough Head. It transpired that it had bombed and sunk the Grimsby trawler *King Stephen*, leaving its crew to perish in the icy sea. Then this month, Hull had been bombed. A week later, Danby High Moor had been bombed by mistake. So the canny moorland folk were taking no chances.

'How is Mother?' Polly asked. 'She rarely writes, you know.'

She heard her father sigh. 'I'm afraid she's no better in mind or body. No, she will never be the same again, I fear.'

'But is it an illness? Can't she be treated for it?'

'How can you treat a broken heart? The mainspring of her life has been broken. Dick was her darling from the hour of his birth.' His voice shook and Polly slipped a hand through his arm, squeezing it comfortingly. She wished she understood. Dick, her elder brother, had been spoiled and selfish, charming but arrogant. He had demanded and got the best out of life and had been killed at the age of twenty-four, leaving a wife and unborn child to be cared for by his parents. 'You loved him too, Dad, but you carry on.'

The rector smiled painfully. 'Only I know how falteringly! But I do have my faith to sustain me – to give me hope. Your mother has entirely lost hers. She never enters the church now and didn't even for Dick's memorial service last year.' Over his thin face with its quizzical look an expression of infinite sadness had descended: Nell had become a stranger and he could find no key to open up her heart to him again. It was as if she resented his very presence now; a great silence had opened up between

22

them. 'We mustn't bother her, Polly, if she wants to be left alone.'

'No,' Polly answered obediently but inwardly she was full of resentment. How could her mother behave as if Dick were her only child? She had four others all needing her in their different ways. Imogen had seen how the land lay and had taken care not to spend her precious leaves in Yorkshire any more, and who could blame her? Alix needed her with her first baby due soon; Archie needed her encouragement to help him face life with his one arm. Then there was herself. How wonderful if she could have gone to her mother tonight and talked to her frankly about leaving Girton for a time. But Nell Paget was no longer there to help her remaining children; there was only this empty shell dwelling in the past.

She's gone away from us all, Polly thought with a sigh. Grief doesn't bring people closer, it simply puts them in separate compartments to grapple alone with their despair. It's Father I'm sorry for.

The pony was slowing down and they were crossing the packhorse bridge that spanned the Esk at this point. A sharp turn to the left and they were passing the church and turning through a five-barred gate into the rectory.

'There's Archie!' Polly cried.

A tall young man in a Norfolk jacket was standing on the steps under the portico. He was twice the size of his twin and not in the least like her with his forceful nose, curly brown hair and freckles. His left sleeve was empty and neatly pinned up. As they came to a halt, he jumped down the steps and pulled open the dogcart door to help his sister down. They exchanged a hug.

'Hullo, pugface!'

'Archie, I do believe you've grown again!'

'My new arm hasn't sprouted yet – I can't think why!'

23

'Tch! Tch!' said the rector, shuddering at this black humour.

'Father, Katy and I had almost given you up for lost. What happened?'

'What do you mean, boy? We've made very good time considering.'

'We haven't even brought my luggage,' Polly hissed in Archie's ear. 'I thought we'd never get here. The *agony* in my cold feet! The blood hasn't got below my knees for an hour.'

'Run in, child. Your mother will be waiting for you,' her father urged.

But it was Katy, Dick's young widow, who came running out of the drawing-room to kiss and exclaim over her. 'Darling, you're frozen. Come in, I've built up a good fire with some logs the squire sent over.' Katy's beautiful face was alight with welcome. She had been part of no family until she married and now Dick's family meant more to her than if they were blood relations.

The fire was indeed roaring merrily and there were pots of yellow daffodils scattered about so that instead of looking dark and shabby the room presented a welcoming sight.

'Oh, it's good to be home!' Polly was surprised to hear herself say, stretching her hands to the blaze. Then her eyes met Katy's. 'I must go and see Mother.'

'She's in there as usual,' Katy said, indicating the closed door at the back of the room. 'She won't come out but I know she's looking forward to seeing you.'

Polly looked at the door despairingly. 'How can she go on month after month like this? It won't bring Dick back. She's punishing the rest of us for being alive,' she added resentfully.

Katy put a hand on her arm. 'How do we know what

her thoughts are? I don't think she can help it. It's some form of breakdown.'

Nell Paget was sitting in the little morning-room she had adopted as her own. She no longer even joined the family for meals. It was as if she were a lodger in her own house. She took no part in running it and seemed to live an entirely separate life. Before her son's death she had been a blooming middle-aged woman, busy from morning till night with her large family and work of the parish. Now she was a silent wraith for whom the doctor had no remedy. Yet he understood her better than most because he too had lost his son. The squire, Wilfred Filey, who had been up at Oxford with the rector and whose living this was, came in several times a week 'to cheer up poor Nell' but even he had had no success. He even smuggled in patent medicines. 'Try this, Nell m'girl. Guaranteed to get you on your feet again. Says so on the bottle. Can't have you indoors another summer.'

Sometimes she sat with the morning-room door open so that she could hear what was going on in the house, but that was only occasionally. She preferred being alone with her own thoughts.

Now she heard the bustle of Polly's arrival but didn't move, her hands mechanically knitting a jersey for her grandchild who was known as Little Dick. Sometimes this sent her back into the past when she was expecting her own first child and had sat for hours happily making his layette. Everything of the finest in smocking and knitting had been made for Dick and was now being worn by his son, who had been born in May 1915. Sometimes, Nell muddled up these two babies in her mind and those were the happiest times. She hated to be shaken out of these reveries and forced to face up to the unquiet present.

Now a small peevish frown formed between her eyes: why didn't they shut the front door? A draught like a hurricane was sweeping through the cracks and about her feet. No one seemed to care that she was such an invalid.

Laughter – inane female laughter, she thought savagely – broke out in a gust, then Archie's deep voice called out. Nell's lips tightened. Of course they had all forgotten her . . .

'Hullo, Mother.' The door from the drawing-room was opened timidly and Polly's face came round it. 'May I come in? What a journey! I thought I'd never get here. How are you, Mother darling?' She kissed her mother but Nell made no move to kiss her in return.

'I hope you've shut the front door?' she said anxiously. 'I could feel the draught in here. I'm not at all strong but no one remembers that. Well, Polly, you're in your usual rude health and spirits, I see, despite all your grumbles about the college food.'

Polly forced a laugh. 'Why is it always known as *rude* health – I've often wondered,' she added lamely as her mother gave her a withering look. 'I hate to mention this but I'm starving. There wasn't a scrap to eat on the train and everything in York station had been cleaned up. War shortages are beginning to bite – oh, I've made a joke!'

'Did you see Alix?'

'Yes, and she sends her love. She looks gigantic but wonderful, a sort of earth mother – '

'Oh, do stop talking such nonsense, Polly! Did Nora send any messages? She knows how ill I am but she never does anything about it.'

'Uncle Dolly and Aunt Nora were away. They've gone up to Scotland. Celia's gone, too.'

'Scotland!' There was a raw envy in Nell's voice. What a charmed life her sister Nora had! No son to get killed in the war and plenty of money for frequent holidays. It was quite five years since she and Arthur had gone away on holiday. Of course, there was Celia . . . One of her heavy sighs shook her. Strange that she had had five healthy children and Nora's Celia had been born backward. So beautiful to look at, too.

'Mother.'

Nell focused on her with difficulty. 'What is it?'

'I think I'll go up and wash. I smell of the train.'

'Tell Katy I'll have my meal in here.'

'Oh, Mother, do join us on my first night home!' Polly pleaded. Then she saw that she had said the wrong thing. Something like fear showed for a moment or two in Nell Paget's expression.

'Do as I ask and tell Katy to send me in a tray. Try not to be a nuisance, Polly, while you're home. We have quite a pleasant little routine now and I won't have you interfering and upsetting us all.'

Polly winced as if she'd been struck. 'No, I'll try,' she said quietly but she was furious. How could her mother greet her in this cruel fashion after two months? The only explanation was that she was worse – much worse. Did the others realize it?

Katy's eyes met hers as she left the room. 'You mustn't mind what she says, Polly darling. She's the same with all of us. It's your father I'm sorry for. You must remember it's a sort of illness. She'll get over it but it takes time, you know.'

'I don't know how you can stand it!'

Katy smiled, shrugging her shoulders. 'The home I have here makes up for everything. To be able to bring up my little boy in a place like this – well, it's worth a very great deal to me. Besides, your mother can't help it, I'm sure.'

They were mounting the stairs together when down below them the green baize door leading to the kitchen regions burst open and Mrs Linsey, the cook and sole remaining retainer, came hurrying out.

'There you are, Miss Polly! My word, don't you look

27

well! Make two of Mr Archie, you would. I don't know what they're feeding you on at that there college but something's making you quite portly. Your favourite pudding tonight, miss, Queen of Puddings. The last of my strawberry jam's gone into it but by the look of you, you'll do it justice.'

Polly said, 'Oh, thank you, Mrs Linsey. It's lovely to be home,' hurried up the stairs and collapsed on the top. '*Portly!* I ask you. I feel about forty and ten stone in weight! It's my cheeks: they're too pink and plump,' and she pinched herself disconsolately.

'I shouldn't worry, love. You look very pretty and nice. Mrs Linsey's a holy terror for blunt speaking. She told me the other day that Dicky was very plain, not at all like a Paget and who did he resemble on *my* side of the family! She also thinks he's got consumption as his red cheeks remind her of her niece Elsie, the one that died in a sanatorium.'

Polly gurgled with laughter. 'Whenever Archie and I aspired to something really grand and earth-shaking, trust old Linsey to prick our pretensions! Do you believe in all these nephews and nieces of hers? Strikes me she's got one to fit every situation. She brings out My Niece Beatie now and again to frighten me. Beatie liked the boys too well – she thinks I do! – and Beatie now has two illegitimate children by two soldiers. She's always telling me to "get a ring on your finger first, Miss Polly"!'

They had reached Polly's bedroom and Katy threw open the door with some pride. 'Spring-cleaned by me and Mrs Umpleby!'

'Goodness, how – er – antiseptic it smells.' Polly's tone wasn't enthusiastic. Every term Mrs Umpleby and Katy ruined her room while she was away; now she wouldn't be able to find a thing. She noticed at once that her large collection of books had been gloriously jumbled up in the spring-clean. It would take hours to get them right again.

Katy followed her eyes. 'I did those myself because I know how fussy you are – and, goodness, what a lot of them you possess! Don't you ever throw the shabby ones away?'

'No, I don't believe I do,' Polly admitted, saving this up for Archie. She was very fond of her ex-Gaiety Girl sister-in-law but until she had come to the rectory, Katy had had no more than a passing acquaintance with books. In her sturdy opinion you had to be ill or odd to own one.

'I'm afraid you're going to have to keep it clean yourself now,' she apologized. 'Mrs Umpleby only comes two mornings a week because she's got Ernie home recovering from a bad wound.'

'Poor old Ernie. Is he going to be all right? He was one of the bellringers before the war. I'll clean Father's room too if you like.'

'Oh, would you? That would be a real help.'

'I suppose Mother still does nothing? It's awful, Katy! D'you remember what she used to be like? A positive dynamo. It isn't as if she's physically ill!' Polly rumpled her hair and sat down on the bed. 'Just look at Father's face! He's *suffering* and she doesn't seem to care. He loved Dick too – and so did you.'

'Yes, but I'm young,' Katy pointed out. 'You usually get over things better when you're young.'

Polly looked at her curiously. 'Would you marry again, Katy?'

For a moment, Katy hesitated and colour ran into her face. 'No one could ever take Dick's place, Polly: I just adored him.' Her voice shook. Clearing her throat she added: 'But if someone offered who would be good for Dicky and – and whom I liked, well, I'd have to think very hard. At my age, I would likely be a widow for fifty years. It's a long time.'

'Yes,' Polly agreed. She fiddled with the fringe on her counterpane and then said casually: 'What does Uncle Wilfred say about Mother?'

'He thinks she'll mend in her own good time.'

'That sounds like him! He adored Dick, you know, as if he were his own son. He was his godfather and being an old bachelor with no children, he rather adopted us. He and Father have been like brothers for years and this is his living.'

'Yes, Dick told me. He's very good to Dicky, too; he wants to educate him when the time comes. Well, I'll go and hurry supper along. Don't be long, Polly.'

I wonder, Polly thought, looking at the closed door. She winced when I called the squire an 'old bachelor'. He's years older but she'd be safe for life with him. What's the alternative? Being at Mother's beck and call and running this huge house on her own?

Thinking of the squire's little nut-brown face and balding head, his skin weatherbeaten from the hours spent shooting or riding his horse, Polly shook her head: Katy would never look at him!

Their evening meal was plain but good: thick lentil soup, fresh fish from Whitby and the vaunted Queen of Puddings covered in hot jam and meringue. Afterwards, the rector went to his study to work on the Easter sermon, Katy went upstairs to look at her baby and the twins were left to themselves. They were supposed to be doing the washing-up, Mrs Linsey and her varicose veins having gone to bed. Instead they propped their elbows on the table and talked. Almost immediately Polly blurted out that she had asked for leave of absence from Girton.

Archie looked gloomy. 'The governor will be furious, you know. He's been banking on getting you off his hands

30

financially before embarking on the task of keeping me at Oxford for four years. He reckoned you'd be earning in two and a half years from now. This is going to be a blow. Trust you, Polly, to put a spanner in the works!'

'But it's only for the duration. If the war ends next year – '

'It won't.'

Polly looked at him, irritated. 'How can you possibly know?'

'Because I believe Kitchener. He's the only chap with his feet on the ground and he says it's going to last at least three and possibly four years.'

'Four years!' Polly was horrified. 'There'll be nobody left alive! No male under thirty anyway.'

'Perhaps we're all bent on destruction,' Archie said, playing with the spoons on the table, a little frown between his eyes. 'I'm worried, Polly. Father's keen on my entering the church but shouldn't one have "a call" or something? That's what happened to Father at Oxford. He went to a revivalist meeting and knew he must become a parson.'

'Then why not tell Father that? You could turn your hands to anything – '

'Hand,' Archie corrected gently. 'Mind you, I sometimes feel it's still there. Queer, isn't it? I always wanted to drive a motor and the squire promised he'd let Woodcock teach me some day. Now I never can. It's things like that that hit you unawares, as well as being out of the navy for good.'

Polly looked at his averted head, her heart burning to help him who was closest to her in life. 'Think how much worse if it had been a leg,' she said persuasively.

Archie's spirits revived as he turned on her sharply. 'Well, if you think that, you're a little ninny! You can hide a leg. A limp would be just the wounded hero touch

31

but a hand – an arm – why, it's like losing half your face! People avoid looking. I've noticed them. And if they succeed in making me wear that ghastly contraption they showed me down at Richmond – it ends in a pair of snapping claws like an angry lobster! – Little Dick will run a mile from me.' He laughed shakily and Polly could see that he was what she privately termed *emotional*. She didn't touch him for they had always been undemonstrative although devoted to each other, but the waves of silent sympathy coming from her seemed to comfort him.

He had never confided his worst fear: that girls would turn from him in horror when they knew he had nothing on his left, right up to a scooped-out shoulder. Archie had always rather fancied the most popular type of young woman: pretty, good at games and dancing, sought after. He had been known as 'a damned flirt' among his fellow midshipmen. Now he wondered miserably if he would have to marry a plain dull girl because no one else would look at him. Of course, a plain dull girl would make an excellent vicar's wife – but he'd be hanged if he would! He wanted somebody to set his heart racing again; he wanted to play the game on equal terms with his friends and snatch a prize from under their very noses – oh, hell! he thought savagely. His taste still ran to impish girls with saucy faces who dared him to kiss them. There had been his captain's younger daughter for one – he sighed and then grinned, trying to shake off his depression.

'We were talking about *me*,' Polly reminded him. 'When am I to tackle Father?'

'Well, my advice is: don't say a word about it until the end of the vacation. Just spring it on him before you go back and that will give him time to digest it – and get over his first burst of anger!' Archie added. 'You know Dad: he'll send you one of his long letters and you'll reply and so on and so on.'

32

'I'd rather have it out with him at once.'

Archie rose and began to pile the plates. 'Oh, yes, madam, I daresay you would! The house would be ringing with your voice and Father's locked in battle for *four weeks*! Have a heart, Poll!'

CHAPTER TWO

The Ransoms

Elaine Ransom finished writing a letter to her husband, signed it and sat back in her chair. Her desk was placed before one of the three windows in the parlour, as the living-room was called up here on this Vermont farm. It was March but, because they had come up to the farm much earlier this year, the double windows were still in position, as were the heavy curtains of scarlet serge.

There was a frosty film on the glass panes but she could still see across the yard to the meadow and the brook running along the bottom where it was marshy. A thin spiral of smoke above a grove of bare-branched trees told her that the children had made a bonfire to roast their potatoes. Dan had asked her a little uncertainly before setting out: 'Do Indians eat roasted potatoes, Mother?' He was wearing the Indian chief's head-dress that had been in his Christmas stocking and was still wheezing from the whooping cough that had dogged them all winter. It was the main reason they had come up so early to the farm this year: Nanny had predicted that the thin mountain air would soon clear their coughs.

Snow still lay on the ground and there was a hard frost each night but already the children were much healthier. Dan had started to eat again and was losing the white, pinched look that had alarmed them so much. Today there was brilliant sunshine and the snow-capped hills – so clear and blue in warmer weather – sparkled against the sky.

Watching the spiral of smoke, Elaine smiled to herself. If Nanny would only allow them, the children could get healthily grubby again and would come home to their midday dinner with sharper appetites than they had had for weeks. Elaine wanted her children to grow up hardy and independent: Nanny deplored independence and quashed it ruthlessly as soon as it appeared. She would now be sitting stubbornly in the doorway of the toy log cabin, their outdoor playroom the size of a summerhouse, knitting mechanically, her eyes never leaving the children, issuing sharp injunctions: 'Laurie! Stop teasing your little brother,' or 'Be careful, Dan! Remember what Nanny told you – there, look! You've got mud on your coat!'

At nine years of age, Dan was too small and delicate and Nanny coddled him tenderly. Her attitude to sturdy six-year-old Laurie was entirely different: Laurie, as often as not, was to be found serving time in a corner of the nursery for misdemeanours that came under the heading of 'pertness'.

Elaine shook her head silently. Something was going to have to be done about Nanny in a year or so. Reggie said so very adamantly. 'She's ruining the boy, Elaine. He's too girlish by half.'

She rose, stretching her arms wide. She had been sitting too long and was now feeling uncomfortably stiff. Oh, God, was this the beginning of the ageing process? She hurried across to a mirror over a pine chest and scrutinized her face anxiously, trying the effect of a smile, of holding her chin at an angle. A small sigh escaped her. No use pretending; she was getting older by the month now, and by this she meant that it was showing. Was that another wrinkle by the corner of her left eye? It was no use pretending any longer: she was forty-six – no, forty-seven next month. She and Reggie had been married for twenty-two years . . . 1894. She had been twenty-five, divorced and with a child of three who was in her husband's custody because *she* had been the guilty party.

35

The child, her eldest of four, was a man of twenty-five now, her age when she married Reggie. How horrifying to have a son of twenty-five! It simply gave her age away to the world. And – hideous thought – Anna who had married Carl Wehner III in the autumn would no doubt be making her a grandmother before long. Reggie positively revelled in the idea but at sixty-six he was the right age for grandparenthood. She wasn't. She felt too young.

She stared again at her reflection. *Much* too young! The familiar gust of depression that often assailed her nowadays suddenly swooped down once again. She banged knotted fists against her eyes, fighting tears. It wasn't fair! Life went past one too fast; one grew old too quickly. Soon no man would turn his head to look covetously at her, and it was this power she knew she possessed that had made life sweet. Now it was slipping from her fast, never to return.

She drifted back to her chair, shivering inwardly.

Had she but known it her fears were groundless. She was still a beautiful woman with the skin, hair and sparkling eyes of one much younger. Clad in the youthful fashion of 1916 with its shorter skirts and lower necks, she looked ten years younger than her age. Her dark green dress of smooth facecloth had a high waist and full skirt. Her shapely legs were clad in heavy grey silk stockings and her narrow feet wore Louis-heeled shoes of grey with a double strap. The dress had a *fichu* collar of white georgette, that delicate silk crêpe that had originated in Paris and was worn everywhere now. Her dark brown hair showed a faint lightening round the temples: in a year it would have changed to grey, but not yet. She spent a great deal of money on face creams and never went out in the sun without a hat but despite these efforts she had nearly convinced herself that she was descending rapidly into old age. Soon – next week or next month – age would pounce on her and change her to an old crone overnight. Daily she prayed that that evil day be put off for just one more year . . .

When she got back to Boston she would order lots of clothes for the summer, she promised herself. Thank goodness Reggie was so rich! Every summer (until last year) they had sailed for Europe at the end of May for the London season; for Ascot, Cowes, for balls and charity concerts, for their own ball they gave each year from the house they rented. The Ransoms were seen and known everywhere. In August they would go up to Scotland to join friends for the grouse shooting, returning home to Boston at the end of September. No longer did the cloud of that ugly divorce case hang over Elaine's head: the smart London set were more tolerant and less stiff than their parents had been. Reggie's money – old American money – counted for a great deal and they were accepted everywhere, even in the Royal Enclosure where, because they were Americans and had been close friends of King Edward, the Lord Chamberlain had to pretend not to know anything about the divorce.

1914 had been the gayest season for years, a veritable swansong to their way of life had they guessed it at the time. This European war was really too bad! All the Germans they had known – even the Kaiser at Cowes – had been so charming, too. Of course as an English-woman she felt for her country deeply. Nevertheless she was as isolationist as most Americans and more so than many. The war in Europe was not America's business and the sooner it ended the better. They could then resume their pleasant life again.

She longed for an end to the war because of David. She was so terribly afraid it might draw him in before it ended. She adored this elder son because she had so nearly lost him for good after the divorce. Besides, he was handsome and charming, a young man to be proud of and if she uttered any prayers they were for him. He had left Harvard determined to enter the law and a few months ago he and his partner, Sam Murray, had put their plate up in Washington Street and appeared to be doing well. Now if he would only get married and put down roots of his own, she would feel more certain of him. Lately, he had been restless and unhappy as he read about the battles on the western front . . .

The parlour door opened suddenly and broke into her thoughts. Old Enoch, in the felt overshoes Carrie insisted on him wearing indoors, shuffled in bearing a large basket of sawn apple logs for the open fire. Seeing his employer at her desk, he grinned as he dumped the basket noisily. He still wore his greasy old cap on the back of his head and his face was red with cold. 'Mister David out there'm,' he announced, shifting his cap an inch back on his head. 'He come fast in that auto of his'n.'

She was startled: her thoughts had been so deeply involved with her elder son and now here was the old man mentioning him. It was nonsense of course; he was just imagining things. He did sometimes do this and was utterly unreliable because he was 'touched'. He was the housekeeper's brother: where Carrie went, Enoch had to go, too. The poor woman had been burdened with Enoch since their parents had died. 'Him out in the yard.' Enoch jerked a stubby thumb, his loose mouth stretched in a grin.

He means Dan of course, she told herself, smiling indulgently.

Enoch scratched his head under the cap, deeply puzzled. He knew how fond Mis' Ransom was of that young scallywag. Why, then, hadn't she jumped up and run to meet him like she usually did? Often he had seen her do just that, running like a gal, her arms out to envelop the

38

young giant. It had given him a warm and happy feeling to see them. 'Young Mister David,' he repeated hopefully.

Something in his voice brought Elaine to her feet. It couldn't be, could it? Oh, God, something had happened to Reggie! David had come up from Boston to break it to her! She brushed past Enoch and ran down the narrow passage leading to the light and roomy farm kitchen where they ate all their meals. A delicious smell of Carrie's stew and fresh hot biscuits filled the air. The bare pine table was laid for the meal and a couple of large saucepans simmered on the stove. But Carrie herself seemed to be out in the yard, her shrill voice came from that direction. A familiar deep voice was answering her. It *was* David's voice – his laugh! He must have started at dawn in his powerful Napier. But why? And why no telephone call?

Reggie's dead and I'm a widow! her wild mind informed her dramatically. With a vague idea of comporting herself with dignity and restraint, she composed her face before stepping out into the yard where the icy air hit her like cold sheet metal, taking her breath away and causing her eyes to water.

Her son, wearing his motoring goggles on his forehead, was standing beside the car; he wore a long racoon coat and a tweed cap. As he argued with Carrie he worked his arms about: although the Napier was a fast six-cylinder roadster it was not the best time of year for motoring long distances and he was pretty well frozen.

Carrie, her white apron blowing in the wind, was giving him a piece of her mind in her shrill voice. She was outraged at the prospect of 'stretching' her stew: she knew David's hearty appetite only too well.

'Now, Carrie, you know very well a crust will do!'

'A crust? You? Well, I guess I'll have to spread things a little by opening a can o' my beans – '

'David!'

He turned, pulling off his cap and goggles. 'Mother darling, how well you're looking!' As he bent his glowing face to kiss her, he added laughingly: 'Save me from Carrie! I've told her a slice of humble pie will do me very well for luncheon. What a termagant she is!'

Elaine anxiously searched his face. 'Dad's not ill?'

'Lord, no. Fit as a fiddle. I wouldn't let him telephone because I wanted to tell you myself.' He took her arm and steered her towards the house. 'Let's go in or you'll freeze in your thin shoes. Yes, beans will be fine, Carrie, with lots of bread to mop up the gravy. I'm allowed a slice of bread, aren't I?' and he looked with mock humility into Carrie's face.

'Oh, you!' She tapped him with the wooden spoon she had carried out with her and then hurried into the kitchen calling loudly for Enoch to fetch her a can of beans from store.

Her first panic subsiding, Elaine led the way into the parlour. He followed, shedding clothes as he went. She thought she could guess why he had come up unexpectedly from Boston. *I wanted to tell you myself*. He was going to be married! It must be Beth Evett; he and Beth were such good friends and Beth's parents were well known in Boston society. Not as old a family as the Ransoms, but old enough. It was time he was married – 'Oh, I'm so glad!' she interrupted her own thoughts impulsively. 'When is it to be?'

He threw the racoon coat on to a chair and turned to stare at her, straightening his tie automatically. 'When is what to be, Mother?'

'You're engaged, aren't you? Engaged to be married?'

Blank astonishment pulled his face into rigid lines. '*Engaged?* Why, it wouldn't be fair on any girl at a time like this!'

40

It was her turn to stare uncomprehendingly. 'What can you mean?'

'Have you forgotten the war in Europe, Mother? I'm an Englishman born and bred although I've taken the name of Ransom. I've been back there twice – no, three times since I left at the age of four and I own property in Yorkshire. What could be more English than that? The war is nearly two years old. You made me promise not to enlist until I had established myself.' He paused and looked at her; she had gone very pale.

'Your stepfather,' she said faintly, 'has gone to England for the Season all his life but that doesn't make him an Englishman, does it? He's as well known at Cowes as – as the late king but *that* doesn't make him an Englishman! If you think an accident of birth makes it imperative for you to die for England, you're mad! You're an American! You've lived here all your life!'

'No, Mother. We're British, you and I. Born and bred British. My roots – the roots of your family, the Norths, are in Yorkshire. And my father was Gilbert Argyle, an MP with *his* roots in Sussex. I'm a sham American and I've always been aware of it. I know you hoped the war would be over by the time I qualified but it isn't. There's no sign of it ending. I qualified last summer and I've set up a firm with Sam Murray; it'll be something to return to when the war is over.' His good-looking young face grew stern. 'If this bunch of isolationists who call themselves a government can't see their folly that's their look-out. I sail for home on Saturday – that's what I've come to tell you, Mother. I'm going back to England to join the British army.'

She was stunned. No words came to her aid and she covered her face with her hands. There was silence.

He moved towards her and put an arm round her: she was shuddering. In the distance he could hear the shrill voices of the children coming home for their midday meal. 'I had to do it. Don't you see? It would have been impossible to live with myself if I didn't do this thing. So I got everything fixed yesterday. There's a berth for me on the *Avonia*. She leaves Boston Saturday afternoon so I shall have to go back tonight. There's a lot to fix up. I've only come to say goodbye. Please, Mother, don't let's part bad friends. I'm a big boy now, remember? Old enough to make up my own mind and to act on it!' He smiled suddenly, his whole face lighting up. He was a handsome fellow and perhaps knew it; because he had a string of young women who all thought themselves in love with Davy Ransom.

His mother looked at him as if trying to imprint his face on her memory. *He was going away to war. She would probably never see him again.* The anguish of her thoughts must have showed in her white face and sad eyes because he hugged her suddenly. 'I knew you'd understand,' he muttered hastily.

Oh, he had all the charm and all the looks of that scamp, Johnny Saxon, his natural father. Yet the steely strain of obstinacy and self-confidence came from her own father Leo North. But the headstrong recklessness was Johnny's and she had never guessed that David had inherited it until now. She bit back the hot reproaches that nearly spilled from her lips and released herself from his grasp, saying with a light laugh: 'Well, what a surprise! But you're right: you're a man now and must make your own decisions. I dare say war appeals to you as a sort of adventure, doesn't it? You'll find the reality very different, I fear.'

He drew away, a frown knotting the muscles above his hazel eyes. 'I'm not a child, Mother! I do understand what this war's about. I've been thinking about taking this step since last fall. Now I can no longer delay taking action.

You see, it's not going to end this year – maybe not next year, either! I'm not going to continue sitting on my butt while my fellow countrymen die in their thousands. My God! I've never felt less of an American than now. It takes a business like this to show one where one's loyalties lie. That's why I'm going home.'

They ate with the children in the big warm kitchen with its crisp muslin curtains and shining copper pans. Some of David's earliest memories were centred on this room; he could feel in imagination every knot and whorl in the pine table and he looked round now with an intensity that was meant to imprint the scene on his mind for the rest of his life.

The only member of the household who didn't share the meal was old Enoch; he preferred to take his meals on his own tin plate in his own room over the stables. He fetched it at the door and carefully carried the hot food across the yard with Tug, his mongrel, at his heels.

Laurie, her hair pulled back in tight pigtails, sat between her mother and half-brother and fought for his attention. David was popular with his young step-family: no one had better schemes for fun than David and they pestered him to stay longer. 'You can't go back tonight – I won't let you,' Laurie said. She gave him a conspiratorial smile. 'We'll hide in my secret place – even Dan doesn't know where it is – '

'Do, then!' Dan's mouth was full and Nanny said mechanically, 'Swallow, first, Dan, then talk.'

Helping his little sister to more stew, David rallied her laughingly. Elaine hardly heard them. With a very still face, she half-heartedly ate some food and the other adults glanced at her and talked louder and with a gaiety they didn't really feel.

Afterwards David excused himself and went up to his

room to collect the few things he would need with him in England. The place was a record of the years he had spent in it: every spring vacation and other times too when he was swotting for his finals and needed a quiet spot. He loved every inch of the farm but it was here, in his old room, that he was happiest. It was pine-floored with rag rugs strewn at intervals and with a casement window opening on to an ancient pear tree. How often in childhood he had opened that window with guilty stealth to let in Sidney, the battle-scarred marmalade cat he was strictly forbidden to take to bed. Sidney had fleas, Nanny had emphasized, but David had slept snugly with Sidney for years and had never seen a flea.

Looking out at the bare tree, he smiled to himself: the dear old cat had been buried, full of years, under that tree five years ago. There were ghosts too of the family dogs haunting this room: Rufus, Mick, Sam, of indeterminate breed and large natures. Opening a leather case he began to throw in photograph albums, books, a college mascot, the pennant off their victorious boat and, rather shamefacedly, the little brown bear that had been his first Teddy and only comfort when he was three. It was called Lordy and had long ago lost an ear.

From a cupboard he took his shotgun; there would, he guessed, be plenty of rough shooting to be had at Northesk; the place must be swarming with rabbits if not with game. He would buy fishing rods at Hardy's when he got to London: that was where Reggie always went for his, he remembered. He believed there would be a lot of time to fill before he saw the front line. Northesk House, left to him by his maternal grandfather, was to be his base in England. He was looking forward to seeing the place again. He had come into it fully at twenty-one and as Leo North had left him plenty of money to keep the place up, he reckoned he would be able to pull the land and house back to its former standard before long. How lucky he was! he thought with mounting excitement. Whistling softly under his breath, he proceeded to dismantle the gun and pack it into its case.

He was giving the room a last look round when he heard his mother's step on the landing.

'David, I must talk to you.' She shut the door behind her, leaning against it. 'You can't possibly rush off to England at a moment's notice like this. The Elliots won't have had a chance to prepare the house for you. They've been living in the flat over the stables. Think how damp the place will be! It will need a thorough cleaning, probably some painting too and certainly everything will need airing. If you descend on them without warning –'

He interrupted her ruthlessly. 'No, I shan't be doing that, Mother. Dad cabled them yesterday on my behalf. They'll have about ten days to get the place shipshape.'

Elaine opened her mouth and then closed it again as she struggled with a feeling of bitter anger. How could Reggie have done this to her? Making plans for *her* son behind her back! Not giving her a chance of persuading the boy into some common sense! 'You and Dad have kept me in total ignorance of this plan and I'm very hurt.' Angry tears glazed her vision.

'Please don't be angry, Mother. Women can't be expected to understand how a man feels about war. It's a decision I must take alone. Dad understands that. That's why we didn't telephone you. And of course I wanted to come and tell you myself. Quite unexpectedly I heard of a berth on the *Avonia* and – oh, I don't know how these things happen so fast, but this just snowballed in twenty-four hours. I had to decide to take the berth, see Sam and talk him into holding the fort – a hundred-and-one things to be seen to, as you can guess.'

'It's such a big step and you've given me no time to consider it – '

'Mother! This is my decision and no one else's.' He was suddenly looking exasperated. Did she think he was a kid of sixteen? He put his hands on her upper arms and looked very eloquently into her hurt and angry eyes. 'Please help me to do this thing properly and with a minimum of drama.'

She choked angrily. 'And if you're killed, what then?'

'You'll still have Dan. Thank God he's too young for war.'

'You don't understand – you don't understand at all!' To her, his action was a quixotic gesture he would bitterly regret when it was too late. He was, she admitted to herself, far more precious to her than her Ransom children because she had lost his babyhood. Perhaps this time she was going to lose him forever.

'Sam will look after the firm while I'm away,' he told her again in an uneasy bid to turn the subject. 'He's a good fellow, old Sam, and I shall rely on him not to lose our best clients! After all, it's only for a year or two.'

A year or two! She felt a twinge at her heart. How could he leave them so gaily at a moment's notice! War was folly, war was madness, war broke women's hearts. She remembered suddenly how a woman friend had once said wistfully: 'We love our children far more than they love us.'

It was so true! Her life was bound to David's in every possible way, but his was not bound to hers. Already his excited thoughts were running ahead of him to wartime England. It was an adventure and he could hardly wait to get into uniform.

'Don't let's part bad friends, Mother.'

She shook her head, her throat aching. 'We could never do that, my dear boy. But – ' She took a deep breath.

46

'I'm not going to let you go to England alone. We might never see you again.'

He hugged her, laughing. 'Of course you will!' He was, she could see, supremely confident of his own invincibility. To her, he seemed suddenly very young, headstrong and thoughtless. Didn't he understand what that European war was like with its gas attacks, its thousands of pounds weight of shells falling on men in the trenches? She knew how many of her English friends were mourning their sons and husbands and lovers. For nearly two years she had been writing letters of sympathy, not knowing what to say, the words refusing to come from her pen. And now . . . David. 'If you go, we all go.'

He stared. '*Mother!* You can't uproot the family just like that! Besides, England's not a safe place with Zepp raids – '

'I know. We'll take our chance like everyone else.' Her spirits were rising like yeast. 'It will be good for Dan and Laurie to have a taste of English education. Dad's just given another ambulance: won't he just love delivering it in person! We have a house empty and waiting at Northesk and we can have it redecorated after we get . . . there.' Somehow she couldn't use the word *home* for Northesk House: she had hated it as a young woman and had never got on with her father. That's why he had left it all to David. But she had no intention of letting David see how she felt so she clapped her hands and said brightly, 'That's settled, then. Isn't it a splendid idea?' She left the room and almost immediately he heard the *ping* of the telephone as she put a call through to their home in Bay State Road. 'Is Mr Ransom in, Stanley? Get him, please.'

He sat down on his bed biting his lip. Oh, Lord! What

an impulsive person his mother was! How was his step-father going to take it? And then there was his half-sister Anna Wehner. He hadn't dared tell his mother about Anna.

CHAPTER THREE
Divided Loyalties

He had gone the day before to see Anna to say goodbye. She was nearly five years his junior and on her twentieth birthday last October had married Carl Wehner III, a rich young man who had recently become head of the family at his father's death but who still lived with his mother. There was the rub. The young couple shared the house on Beacon Hill with the older Mrs Wehner on a permanent basis. Carl had no intention of setting up another establishment: his relationship with his mother was too close for them to part.

The house enjoyed some of the best views in the city; not that anything of this could be seen from its windows, which were shrouded in heavy lace curtains. It was a white house, rich in gable ends and stucco, and always reminded David of an outsize wedding cake. Its more restrained brick neighbours looked like poor relations beside it and were meant to, for Carl II had built it in 1875 with the intention of annoying the other inhabitants on Beacon Hill who were reluctant to accept him or his family.

Now covered in snow it looked more like an iced cake than ever, David thought, running up the flight of stone steps and ringing the bell. The door opened immediately and Flanagan, the lantern-jawed Irish butler, appeared.

'Good afternoon, sir. I'm afraid Mrs Wehner is not at home to anyone this afternoon.'

Taking off his driving gloves, David said coolly: 'I'm not calling on the elder lady. Please inform my sister I am here.' He had encountered a welcome like this before and supposed that Carl's mother was trying to keep Anna's family out of her life.

For a moment the man hesitated but David looked at him levelly. 'And I'm in a hurry,' he added gently.

Reluctantly, Flanagan allowed him over the threshold. The strains of a gay Chopin mazurka came from the back drawing-room. Shrugging out of his coat, he said curtly: 'You needn't announce me. I know the way.' Running a hand over his hair, he left the man standing with his coat and walked across the white tiled floor of the vault-like hall to mahogany double doors. The drawing-room was seldom used except on At Home days and smelled as damp and cold as the hall. It led through to a small room that overlooked the garden and housed the grand piano Anna had brought with her when she married. His half-sister's back was towards him, her concentration on the music.

He paused, listening to the sounds she was making. He knew very little about music but knowledgeable music critics, who had heard her play at charity concerts before her marriage, had agreed that Anna Ransom had a formidable musical talent. They had confidently predicted a brilliant future for the girl should she choose to follow a career as a pianist. The Ransom family had been horrified; it was tantamount to going on the stage! Aunts, uncles and remote cousins had written gravely and at length to Reggie, begging him to think of the family name. Not one of them knew much about music but their message had been unanimous: get the girl married as soon as possible and stop this music nonsense.

Poor Anna, David thought. What had made her consent to marry such a dull dog as Carl Wehner and come to live in this depressing mausoleum? Poor little devil!

She had stopped playing and had let her hands drop. A long sigh escaped her.

'Hullo, Anna,' he said softly.

Her head jerked round and her full, rather sultry mouth parted in a smile of delight. She was a very pretty girl but quite unlike the other Ransoms with her lustrous dark eyes, pale skin and sensuous mouth. She was in fact the image of her French grandmother, Otile Ransom, Reggie's mother. It was from Otile that she inherited her melancholy temperament.

Rising, she ran forward and flung her arms round her brother. 'Oh, Davy, I'm glad to see you! If you only knew how bored I've been!'

He cocked an eyebrow. 'That music didn't sound bored.'

'If I didn't have my music, I'd go mad – stark staring mad! And Mother Wehner wouldn't like that, would she?' She flopped on to a sofa and tried to laugh: instead her eyes filled with tears.

Alarmed, he sat down beside her and examined her expression.

'Don't stare at me!' she said sharply.

'Sorry, ma'am. I was just looking for signs of madness.'

She flung a cushion at him. 'I know you think I'm exaggerating but you don't live here. If you did, you wouldn't stand it for half a day. Oh, Davy, what a fool I was! I ought not to have married Carl – it was the greatest mistake. I still don't feel married because – well – oh, don't look so disapproving! If you were married you would understand what I'm trying to say.'

'I don't need to be married to know what you mean, you little idiot!' He looked at her in amused exasperation; what an innocent she was! No wonder she was unhappy. 'Perhaps you haven't given your marriage a chance yet; after all, it's only five months old. I'm sure Carl is a very good fellow really. You've got this lovely house and some day you'll fill it with children.' *I sound like a do-gooding* old lady, he thought amusedly. But there was something so dangerous underlying Anna's sulky mood that he had to say something, however banal, to mitigate the situation.

'*Children!* I hope not. If I have a child I'll never be able to leave Carl – '

'Leave? Are you mad? You'd be ruined socially – the Wehners would see to that. And you know how you enjoy Boston social life, Anna.'

She looked at him scornfully. 'You're so conventional, Davy! I suppose it's your law training. I don't give a dime how I stand in the world. I want to live, to do something worthwhile with my life like the study of music. And it's not my house, it's Carl's mother's. Even our bedroom isn't furnished as I would like it. I go out calling with her some afternoons and – ' She stopped abruptly, her angry eyes suddenly fixing on a point beyond his left shoulder.

'So it is you, David. Welcome. Why was I not told I had a visitor,' a guttural voice said with feigned pleasure. 'Why did not Flanagan inform me, Anna? I was not asleep. Indeed, how could anyone sleep with the piano being played so loudly beneath me?'

David got to his feet and shook hands with the real mistress of the house who had glided so quietly into the room. He wondered if she had overheard Anna's outspoken remarks before announcing her presence. Anna was so indiscreet! It was as if she no longer cared about preserving her five-month-old marriage, he thought uneasily.

Carl's mother had been born Countess Margaret von Herssen and had come straight from Prussia to her marriage – an arranged affair with the much richer Wehners who had been settled in Massachusetts for nearly forty years. Although she spoke careful and perfect English, she still retained an accent. When her only son was with her, they lapsed naturally into the mother tongue and rudely excluded Anna who knew no German. A stout, well-built woman with a head rather too large for her height and with a small hooked nose, she possessed a devious nature kept hidden behind a permanent smile. She was not unlike the Kaiserin of Prussia to look at and she claimed kinship with her, referring airily to 'my Cousin Dona'.

'I've only looked in for ten minutes, Mrs Wehner. I came to tell my sister that I leave for England on Saturday.'

Anna leaped out of her chair and kissed him. 'Davy! You never breathed a word! You're going to join the British army? Oh, I knew you would – I knew it! I told Carl so. Oh, Davy darling, how brave you are – but of course you're an Englishman!'

Here we go, David told himself resignedly.

'Anna, must you be so excitable? You quite make my head ache.' Mrs Wehner's smile was even broader now.

'I'm not being excitable. I'm just telling my brother how proud of him I am. Thank goodness, someone in the Ransom family is prepared to go and fight those beastly Huns!'

Damn it all, she's being deliberately provocative, David told himself irritably. I'm blessed if I'll stay here to be torn apart by these two strong-minded females.

However, Mrs Wehner was too experienced to be provoked. She continued to smile, saying with honeyed sweetness: 'My dear David, it's a very worthy thing to be loyal to one's own country. You are English by birth, I know. But I fear you are too late. My Cousin Dona writes that the war will be over this spring. Her eldest son – the Crown Prince, you understand – is in command of the Fifth Army and he says – '

'Pooh! Little Willie!' Anna interjected scornfully.

' – he says that Germany will be the victor this summer

when they have driven England and France into the sea.'
She laughed. 'So you see, you are only going to get your
feet wet, David!' Bending towards the bell on the wall,
she gave it a tug. 'You will take tea?'

'Thank you, no. I'm going up to Vermont to see my
mother very early tomorrow morning and I have a great
deal to do before I go.'

'So? A hundred miles in your motor? You will be very
tired – but you are a strong young man and will come to
no real harm.'

'My Napier's the strong one. Of course the roads up to
the farm have improved a great deal now with everyone
motoring. It's a really pleasant run, Mrs Wehner. You
must try it.' He shook her hand. 'Goodbye. I've got a
strong feeling we shan't get our feet wet! Please say
goodbye to Carl for me, will you?'

In the hall Anna was tapping a foot impatiently. 'Isn't
she an old beast? Can you imagine what it's like being
shut up with her all day?'

'Why don't you and Carl have your own place?'

'That's what I say. But he won't: he says she'll be
lonely. Oh, I wish I hadn't married him!'

Alarmed, he steered her to the door. 'Ssh! She'll hear!'
But he felt deeply sorry for his half-sister and longed to
give her good advice, to help her in some way. 'You can't
go on like this. Talk to Carl again. Tell him how unhappy
it's making you to live in his mother's house. Did you
know that the Grants' house is for sale? They're going to
Washington. It's a charming place.'

Her eyes lit up. 'Oh, it is. I remember it from the days
I went there to their children's parties. I'll ask Carl again.
Dad would buy it for us, I know.' Impulsively, she hugged
him. 'Oh, Davy, you always do me good! I do wish you
weren't going away but I am proud of you, you know
that? Is – is Sam Murray going?'

'Sam? No, why should he? America's not at war. I'm relying on Sam to keep things going until I return.' He looked down at her with narrowed eyes. 'Why this interest in Samuel Hart Murray all of a sudden, eh? Now, Anna, you're not starting anything there, are you?'

'Really, David, how vulgar you are!' She had gone very cool suddenly and was raising her well-defined eyebrows at him. But he knew her of old. Giving her a little shake, he said warningly: 'Well, just watch yourself, Mrs Wehner! Sam's a good fellow, not the sort to get involved with a married woman.'

She looked at him broodingly. 'When you're locked up in jail you have to examine every means of escape,' she said cryptically, then laughed at the concern on his face. 'Don't worry, Davy, I'm not an idiot.'

'I'm not so sure of that.'

She kissed him briskly. 'I'll come down to the docks to see you off on Saturday, never fear. Give my love to Mother when you see her tomorrow.'

As he started the Napier's engine he glanced back: she was still standing at the open doorway, one hand raised. But even as he watched, Flanagan appeared and closed the door very firmly. The sound of the slam was indeed like that of the door of a secure jail, David thought as he let out the clutch.

So he had gone up to the farm to say goodbye; no one was more surprised than he to be returning with his mother beside him and her luggage strapped on the grid. It was freezing in the Napier but wrapped in furs, only the pink tip of her nose and a pair of bright eyes showing, Elaine was in her element. She was at her happiest when things were happening but David could only marvel at her spirits.

It was dark when they reached home and the house was

ablaze with lights. A rush of warmth came out as Stanley, the coloured butler, opened the door and beamed a welcome.

Reggie came hurrying out of his study, a glass of whisky in his hand, to scold. 'Elaine, you mad little fool! Let's hope you haven't given yourself pneumonia. David, what were you about to allow your mother to travel in an open motor in this weather?'

'Don't blame me, sir!' David grinned, shrugging off his racoon coat. 'I was only the chauffeur! You know what my mother's like when she gets her teeth into something she really wants to do.'

'Stop fussing, Reggie. It's a beautiful night for a drive and I enjoyed every minute of it.'

'Do you know, Dad, she did forty miles an hour all the way?'

'Who did? Your mother?'

'My Napier, of course! I shall be pretty sorry to leave her behind,' he added with boyish regret and his step-father realized with affectionate exasperation that he was still talking about his motor car. He put an arm round Elaine and led her into the study. 'I insist on a finger of whisky before your bath. Got to keep the cold out. How about you, David?'

'Please.' David sat down on the arm of a chair, watching them both with affectionate amusement. They made an attractive pair, both seeming much younger than they really were. Reggie Ransom was still tall and slim with abundant white hair and a good colour. As for Elaine, her son thought she looked like a girl in the soft light as she talked animatedly of the plans she had made for them to follow him to England.

'David!' She turned to appeal to him over some point, drawing him into the discussion. The young man came and sat on the floor by her feet, as they good-humouredly

56

argued, their faces brimming with amusement and now looking very much alike.

Now it was Reggie who watched them both silently, his eyes on the young man who had been like his own son for years. The boy was the apple of his mother's eye and here he was about to throw his life away for an ideal. It was what had sent the British to war: *fair play*, they called it, Reggie told himself glumly. Poor little Belgium had been kicked in the stomach by her bullying neighbour and so the British had gone to war. God knows, they weren't a warlike race but it looked as if they were determined to go through with it, come hell or high water. Reggie sighed under his trim moustache; the British saw war as a game to be played to certain rules. He doubted very much if the Germans saw it this way. The boy's gesture, and he had a certain sympathy with it, meant that Reggie's quiet well-organized life was disrupted beyond repair and Elaine's happiness shattered, too. Where would they all be next year?

'Don't look so glum, darling!' Elaine's quick eyes missed nothing. 'You know you're longing to see England again! The war can't last much longer, surely? Everyone says so. And if you were thirty years younger you'd be putting on a uniform too – '

'I'm an American citizen, my dear one! What I can't understand is that you left here a week ago a determined isolationist and return tonight breathing belligerence like a recruiting sergeant. You've got me spinning.'

Perhaps it was as well that at this moment Stanley came in and bent his great bulk over his mistress. 'Ma'am, it's our Miss Anna jus' telephoned. She wants she should come round – '

'Oh, no! I'm too tired to see anyone tonight. Tell her, Stanley, that I'm going to bed and will ring her – '

'She's on her way, ma'am.' Stanley's face creased in a

grin. 'Jus' no way of stoppin' our Miss Anna when she done get her teeth in sumfin',' he murmured warningly.

'Oh, how tiresome of her!' Elaine jumped up. 'I'm going for my bath.' She put her glass down, her face suddenly tired. She had a vague idea that Anna would be awkward when she heard that the family were leaving for Europe. She could have coped tomorrow; now, suddenly, she was feeling middle-aged.

'Come in, Anna darling!' she was calling fifteen minutes later through clouds of steam. 'That will do, Bridget, thank you. Put out my old black and white dress tonight as it's only family. I'm sorry I disrupted your holiday by coming home so unexpectedly.' For she never took Bridget up to the farm.

'That's all right, madam,' Bridget said in her soft Irish voice and collecting her mistress's discarded underwear disappeared through the door by which Mrs Carl Wehner III had entered. Anna looked magnificent: pent-up anger made her eyes more luminous and her deep bosom heaved with emotion. She wore a lovely scarlet dress, part of her trousseau, with a *fichu* neckline and long tight sleeves, her only jewellery being the large pearls given her by her father. Her mother stared at her, realizing for the first time that at twenty Anna was at the height of her beauty. What a fool Carl was not to make her happier!

'What brings you here in such a bustle, darling?' Elaine asked nervously. She had a shrewd idea what was causing her daughter to look like a Valkyrie.

Anna's underlip trembled suddenly. 'Mother, how could you? Stanley told me this evening when I telephoned that you were all going off to live in England – '

'Stanley's a gossiping old darkie!' Elaine said crossly.

'But of course he told me! He's known me all my life. He knew that I couldn't stand it! Mother, I'm coming

58

too!' She fell to her knees on the black-and-white tiles and beat her hands on the bath ledge. 'Mother, I must come too! I'll *die* if you leave me with these awful people – '

Elaine sat bolt upright, water streaming off her plump shoulders and bosom. '*What* people? Who are you talking about?'

Anna's dark eyes stared directly into hers. For a moment she said nothing. How could she explain that she had only agreed to marry Carl because he was so handsome? Tall and fair with cool grey eyes and the profile of a Greek god. Her family had wanted her to marry into this rich solid family (for like rich people the world over they were attracted to their own kind) and when at last she had met Carl, she had been ashamed to feel all her senses leaping. She had *wanted* him. Ought she to have felt like that? Bewildered and ignorant, she had hidden this fact from her mother and had agreed with pretended indifference that she would consider him. All last summer he had courted her with great correctness while she had trembled at his touch. But on their honeymoon, her eager delight in gaining this handsome boy as a lover had turned to frustration and chagrin on their first night. Carl was frigid. Despite his looks, here was no eager young lover but a disinterested, under-sexed man who knew he had a duty to perform, did it roughly and went to sleep. For the five months of their marriage it had been like that. And Anna was still not pregnant.

Pride and embarrassment had sealed her lips for months. But now something catastrophic had happened: her family were going away to live and she was being left to face an unhappy future on her own. 'The Wehners,' she muttered. 'Carl and his mother. They're not my family! You and dad and the children and Davy are my family and I can't – I *won't* stay behind!'

'Anna! Carl is your husband – how can you talk about him as if he were a stranger?'

'He is a stranger! I shall never know him! Not as a husband, not as a friend – he's – he's a stranger! We've been married five months and I've never yet seen him naked. He hates being touched – ' She broke off, examining her mother's white, tense face. 'I've shocked you. I'm sorry.'

'Not in the way you think,' Elaine said with difficulty. She felt suddenly sick. She had been here before, only it had been *her* cry of 'He doesn't like me to touch him!' to her mother. And what help had her mother, a rigid Victorian, been to her? She had said crisply that Elaine must do her duty and behave as her husband wished. If he didn't like being touched, then he must not be. Duty, duty, duty, her mother had intoned and Elaine had crept away, ashamed of the physical feelings she was not supposed to have. Until Johnny Saxon had come into her life.

'Pass me my towel, darling.' She stood up, wrapping herself in the bathsheet and allowing her daughter to help her out of the bath. Remaining outwardly composed, she tried to calm the girl who was now crying openly. 'Carl is obviously being very selfish and foolish. Dad will talk to him – stop wailing, Anna! Do you want Bridget to hear you? You can't come with us because it would destroy your marriage. Give Carl a chance. He may be very shy – some men are – '

'No, he's not shy!' Anna shouted angrily, throwing off her mother's hand. 'He just loves his mother more than he loves me!' She began to walk round the bathroom like a young lioness. 'Sometimes I look across the table at dinner and think: *Can I really be married to that indifferent stranger?* Yes, Mother, that's what he is – a stranger. He knows nothing about me and doesn't try to find out. Why

60

do we have to have his mother with us? Why can't she go and live somewhere else? It's Carl's house and she is still the mistress of it although old Mr Wehner has left her millions of dollars and she could well afford a place of her own. She gets more and more Prussian with every week that passes. D'you know she makes us pray for the Fatherland at morning prayers? I won't do it. To myself I say: *No, Frau Wehner, I'll die before I do it!* She and Carl talk to each other in German at every opportunity and that very successfully excludes me. Then he sings *Lieder* to her after dinner – oh, sometimes I feel like screaming!'

Elaine listened to this outburst with terror, her rapidly chilling body remaining undried under the towel. Blinking the damp tendrils of hair out of her eyes, she heard herself croaking pleadingly: 'No, no, Anna darling, you don't mean half of this! Poor Carl isn't really a stranger. I'm sure he loves you. You must realize that they have as strong ties with Germany as we have with England. Perhaps in Carl's eyes, because you're his wife, he considers you are German-American now. Perhaps you ought to learn German – '

'Never!' Anna shouted, whirling round the bathroom.

'Oh dear, what a headache you're giving me! Sit down, darling, and listen to me for a moment – '

'Those Wehners are not my family and never will be!'

'You mustn't say that, Anna. When your children are born – '

'Children? What children?' Anna gave a cold little laugh. 'We shall never have children because he doesn't – doesn't like doing it. There, I've told you. The whole marriage is a sham and a farce.'

Elaine sat down heavily on the edge of the bath and tried to think clearly. She was desperately tired and her head throbbed. All the wasted years she had spent as Gilbert Argyle's wife came back with a rush; she felt sick.

Surely this could not be happening to Anna, too? Not Anna who was made for passion and who with the right man would be a happy, fulfilled woman? And for it to burst on her just when she had heard about David's folly in joining the army. No, she couldn't take this on her shoulders as well! Anna was a woman now and must make her own decisions.

Tightening her expression, she looked sternly at her daughter. 'Stop this nonsense, Anna! No, not another word, please. You're making a mountain out of a molehill simply to create a scene and force me to take you with us to England. You've only been married five months and you haven't given the marriage a chance. You're a Wehner now whether you like it or not. Do remember that the States are not at war with Germany – and I pray never will be – and the Wehners are not alone in expressing the views they hold. You cannot really blame them when they have German blood – as your children will have when they start arriving, which I hope will not be long. You've too much time to think about yourself.'

If she had struck her daughter across the face, Anna would not have looked more devastated. Her huge eyes flared angrily and then died down; her face was now only sad and defeated. 'Very well, Mother, I won't mention it again – ever. I know now that you don't love me as you love Davy – no, I'm not being jealous, I'm simply stating a fact. It makes a difference, doesn't it? Goodbye.'

The door closed behind her. It had a very final sound.

CHAPTER FOUR

Farewell!

Elaine closed her eyes against blinding tears as she stumbled to her bedroom. Bridget had left her lace and chiffon peignoir on the bed and she slipped it over her still damp shoulders and sat down heavily on her dressing-table stool. She looked at her reflection and saw, without surprise, the face of a despairing stranger. If her daughter had been physically ill would she have turned from her, dismissed her so heartlessly? She knew she wouldn't have done. Anna had turned to her and she had refused to help. It wasn't as if she didn't know with every fibre of her being what the girl was suffering; she had gone down every step of that road during the brief years of her first marriage. How the black memories had come flooding back at Anna's cry of 'We shall never have children because he doesn't – doesn't like doing it!'

She and Reggie had pushed Anna in Carl Wehner's direction because it had seemed to hold such excellent prospects for her. So had *her* parents pushed her into marriage with Gilbert Argyle, the rising young MP and his party's bright hope. Her mother emphasized his charm, her father his 'soundness'. 'Gilbert is thoroughly sound,' Leo North opined.

Only after marriage did she fully understand Gilbert's reasons for marrying her: it was to stifle gossip. Strange things were already being said about him. His private life was unorthodox if rumour was to be believed. He nurtured hopes of getting into Lord Salisbury's government; he was politically ambitious and the beautiful daughter of a Yorkshire county family with Tory strings they would be willing to pull for a son-in-law was the perfect choice for him. He stifled all gossip by his marriage with Elaine North.

Three years later had come the scandal and the divorce case that was featured in all the papers.

It was Argyle who was forced to bring the case: the *affaire* between his wife and Johnny Saxon, Lord Southsea's youngest son, was known and talked about in society. 'You must *do* something,' his male friends urged him. It would have looked extremely odd if he hadn't; so he brought an action for divorce, claiming custody of 'his' son.

David had been born out of Elaine's desperate need and loneliness. Johnny Saxon, a man-about-town and permanent bachelor, had a string of conquests to his name. His progeny were said to be in many a noble nursery but bearing the name of the husband who had been cuckolded. He wasn't a bad man; his charm and good looks added to a happy-go-lucky nature proved too much for the women he wooed. Elaine and he had met at a Friday to Monday houseparty; before she knew where she was, the beautiful and lonely Mrs Argyle found herself in his bed. He had been astonished to find her a virgin. Their *affaire* lasted a year and a half; at the end of it, she bore his child whom Argyle, to save his face, called his own. He was thankful to be the purported father if only to still the growing rumours about his lifestyle that were threatening to ruin his political career. Homosexuality was an indictable offence in England although not in France where he kept his lover, one Luiz Mendoza, an indifferent painter.

But then Elaine talked of leaving him for good and taking the child whom he could not pretend was his. So because he must do something to save his name, he brought his action, claiming damages from Saxon, and the custody of the child.

Elaine had pleaded with him, then threatened. 'If you attempt to take David from me, I'll tell the world our marriage was never consummated. Johnny is prepared to testify that I was a virgin when I went to him. It's the truth and the rest will all come out.' For Johnny had explained to her what was wrong with the man she had married; he only cared for men and would never be able to touch her. She had been amazed because she had never heard of homosexuality – but what a weapon she had been given!

Keeping his cool nerve, Argyle had dismissed her assertions in court with a great show of horror and amazement. It was totally untrue!

The cheaper papers had pounced on Elaine's reputation with glee, shaken it and thrown it to the wolves. In court Argyle looked the very picture of a betrayed husband; pale, bewildered and sorrowing. For the two-week duration of the trial he lived, despite his calm front, on a knife's edge: were the jury going to believe him or Elaine?

It soon became known that Argyle had expected to be in the next cabinet. 'This foul accusation' was manufactured by a vindictive woman to destroy the reputation of a fine man, his counsel, a famous QC, had thundered. Back copies of *Hansard* were studied and it was found that, time and time again, Argyle had gone on record as inveighing against the weakened morals of his time. His probity could not be questioned.

So public opinion swung to and fro and filtered to the jury. Elaine lost her case and custody of her adored little son. The papers recorded with relish that the respondent had cried out and fainted on hearing the verdict, that the co-respondent, the Hon. John Saxon, had leapt to his feet and shaken his fist at Argyle. 'You damned hypocrite!' he had shouted. There had been something of a sensation in court. On no account, the judge had pronounced, must Mrs Argyle be allowed near her son again. She was a woman of vicious morals.

For once, Johnny Saxon had come up to scratch and offered marriage. He was fond of the poor little thing and her old beast of a father was being particularly nasty to her (her mother had died a year or two before). 'But we'll have to go to Australia,' he said gloomily. 'The governor will only finance me if we take the next boat.'

To his secret relief, Elaine refused him. Instead, she had gone to Boston to stay indefinitely with close friends who offered her sanctuary from wagging tongues. She didn't return to England until she had become Reggie Ransom's wife. His own first marriage had ended in divorce but, unlike England, in the States he was accepted everywhere still. For the first time in her life, she tasted happiness with a very rich man who delighted in giving her her heart's desire – even her lost child in the end.

They had heard that Argyle had resigned his seat in the House of Commons a year after the divorce. He now lived almost permanently with Luiz in Paris. David, in the care of a nurse and a housekeeper, continued to be brought up in his house in Sussex. It was just after his fourth birthday that a beautiful woman accompanied by two men had swooped on little David Argyle when he was out in the garden of his home and bundled him into a large motor where he was kissed and hugged until he was breathless. The woman said she was his mother and that they were going to Southampton to board a big liner. The man with the head of thick grey hair had laughed as if it was all huge fun and had puffed a cigar: ever afterwards the smell of Reggie's cigars and Elaine's flowery scent had spelled security to the boy in whose life affection had been sadly absent for three years. The second man said nothing: as Reggie's English solicitor he simply looked unhappy and scared. This was a mad scheme!

But it worked. Threatened with a new lawsuit, and this time Elaine had a very famous QC to represent *her*, Argyle put up no fight. The child's name was changed to Ransom by deed poll and the whole unhappy episode was soon forgotten by everyone.

Except by Elaine; she felt the scar on her heart ever afterwards and it bled occasionally, as it was bleeding now. She shivered under the chiffon peignoir. There was no child involved in the Wehner marriage but Anna was just as unhappy as her mother had been at the age of twenty. What a fool I was not to spot what it was that Carl lacked! she thought and wearily began to brush her hair. But I can't help her – I can't! I'm going to England, following David. He is terribly important to me . . . Her thoughts trailed off and she was aware of deep shame: Anna, her first child of the Ransom marriage, did not mean as much to her as the boy she had lost for three years. She had been *glad* to have Anna married and someone else's responsibility . . . Perhaps it's only a storm in a teacup and it'll soon blow over, she always was a temperamental child, she added to herself. But she knew she was being less than honest.

The weather had changed by Saturday and there was a relenting breath of spring in the air. The SS *Avonia* would sail under a cloudless sky at four-thirty that afternoon.

They drove to the docks in good time. Elaine felt sick. 'I do wish you weren't going, David,' she said for the third or fourth time. 'This is such a romantic gesture, rushing to the colours of a country to which you owe nothing – '

'Leave the boy alone, Elaine! He's old enough to make his own decisions.' Reggie frowned at her warningly.

'Please try and understand, Mother,' David begged. He squeezed her hand persuasively and she tried to smile.

'But I find it so difficult to understand! After all these years you ought to feel more of an American than an Englishman!'

'Just try and understand,' David repeated.

Her lips were aching and stiff but she managed another reluctant smile. Had she ever been able to resist him? she asked herself wistfully. 'I must try and remember that we shall all be following you shortly.'

'I wish you didn't think it necessary to uproot your-selves – '

'Uproot?' Reggie waved his cigar indignantly. 'Good God, boy, we aren't in carpet slippers yet! I'm giving the American Ambulance Service another couple of vehicles and this time I'll be able to see them in action – '

'What on earth do you mean, Reggie? You're not going across to France?' Elaine gripped his arm, her face alarmed.

Reggie puffed his cigar. 'Might do just that,' he drawled, his eyes glinting. 'I tell you what, boy, it'll do us good to be shaken up a bit. I was getting bored with being cooped up in the States. It's two years since we were over and there are a lot of people to look up.'

'Everyone says England's starving,' Elaine reminded him gloomily.

'Then maybe you and the children had better stay at home, my dear.'

'Reggie! Are you suggesting going alone to England?'

'Why not? I guess I ought to know the way by now!'

'Oh, you're impossible!' But he had restored her spirits, David saw gratefully, and he winked at his stepfather.

They found Anna, pale and composed, waiting for them with Carl. Anna looked very pretty in mistletoe green facecloth with a deep-brimmed velour hat hiding her dark hair. Carl, who was only twenty-three, looked middle-aged and stiff in his dark overcoat with an astrakhan collar, cream spats and a black Homburg hat. He made several heavy jokes about the Germans having won the war by the time the *Avonia* docked in Liverpool but the Ransoms had made a pact not to rise to them and smiled politely. Anna appeared not to hear and simply cut ruthlessly across him to talk to her half-brother.

Elaine watched them covertly. She was fairly sure that Carl was not homosexual but just cold-natured: he wore 'correctness' like an extra overcoat and clicked his heels when she spoke to him. His manner towards his wife was courteous but hardly warm. Could the man make a real joke? Make a fool of himself and laugh? Elaine doubted it and thinking of warm impulsive Anna crying out for passion and excitement she realized with a feeling of guilty dismay that she had been wrong to encourage such a union.

They went on board and inspected David's cabin. He was sharing it with a man called Munro who was something to do with the shipping line in Liverpool. He proved to be a jolly, round-faced man with a bowler hat on the back of his head. He snatched this off as he bowed over the ladies' hands.

'It's pretty crowded in here,' Reggie said. 'I think we'd better go to the saloon. Mr Munro, will you join us in a glass of champagne?'

'I'd be delighted, sir. It's not my tipple – you can't beat Irish whiskey, y'know! – but I'll certainly join you in a farewell glass.'

'Are you over here on business?' Reggie asked as they strolled along the companionway.

'You might call it that,' Mr Munro agreed. He winked. 'I've just overseen a shipment of guns aboard. Sort of government work.'

69

'Guns?' Reggie stopped. 'On a passenger liner?'

'Oh, m'dear sir, we've been doing it for a long time. Every little helps.'

'But if the enemy knew – ' Reggie was aghast. My God, and with David on board! I won't tell Elaine about this. Aloud, he said: 'Where's that champagne? We'll drink a toast to the travellers.'

Almost at the last minute Sam Murray, David's partner, dashed on board. He had been held up in court, he said.

Elaine glanced across at her daughter and saw that fresh colour had reddened her paleness, her eyes sparkled and she was suddenly animated.

Young Murray was a plain, fresh-faced young man with freckles. He was over six feet tall and had rowed for Harvard. Suddenly with his arrival, a new gaiety was in the air as he and David joked together and more bottles of champagne were opened.

'You see that you "mind the shop" while I'm over there,' David warned him, punching young Murray on the shoulder.

'My dear old fellow, have no fears! Remember what old Caleb Robinson is going to have to pay in fees when I win this case for him!'

Reggie was glancing at his watch and Elaine's heart skipped a beat. Any moment now they would have to say goodbye.

'Jove, I wish I were coming with you!' Sam said enviously. 'I've no doubt I'll be following you before long. We're sure to be in by the fall – just look what the Huns are doing to our shipping!'

Carl rose. 'Come, Anna, we must be leaving. I have an appointment in one half hour. Say your farewells to your brother.' And he went round to everyone, clicking his heels and bowing his well-groomed head.

'I want to see the boat sail,' Anna said obstinately. 'You go. I'll get a cab later.'

Carl opened his mouth to protest but Sam said hastily: 'If it's all right with you, Wehner, I'll drop Anna off when I go back to the office. I've got my runabout here.'

Carl hesitated, looking across at his wife with a frown of annoyance. 'Anna should come now,' he began stubbornly. How dared she let them see how disobedient she was? 'Anna –'

'Do go, Carl,' Elaine interrupted ruthlessly. 'You'll be late for that appointment. Her father and I will take care of her. Give my regards to your mother.' She was pushing him gently towards the door as she spoke: surely he must soon see what was so plain to them all now. *Anna and Sam Murray.* Whether it was simply attraction, infatuation or love they felt for each other it was there on their faces for all to see. They had eyes for no one else.

Carl allowed himself to be persuaded and with his departure the atmosphere lightened considerably.

'It's late,' Reggie grunted presently. 'A quarter before five. What's holding things up?' and he moved across to stare out of the porthole.

'I told you some extra cargo is being brought aboard,' Munro explained, smiling blandly. 'A contribution to the European war, you know.'

There was silence as they avoided each other's eyes. If Munro, who was after all an employee of the Line, could make such a confident assertion, Reggie Ransom was thinking, then the *Avonia* was a vulnerable target. Good God, she was a passenger liner! What were they all playing at?

Elaine looked down at her hands: tears swam in her eyes and all she could see were the dark waters of the Atlantic and the U-boat wolf packs waiting out there.

Arms on board made the ship a legitimate target for the Germans. She was sick with apprehension for her son.

The ship's klaxon suddenly startled them. It had come, the moment she had been dreading. Her heart seemed to be falling into her shoes. Smiling with difficulty she kissed David composedly, to his heartfelt relief. 'Goodbye, darling. A safe passage to England. We shall be seeing you in a month's time, I daresay. Telegraph as soon as you arrive, won't you?'

Looking down on the quay as the great liner was pulled gently away by tugs, David sought for and found the four familiar faces tilted up to him. Taking off his soft hat, he waved it first to his parents and then to Anna and Sam who stood a few yards away in the crush of heads. Surely Sam had his arm round Anna? He was certainly looking down at her very intently and not bothering to wave his partner off. How intimate they looked! Sam was proffering a handkerchief – no, he was wiping away Anna's tears himself!

Yes, David thought with sudden insight. That's how it should have been: Sam and Anna. They were made for each other. And he raised his hand as if in benediction over them.

Soon, the figures on the shore had blurred and faded together with the shoreline, the distant buildings and derricks. A sharp breeze nearly deprived him of his hat and he laughed exultantly. At last he was on his way! He was going to war!

CHAPTER FIVE

Remember Belgium!

Polly's home, Eskton Rectory, was a large Victorian house built from local grey stone. It stood on the edge of a moorland village next to its small Norman church. The village, just ten miles inland, had a famous salmon river running through its centre from which it took its name. This was spanned by a large bridge in the village and by a narrow packhorse one on its outskirts. The church, standing high on a knoll, could be seen for miles round on a clear day. To those weary travellers on the moors in medieval times its tower had acted as a guiding beacon.

For most of the year, bracing east winds blew in from the sea but when the weather was fine, as it was this April, it could be a delightful place to find oneself in. The last of winter's snow might still linger in the shadowed ghylls, but on the open moor bees were already skimming over the spongy turf that was covered by patches of yellow and white flowers. Sheep dotted the greening turf as far as the eye could see, each distinctly marked with the owners' brands. Grazing was free to every parishioner and the land was common to all so over-grazing was carefully monitored by local courts of villagers who sat once or twice a year. Unlike New England, spring had arrived early. With a shortage of fuel of all kinds this was a blessing up here in the North Riding where sometimes winter lingered into May. Every day something new unfurled.

The rectory garden was awash with daffodils and paper narcissi; as the warm breeze swayed them, the scent of the narcissi filled the air. It was nearly as warm as a day in summer. Old Hoggett who helped out in the garden shook his head pessimistically; depend on it, he told everyone who would listen, they'd have a sharp frost one night and a blackened garden next morning. He didn't like the look of things up here, he didn't. It reminded him of that spring in 1892 . . .

Polly had now been at home for a fortnight: she was bored to the point of losing her temper over trivialities. The warm sunlight filtered through the window of her bedroom where she was working and tickled the end of her nose. Through the open window came the liquid notes of a blackbird. It was too much. 'I can't do another page!' she cried and hurled her book with its three-decker title of *A Study of Medieval Customs in Northern European Monasteries with Especial Reference to etc. etc.* across the room on to her unmade bed. Impossible to read that stuff with sun pouring in like molten gold and a little breeze wafting past the curtains, smelling of the moors. There was even a wild honey bee caught up in an uncurling virginia creeper leaf on the windowsill. With a gingerly touch, she freed the fat yellow ball and it flew away, buzzing angrily. Leaning against the sill, she glumly surveyed the room. Where did all the dust come from? And how had the room got so untidy? She was expected to keep her bedroom clean herself and had always been about to do it when something else distracted her attention. Now she faced an unmade bed, piles of books everywhere, a half-eaten apple turning brown and an accumulation of fluff under every piece of furniture. What a tyrant a house could be, she thought with surprise.

Archie, with his naval training, positively enjoyed keeping his room neat and all surfaces bare. Even with one arm, Polly thought guiltily. Thank goodness no one ever ventured to this floor to view her room! She rushed at the bed and drew the blankets up, punching the pillows with hatred. Once covered by a counterpane the bed looked better and so did the room. I'll go down and get the sweeper and give it a really good clean, she promised herself. It's that sun; if it hadn't suddenly shone on everything, I would never have noticed.

Glancing down into the garden, she saw with surprise that her mother had come out and was settling herself in the shabby old basket chair from the summerhouse. Polly marvelled at the sight. She was pretty sure Nell hadn't sat in the garden last summer: could it mean she was better? It occurred to her that she hadn't yet plucked up courage to tell her parents that she would not be returning to Girton at Michaelmas. Perhaps this would be a good moment. Even so, there were butterflies in her stomach at the prospect of a family row.

She hastily poured water into the basin on the wash-stand and scrubbed the ink off her hands. Then she brushed and re-pinned her hair and after a moment's hesitation decided to change her blouse, too. Satisfied at last, she regarded herself gravely in the cheval-glass. She saw the usual slight figure with the auburn curly head that she had been seeing all her life, it seemed. Why hadn't she changed? She was so sick of herself! Her whole appearance bored her to distraction.

The mirrored image stared sulkily back at her. Her face was too childish – her whole appearance not what she wished to be at all. She had always longed to be statu-esque and dignified with black enigmatic eyes that strong men would go mad about. Heaving a sigh, her blue eyes filled with dreams: tall and willowy with hair the colour of flax. Anyway, strong men would go mad about her one way or another; and it would be such fun brushing them away like flies. Her voice would be low and sweet like one of Mrs Henry Wood's heroine's and never, never raised in shrill argument with Archie. She would have a nature to match her appearance and the poor of the parish would beg for a glimpse of her on their deathbeds. She would come in with a cloak over her head carrying broth and the parish magazine and would show such Christian patience to poor Mother that her parents would beg her not to return to Girton –

She stopped and made a face at herself, laughter spilling out. Oh, well, that's what came of reading Charlotte Yonge late last night! She remembered with a jolt that the time had come for her to confront her parents with the truth: after next term she wouldn't be going back to Girton until the end of the war.

Slamming her bedroom door she ran helter-skelter down two flights of stairs (only two years ago she had been wont to slide down the banisters and shoot out on to the mat outside the study door) and out by the garden door. Here on the broad gravelled terrace her mother was sitting for the first time this year.

Nell Paget was darning mechanically, her thoughts busy and far away. She was neatly dressed in a style that of necessity hadn't changed for years. In honour of the sudden arrival of warmer weather she had brought out her cream straw hat; after ten summers it had taken on the colour of old ivory. She wore a brown frieze skirt that had come down to her from her rich sister, Lady Gromont, and a silk blouse made up from a remnant by the village dressmaker. Her black kid shoes were made for her in Harrogate and were the one extravagance she allowed herself. After months indoors her skin was parchment-coloured and she held her mouth in a rigid line of control. She had once, not so long ago, been a plump woman with pink cheeks and a ringi:.g, confident voice usefully employed in addressing parish committees: and it always secretly jolted her family to come upon her suddenly and feel they were facing a stranger. In their minds she existed quite whole and healthy like the photographs of her that still lay about. This fragile woman was a stranger.

'Mother?'

She looked up to find her youngest child in front of her. Really, how shabby the girl looked, Nell thought, reaching out to tweak the worn serge skirt. 'Where's your belt, Polly? Dear me, the back of your skirt is covered in William's hairs! He must have been sitting in your bedroom. You and your father are far too soft with that cat. He gets everywhere. Now turn round – '

'Oh, please, Mother, don't bother. I only wear it in the mornings when I'm studying. I want to talk – to tell you something.' She dropped to her knees beside the chair. 'Mother, I've been granted leave of absence from Girton – from the end of next term. I shan't be going back at Michaelmas. I'm going to get a war job.' Anxiously, she examined her mother's face, saw the slow change of expression and felt her heart sink. Had she succeeded in winning over her mother, she would have won the battle hands down, she realized. But Nell was startled and then angry.

'Polly, are you in trouble with the Girton authorities? What have you done?'

'Nothing! I just feel I can't concentrate on medieval history while the war news gets worse and worse. Archie's badly wounded, Dick is killed and I'm supposed to feel indifferent to what's going on round me. I can't do it. I've spoken to Miss Conway and she's promised to let me know if they'll let me resume the studentship at a later date. Other girls are doing it all the time. I met one at the end of term called Thelma Lacy. She's an ambulance driver with the Serbian Unit from Girton – she says it's tophole and that's what I want to do if they'll have me.' Again she studied her mother's face.

77

Nell sighed heavily. 'I really don't know if this is wise. There's no money to spare, Polly, and I daresay these are rich girls whose parents can afford to give them a good allowance. You won't get paid much, you know.'

The eager light was fading from Polly's eyes. Money. Always the same thing: money – or rather its lack – was held in front of one like a bogey. They had said she couldn't get to Girton because there was no money to spare. The squire had been glad to educate Dick at Wellington and Sandhurst and Gerald Parsons had paid for Archie at Dartmouth. But the squire had never offered to help the rector's daughters to a little education; he didn't believe in it for women . . . It was like the Dark Ages in Eskton, Polly thought with fury. Young women were supposed to stay at home and sew shirts or tend their spinning wheel. She opened her mouth to say as much and then closed it again. It was no use arguing with her mother; she would just have to grit her teeth and look for ways and means of getting what she wanted. That's what she had done about Girton: won a studentship and taken the wind out of their sails. If necessary she would do it again.

'Then I'll look for paid work,' she said. 'Where's Father? I'll go and tell him at once.'

'He's gone to Ugglebarmby to a funeral.'

'Then I'll tell him tonight,' Polly said firmly. 'By the way, there's a sale of work and fair in the grounds of Northesk House this afternoon. It's in aid of the Belgian Refugee Fund. Cassy Byrne is organizing it. Don't you wish I were just such a daughter as Cassy?'

'She is certainly her father's right hand in the parish. Personally I dislike bossy young women who insist on knowing better than their elders.'

'Oh, Mother, how can you?' said Polly in mock reproach. 'Mr Byrne would be *lost* without Cassy; he's said so thousands of times and methinks he protests too much. Look, she's sent this card in her own hand. I think we should go along this afternoon to support her.'

'You know I go nowhere now. Cassy wouldn't expect me.'

'But, Mother darling, you must start coming out soon! It will do you good to come this afternoon – '

'Nothing of the kind!' Nell snapped. 'It would hurt terribly for people to come up and mention my Dick – I couldn't face it. Don't ask me to come with you, Polly, for I can't do it.' She had gone paler than usual and there was suppressed panic in her voice. Pulling out more wool, she let the ball fall from her trembling hands. 'Look how you've upset me!'

Polly picked up the wool. 'I don't mean to, but it's got to be said. Someday you'll have to face people again – '

'Why?' Nell's voice was hard and cold like her eyes.

Polly laughed uncertainly. 'Because you can't stay behind these walls all your life! For one thing, we need you. Don't you wonder why Imogen spends her leaves in London with Aunt Nora? Why Alix hasn't been home for months? Why – after only a fortnight – I'm only too ready to leave again? Then there's Father – '

'Leave your father out of this and *don't interfere!*'

'We all hate seeing you like this,' Polly went on inexorably. 'But I hate especially seeing poor Father pushed out of your life – '

'Polly! How dare you talk to me like this?' Hunted, Nell began to gather her things together, to rise from her chair and prepare to go back indoors. Her pale face had now flushed and her eyes were bright with anger. 'Leave me alone! I don't want you home if all you can do is badger me! Stop interfering. Going to Girton hasn't improved your character. You were always the most difficult of my children, the one I found hardest to love.'

79

There was silence. Something in Polly recoiled as from a sharp blow. And yet she had always known that her mother couldn't care for her as she cared for her other children. Even as a child she had felt rejected by her mother whose attitude had always been one of impatient dislike for her youngest. It was from her father that Polly received the affection she needed. She laughed shakily and rose from her knees. 'Yes, I've always known that,' she agreed. 'So you won't come with us? Very well, Archie and I will go together.'

Nell relaxed, relief showing itself now that she was certain Polly wasn't going to force her into the outside world. 'It will do Archie good to get away from his books for an afternoon. You and Cassy are great friends and you should give her support.'

Going indoors, Polly thought: Why does everyone persist in thinking Cassy and I are bosom friends just because we went to school together? I can't stand the woman and I don't suppose she's any fonder of me.

Cassandra Byrne, a large energetic girl who was good at every sort of game, ran her widowed father and Northesk parish with a capable hand. The Rev. Mr Byrne was the envy of all parents with daughters at home and with time heavy on their hands. 'Just look at Cassy Byrne!' they would say reproachfully. 'She's not always hankering to go to London or to nurse or to have a career,' or whatever it was their Marys and Isabels and Doras hankered after. Cassy Byrne was the idol of distracted parents and the bane of her contemporaries: Who wanted to be like old Cass? they asked scornfully.

But no one could deny that Northesk's sales of work and bazaars were known for miles round: they were well worth flocking to and people flocked in their hundreds.

As Polly ran indoors she heard voices and laughter issuing from the dining-room. Putting her head round the door she found Katy feeding her child in his high chair. As she spooned baked apple and custard into the child's mouth, Archie sought to distract him by doing tricks with the family napkin rings. Little Dick, with a scream of mirth, brought his fist down into the middle of his apple which splashed out over his mother, Archie and the nearby wall.

'There, look at the mess! Archie, you're the limit!' Katy scolded laughingly.

'It was pretty good. I bet you couldn't do it with one hand like this – '

'Archie! Not again.'

Polly came in and scooped up the napkin rings. 'Idiot! Just look at the wall.'

They looked guiltily, and even the baby seemed startled by the sight of apple and custard slowly trickling down on to the floor.

'And look at my hair!' Katy laughed. 'Take him away, Polly, before Dicky has hiccups.'

Taking his arm, Polly pulled her twin into the hall. 'I thought you were supposed to be studying.'

Archie made a face. 'The fact is, Poll, I'm finding it darned difficult. I haven't done classics since I was fourteen. I'll never pass next November.'

'I'll help you after supper tonight. All work and no play makes Jack a dull boy so I propose we go over to Northesk to Cassy's sale of work. On the bicycles as Father's taken the dogcart.'

Archie looked uncertain. 'I haven't ridden a bike since I lost my arm. I'm still a bit unbalanced and I'd hate to topple off and fall on my stump. It can hurt like hell.'

'You won't. I'll go ahead and when we have to turn left I'll stick my hand out for us both.'

* * *

Nell had the grace to feel ashamed as she put away her knitting and prepared to go in to lunch, which she would take alone as usual. She knew she shouldn't have said what she did to Polly: *the one I found hardest to love*. It was true, of course, but she shouldn't have said it. But Polly was a difficult person: she had this uncomfortable bluntness that was so hard to parry. Nell found little white lies necessary to her life; Polly always saw through them. She lacked decent reticence, Nell told herself, leaning back in her chair with closed eyes. She could feel the turmoil in her brain threatening to become an engulfing tidal wave. Why couldn't Polly leave her alone? The others did so. They realized how impossible it was for her to go out and meet people again. No one should expect it after all she'd been through!

Opening her eyes, she looked across at the daffodils swaying under the apple trees. Everywhere there was renewal of life in the unfurling of leaves, the opening of flower heads. Somewhere in Flanders, Dick's body was rotting in the ground – 'Oh, God!' she shuddered and pressed her hands against her eyes.

Dick is dead. I'll never see him again. My lovely son, the best of them.

She had only to say these words in her mind for the day to lose its light and colour.

Sometimes when she looked back, Nell remembered how she had grumbled about their poverty. Five children to bring up on a parson's stipend was no mean feat. How wonderfully happy they'd been all the same! They had been a family, whole and unblemished. How really rich she had been without realizing it; now it was too late.

Everywhere in Britain one came across women like Nell Paget. Their life in ruins, they wore the same frail look of bewildered grief. Most of them carried on despite their dumb despair for they had others dependent on them. By staying inside the rectory's walls and letting life go on without her, Nell was taking the easy way out of her obligations. There were few who could so indulge themselves, but this didn't occur to Nell Paget. She had given up, earned the right to be selfish, she told herself.

It was still sunny at two o'clock when they set out. On such a day, Polly felt justified in wearing the tussore silk outfit after Cousin Celia. She had altered it hurriedly two days ago and as she wheeled her bicycle out of the shed, her mother rapped on the morning-room window.

'Polly! Polly!' She threw the window up. 'How could you? You've ruined that lovely coat and skirt! It's much too short now – what possessed you? That skirt must be at least ten inches off the ground – oh, *Polly*!'

'Twelve actually.' Polly threw out a leg. 'Nice, isn't it? Everyone's wearing shorter skirts in London, Mother.'

'London! That's all I want to hear! I don't know what the village will think. Besides, you've cut into perfectly good silk and there's nothing left to let down. Good coats and skirts like that don't grow on trees,' Nell pointed out, sighing dramatically. 'I was going to ask Miss Bonner to do it properly but what's the good? You've ruined it. And is that a pin holding the waist?'

'Don't worry, Mother, no one will see.' Polly hurriedly buttoned the jacket. 'It was much too long and that's why Aunt Nora sent it. She knew it was dowdy. Besides, I've got nice legs and it's a sin to hide one's best asset. This new fashion suits me down to the ground.' She chuckled gleefully.

'I do wish you'd remember you're a daughter of the rectory,' Nell said, closing the window with a bang.

Polly made a face. Wonders would never cease. She could swear that this was the first time her mother had stirred out of her torpor; all for the length of a skirt! She must do something else before long. She wheeled her bicycle to the front where Archie was experimenting on his vehicle round the central flower bed.

'Look, no hands!' he yelled and nearly fell. Cursing under his breath, he climbed on again. Then his eyes fell on his twin and he whistled. 'I say, old girl, dressed to kill, aren't we?'

'Mother's just told me to remember I'm the rector's daughter so I must be looking fairly decent for once. Like the hat?' Her hair was crammed inside a round straw hat sporting a velvet rose. Only two curls were allowed to show and these were pressed to her cheeks on either side in the Castle Clip (as worn by Irene Castle, the dancer).

'Not bad,' Archie granted. 'Don't let Mrs Linsey see you or she'll tell you parsons' daughters invariably go to the bad and you're halfway there, Miss Poll, by the looks of you!'

'This house is filled with Mrs Grundys!' Polly said crossly. 'Are you ready? Then let's go or we'll be late.'

It was two miles to Northesk over a rather rough moorland road and Polly guessed that Archie was feeling the bumps although he didn't complain. He soon mastered the feeling of weighing heavier on one side and although he veered to the right several times, he managed well. Polly, remembering his damaged heart muscle, made him walk slowly up the two small hills that lay in their path and they were passed by several gigs and motor cars, all bent on reaching Northesk in good time.

The iron gates of the manor were wide open and gay bunting fluttered from the trees in the avenue. The drive was full of potholes and there were signs of neglect in the moss and weeds, broken dry walls, gaps in the palings and rank grass everywhere. The shrubs had grown tall and close like a jungle and fallen trees hadn't been removed.

'What a pity it's been allowed to go back to nature like this,' Archie observed. 'The owners live in America, don't they? They ought to sell it and let someone else rescue it.'

'Don't you remember old Mr North who lived here when we were children? Rather a frightening old man with whiskers? It was spick and span in his day. He was rather a tartar, I remember.'

They walked up the drive pushing their bikes; it was thronged with people and Polly exchanged an eloquent glance with her twin: how did Cassy do it? As they rounded the last bend they saw the house at last. It was beautiful and seemed to have grown out of the ground and into its background. The original Tudor house had Georgian and Victorian wings but it all blended comfortably because all the additions were in the same local stone. Virginia creeper and roses would scramble all over it by midsummer but now it was bare and its one great stone window that stretched from roof to near the ground would be flooding its interior with light.

'I never realized it was like this.'

'Nor I – look out!'

For Miss Cassandra Byrne herself, resplendent in Red Cross uniform, was bearing down on them. 'Here you are at last, old sports! I'm delighted you've brought the Admiral, Polly – bravo.' Turning her beam on Archie she added: 'I say, I'm glad you've made it, Admiral. Not too tired? Sure you wouldn't like a chair?'

'He's lost an arm not a leg, Cassy, haven't you noticed, *old sport*?'

Archie frowned repressively at his twin while he sought to parry Cassy's over-zealous concern. 'No, thank you, Cassy, I'm fine – no, really, I am – '

Cassy was summoning a Boy Scout with an imperious finger. 'Fetch a chair, Johnny. Can't have the Admiral overdoing it. You're so thoughtless, Polly. Isn't this a ripping wheeze? I always guessed this would be just the spot for a really rousing bazaar.'

Polly sat down on the chair meant for her embarrassed twin. 'How did you get permission? The owners live abroad, don't they? The States, I've heard. Or have you gone ahead on your own and we're trespassing horribly?'

'Don't be a little idiot, Polly!' Cassy's expression hardened. 'Dad wrote to Mrs Ransom – she was Mr North's daughter, you know – last Christmas and she gave her permission at once, of course. Oh, there's Dad now!'

The Rev. Mr Byrne could be discerned meandering across their line of vision among the coconut shies, his long pink face shaded by the yellowing panama hat he brought out annually. Above their heads floated the biggest banner of all: REMEMBER GALLANT LITTLE BELGIUM it proclaimed in wobbling cut-out letters. Girls in red, white and blue carried baskets filled with handkerchiefs, pincushions and other knick-knacks the parishioners had spent the winter making under the driving force of Miss Byrne herself. Buns and a bright yellow lemonade made from fizzy powder were being sold at one stall; there were several others selling garden plants, toys, secondhand books. A balloon seller stood on the terrace, a roundabout had a queue of chattering children awaiting turns and a shooting gallery was doing splendid business. The Northesk Silver Band played popular wartime songs under a red awning and was surrounded by a circle of admirers.

'I must say, Cassy, you've done marvels.' Polly looked round, overawed by the spectacle. Eskton would never have been able to put on such a show, she admitted to herself.

'Haven't I?' Cassy agreed calmly, her flat broad face complacent. 'It's taken months but – although I say it myself – no one else would have been able to do it half so well. I'm a splendid organizer.'

Archie's facial muscles worked hard to keep his laughter from bursting out and he avoided meeting his sister's eyes: she had been out-trumped by her old enemy for once.

But Cassy now had only one object in view: to keep Archie Paget by her side for the whole afternoon. Taking him by his arm, she led him away. 'Come on, Admiral, I want some lemonade.'

Archie's back looked very reluctant, Polly noticed, and he cast her one appealing glance that said *Help!* very plainly.

But even as she attempted to rescue him, she found the vicar himself by her side, enquiring after her parents as he shook her hand and turned her firmly round in the opposite direction. He threw a glance over his shoulder as he murmured: 'She's a wonderful girl! Splendid in the house – quite a little cook now. Runs the vicarage and parish like clockwork. I shall be quite lost when she marries, you know.'

'Is Cassy engaged? She's never mentioned it.'

'No, no. But she's bound to be before long,' Mr Byrne pointed out with satisfaction. 'She's going to make some lucky fellow a splendid wife and support – especially someone wounded in this dreadful war. She's an excellent manager – good nurse, too – and she's sure to be snapped up by some poor wounded officer who's in need of care and attention.' His gaze followed his daughter and her reluctant escort with great content. 'Archie's going into the church, your father tells me. Splendid, splendid. Just what I would have advised for him myself. Goodbye, Polly, remember me to your parents.' Mopping his brow with his handkerchief, he wandered off.

Polly stored up this snippet intending to tease Archie

with it on the way home. Cassy had had her eyes on this particular 'poor wounded officer' for some time and Archie knew it. His family thought it very funny, especially as Archie's taste ran to the sort of girl who was the exact opposite to Cassy Byrne. She would tell him Mr Byrne wanted to put up the banns on Sunday, she thought gleefully, as she wandered off to sample the fair herself. She bought lace handkerchiefs for her mother and Katy, a woolly ball for Little Dick and a secondhand book for her father. She further loaded herself with a geranium in a pot for Mrs Linsey and then having done her duty by the bazaar and her family, she walked purposefully towards the house. She had always wanted to see inside and this seemed a golden opportunity to do so.

But the front door was firmly closed against visitors. She peered through the windows and found herself staring into a large dining-room. A woman in an apron was polishing the furniture and stared back hostilely. Polly's mouth opened slightly; she had expected dust, furniture under dustsheets, carpets rolled back, in fact the bare ribs of an abandoned home. Instead there was activity, the look of a house where people were expected at any moment. Even as she stared, a younger woman in a pinafore brought in a bowl of flowers and placed it in the centre of the dining table. Polly hastily backed away. She must ask Cassy what was going on.

As she looked round for the familiar Red Cross uniform, her eyes fell on the locked and barred iron gates into the rose garden where the broad paths were covered in deep moss. Peeping through the bars, she could see stone benches and urns, a sundial, overgrown rose bushes in a tangle, some yellow forsythia just coming into flower and a tempting vista disappearing round a corner. It reminded her forcibly of an illustration in her Andrew Lang book of fairy stories she had loved so in childhood.

Just such an illustration had made her long to see more of the golden garden where the Beast prowled and the Princess lay sleeping. A captive princess ought to be languishing on the stone bench . . .

She blinked suddenly. There *was* someone there. A man was strolling nonchalantly towards her up the grassy path, his hands behind his back, a tweed cap on his head. He was tall and broad with a healthy glow in his cheeks and a smile that was obviously inspired by her wide-eyed interest in him. His appearance was so unlike the faces one saw in wartime that she could only stare speechlessly. Was he real? He was so well-clothed, well-nourished and ruddy that he might have walked off a poster advertising body-building health foods. She wondered if she was seeing a manifestation from the past, like the ghosts those two maiden ladies had sworn they had seen at Versailles . . . But then he spoke.

CHAPTER SIX

The New Englander

'Hullo, there!'

Polly found her voice. 'How on earth did you get in? It's locked.' And she rattled the gate in proof. 'Did you climb over? You *will* get into trouble!'

The young man had come directly up to the gate and was staring appreciatively at her through its bars. There was an impish light in his eyes. 'Think I'll be sent to jail for trespassing, do you? Or do you still hang, draw and quarter people in this country? Guess I'm shut in for good,' and he drooped visibly. 'Will you come every day and poke food through the bars for me?' He laughed, displaying white teeth, and removed his tweed cap. 'Who are you?' he asked with great directness.

She was staring, her mobile face registering doubt, then curiosity, then burning interest. He looked so splendidly untroubled, like a creature from another world. Then there was that tinge of accent. Her eyes took in his well-cut country suit of fine brown tweed, the thin gold watch chain linked across the waistcoat. Was he someone from the colonies? He seemed extremely well turned-out with an air of being in charge that she couldn't quite understand.

His amused eyes were reading her thoughts. 'I'll tell you what I'm thinking if you tell me first what you're thinking. That's fair, isn't it?'

She coloured. 'I thought you looked as if you'd arrived from another planet.' Then as he raised his brows, she added quickly: 'Do tell me how you got in. I'd love to see inside that garden. I suppose you realize you won't be able to get out this way? Look at the padlock.'

'Sure about that?' He searched his pockets and produced a bunch of keys on an old-fashioned ring. 'Now how in the name of Old Glory do I find the right one? I got in by the stableyard, by the way. It's a long way round but you do arrive at this point eventually! I'd forgotten my way about, I'm afraid. It's been some years since I was here but it's coming back to me gradually.'

So that's who he was! Old Mr North's Yankee grandson to whom all this belonged. His clothes gave him away: good, but slightly different from an Englishman's. For one thing, his brown boots were yellowish in colour – no Englishman would be seen dead in them. His tie was extra floppy and his collar soft. Now she looked closer, she saw how very different he was from the conservative males she was used to. Then there was that tinge of accent and his manners which were far more friendly and open than any other stranger's would have been. Far too friendly, her mother would consider. Polly's spirits rose with a bound. 'You've come home! Are you one of the Norths – no, your name must be something else because your mother was Miss North.'

'My name is Ransom – David Ransom – and my mother was Leo North's daughter. I heard there was to be some sort of circus here today so I'm keeping out of the way – there, got it!' With a squeak and a groan the padlock yielded and he pulled back the gate with difficulty. Polly was through with a bound and looking about her with eager eyes.

'Oh, what a gorgeous spot! Do let's explore!'

'Sure. I'll show you round.' His eyes inspected her with approving interest. Who would have thought the village would have yielded up a little stunner like this? he asked himself. 'Who did you say you were?'

'I didn't say,' Polly said over her shoulder. 'My father's the rector of the next parish and I'm Polly Paget, a friend of Cassy Byrne's. She's the girl in the Red Cross uniform who's running this show today.'

They strolled along most amicably, both talking fast as they exchanged details about themselves. She learned that he had come over to join up only to find that under the new conscription act he was having to cool his heels. He had put his name down for the county regiment though there was a waiting list for officer training. The rest of the family were coming over – indeed had already sailed – and they were going to make Northesk their base for the duration.

'Your family?'

'Yes, my mother and stepfather and the two youngest children. My elder half-sister is married so she'll stay on in Boston – that's where we all live.'

As they strolled on Polly told him about her own family and about the district. 'By the way, we mustn't show lights at night even though we're in the country. Danby High Moor – that's only over there – had a huge bomb dropped on it only a month or two ago. They were looking for the munition works at Middlesbrough, I suppose.'

'And when's this thing called summertime going to start?' He was enjoying hearing her talk in her clipped voice, the words tumbling over one another and yet as clear as a silver bell. He was enjoying looking at her too. Her skin was like fine, delicately tinted stretched silk, he told himself. And that glorious red hair escaping from under that silly little hat meant she probably had a quick temper. Then her eyes – confused, he saw that she had stopped and was putting a hand up to her face, tweaking her hat.

'What is it? Have I got a smut on my nose or broken out in a rash?'

He laughed. 'Sorry, I was just admiring an English skin. I guess it's all this rain you get over here.'

She burst out laughing. 'That's really funny! Do you know I've been wondering how you manage to look so healthy and blooming. Haven't you noticed how grey most people look? Grey-skinned and grey-spirited for the most part.'

He nodded. 'I have. The older people especially. It's the war, isn't it? By this time next year I'll look grey too if the food I had in London is a sample of what I must get used to in wartime. Yuk! It was awful!'

By this time next year. She turned, pretending to inspect the tangled forsythia overhanging an arch. He didn't understand a thing or he wouldn't talk like that! By this time next year he could well be dead.

'What's the matter?'

'Oh, nothing.' She picked a piece of forsythia and put it in her buttonhole and he found himself wishing he had been bold enough to do that for her. 'Lots of men wouldn't have uprooted themselves to come over and fight,' she said as they strolled on. 'After all, you've lived over there all your life, haven't you? You're only an Englishman by birth.'

'Maybe but my roots are deeply here in the north of Yorkshire –'

'The North Riding of Yorkshire.'

'Sure. The Ridings: North, South, East and West –'

'Oh, no! There's no South Riding but don't ask me why! England's full of anomalous facts like that. As for surnames, or names of villages, it would take a lifetime to master them.'

The path narrowed and they went now in single file. Over her shoulder she said: 'I suppose your mother will be happy to be home again.'

He looked doubtful. 'I wonder. Of course she and Dad

93

came over most years and took a house in London for the Season. But my mother's become a thorough New Englander now and she'll pine a bit, I think. I'd like to persuade them to go home again after a few months but I don't suppose I'll be successful. You see, she's determined I shall have a base to come back to when I'm on leave and I suspect she wants to be here in case I'm wounded! It's silly really; there are thousands of Canadians and Australians and New Zealanders here – and miles from home, too – but they haven't brought their families with them!'

She sensed that he was chafing against his parents' determination to accompany him to England, much as a boy would whose parents went with him to parties.

'And she doesn't realize what a bad state the place is in. She's going to have a shock. Mrs Elliot, the coachman's wife, is looking after me and she says it's impossible to get servants now. I can't see Mother running the house single-handed!' He grinned, satisfied that that would send his mother home if nothing else did.

'You should ask Cassy Byrne to help you find someone. She's sure to know where you can get extra help. There she is now – my twin's with her.' They had walked out of the gardens through a door in the wall and were now in the stableyard. Cassy and Archie were looking over the tops of the loose boxes. Now Cassy beckoned excitedly.

'Polly, come and look! There's the jolliest little roadster in here. Whose can it be?'

'It's mine,' David Ransom said.

Cassy's bulbous eyes inspected him closely. Speechless for once, she turned enquiringly to Polly.

'This is Mr David Ransom, Cassy. Miss Cassandra Byrne, Mr Ransom. And my twin brother Archie Paget.'

As they shook hands, Cassy said hurriedly: 'Now I know who you are, of course! Mr North's grandson. But how is it we knew nothing of your arrival? I do think Dad should have been told. After all, he is the vicar!'

David smiled with all the charm he could muster. 'I'm afraid I did it all in a hurry. I've come over to volunteer.' His eyes rested on Archie's empty sleeve. 'I know you can tell me all about it,' he said quietly. 'Army or navy?'

'Navy. Not an exciting engagement – fact is, we haven't met the German navy in a full-scale battle yet – just pure bad luck. We ran into a minefield in stormy weather and some of us caught the full blast.'

'I do think we should have been told!' Cassy persisted, her face red with annoyance and injured pride. 'This is a Northesk living after all and Dad and Mr North were the greatest friends. Dad *will* be surprised when he learns you've turned up without a word.'

David's eyes turned on her in mute astonishment. Polly could see that he was wondering why he was supposed to have sought permission of the Rev. Mr Byrne before returning to his own property. That Cassy was cross because she'd been caught unawares was plain to the Pagets.

'Oh, do dry up, Cassy!' Polly snapped. She looked meaningfully at her twin. 'We must go. We're on bicycles and it's all uphill going home.'

David's spirits sank: this stunning girl was disappearing out of his life as abruptly as she had entered it. 'Home? Where is that? I do hope we can meet again soon.' He glanced imploringly at Archie and Archie, who often wondered why his men friends fell so swiftly under the spell of his twin sister, sighed and said obediently: 'You must come and play tennis. The court's pretty ghastly now and I haven't learned to serve with one hand but I daresay Polly can give you a game.'

'Now come and meet Dad.' Cassy put a masterful hand

on David's arm. He stiffened, determined not to be rushed away by this gorgon to whom he had already taken a great dislike.

'Goodbye, Miss Polly, I'll be in touch. Goodbye, Paget, we'll have that game of tennis before too long.' Snatching off his cap he had only time to shake hands before being marshalled by Cassy Byrne and marched off in the direction of the vicar who was still wandering from stall to stall uttering words of encouragement to the sellers.

'That's a nice chap. He's certainly taken a shine to you, *Miss Polly*! What lovely manners.'

'I think he's very friendly,' Polly said. She couldn't resist adding boastfully: 'And I found him all by myself! We've been walking about for ages, talking. Ever since, in fact, you basely deserted me for your – er – childhood sweetheart.'

'There are times, *Miss Polly*, when I could cheerfully hang you from the nearest tree. You threw me to that she-wolf the moment we arrived. A dirty trick if ever there was one.'

'Oh, you could do worse than old Cassy,' Polly observed with deceptive blandness. 'Her father tells me she's looking round for a wounded officer to marry. As she means to have you anyway, why not give in gracefully and let her put up the banns?'

Archie, assuming an air of patience that was as foreign to his nature as to his twin's, stalked ahead in chilling silence.

Polly, assuming an air of large-eyed innocence, followed in his wake.

It was almost dark when they reached home and Polly guessed that Archie was very tired. 'I'll put the bikes away,' she said. 'Go in and tell them about our afternoon – and, Archie, remember that Doctor Mallory said you were to have a glass of whisky and water when you'd done rather a lot.' The splinter near his heart muscle had done more damage than Archie realized but she and the family knew and worried about him.

'All right.' He sounded exhausted and she cursed herself for forgetting his delicate state. As she put the bicycles away she saw how untidy the sheds had become; there were cobwebs and mouse droppings everywhere. There was no longer Joe, the young gardener, to look after things: he was now out in France and Annie, the housemaid whom he had courted for years, had left at the same time to make munitions in Middlesbrough. It was rumoured that she was earning more money than the rector. As for old Hoggett, Joe's grandfather, who had come back to help out, he was worse than useless, Polly told herself angrily as a festoon of cobweb hit her in the face. She loathed spiders.

She walked back though the overgrown garden to the house and encountered her father as he came down the path from the church wearing his cassock and carrying a pile of books.

'Is that you, Polly?'

'Yes, Father.' She linked her arm in his and said persuasively, 'Let's take a turn round the garden. I want to discuss something with you.'

The lawn was heavy with dew and the rector's cassock brushed the overlong grass as they paced.

'Father, I've asked Girton to release me from my studentship for the duration of the war.'

Arthur Paget stopped dead. 'What did you say?'

'Oh, please, Father, don't start raising objections until I've explained everything.' Polly hung on his arm, looking pleadingly into his face.

He listened in silence and then shook his head. 'My dear, I understand how you feel and if we were rich people I would encourage you to take this step. But, you

97

know, these private units are not likely to pay you or pay for your uniform and your fare to and from France and so on. I can't promise you much of an allowance with Archie going up to Oxford next year.'

It was on the tip of Polly's tongue to say that Archie hated the idea of Oxford; knowing how this would upset her father, she changed her mind. Instead, she stood on tiptoe and kissed him. 'Don't worry, I'll find a way not to be a burden to you. There are bound to be some jobs that pay something. I'll find one somewhere. But you do understand, don't you, Father?'

He sighed, looking earnestly into her face in the dusk. 'Yes, darling, I do but I still think it's your duty to get a degree and a job as soon as possible. I want you to promise you won't do anything rash without consulting me. Will you do that? You see, darling, these things have got to be thought out, not rushed into, and, you know, you are inclined to be impulsive.'

Polly withdrew her arm. 'No, I'm not, Dad! Oh, how can you try and bind me with a promise! It isn't fair! How do I know what I'll be feeling next year? I'll still want to do something – I know I shall!'

The rector, who was used to these outbursts, patted her shoulder and by doing so maddened her further. 'Now, darling, be sensible and let yourself be guided by me for once. I pray daily that this horrible war will be over soon. Then you won't have to make a decision, will you?' And the rector, nodding in a satisfied way, made a beeline for the house and the smell of supper.

CHAPTER SEVEN
To Our Generation!

It was Easter the following week and on Tuesday David drove over to Eskton rectory in his smart black roadster with the red wheels. He was immensely pleased with himself for having found this American-made 1913 Fiat brought over from the States just before the war and, as it had just arrived from its last owner in Lancashire, he was anxious to show it off. Petrol was getting difficult to obtain but he had saved enough to take Polly Paget for a picnic on the moors.

He had thought of her constantly since meeting her at the bazaar and her piquant face with its large expressive eyes had floated before his eyes each night before he drifted off to sleep. He was uncertain how long it would be before he was called up for training but he meant to make the most of that time pursuing Miss Paget. He had sensed she might be difficult to capture. There was something capricious about her that drew him like a magnet – that and her undoubted physical attractions. She had beautiful, slim legs, he remembered with a chuckle. He wondered what her skin would feel like if he touched it: it was flushed and smooth like a nectarine's and he guessed it would be warm and moist to his touch. And what a pretty laugh she had: it was husky and so infectious that one was bound to join in.

He had learned a great deal about the Pagets from Mrs Elliot who worked in the house; she appeared to know everything there was to know about the family. She would bring his breakfast to the vast dining-room where he sat in lonely splendour and linger with the tray balanced on one hip while she prattled about the Pagets, giving him details of all of them except the one he wanted most to hear about. She was, it transpired, aunt to the housemaid Annie who had gone away to make munitions in Middlesbrough.

'The money that girl's making, Mr David! T'aint right and that's what I told her last time she were home. Tossed her head at me she did, her with silk stockings on her legs! Mind, she'll pay for it when her skin turns as yellow as a guinea as it will, you mark my words.'

'Er – which was the Paget daughter I met yesterday?' he asked casually when he could get a word in.

'D'you need more toast, Mr David? Sure? It won't be a bit o' bother – oh, that was Miss Polly, twin to Mr Archie. Nineteen they are and poor Mr Archie limbless already – '

'Only one arm, Mrs Elliot. He's perfectly all right otherwise.'

Mrs Elliot shook her head pleasurably. 'No, he in't, Mr David: there's a wicked splinter from the explosive drove right next his heart, my niece Annie says. Expected to die any moment he is. Poor Mr Archie, just waiting – like.'

'For an operation?'

'For the church-yard, Mr David.'

'Oh, surely not! He looks very well. They can do wonders nowadays – '

'Not with Mr Archie. He's got death in his face, poor lad. That'll be the second boy the poor rector will have lost. Now, Miss Polly's a different kettle of fish altogether. Too clever by half. It doesn't do a young lady any good to be too clever, I always say. Gentlemen don't like it. Nay, never smile, Mr David, I'm right about this. She'll not marry if she's not careful. Why, you've only got to look at that lady doctor who came to help Dr Mallory last year – just like a man she was – '

'Come now, Mrs Elliot, you couldn't say that about Miss Polly!' He buttered his toast with a slightly guilty feeling: how often had his mother told him not to gossip with the servants? But she was a fine one to talk: old Stanley at home in Boston knew everything there was to know about the family. Anyway how else was he to find out about Polly Paget?

'No, indeed. Now it's not for me to say, Mr David –' *But you're going to say it all the same, Mrs Elliot.* ' – but when I saw that short skirt on her yesterday, I blushed for her. It's not right, her a parson's daughter an' all. Our Miss Byrne's not like that.'

'No, indeed she isn't!' David agreed feelingly. 'But Miss Paget looked charming, I thought. She's very pretty. Glorious hair. Titian red from what I could see.'

Mrs Elliot sniffed as she opened the door into the hall. 'That's what all the young gentlemen think, Mr David. I reckon she's fast. It's to be hoped she doesn't come to a bad end, her and her short skirts!'

She left David laughing silently to himself. Poor little Polly Paget! To be pretty and a bit daring caused a girl to be regarded suspiciously by these simple country people. It was much the same in New England: an irremediable strain of puritanism ran through their characters, making them suspicious of the lighthearted young who must surely be heading for an evil end. He poured himself more coffee and decided then and there that he must call on Miss Polly Paget at once.

It was Polly's turn that morning to supervise the household and allow Katy a little holiday from her domestic duties. The squire had taken her in to Whitby to see the holiday crowds and to stroll in the sunshine. No one seemed to think this strange except Polly.

'The squire's taking her out, Mother? But Uncle Wilfred's such a stick-in-the-mud! It won't be much fun for her. Why couldn't we all have gone? There's heaps of room in the Rolls and I could have sat next to Woodcock and got a few tips about driving.'

Her mother, sitting with her hands in her lap, had smiled indifferently. 'He knows I don't go out. But you'll be up early tomorrow, Polly, to take charge of Little Dick?'

She had promised not to oversleep and now, clad in a large pinafore, she was dusting the hall and keeping an eye on the baby asleep in his wicker pram in the garden. Shafts of sunlight lay in bars across the hall floor and the grandfather clock wheezed and struck just as she heard the sound of a motor approaching across the packhorse bridge. Petrol fumes drifted in through the open door as a smart little roadster roared through the gates and drew up in front of the house.

Who on earth would come calling so early in the morning? Perhaps it was someone wanting to examine the church records: the fine weather always brought such people to the rectory door looking for their ancestors. No one in the village except Dr Mallory and the squire owned a motor car. Still holding a duster, Polly went out on to the steps preparing to frown inhospitably on the early visitor. She was considerably taken aback to be confronted by David Ransom. Painfully aware of smudges of dust, and hair that had escaped its pins, she stared at him in wordless exasperation.

David's face lit up ingenuously with pleasure at the sight of her. 'Hullo there! I'm so glad to find you at home. I was wondering if you'd be very kind and show me the country round here? It's a sin to stay indoors in weather like this,' and he glanced eloquently at the blue sky as clear as stretched canvas. 'I'm getting more English, aren't I, talking about the weather! I've been saving up gasoline for this trip so don't you dare disappoint me.' Then, remembering Mrs Elliot's gloomy prognosis of Archie's condition, he felt forced to say: 'I'd be glad if your brother would come too.'

'I'm sorry but Archie's gone into Scarborough for coaching in Greek. A master from the High School teaches him during the holidays and my father does it when he can spare the time. He's going up to Oxford next year if he gets in.'

'Oh?' He looked blank. 'If his health allows, I suppose you mean?'

'His health? His one arm won't stop him!'

'I heard he had a critical heart condition?'

'You mean the splinter that grazed his muscle? A wonderful man in London operated and he's mending fast although he's not completely mended yet. If the splinter had gone an inch further, it would have killed him. As it is, he's getting over it well.'

'Well, I'm glad to hear that!' He hovered on the doormat looking over her shoulder and reluctantly she stood aside to let him in. Bother the man! There was a brush and pan on the stairs and the state of her hands was awful: hurriedly she thrust them into her pinafore and led the way into the morning-room which was clean, with flowers and plants in profusion and the cushions on Nell's chair well plumped-up. But as Nell never came down before eleven the room was now empty.

'I really don't know if I can come,' she began. 'I'm doing duty for my sister-in-law who's out for the morning.'

'But I'm counting on you! Besides I'm leaving for camp very soon,' he added mendaciously and took one of her grubby hands. Looking her straight in the eyes he said: 'I want to get to know you better.'

Such a precipitate announcement took her breath away.

She found herself stammering, something she seldom did. 'But – but who's to look after the baby? Katy left me in charge.'

'Your mother will help out, I'm sure.'

She opened her mouth to deny this but thought better of it. Instead she said meekly: 'I'll tell my mother you're here. Please sit down.'

As she fled upstairs she was aware for the first time in her life of being hunted. She was utterly at a loss as to how to deal with him; her experience of young men was minimal. Besides, he seemed to her so much older than the callow youths she had come across; older and much, much more confident. It was rather frightening. She found her mother up and dressed and rapidly explained the situation to her.

'But you know I never see strangers!' Nell's voice held badly suppressed panic and her taut hands clasped each other in an agonized knot that expressed her feelings more eloquently than words. 'You must explain to him – '

'Oh, Mother, *please* come down!' There was panic in Polly's voice. 'He'll think it strange if you don't – oh, Mother, just this once. He's – he's awfully nice and easy and you knew his mother, didn't you?'

'Elaine North? But I haven't seen her for years.'

'But you can talk to him about her. Everyone else is out and I've simply got to tidy myself – see what a sight I am? He wants me to go out with him.'

Nell, looking harassed, walked agitatedly up and down the room. Then she said: 'Very well, but it will be an ordeal and I shall have one of my terrible headaches and be of no use for the rest of the day. So be it,' she added in a tragic undertone and walked out of the room as if to the scaffold.

David saw nothing strange in the demeanour of the rector's wife as she greeted him composedly. She sat down opposite him and smiled. 'I knew your mother years ago when I came first to this village. Is it true she's coming home at last?'

'Yes, it's true.' He gave a short laugh. 'Although I don't think she regards it as *home* any more! My mother is a convert to the American way of life – especially the plumbing. She's not going to like Northesk House in its present state and I'm told I shan't be able to get hold of a workforce very easily – most people have gone into the army. My stepfather and my mother and my brother and sister should dock at Liverpool early on Wednesday.'

'That's very exciting.' She moistened her lips, searching for something to say. 'Er – will the United States come in on the Allied side soon? We need her badly.'

'I doubt it. President Wilson doesn't understand what's at stake. It seems so remote to the average American citizen. After all, Europe's a pretty long way off! Life hasn't changed a jot in the States for most people.'

'Fortunate people! If they don't feel the need to come in on the Allied side, then let us hope one corner of this planet will survive the holocaust!' She was leaning towards him, tense in her earnestness, and he could see how thin, pale and worn she was. 'Did Polly tell you about her brother? I've lost my son – the most dear of my children – and life is over for me.'

As he listened, he felt the hair on the back of his neck rising. Her voice, low and rapid, brooked no interruptions. It was as if she were talking to a mirror, her whole being concentrating on remembering her dead son.

Upstairs, Polly was regarding her wardrobe with dismay: she hadn't a thing fit to put on! Why hadn't he let her know he was going to ask her out today? She could have put the missing buttons back on that blouse, mended the tear in her better skirt. Some day, she promised herself angrily, she was going to throw away all her wretched clothes and start again. It was no good pretending any longer: she couldn't go. The tussore coat and skirt she had worn at the bazaar had been sent to Miss Bonner for renovations, not that it would have been suitable for the moors. But she must go! David Ransom attracted her and she wanted to know him better. She couldn't throw away this chance of a day out with him because her shabby clothes weren't fit to wear.

Suddenly, inspiration came: she would borrow something of Katy's. Katy wouldn't mind; indeed she would be pressing her most treasured possessions on her young sister-in-law if she were home and knew of the dilemma. Katy had trunks full of clothes from her days at the Gaiety Theatre and she was always altering and mending them, rendering them more fashionable.

In no time at all, Polly had raided Katy's wardrobe and had arranged herself in a blue linen skirt, white ruffled blouse and a blue cardigan with a belt. Her own knitted tam was exactly the right blue. Oh, bliss, to look right for once!

In the rectory kitchen, Martha Linsey was having a rest in her favourite rocking chair by the stove. A savoury smell of rabbit stew was gently wafting through the room, which was very warm but extremely tidy. It had been very tidy since the departure of Annie for her munitions factory: now the cook knew where every shining spoon was kept. She looked round her domain with satisfaction. Young people nowadays were real bad in the house – just look at Miss Polly. Hopeless – no interest, neither. She and the mistress had done their best to train Miss Polly to be a poor clergyman's wife some day but she just hadn't taken to it, more's the pity. It was books, books all the time with that young lady and what was the good of *them*?

She rocked comfortably to and fro, keeping an eye on the boiling potatoes while enjoying the sight of the shining blue-and-white china plates on the dresser and the best copper pans adorning a wall. Crisp blue check curtains on the window framed a view of the yard where William, the rector's cat, sat majestically on the wall awaiting his master's return for lunch. Yes, the whole kitchen shone like a jewel, Mrs Linsey told herself happily, although goodness only knew what the rest of the house looked like now the family had charge of it and it was mostly left in the hands of that slatternly Mrs Umpleby who went off leaving filthy dusters for someone else to wash out. Mrs Umpleby had nine children and never went home without a bowl of soup or a bit of something to feed all those hungry mouths.

The cook got up to throw diced vegetables into the stew. Eleven-thirty. It would be nicely done by one o'clock. The rector needed his vittles, poor dear man. Thin as a rail he was and the mistress not seeming to notice. Well, she'd made him a nice custard tart with plenty of nutmeg on top. He'd like that.

The rector was first favourite with his cook; after him Archie stood high in her favour. The women of the house, however, only aroused Mrs Linsey's impatient pity.

As she went to open the back door and let a little air in, she raised her head and stared at the ceiling: just listen to Miss Polly running to and fro opening and shutting drawers! That's where being sinfully untidy got you. Who was the young fellow in the morning-room with the mistress? He'd fair put Miss Polly in a panic by the sound of it; she probably couldn't put her hand on the right garments now she needed 'em – just like Mrs Linsey's niece Hannah Makepeace who had had many a scold for the same fault. Well, well, thought the cook, that was the young for you. Never listened to a word of advice, they didn't, not till it was too late.

Nell didn't blink an eyelid when at last her daughter re-appeared wearing borrowed garments.

'I'll take good care of her,' David promised as he opened the roadster's door to hand Polly in while Nell watched from the steps.

'Are you going to the sea?' she asked.

'No, I think I'd like to inspect the Roman road near Wheeldale moor – if that meets with your approval?' he said to his passenger. He gave the brass-handled starter in front of the bonnet a couple of violent turns and the engine burst into life, shaking the vehicle so much that Polly almost fell off its leather seat. She concealed her misgivings that the motor would run away with her before the driver could leap in and control it, and managed an airy wave of the hand as they rattled out of the gates and on to the white dusty road leading to the moors.

As Nell watched them out of sight, a small smile lifted the corners of her mouth; the first time she had felt like smiling for months. What a marvellous thing it would be if this eligible young man and Polly had taken to each other! All sorts of dazzling possibilities occurred to her. She had borne for years her rich sister Nora's pity; now she longed to be able to say airily: 'Oh, Polly's engaged to old Leo North's grandson. Didn't you see it in *The Times*? Yes, Northesk House is quite lovely and it's been in the family for hundreds of years . . .'

Nora, silly woman, would look quite green with jeal-ousy and – and – but I mustn't think like this, Nell told herself regretfully. It's too soon. But it would be wonder-ful. She dragged herself from the dream and went across the garden to take a look at her grandson. He was awake, yawning widely and staring up at the leaves waving above his pram. Seeing her, he grinned, showing his four teeth and struggling sleepily to sit up.

'Granny's going to wheel you up and down, darling, until Mummy comes.' She propped him up, finding him surprisingly heavy as she hadn't handled him for a long, long time. Katy usually brought him in to her each morning and evening and she would drop a kiss on his head. But now she was handling him herself and finding all her expertise with babies flooding back. Singing snatches of nursery rhymes she pushed the pram up and down the gravelled paths and Little Dick stared up at her, fascinated by this new voice raised on his behalf. Slightly hoarse and out of tune it was but it afforded both of them a certain satisfaction. 'More,' he said as she stopped and, flattered, she hunted through her mind for yet another rhyme.

For a short time that morning, the grief that had so nearly vanquished her receded and she was filled with a new sensation. Hope in the future was beginning to lighten her step. This little child of Dick's. Soon, Alix's baby would be here.

It was not to last long. A strange and rather alarming noise on the road outside made her turn her head, her song dying away. A horse was being ridden very fast over the packhorse bridge; it was either running away (and remembering that the gates were wide open, she pushed the pram quickly against a wall) or it was being galloped in a dangerous manner through the village. Even as she wondered, a horse was pulled up sharply at her gate and a man hurled himself off its back, threw the reins over one gatepost and came running towards her. He was a long-faced man with veined red cheeks and he wore a billycock hat that he snatched off as he approached her.

'Is Mr David here, ma'am? Mr David Ransom?'

Nell stared at him, her hands suddenly tight on the pram handle. An old familiar feeling of dread was making her heart flutter. 'No – not now. What is it? Is something wrong? What's happened?'

The man was moistening his lips, trying to get his breath back. 'I'm Elliot, t'coachman from Northesk House. I need Mr David urgent. It's bad news.' He gulped and Nell saw the naked grief in his eyes.

'He's out with my daughter. They left half an hour ago. Has there been an accident?'

'There's bin a message from Liverpool, ma'am, a telegram that my wife opened. She hates the dratted things and wanted to spare Mr David. It's from shipping line: the *Oceana*'s bin torpedoed – sunk by them bloody Huns early this morning – I beg pardon, ma'am, but I'm that upset.' He took out a large bandanna and passed it over his face. 'Miss Elaine and Mr Ransom and t'bairns were aboard – them bastards have drownded the lot!' Tears fell down his red cheeks. 'Miss Elaine that I've knowed since she were a little 'un,' he murmured brokenly.

'Oh, my God . . .' Her eyes wide with horror, Nell stared at him. That nice boy, so laughing and carefree in her house less than an hour ago, was now facing a tragedy as great as her own. Who was going to break this black news to him? She couldn't do it. He mustn't ask her to do it. 'Elliot, you must go and find him. He's driven up to the Roman road – you know where that is, don't you? On Wheeldale moor? Go on, man – hurry! And try and tell him quietly – give Mr David time to take in the telegram – ' But he had already gone, flinging a muttered 'Thank you, ma'am,' behind him.

Her hands were still clamped to the pram handle as if

they had been soldered to it, all the old tragedy of Dick's death sweeping over her again.

They had found a sheltered spot on the moor, a grove of ancient scrub oak twisted over hundreds of years by the winds rushing over the land from the north-east. But under their shade it was cool on a hot day, sheltered on a wild one, and always it was peaceful, the only sounds the bubbling water and the bleating of the sheep. A few primroses nestled in the wet moss by the water and their sweet honeyed scent was strong on the air. The Roman road was half a mile or so away and they proposed to eat first and view it later.

David had unpacked Mrs Elliot's hamper and discovered homemade pork pies, slices of tongue between bread rolls, boiled eggs and a whole fruitcake. Polly stared at such largesse: it would have provided several meals at the rectory. And that cake was stuffed with almost-unobtainable dried fruit . . .

He was unpacking glasses and a bottle of hock in a long-necked green bottle that he thrust into the water to cool. Then he had a thought. 'Er – you *do* drink, I hope?'

Amusement gleamed in her eyes. 'Yes, of course. Do you think that the rector's daughter ought to be teetotal? There is a Band of Hope in the village but they've not succeeded in netting anyone in the rectory yet. I suppose you also think I ought to wear dowdy clothes and think only of the poor?' Her challenging glance scorched him.

'Of course I don't!' he denied quickly. 'I'm pretty glad you're not like that.' His eyes admired her: that blue thing suited her no end, he thought.

'Not that I don't think of the poor from time to time,' she added perversely. 'But there are poor people and *really* poor people, you know. We haven't any of the real poor in Eskton, thank goodness. Eskton folk are a thrifty lot and the wives know how to stretch the money by baking their own bread and pies and growing their own vegetables. You'd have to go to York or Hull or Middlesbrough to see real slums and hardship and ignorance.'

'That's how it is at home.'

She raised her brows. 'You still think of it as home even though you've come back to fight for England?'

'It's been my home since I was four. If the States had gone to war I'd have fought for her. My parents were divorced, you know.' He glanced at her quickly to see how she reacted to this. 'I have a father living in Paris whom I don't remember. My name is really David Argyle only when Dad – Reggie Ransom, I mean now – adopted me he changed my name to his.'

She nodded, pitying him a little for not knowing his father, and studied his face as he leaned over and retrieved the dripping bottle from the back. Whoever the Argyle man was he must have been very handsome – or did he get his good looks from his mother?

He opened the wine expertly with a quick twist of the corkscrew, poured a little, tasted it and filled her glass. 'To us!' He raised his glass, smiling at her with his friendly eyes.

'To our generation,' she amended.

'Why d'you say that?'

'Because our generation is going down the drain faster than flood water.' She looked round on the peaceful scene: at the small moorland sheep cropping the turf with their lambs at their side, at the greening of everything for another spring. He was astonished to see her blinking tears away. 'Not quite two years ago – I think it was in July 1914 – we all came up here for a picnic at the Druid's Stone. There was my brother Dick and his new bride, my sisters Imogen and Alix, Ned Mallory, our doctor's son, and the village schoolmaster's son who is called David

112

like you, and a very smart brother officer of Dick's called Guy Tancred. Archie wasn't with us. He was still with the Grand Fleet at Malta. The war hadn't started. It was a wonderful day and we enjoyed every moment of it. I remember every detail as if it were yesterday.'

He was leaning on one elbow, his face very near, his eyes fastened to hers. 'And?' he prompted.

'Oh . . . just that out of the four men, three of them are now dead.'

He took his eyes off her face and let them dwell on the beauty round them. For the first time, the tragic reality of the war struck home. Those exciting episodes he read in the papers, the carefully censored pictures – those weren't the real war. The real war was here in the sense of loss evident in Polly Paget's eyes, her forlorn voice: her brother, her friends. *To our generation*. Who would be the survivors? he wondered.

'I'm not going back to Girton next Michaelmas.'

He looked up, startled. 'Your college? Why?'

'I've decided to go to the war, too. I'm joining one of the medical units if I can. Preferably one run entirely by women like Doctor Elsie Inglis's Scottish Women's Hospital.'

He sat up, spilling some of his wine. 'Not one of those suffragette affairs!' There was deep suspicion in his voice.

'Yes, why not?'

'You don't know what you'll be letting yourself in for. Don't do it! I've seen pictures of those women – battleaxes every one of them. You may not realize it but we men like to think of our womenfolk safe at home. It's what we're fighting for.'

Polly had restrained herself with remarkable self-control as she listened but now she burst out with an explosive 'What utter balderdash! It's like something out of *Little Women*! As for being a suffragette I am one already and

113

we would have got the vote by now if it hadn't been for the war and because we're doing the decent thing and shelving our demands until the war's won. But woe betide any prime minister who tries to brush us under the carpet when that day comes. I wouldn't like to be in his shoes. These are wonderful women I'm joining, women who have had to get their medical skills abroad because the Establishment doesn't like women doctors and surgeons. My blood boils at the thought of all those self-satisfied men who think we're only fit to scrub the wards and run and do their bidding. You can't mean it!'

'I guess I do mean that,' he said flatly. 'If I thought my sister Anna was likely to rush into war service over here, I'd do my best to stop her.'

'And would she take notice of what you said?'

He faltered, remembering his wayward half-sister with that strong will of hers. 'I don't know. War is a horrible business, best left to men and those professional nurses who have trained for the job. What can you join? You've told me you don't drive a motor, you're not a nurse – you're not trained for anything yet! Enthusiastic amateurs do more harm than good – '

'And what do you call yourself?' she flashed, her eyes narrowing dangerously. 'You're an enthusiastic amateur too when it comes to soldiering!'

'That's different. Besides, I've already had some training with the National Guard back home – that's like your yeomanry here. Sure, I need more training and that's why they'll be sending me to Salisbury Plain next month.' His eyes examined her face wistfully: she was so pretty! He was already attracted to her – if only she'd keep her mouth shut! It would be impossible, he now realized, to have a short flirtation with this girl just to fill in the weeks before he went into the army. She had a prickly personality; he couldn't see her being a willing partner to a little

114

gentle philandering. He now understood what Mrs Elliot had meant when she said, 'Miss Polly's too clever by half.'

'You're very old-fashioned,' she observed, regarding his disturbed face with composure now that she had succeeded in ruffling him. 'You've got charming manners towards women but you've no opinion of us. You're closer in thought to my father and our Squire Filey than you are to me and you ought to be ashamed of that. They are a different generation but you're *young* and your head ought to be filled with new ideas to improve the lot of the human race – we women are members of the human race, you know! But you'll learn,' she finished in a kind tone that he found infuriating.

He snatched at her hands and held them tightly as he said emphatically, 'I'm no different to thousands of men who feel as I do. War's not for women and it would be far better if you all stayed at home and remained sweet and kind and womanly – ' He broke off because she had collapsed into laughter. Flushing angrily, he dropped her hands and turned away. 'The idea of a woman surgeon makes me sick!' he flung at her.

'I'm sorry,' she apologized because she could see he was deeply offended by her laughter. He was looking sulky as he hacked at the cake. Obviously, like most men, he hated to be laughed at. To be honest, she hated to be laughed at, too. But she had been very attracted to him and it was a bitter disappointment to find that he held such out-of-date theories about women. She could never care deeply for any man – however good-looking – who held such old-fashioned ideas. She would have to fight her physical attraction to him: he really wasn't her sort. Rich young men like David Ransom had never had to think things out so they just blindly accepted the shibboleths handed down to them by their own kind. She wasn't very good at flirting and she knew it. He had probably only wanted to spend a few days in lighthearted amusement before going away and she had been more serious in her approach – fool that she was! She was no man's plaything and if their minds couldn't meet at any point, then the whole friendship collapsed. He was, she told herself bitterly, a good-looking ninny and nothing more.

He too was silent, studying the sweet full mouth that was made for passion. She had looked so yielding with her expressive blue eyes and dimpled cheeks when she wasn't arguing. Then her whole face changed. And she was so sure of herself, too! She wasn't a bit what he had thought and now he felt cheated. Yet he knew with every instinct that when this girl gave her heart, it would be with a passion that would satisfy any man. But she wouldn't give it easily nor would she give it to him without a battle.

So what the hell? he thought suddenly. He'd change her feelings towards him if it was the last thing he did! He'd make her fall in love, he'd make her want him as much as he wanted her. And he intended starting this very afternoon –

'What's that?' She had turned her head, listening.

He heard it, too. 'Sounds like someone's bent on ruining their horse's legs on that flint road.' David stood up, staring down to the road below. 'It's Elliot – our coachman. What the devil's he up to following me here? He's seen the motor. He's coming up.' Taking off his straw boater he waved it at the approaching horseman. As horse and rider scrambled up the rough track towards him he saw how strained Elliot looked, how dark with sweat was the horse. Elliot never rode his horses into the ground like this!

His nerves tingled warningly. Something had happened. Suddenly he knew as surely as if he had been told that things would never be the same again: Elliot's face spoke volumes before he opened his mouth.

Standing his ground, David braced himself as if beneath a descending sword.

CHAPTER EIGHT

The Wolf Pack Strikes

Anna was downtown having her hair washed when she heard. Time hung heavily on her hands now that her own family had gone to England. Many of her young friends had married and moved away; those who were left came to lunch occasionally or she visited them. In between there was nothing much to do. She was not allowed to run the house or order the meals: that was her mother-in-law's province. Her large trousseau was still mostly unworn so it would have been capricious to call in her dressmaker. So as often as possible she went to Madame Yvonne to have her hair washed and dressed or to buy scent or new combs. Today Madame Yvonne was pressing on her the very last bottle of *Jicky* from France.

'Positively the last I can get, Mrs Wehner. French imports are getting more difficult all the time now. Yes, what is it, Myra?'

The girl who had washed Anna's hair was hovering outside the glass screen, her face full of bad news. 'Oh, Madame Yvonne, it's being shouted on the streets! The *Oceana*'s been torpedoed and it only left Boston last week – '

'Oh, no!' Anna had sprung up and the last bottle of *Jicky* smashed to the floor. Afterwards she could never smell it without the scene coming back to her with sickening clarity: her own white face in the mirror and Madame standing clutching at the chains she wore round her neck. 'Who says so?' She had grabbed the girl by the arm. 'Where did you hear this?'

'There's a crowd outside – see, Madame? One of those

118

darkies told me and a gentleman walking past confirmed it when young Maisie ran after him. They say it's lost with everyone on board. Dreadful, isn't it?'

Anna's lips were as white as her face and the room seemed to be spinning. She hid her face in her hands. It couldn't be true! Not her family! Oh, God . . .

'Quick, Myra, run and fetch the brandy I keep in my cupboard – here, girl, here's the key! Now, Mrs Wehner dear, just put your head down – right down. That's it. Myra! Hurry up, girl, she's going to faint –'

Anna heard them from a distance: Madame Yvonne had quite lost her assumed French accent and was revealed as from the mid-west. Gradually her head cleared and her heart stopped racing and she was able to refuse the brandy Madame was offering her. She must get to Sam.

'Shall we call your chauffeur, Mrs Wehner?'

That would never do, Anna thought, pressing her fingers to her temple. The chauffeur's eyes and ears worked overtime for Mrs Wehner senior. He would report her visit to Washington Street. She had only come in the family motor this morning because she and Carl were going to lunch with friends and she was to pick him up at twelve-thirty. 'A cab – yes, fetch me a cab, please. I'll come back for my motor later. If my chauffeur calls to collect me, tell him – tell him I'm not yet ready – oh, tell him anything!' She was pinning on her hat with frantic fingers that seemed to be quite numb; pricking a finger, she barely felt it. She was trembling violently now and was suddenly so helpless that Madame Yvonne and Myra had to dress her themselves while she supported herself with the aid of a chair. 'Oh, hurry, please! The cab – has the cab come?'

'I don't like the look of you, Mrs Wehner. Let me telephone your home –'

'No!' She straightened, making a valiant effort to appear in charge of herself again. 'It's very kind of you but I'm perfectly all right now.' She gave them a wavering smile and walked steadily to the door and into the cab. In no time at all she had reached the office. Paying off the cab she pushed open the door into the vaulted hall with its small elevator worked by a tiny boy in a brown uniform. Sam's and David's office was on the third floor and running from the elevator she burst into the outer office like a meteor. The two clerks stared as she hurried past to open the next door without knocking.

'Sam! Sam! They've been drowned!' She went round the desk and flung herself into his arms, bursting into violent tears as she did so.

'Dearest Anna, what is it?' With one deft foot he closed the door in the astounded faces of his clerks. Then he hugged and rocked his unexpected visitor, murmuring words of comfort as he took her hat off and smoothed back the damp hair she hadn't stayed to have dried at Madame Yvonne's. 'Now, darling, please stop crying for a moment and tell me what has happened.' If Wehner had so much as laid a finger on her he'd go up to the house and punch his head, he promised himself savagely.

The face she raised from his shoulder startled him by its look of stark hatred. 'Those Huns! I hate them – hate them! I can't go back to him, Sam – I can't! They've killed Mother and Dad and the little two – yes, the *Oceana*'s been torpedoed by those fiends and my family's gone!' With a terrible cry of grief she turned and flung herself across his desk, hammering with her fists on the wood. 'I hate him! I hate him!'

In her mind, Sam Murray realized, the Germans in the U-boat and Carl Wehner had become one.

* * *

120

By the time the *SS Oceana* prepared to sail out of Boston on Monday evening, Elaine felt emotionally worn out. So much had had to be seen to and although Anna had kept her promise not to pester her parents to let her accompany them to England, her face had looked much older and laughter had left her eyes. Somehow this had been worse than tears and pleading.

Now as Elaine sat in her stateroom she looked round at all the flowers and fruit sent by friends and smiled wearily at Sam Murray who was seeing them off. 'I can hardly believe we've managed it! There was a time last week when I all but gave up and decided not to go. You've been a tower of strength, Sam, and I can't thank you enough.'

'I hate to see you go,' he admitted, 'and I envy David being able to do something. However I feel sure we'll be in ourselves before long.'

'I devoutly hope not! Are you young men never satisfied unless you're fighting?' Elaine exclaimed crossly. 'I hope America will have the good sense to stay out of this war. It should be over quite soon. Reggie says it's now a stalemate and poor Europe will be impoverished beyond belief.'

Sam looked sceptical: he had heard this very same argument from other well-heeled Bostonians. He wondered if Mrs Ransom had any idea how miserable Anna was in her marriage; if she had, then how could they all go away and leave her to her fate and the Wehners? He watched Mrs Ransom rise and go across to a mirror to tilt her hat a little further to the left and to settle her furs more comfortably about her shoulders. *She's a selfish, vain woman*, he told himself with young intolerance. *Poor little Anna with a mother who simply couldn't care what becomes of her!*

As if conjured out of his imagination, the door opened

with a jerk and Anna almost fell into the stateroom. She was breathless, the colour in her cheeks making her lovelier than ever. 'Mother, I'm coming with you!' Then she caught sight of Sam Murray. 'Oh, Sam, you do understand, don't you? I've got to go, too – I can't stay here with Carl and his mother – I *can't*!' Turning eagerly back to her astounded mother she added: 'My luggage is being brought on board now and they've squeezed me in to share a cabin – '

'Anna!' Elaine came across in a rush and shook her. The two women stared at each other. 'You little fool! What are you playing at? What about Carl? You're a Wehner now – '

'No – never!' Anna burst into tears.

'Sam, will you fetch my husband, please?' Elaine put her sobbing daughter in a chair, feeling shaken and depressed. She hated the thought of leaving her behind but she couldn't encourage her to take the step that would lead to social disaster. Women like Anna *couldn't* leave their husbands; life would become impossible for them: the Wehners would see to that. She herself knew too much about the pitfalls to want to see her daughter fall into the same trap.

She did understand how Anna felt about the Wehners. Two nights ago she and Reggie had gone to a farewell dinner and the old lady (for at fifty-eight Mrs Wehner had settled for widowed old-ladyhood with a vengeance and invariably wore black and jet beads) had not been able to resist a dig or two. 'How very foolish of you both to go to Europe at such a time! Everyone knows that Germany has starved out your country and the children are dying in the streets. It's only a question of weeks before the Allies capitulate, my cousin Dona says. I understand France is ready to do so but the stubborn Anglo-Saxons are refusing to comply. That Mr Asquith is a fool! He must know he is beaten! The Kaiser intends being in London before the summer is through – Dona was very amusing about it!'

Reggie's foot came down warningly on Elaine's toe and she swallowed her indignant retort. Reggie was looking cynical, his eyebrows raised with deliberate scepticism although he kept politely silent. But colour had flared in Anna's cheeks and she had directed a look of angry dislike at her husband who was complacently listening to his mother's remarks.

The marriage is doomed, Elaine told herself with despair. That stupid old woman wants it to fail, darn her! I could kill her.

They had left soon after that.

Turning now to her daughter, she softened her voice for the girl's palpable unhappiness touched the very core of her own being. She remembered her own first marriage vividly! And now here was her own little Anna trapped in a very similar situation and yet, she thought miserably, it was her duty as a mother to keep her trapped in it for the girl's sake. Anything else was unthinkable. 'Listen, darling, be good for a short time. Make up your mind to get on with Mrs Wehner and when I come back – and perhaps it'll be in the fall – we'll have another discussion. How does that strike you? I'm too worried about David to think of anything else at the moment.'

'It's always been David first,' Anna said resentfully. 'You've never had any time for me, Mother.' She wiped her eyes. 'You were glad to get me married and out of the way – oh, I know it's true!'

'You're talking rubbish. All I'm asking is that you give your marriage a chance – Reggie, thank goodness you've come! Make Anna see sense.' In a low voice she added: 'She must be got off the boat quickly. There's only ten minutes or so left and she has luggage –'

'*Luggage?* Anna, what in God's name are you thinking

of?' Reggie seldom spoke harshly and Anna looked frightened, twisting her handkerchief in nervous fingers. 'Does Carl know you've come? No? Then he will be very angry and with cause. You are married to him and you can't – on a sudden whim – decide to come with us before we've all gone into the reasons behind this flight. Did you come in a cab? Then Murray shall see you home. One last kiss, my dear, then you must go.' He opened the state-room door. 'Sam, will you see my daughter back to her home? We must get her luggage off.'

Sam Murray offered the red-eyed girl his arm which she squeezed comfortingly. Elaine, swallowing tears, kissed her and nodded at young Murray. Taking a firmer grip of his charge, he hurried her down the gangway. At the foot he said: 'Shall we stay and wave them off? Or would you prefer to leave at once?'

She looked up, meeting his kind and understanding eyes; her own filled again and she sobbed aloud. 'A little piece of me is dying,' he heard her say under her breath. He believed her. It was her first sorrow in a life that had been singularly carefree up to the time of her unfortunate marriage. It was changing her as sorrows, however small, did. She was growing up and it was hurting badly. 'Let us go home.'

In the cab he took her hand, peeling off the glove and kissing the palm. 'Anna, my dearest . . .' It was only a whisper because of the cab driver and she turned and whispered back: 'Oh, Sam, Sam, if I'd gone to Europe perhaps it would have saved us – but now!'

His heart leapt and he felt a warm wave of happiness as his arms tightened round her. 'Nothing can save us, darling, because we're up to our silly necks!'

For Elaine the voyage was a much-needed rest after a hectic three weeks of preparation. The children, as children readily will, had adapted themselves to the idea of living in another country. Nanny was glad to be going back to her native Yorkshire and filled them with exaggerated tales of its being the only place in England to live. Secure that they were travelling in a neutral ship that was lit from stem to stern at night, they were all enjoying the voyage in perfect weather.

On the seventh night, they were dining as usual at the Captain's table. Tomorrow they would reach Ireland and berth at Queenstown for twelve hours. A day later they would sail up the Mersey to reach harbour on the ninth day out of Boston. Captain Bruce, twenty-five years with the Line, was describing to his guests the precautions they were taking now that they had reached the danger-zone for U-boats: neutral ships, he admitted, had been attacked in the past year and it was said that the Germans were increasing their campaign against them in order to stop supplies reaching the Allies. All the lifeboats were now swung out from the davits and all the bulkhead doors were closed.

'I've doubled the watch, of course, and the bridge is double-manned,' he told them with breezy confidence, signalling to his steward to refill glasses. He raised his to Elaine. He had a soft spot for 'the pretty little woman' as he termed her and his practised eye gave her a twinkling look of appreciation. 'No need to lose any sleep, Mrs Ransom, you're in good hands!'

'I know that,' she agreed, smiling at him. 'This will be our tenth voyage with you, Captain Bruce! How exciting it is to think we'll be back in England in a couple of days.'

'Yes, it's full steam ahead for us now. We shall reach Liverpool at dawn the day after tomorrow. That will enable us to catch the tide and cross the bar.'

Reggie had leaned across to join in the conversation. 'Have there been many incidents lately? Surely since the

125

Lusitania tragedy last year, the Germans have been more careful about sinking passenger liners?'

Captain Bruce looked sceptical. 'I'd certainly like to think so but we can't afford to relax our vigilance for one minute. You see, Germany has been scenting victory lately. Their U-boat campaign in the Atlantic has been highly successful in sinking grain ships – in fact, supply ships of every sort. They haven't yet confronted the British navy in a pitched battle, strange to say, but they've done every sort of damage to ships carrying food and oil and essential supplies. It's a clever campaign: cut off supplies to the Allies and starve 'em out. It could work.'

Elaine looked anxious, remembering Mrs Wehner's malicious words. 'But they're not really starving in England, are they?'

'Oh, don't misunderstand me! They're not starving by any means but they're certainly tightening their belts. There are queues for most commodities – and a thriving black market too, I'm told. If you're thinking of motoring, I'd advise you to go back to the good old horse. Gasoline's scarce over there.' He speared a piece of cheese and sighed in his beard. 'Even though the States aren't at war with Germany, they know full well where our sympathies lie. They suspect us of carrying war cargo for the Allies in our holds, you know.'

'And are you?' Reggie asked bluntly.

Captain Bruce smiled. 'Not that I know of, Mr Ransom! That doesn't mean that certain things don't get carried that *might* be useful. The Allied agents are a crafty lot and they certainly come to and fro a great deal. See that grey-headed gentleman over there? Looks like a college professor, doesn't he? He's a buying agent for the British government.'

Oh, God, I hope not this time! Elaine thought apprehensively, looking round the crowded first-class dining-room with its gold columns with acanthus leaves and caryatids, its long Venetian mirrors, beautifully dressed women passengers glittering with jewels, the smell of rich food, the attentive stewards: it seemed too secure to be consigned to a watery grave and she smiled at her folly. She couldn't help wondering when she would eat such food again if all they said about Britain was true. Well, they could be sure of game at Northesk and they could keep chickens for eggs and perhaps a pig or two. England certainly sounded very drab and she couldn't help feeling annoyed with David for volunteering: it was totally unnecessary, she was certain.

Behind potted palms, the ship's orchestra was playing softly. She knew that haunting tune, a relic of 1913 called *Destiny*. A shiver went down her spine. What would be *their* destiny for the next year or so? Would David survive to have a future?

But Captain Bruce was trying to get her attention.

'Tell me, Mrs Ransom, was it a great wrench to leave Boston for such a long sojourn abroad? I believe you intend staying until the end of the war – whenever that may be.'

She accepted a cup of coffee from the steward. 'It was. But I was brought up in Yorkshire and I tell myself I'm going home!'

She saw his smile, saw his mouth open to reply but she heard nothing except a tremendous thud like the clash of thunder. The huge vessel shuddered from stem to stern. China and silver crashed in the background; the wine was spilt and the chandeliers, blinking wildly for a few seconds, suddenly went out.

In the short silence that followed she realized that the great engines had stopped. She felt Captain Bruce roughly pushing back his chair and stumbling away in the darkness. She half-rose but could see nothing: it was as if she had gone blind without warning. Then a woman shrieked in terror; a shriek that was cut off by a hand across her mouth. A subdued murmur gained in strength and there was a nervous laugh or two as people began to leave their tables and grope their way to the stairs. She felt Reggie's hand gripping her firmly.

'Elaine, sit down.'

'*Sit down?* Reggie, I want to get out – '

'Not yet,' his reassuringly calm voice said out of the darkness. 'There'll be a rush and you'll get trampled. *Wait.*'

Suddenly, real panic broke out. The subdued voices became screams as people clawed their way up two staircases and fell and were trodden on in the total darkness.

'Let me out! Let me out!'

'God help us! Oh, Harry, where are you?'

Elaine felt terror suffocating her and every instinct in her wanted to run too; but Reggie's hand still held her down in her seat. 'Just a little longer, darling. We might get parted. Nanny knows what to do; we've talked about it and the children have done their boat drill.'

She obeyed, trusting his judgement completely. 'We – we've been torpedoed, haven't we?' Her tongue seemed to be sticking to the roof of her mouth so that she spoke with difficulty. Her mind kept repeating dully: The bulkheads are closed . . . the bulkheads are closed . . . She knew now what naked fear was like: it stripped one of the thin veneer that civilized society painted on one's personality. Now she was ready to fight and cheat – maybe even kill – to save her children and herself. Heroes and heroines were selfless: she was not.

'Come on.' His voice was cool and firm and he held her steady as she stumbled against him. But as he had predicted the stairs were almost cleared of passengers and

128

the way to their suite was free of other bodies staggering against each other in the dark. There was already a decided list to the vessel and they were thrown to one side of the companionway as they lurched along. They fell into their cabin and Reggie said curtly: 'Stout shoes and your thickest coat. This scarf round your head. Quickly.' He pulled on her lifejacket and tied the tapes with firm, sure hands and she tried to do the same for him. But she made a poor job of it, her hands trembling with fear. She felt deadly tired.

Into a small leather pouch he swept her jewels, plucking them off her breast and hair with rough fingers. He stuffed them into the deep pocket in her broadtail coat and pushed her through into the other cabin where the children were being dressed by Nanny. With Yorkshire phlegm, Nanny was finishing buttoning coats on her charges, her voice and hands steady. The children weren't frightened, regarding it as fun to be roused in the night. She had taken the storm lantern out of the cupboard with the lifejackets and now lit it with Reggie's matches.

'I want Drongo!' Laurie cried obstinately, escaping from Nanny's hands and rushing to her bunk. Ruthlessly Reggie's scooped her up, saying: 'Ready, Nan? Daniel, take hold of your mother's arm and *don't let go*. Come along, Laurie, we're going in the lifeboat. You know how much you wanted to get in one – well, now we're all going.'

It was only with difficulty that he opened the stateroom door for the *Oceana* was listing heavily to starboard: it was obvious to the adults that she was sinking fast. People were still surging up from below and boats were being got away from the starboard side as each one was filled.

A milky radiance was filling the sky; a full moon covered by a thin layer of cloud. As they emerged on to the sloping deck, Elaine was unnerved by the four tall

129

funnels leaning over their heads, belching forth black smoke and showers of red sparks. They all choked, feeling the stinging ash at the backs of their throats.

Reggie now realized with horror that the ship was sinking even faster than he had calculated. Their lifeboat, already nearly full with people, was now only a few feet above the water as it hung from its davit. The need to get all the lifeboats away before the ship keeled over and dragged them all with it gave added urgency to the crew as they worked frantically to round up all the passengers.

'Get in, Nan,' Reggie said crisply. 'Never mind showing your legs, woman! Now, Elaine, hand Dan to me – all right, old man? Here, Nan, grab him.' Reggie tried to keep his voice reassuring for he saw that his young son was dumb with fright; his hand grasped convulsively at his father's coat and Reggie had to shake himself free. He began to hand Elaine in after them, holding Laurie by his other hand. Suddenly she cried: 'I want Drongo! I must have Drongo!' and she wriggled free, making a dash for the companionway.

'Laurie!' He released himself from his wife's clasp, pushed her roughly in beside the others and rushed after the child. He caught her by her skirts and administered a sharp slap, plucking her up into his arms as he did so. But she shrieked so much, making herself rigid with temper, that he nearly dropped her.

As he struggled back to the lifeboat, a group of six people came bursting from below, swept him aside and jumped into his lifeboat, filling it completely. A sailor cut the retaining ropes and it fell into the water.

'Reggie!' Helplessly, Elaine held out her arms. 'Laurie! Reggie! Oh, God, they've been left behind!'

Rough hands pushed her back into her seat as, with frantic haste, those manning the oars tried to get the lifeboat away as the big liner began slowly but inexorably to keel over.

Holding his child locked in his arms, Reggie watched them go.

'Mother! Mother!' Laurie was crying with fright now.

'It's all right, Laurie girl, we'll find another boat,' Reggie said cheerfully but he knew without looking that there were no more. All round him, the crew were sliding down the decks into the dark waters. Water was washing round his feet and then his legs. 'Take a deep breath and hold on tightly,' he told his daughter, kissing her before sliding with her into the sea. The child shrieked as the cold water reached her, struggling frantically as he attempted to keep her head in the right position above the lifejacket. He was fighting for both of them as he swam away from the doomed ship, and he felt the tug on his heart muscles as he tried to push out with his feet and one arm for he dared not risk letting Laurie go with the other. When he judged them far enough away, he let her float gently beside him, pulling her after him as he swam on his back and tried to get his breath. She was roaring with fear and cold but her head was safely above water.

People were all around him in the water, crying out and trying to make contact with their families. Laurie, he knew, would not survive long in the icy water. He wondered how near the Irish coast they were and if their distress signals had been picked up: he thought he could see a winking light in the distance. Perhaps it was a lighthouse, he thought, as he tried to wipe salt water from his eyes and tread water for a few moments to rest. His heart seemed to be on fire as he pulled the little girl after him, trying to put a safe distance between them and the huge liner that had now reared up and was preparing to plunge to the bottom. Suddenly, there was a screaming hissing sound followed by a tremendous roar as the sea entered the ship's funnels and the straining boilers burst. He struggled frantically, feeling even at this distance the strong pull of the waters round the ship. For those remaining souls on board he sent up a silent prayer: Captain Bruce would have remained on the bridge because there were others helplessly marooned on board. The men in the engine room would have been trapped too. 'God help them all,' Reggie said aloud. 'God help us.'

An unearthly silence had descended on the scene with the disappearance of the *Oceana*. Awestruck, the survivors could only stare. Then suddenly close at hand, Reggie heard the splash of oars and voices. Summoning all his breath he yelled: 'Help! There's a child here – for God's sake stop!'

The lifeboat loomed up behind him. 'Sorry, we haven't an inch of room. We're dangerously overloaded.'

'Take my child! For the love of God, take my little girl! I beg you – *please*! She'll die in the water!'

A woman's voice cried, 'Yes, take the child! Someone grab the child!'

Hands came out of the dark and he pushed Laurie towards them, felt her lifted out of his arms. 'Her name is – Laurie Ransom,' he gasped. 'Six years – old. Contact the shipping line – her mother – look after her!'

They had gone. He was alone in the water. Relief made him light-headed and he sank beneath the next wave. But coming up he took in a vast gulp of air and felt the muscles round his heart relax. Laurie had a chance now. Someone would reunite her with Elaine. *She had a chance*.

Something bumped into him as he lay on his back. It was a basket chair from one of the lounges on board the *Oceana*. He held on to it and together they bobbed along, passing shapes that could have been dead bodies or pieces of wreckage. The voices of people in the lifeboats had vanished. He seemed quite alone in a vast expanse of ink-black sea. He looked up at the sky, wondering how long it would be before dawn and if it would ever break for him again.

CHAPTER NINE
Full Fathom Five

It seemed to David as he travelled to Liverpool that no journey he had ever undertaken had been so slow. At Leeds, where he had to change, the train was crammed with troops going to a camp in Lancashire. They were trench-hardened men with shabby mud-stained uniforms who had recently been taken out of the line and sent home to recruit. He looked at them with an interest that temporarily dulled his gnawing anxiety: they were the first battle-scarred men he had encountered. They talked little among themselves but their eyes stared at their surroundings as if they had not yet come to terms with them.

Poor devils, he thought and returned to staring unseeingly out of the window at the darkening landscape. His mind was heavy with foreboding. He had been inspired to telegraph Munro, the man from the shipping line who had shared his cabin coming over on the *Avonia*, and Munro had sent a two-page telegram back. Although several lifeboats had come to land, he warned David not to be too hopeful. By survivors' accounts, the death-toll promised to be horrific. Booth, also from the shipping line, was on the spot in Ireland and had been asked to meet them tomorrow morning. Meanwhile he himself would be waiting in the bar of the Station Hotel at Liverpool that evening.

Staring out of the window, David's thoughts were of his family and especially mischievous little Laurie and quiet Dan who was her opposite in every way – my God, they couldn't be dead, lying at the bottom of the sea! It didn't bear thinking about. Yet Munro had warned that nearly a thousand passengers were still unaccounted for. It was dark when he reached Liverpool and made his way to the hotel where he had arranged to meet Munro. But when he stood in the foyer he could see no sign of that familiar blue-jowled face with the bowler hat pushed to the back of a balding head.

'Can I help you, sir?' a clerk asked, leaning over the mahogany reception desk. 'Mr Munro? He'll be in the bar, I'm fairly sure. Through there and turn right.'

The bar was crowded with businessmen, with a sprinkling of soldiers and sailors. The air was choked with cigarette smoke and filled with the roar of voices all talking at once and trying to be heard. As he moved into the sea of khaki and bowler hats, David felt a hand grab his arm. He turned quickly, thinking it was Munro, and found himself staring into the podgy red face of an army officer who screamed at him: 'Why aren't you in khaki?' The man was holding a pink gin; by the colour of his face it was evident he had already had several. David's eyes blazed with anger as heads turned to stare. He shook himself free. 'Mind your own bloody business!' he said between his teeth and pushed the man out of his way. 'I don't see much trench mud on yours,' he added and there was a roar of appreciative laughter from those standing near: the officer was a 'dug-out' and hadn't set foot out of England himself.

Then as he thrust through the crowd, he saw Munro. The little man was sitting by himself in a corner reading a sheaf of telegrams, and drinking whisky and water. They shook hands. 'Drink this, lad,' Munro urged and pushed forward a second glass he had had waiting for the traveller. 'You look all-in. I don't suppose you've eaten? I thought not. We'll have a bite in a moment and then catch the midnight ferry.'

135

'Is there any news?' David slid into the vacant seat opposite his erstwhile cabin mate.

Munro shook his head. 'Not of your family. Several lifeboats have landed and a naval frigate sighted another one this afternoon.' He spread out a well-worn map printed on waxed paper; a lot of the names had been rubbed off with use but he seemed to know his way about it. 'See here? Some have landed at this point. Now our ships take this route . . . south here because there are still icebergs about even at this time of the year. So the *Oceana* would take this lane, come up St George's Channel and put in at Queenstown. Provided nothing happened, that is. We believe she was torpedoed off Fastnet – wolf packs of U-boats operate along here and put in at quiet bays for water. I've sent young Booth down ahead of us – he's in my department at the Line – and he's keeping me informed by telegraph.' He pointed a stubby finger. 'Some boats have put in at Bantry Bay here and another lot have been sighted off Courtmacsherry. There's even a possibility that several have beached on these islands. The coastguards have gone to investigate.'

David nodded rather dazedly as he sipped his large whisky. It was not a drink he cared for but it was warming him and lifting his spirits a little.

'So don't you start worrying your head too much yet, Mr Ransom. It's early days,' Munro said kindly. 'Now we'll get that meal inside us and then take a cab to the docks.'

They shared a cabin on the ferry. Fully clothed in case of emergency, they lay awake, the boat's engines shaking them mercilessly. David's head ached with fatigue and anxiety but Munro never stopped talking, reminiscing about the past and the journeys he had taken as a young man.

David fell asleep at last despite this relentless voice and

the strong smell of whisky from the bottle with which the little man fortified himself through the night. They were below the water line and the slap-slap of the sea, that had at first reminded David tragically of where his family might be lying, soon became a lullaby that sent him off to sleep. Munro had to shake him awake as they docked at Queenstown and he was stiff and hot with a very dry mouth, he discovered, as he swung his legs to the floor. It was drizzling with rain as they ate the bacon and eggs Munro insisted upon, 'for you'll do no good on an empty stomach, lad'. He then had his hip flask filled with more whisky 'to keep out the cold'.

At last, all these maddening preliminaries behind them, they walked along the greasy quay to the offices of the shipping line. There was a queue here but Booth was on the look-out for Munro and dodged past everyone to reach him. The early drizzle had become a downpour and the town seemed to be floating on water as they turned with him and walked to the gates.

'I've got news!' Booth blurted out. He had been out since dawn, had lost his cap and now his hair was plastered to his skull and his ulster was dark with water. 'Mrs Ransom and the boy are safe! They were landed about four o'clock this morning. The nurse is dead, I'm afraid. She and two others died of exposure – it was a very cold night for the time of the year and they probably hadn't got strong hearts. I've got them to make a big fire to warm up the rest – soaking wet most of them are.'

'My father? My little sister?' David grasped the man's arm.

Booth shook his head. 'Sorry. No news of them yet. I've had Mrs Ransom and your brother put into O'Donal's Hotel. There's not a bed left empty so they're lying in the lounge. It's down this way.'

David nodded, his mouth tightly controlled. He knew

he mustn't think of dear old Nanny yet or he'd break down: she had been his nurse when he first went out to America and had been waiting on the big liner that took them to Boston after he'd been snatched from Gilbert Argyle's custody. How she had hugged him and loved him, the scared little boy who was wondering what was happening to him! He pulled his mind away from Nanny and applied it to the fact that his mother and Dan were safe.

O'Donal's was a tall white house in a side street. A man in shirt and braces and soaked to the skin was supervising the delivery of fresh barrels of beer being lowered into his cellar but David pushed impatiently past him and into the dark interior. He opened one door after another until Booth, panting, caught up with him and pushed open a door into a dark and dusty little hotel lounge. Elaine was lying on a horsehair sofa drawn up before a huge fire and Dan was curled at her feet. The room, getting warmer by the hour, still smelt damp and mouldy. She seemed to be asleep but Dan sat up crying out, 'David! Davy, it's me!'

Elaine's eyes opened with difficulty: they were red-rimmed from exposure and salt water. She was shivering violently under the army blanket covering her. 'David. Thank God.' Her voice was unrecognizable; rough and hoarse.

David bent and kissed her gently. 'Mother, I'm here,' he said unnecessarily as she clung to him. 'It's all right – everything's going to be all right, I promise you.' He pushed her hair back from her icy face. 'What you both need are hot baths. I'll see what I can – '

'Reggie? Laurie?' Memory had returned and she was sitting up with a wild look of fear on her face. 'Where are they? Are they here? Have you found them?' She was

138

jerking her head from side to side to examine the other prone figures lying about the floor under blankets.

'Is that Reggie? I can see his hair – look!'

'It isn't Dad,' he said soothingly. 'I've no news yet. Were they in the boat with you?'

'No, that's what frightens me!' She shivered, dragging the rug round her shoulders. 'I never saw them get into any boat. They were standing at the rail and we were rowed away and then – and then – ' She choked. 'Oh, God, shall I ever forget it – no, not as long as I live. I was utterly helpless and then that great liner went under like a toy. It – it reared into the air and there was a terrible roaring sound and it was gone.' She buried her head in his shoulder, shuddering violently.

Fear made his voice harsh. 'Please try and think. Did you *see* them go under with the ship?'

She took a deep breath, the tears glistening on her white cheeks. 'I thought I saw them in the water – only because of Laurie's white coat – oh, Laurie, my dearest little girl!' and she broke down again.

He held her frantic hands in his firm ones as long ago she had held his when he was having a childish nightmare. He heard himself making the same soothing noises as she had on those frightening nights of his childhood. Dan, he saw with relief, had fallen into an exhausted sleep in a heap on the floor. 'Look, I'm going to organize coffee and breakfast for you. This is a terrible hole but I want you to stay here until I've finished some investigations.' He released her hands and rose, looking round him with distaste. The hot fire and drying humanity made the small room smell unbearably stuffy so he went across to a window and tried to prise it open. A bluebottle was trapped behind the lace curtain and buzzed as he disturbed it, but he succeeded eventually in opening the window an inch or so, and blessed fresh air, rain-laden and smelling of the sea, at last poured in.

'Young man!' said an angry female voice, and a grey-haired woman wrapped in blankets sat bolt upright on the floor. 'You shut that window right away! D'you understand? Right away! We've had enough sea air to last a lifetime.'

A murmur of assent ran round the room and David hurriedly complied.

'Mr Ransom, are you there?' Munro's hoarse whisper came from the direction of the door and he drew David into the dark hall. 'Me and Booth have found your father. While you've been here we nipped across to the hospital and had a word with the matron.' He took off his bowler and water ran off its brim and dropped on to the floor. Where the hat had rested on his forehead there was a deep red mark but under it his small black eyes smiled encouragingly. 'He's unconscious but that's to be expected, I think. Will you come – the child? No sign, I'm afraid.'

'I'll come at once but I must order coffee for my mother and see about a hot bath – '

'A bath? Lord bless you, there isn't such a thing in O'Donal's, I can vouch for that!'

'Then the coffee and some breakfast and we must get her on the next ferry to Liverpool.'

It was raining heavily when they plunged out into the street again, their collars turned up against the steady downpour. David had never seen such rain; it was descending like straight steel rods, roaring and hissing like a wild animal.

'The *Oceana* went down between Fastnet and Galley Head, we reckon,' Munro gasped as they skidded along the uneven pavement, down which the rain ran like a mill stream. He suddenly stopped and without looking right or left plunged across the street and through high gates set in peeling railings. 'She's gone down in fifty fathoms – just like a stone,' he flung over his shoulder.

David didn't reply, but over and over in his head rolled some lines from *The Tempest*:

> Full fathom five thy father lies;
> Of his bones are coral made;
> These are pearls that were his eyes . . .

Tears blinded him, mingling with the rain. She'd always been a cute little kid, full of spunk and mischief. *Laurie*. Oh, God, how was he to break it to his parents? Damn the war! Only a few weeks ago they had been thoughtlessly happy in New England, the European war simply something they read about. Then he had upset the apple cart and now here they were in Ireland and Nanny was dead and all too probably Laurie as well. Despair and grief choked him.

Munro had done all the groundwork and as soon as David entered the hospital he was led away to the mortuary that smelt of death and formaldehyde. He hardly recognized the face under the sheet: Nanny had lost her false teeth, her closed eyes were sunk in her head and her sparse grey hair had been neatly brushed down each side of her face. She looked terribly old and shrunken.

The cruelty and senselessness of total war as it affected ordinary, helpless people struck him like a blow in the midriff. And he had thought of it as an adventure for young men!

'Yes, it's the body of Margaret Flintoft, nurse to our family and a British citizen. I think she was about fifty-five.' Touchy about her age, Nanny had been. Only last birthday he had teased her as he made wild guesses and in the end his stepfather had intervened: Nanny, like him, must stick to twenty-nine as her last birthday, he had said soothingly.

The attendant muttered something about a mass burial for the victims. Had he any objection?

'No, let her be buried with the others and I hope a memorial with all their names will serve to remind us all what war against innocent civilians means,' David said bitterly. He gave the old face one last searching look and replaced the sheet.

Outside the mortuary a little man in a tweed jacket and trousers was hovering, obviously waiting for him. He was bandy-legged with the face of a sad monkey and had the air of someone who had to do with horses; so David was surprised when he introduced himself as Doctor O'Hara.

'It's a bad business this, Mr Ransom. There's not a soul in Ireland who doesn't feel for these poor souls, I'm sure, although we're all against the English presence here.'

'I'm concerned about my stepfather's condition – ' David prompted impatiently.

'Yes, yes, indeed. That's what I came to see you about.'

'Is he conscious yet?'

Doctor O'Hara gave a lugubrious sigh. 'They've not told you?'

Damn the man! Why couldn't he come to the point? 'No. I know only that he's here and unconscious.'

'I think he's had a stroke. The cold and the strain on his heart and so on and so on.' He spread his hands, leading the way up some stone stairs and down a narrow corridor. 'An artery in his head will have broken. That causes the seizure, y'know. Blood has flooded the brain on the right side and it's his left arm and side that's been paralysed. He'll be unable to speak, I daresay.' He pushed open a door into a very crowded ward.

Reggie Ransom lay with unseeing eyes wide open and

the left side of his face drawn into a curious grimace. Saliva trickled out of a corner of his mouth. All round him there was noise and bustle but he evidently heard nothing, lying like an inanimate hulk under the neatly drawn-up bedclothes. He looked like Nanny, David thought with grief: old and finished with life. Yet he was breathing. The punishing hours of exposure in the sea had found his weak spot and the hearty man who had been young for his age had vanished.

Staring at the man who was the only father he had ever known, David found himself begging forgiveness. If only he hadn't decided to come home and volunteer!

'Dad,' he said, taking a limp hand in his and rubbing it as if by so doing he could infuse it with life again. 'Dad, it's David. Can you hear me?'

'I'm sorry,' Dr O'Hara murmured. 'Best leave him, Mr Ransom. We'll do our best but it will have to be left to nature – oh, yes, nature has to take its course in cases like this. But don't give up hope. I've seen many a patient – indeed I have – come back to life after weeks. Slowly, mind, and with some impairment, but they're alive.'

David's eyes were angry. 'Speechless and unable to move, you mean? I would hate that for my stepfather. He's always been so full of zest for life that anything less would be purgatory for him. I wouldn't have him live on as a cabbage.'

'Now, now, we mustn't talk like that. He's in God's hands, my dear young sir,' and the doctor crossed himself.

Over a quick sandwich and a pot of black-looking tea in a fly-blown café beside the hospital, David and Munro discussed the chances there were of Laurie still being alive. Munro explained that British destroyers and submarine chasers had been called to the area off Fastnet: if any more of *Oceana*'s lifeboats were still out at sea, they should be accounted for today. Five boats were missing.

'After that, I'm afraid it will be hopeless,' Munro said, stirring several spoonfuls of sugar into the dark tea.

'I must go round the villages in the region and find out for myself,' David decided. 'Is there a motor to be hired? I can drive myself.'

He found one at O'Donal's Hotel and Mr O'Donal himself volunteered to drive for it was soon obvious that he didn't trust David to do it. 'This motor car, y'know, surr, has a special way with her – oh, indeed, yes.'

David was glad of his company. Munro had left him to go to a hall where those survivors who hadn't needed treatment were being accounted for. They arranged to meet later to decide on their next action; they mustn't lose sight of the fact that Elaine and Daniel had to be got on board the midnight ferry and sent over to England.

They made first for the Old Head of Kinsale area because there was a rumour that a boat had recently drifted ashore there. There were so many rumours flying about Southern Ireland at the moment that it was difficult to decide which might be authentic. This latest one had a strong claim because it originated from a ship that had spotted survivors in this area being helped ashore.

Ordinarily David would have enjoyed the drive with Mr O'Donal setting a tremendous pace in the Ford that was the pride of his heart. He took all corners on the wrong side and narrowly escaped disaster, scattering pedestrians, laden donkeys and a pony and trap. 'Get out of the way with yer!' he would yell as if in charge of a runaway horse. But David's heart was too heavy to appreciate the humour of the situation or indeed the beauty surrounding him. The rain had subsided and hung in the air, making the blues and greens of spring run together like woven silk.

Laurie – Laurie – The sound of the engine seemed to spell out her name. Mr O'Donal talked fast and fluently, leaving David only the necessity to mutter 'Yes' or 'Indeed?' as they drove down narrow roads to the coast. Hope was burning low in his heart. Soon, on his return to Queenstown he must break it to his mother that Laurie had died. He dreaded the task.

There was a cluster of white cottages with turf roofs nestling round a small quay and it was here Mr O'Donal stopped. 'See that light, surr? There'll be someone there for sure.'

A sharp rap on the door brought out an old woman with a shawl round her head. Peat smoke stood round her like a halo and a smell of appetizing broth escaped round the half-open door. David tried to make her understand what he wanted but she only stared at him blankly. But before closing the door in his face, she pointed to a group of men advancing up the street. Then she retreated to her window to peer out at the scene from between her plants.

'It's true, indeed it's true, sir,' the men said in answer to his query. 'There was a boat on the rocks at first light this very morn. There are many dead.'

'They were – all dead?'

They shuffled, looking at one another. 'Not all,' one volunteered. 'We have laid out the dead in our church and Father McCarthy himself has gone to Cobh to inform the authorities.' He brought out this last with relish; it was obviously what the priest himself had said and he was now repeating word for word.

A younger man came forward hesitantly with many a push and a whisper of 'Go you, Joe Pat,' from his comrades. 'There are two ladies at Granny Harper's and a little gurl lying at Patsy Connolly's. Shall I be showing you?'

'Show me, please,' David said and put a gold coin in

the youth's hand. The others exchanged looks and shuffled after them.

In the dark and odorous interior of a tiny cottage it was difficult to see clearly. A lamp burned on a table and several children moved in the shadows. A thin young woman with a shawl round her shoulders came forward and in answer to a question in Gaelic from Joe Pat pointed to a cupboard bed. Here a child lay motionless under a grubby quilt.

David stared down at the small white face framed in dark matted hair. It was a little girl and her eyes were closed. Sick disappointment enveloped him. Somehow he had felt in his bones that he was going to find Laurie at last. But this little thing with the pinched face wasn't Laurie. Laurie had fat pink cheeks and dimples and a mass of red-gold hair.

He straightened up. 'I'm afraid this isn't the child I'm looking for.'

But the woman didn't understand him. Brushing past him she put a hand to the child's neck and lifted from it a fine gold chain with a coral heart strung on it. She held it out on her palm, looking at him hopefully.

David's breath caught in his throat. Laurie had had just such a chain and coral heart . . . But this wasn't Laurie wearing it.

The woman spoke again to Joe Pat in Gaelic.

'She says the child was flung into the water when the lifeboat hit the rocks but that a lady – an American lady who was in the boat – jumped in after her and pulled her out.' He listened again to Mrs Connolly and translated: 'She says many were not so lucky. Just the American lady, one other and the little gurl.'

Snatching up the lamp, David held it over the child's head. Was it Laurie? Could it be? Gently, he turned her face towards him. 'Laurie, it's David,' he said clearly. 'Wake up! Laurie?'

The child's eyelids rolled back slowly, flickered, nearly closed again. Then suddenly her dazed blue eyes were staring full at him and Laurie's unmistakable voice whimpered weakly: 'Davy? Where's Mother? I want Mother . . .'

The red-gold hair was black with sea water and the child had lost pounds in weight. But it was Laurie all right and with a shout of gladness David gathered up his little sister in his arms. Now he had found them all.

CHAPTER TEN

Return from the Dead

Her vacation at an end, Polly was spending the last morning reluctantly packing her big trunk. But the sun shone so invitingly on the daffodils in the orchard and the sky was so full of small white clouds scudding out towards the coast that it was, she told herself, more than flesh and blood could stand. So she brushed her hair and washed her hands and went downstairs somewhat defiantly.

Of course Nell's sharp ears heard her stealthy footsteps and called from the morning-room: 'Polly?'

Polly frowned rebelliously and went into the room preparing to defend her dire need of fresh air. But her mother was engrossed in *The Times* that had just arrived.

'Look at this picture of David Ransom! It makes him look much older, don't you think?'

It was a rather blurred photograph on an inner page. Polly read the caption aloud: '"Mr David Ransom, stepson of millionaire Mr Reginald Ransom of Boston USA who is reported missing after the SS *Oceana* was torpedoed off Galway Head, Ireland, with the loss of nine hundred and seventy lives." Mother, how terrible! Nine hundred and seventy people dead! What about the rest of his family?'

'I don't know. Look at the list of dead and missing. I haven't got my reading glasses. It's a great tragedy but especially for David Ransom whose whole family was on board, I believe – there was just one married sister left behind. I think you ought to write to him, Polly, I really do. He was with you on Tuesday when he heard the terrible news. It would be friendly,' Nell insisted earnestly.

Polly shot her a glance from under her lashes. Her mother was being too transparent, she thought crossly. Just because she had been out once with David Ransom she was all set to make a match of it. Really, parents were such a nuisance when they began to think like this. Last week her mother hadn't given a second's consideration to her youngest daughter's destiny. Now, just because of a rich young man she was trying to push her into his arms!

'There's a stop-press: Mr and Mrs Ransom and Daniel Ransom are safe. There you are, Mother! The rich are always saved!'

'Really, Polly, you should be glad for the young man's sake. Now about that letter – '

'No, Mother, thank you. That's your task, I think. You can write to his mother and welcome her back at the same time. But perhaps you had better wait: there's the little girl who's still missing.'

'Are you sure?'

'Well, she's not named; only the boy. I'm going for a short walk. Do you want anything from the village?'

As she walked over the packhorse bridge into the village she found herself smiling wryly. It was obvious that her mother was wistfully hoping that she had become close friends with David Ransom during the short time they had spent together on Tuesday. Well, Polly thought with a sigh, that was well and truly over before it started. He was a very attractive man with a charm that was difficult to resist – but she had resisted. They simply had nothing in common, she had decided. David Ransom epitomized every thoughtless male who believed that a woman's place was only in the home and that men were lords and masters. The stupidity of the man! Polly ground her teeth with rage and felt better. Well, she must stop thinking about him. It was going to be difficult because – why not admit it? – she had been very much attracted to him.

She turned down on to the river path where the ducks scattered as she walked through them. Outside the New Inn (new in 1630) sat Herbert Lazenby, the oldest man in the village and a veteran of the Crimean War. In the fine weather he always sat outside the inn hoping to be treated to a pint by anyone who would sit and listen to his reminiscences.

Now he eyed Polly hopefully, smiling toothlessly because although he was the proud possessor of false teeth paid for by the squire, he only wore them on Sundays. 'Morning, Miss Polly. I thought you were at that there college? Had enough of you, have they?'

Polly paused. 'Not yet. I'm going back tomorrow. Have you heard about your great-grandson yet? At Loos, wasn't it?'

The old man nodded. 'Aye. He were a good lad, were Ernie. Just eighteen. Captured by them Jerries and not a word since. I reckon they've finished him off,' and he drew a shaky finger across his throat. ''Tain't no good saying so though. Sue and Albert don't listen to me. I knows about war. Jerry wouldn't have the food to feed our lads – so they finishes 'em off.'

'Oh, I'm sure they haven't done that – and you oughtn't to worry your grand-daughter with such stories,' Polly scolded, sitting down on the bench. 'It takes the Red Cross a long time to get news of them. He'll be home by the end of the war, you'll see. Here you are, the price of a pint.' She found fourpence in the little purse in her pocket and put it on the table.

'Thank you, miss, but it's gone up to sevenpence now. It's the war, they say,' and the old man looked hopefully at her.

She put down a threepenny piece and the old man said earnestly: 'You've a good heart, Miss Polly, just like the rector,' and he pocketed the money to await the pub's opening.

I wish it was as easy to cheer up Mother, Polly thought, walking on past Doctor Mallory's house and up on to the open moor. From a vantage point up here she could look down on the house with its neat garden and disused tennis court. Ned Mallory, the doctor's only son, had been sweet on her, she remembered. She'd been sixteen and Ned two years older, a sweet-tempered, rather dense boy who had just left school and was going to London to study medicine that autumn of 1914. Instead he had gone to France and been killed before Christmas. His father, who had been apt to castigate Ned as a worthless layabout who would come to a bad end, now mourned him silently, working every hour that was possible to assuage the emptiness in his life.

She looked round her as she walked slowly on: every stone on the moor, every patch of heather was familiar and held memories of that last carefree summer. So much had happened in the months leading up to the outbreak of war. Dick had arrived home from India with a bride. They hadn't known a thing about it and had been sitting having tea under the mulberry tree when the station fly had turned in at the gate. Dick had jumped down and turned to hand down a vision in violet and biscuit. 'Hullo, everybody!' a high-pitched cockney voice had greeted them and Katy Odell, late of the Gaiety Theatre and now Mrs Dick Paget, had stepped into their lives.

While the Pagets had goggled, Katy herself had poked her new husband in the ribs. 'Well, aren't you going to do the honours?' she had demanded.

Thus Katy Odell had come into the family. Cheerfully uninhibited, she had taken all of them to her heart and when Dick was killed that October, she had picked up the pieces of her shattered life and come back to Eskton to have her baby and to run the house.

And now we all love her, Polly thought, and I'm beginning to think Uncle Wilfred likes her best of all! After all, he had adored Dick, spoilt him shamelessly and been as shattered as Dick's parents when he was killed: what more natural than if he adopted Dick's little family, perhaps even married Katy? He had a great admiration for 'the little woman' as he dubbed her.

The sound of the church clock striking the hour reached Polly on the rock where she was lazily sunning herself like a lizard. She yawned and swung her feet down. She would have to go back and finish her packing.

When she reached the house, she found a group in the hall. Something had happened. Even Nell Paget had emerged from the morning-room; Mrs Linsey was holding the baby and Katy was holding an orange telegraph form.

'What is it?' Polly leaned over Katy's shoulder and read: '"*Kit missing believed killed coming home today Alix.*" Oh, Mother, how awful! The baby's due next week, isn't it? She shouldn't be travelling now of all times. I can't believe that Kit's dead – he can't be! It will break Alix's heart – ' She faltered to a stop, seeing the expression on her mother's face.

'Yes,' Nell said in a strange voice – almost one of triumph, Polly thought. 'Yes, all our hearts will be broken soon.' She turned and went into the morning-room and as the door snapped shut they looked at each other. In the silence, the baby began to grizzle hungrily. 'More! more!' he shouted, using the only word he had for food.

'Lunch, Mrs Linsey,' Katy said firmly. She folded the telegram and put it on the hall table, then she took Dick from the cook and led the way into the dining-room. As they began to eat, they heard the rector come in and pause by the hall table where he always looked for his messages. The handle turned and he came slowly into the room, holding the telegram. He looked searchingly at the girls.

'How did your mother take it?'

'Come and eat, Dad.' Polly went across to the sideboard and cut him a slice of bacon-and-egg pie. 'She took it very well. We're terribly upset about Kit, of course, but it's hopeful, isn't it?' She put the plate in front of him and added, 'Isn't it?'

Her father sighed, stroking his chin, a habit of his when worried or puzzled. 'I don't know, my dear. It sounds very bad. The telegram was sent from King's Cross: did anyone notice? It means she started at nine o'clock and more than likely will be on the six-thirty at Whitby. I pray she'll make the journey without trouble. How typical of Alix to act before she thinks!'

'She would have felt in need of comfort,' Katy suggested, pushing the salad towards him.

'Let's face it: Aunt Nora's isn't a bosom to cry on,' Polly said caustically. 'Can't you just hear her? "Come, come, Alix, be sensible. The servants might hear"!'

'Your aunt has been very kind to the young couple,' the rector pointed out in a mildly rebuking tone.

At this point, Archie arrived late for lunch and the news had to be broken to him. 'Good heavens, she'll be having the baby here now. Have we room?'

'We can fix up the spare bedroom for the event,' Katy suggested. She was in her element suddenly. 'There are all Dicky's things – the Moses basket, the little bath and a heap more in the attic. Archie, will you help me fetch them after lunch? I'll write at once – no, we must telegraph Nurse Barnes to come immediately. You remember how well she looked after me when Dicky was born?'

The rector wasn't eating. Putting his knife and fork down, he rose. 'I shall have to send a note up to the squire to ask if he can lend us his motor car to fetch Alix from Whitby. In her condition – '

'Oh, rector, what a pity the squire's in Middlesbrough with the motor until tomorrow evening!' Katy exclaimed. She wiped the child's mouth and took his bowl of cereal away, blissfully unaware of Polly's startled look.

How on earth did Katy know the squire's movements when he hadn't been near them for a week? Polly's eyes turned to her father; he at least didn't seem surprised.

'Is that so, my dear? Then the twins will have to go over in the dogcart.' Turning to Archie, he added: 'You'll have to travel carefully on the way back, my boy. Your sister's condition is rather tricky with the baby expected early next month.'

They set off in good time. Once out on the open road Archie attempted to get a little speed out of Pinky but the crafty pony knew who was in charge and was mulish. In vain Archie clicked his tongue and shook the reins: the pony simply broke obediently into a trot for a few seconds then almost immediately slowed down again to a walk.

'Give her a sharp swish that will surprise her,' Archie urged as Polly pulled out the whip from under the seat. 'I know Father makes us promise never to use it but I consider this to be an emergency. Get *on*, you fat slug!' he roared suddenly.

The startled animal got on, her legs fairly twinkling down the road to Whitby.

'See that? A taste of the whip is what she needs.'

'It's a good thing she can't talk,' Polly retorted. 'Think what Father would say!'

They continued in silence for a few minutes then Archie

observed: 'I liked him, you know. A thoroughly decent fellow.'

'This war!' Polly said despondently.

They both knew they were referring to their brother-in-law, Kit Gromont. He had been reading for the Bar but when war broke out, he had volunteered immediately. Long months in the trenches had changed the good-tempered and humorous young man into a grim-faced, silent officer who had come home on leave to marry their sister a year ago this spring. He had been due for leave after the baby's birth: now the twins were silently wondering if Alix would ever see him again. *Missing* had such a hopeless sound to it.

The York train was late into Whitby: they had time to walk up and down the breezy platform several times before at last it pulled in, releasing a huge jet of steam and soot as it screeched to a halt. Doors were flung open and passengers streamed towards the exit. Dodging in and out, peering through the choking steam, the Pagets looked in vain for their sister.

'She can't have caught the connection at York – '

'There she is!' But Polly's eager smile of welcome faded. Could that stooping figure in a dark cloak be Alix? Under a dusty velvet hat, her face was pale and drawn, her eyes dark-circled.

'The baby's started . . . Quick! Get me home!' were her first words.

At this awful announcement, Archie and Polly drew horrified breaths. '*What?* You mean – then it's straight to the hospital for you, my girl,' and Archie took her by the arm.

She resisted. 'No. No, I want to go home – '

'But it's miles – '

'I don't care. First babies – take ages – and I – only went into labour – ' She held his hand as a contraction

155

seized her. 'It started at York.' There was sweat glistening on her face and she brushed it off with a gloved hand. 'Don't look like that, sillies, there's heaps of time to get home.' She smiled suddenly into the two pairs of horrified eyes. 'Don't worry. I promise it won't be born on the way.'

'How d'you know it won't?' Archie demanded angrily. He was furious with her for landing them in this predicament. His naval training hadn't taught him anything about birth and from her wide-eyed look of horror, he shrewdly guessed that Polly knew no more than he did.

Gathering her cloak round her, Alix was walking towards the dogcart. 'Help me up . . . now make her go as fast as you can, Archie.'

'Easier said than done,' Archie retorted grimly.

Nevertheless, with a judicious touch of the whip now and again, Pinky did trot quite briskly to the foot of the hill leading out of the town. Then she all but stopped.

'Get down, Polly. We'll walk and pull her after us.' Archie had seized the bridle and was tugging. Pinky stuck her neck out and her toes in and was deaf to all cajoling. 'If I had my say in the matter, she'd go to the knacker's yard tomorrow!'

'Leave her alone like Father does,' Polly whispered. 'See? She's coming.'

Pulling and driving alternately they somehow covered the ground. It was a chilly evening and dusk was falling rapidly. Next month, the new Daylight Saving Bill would come into being and they would be living by false and not true time and although the Pagets had all poured scorn on this scheme, two of them at least were now beginning to see its possible advantage.

Three miles from home, Alix, who had been very quiet, suddenly gave a loud cry and slipped to the floor of the dogcart. 'Hurry!' she muttered. 'Please hurry – '

'I knew it! She'll have it here on the road!' Archie said despairingly. Pinky had stopped dead and was cropping the new grass growing on the side of the road. Leaping down, uttering naval curses, Archie pulled her head up. 'Give her the whip, Polly!' He clambered back just in time as Pinky, her eyes glinting dangerously, broke into a wild gallop and they covered the empty moorland road faster than they had ever done before.

'Oh!' Alix's voice was muffled but anguished.

'Archie, for heaven's sake, pull her up! This is worse for Alix than going slowly. Don't yell at the creature, she'll only go obstinate – ' Archie deduced that his agitated twin meant the pony now – 'We'll stop and light the lamps. It's getting very dark.'

One-armed though he was, Archie's male pride insisted on performing this task himself. Polly watched dumbly, her hands clenched, as he slowly opened one lantern, lit a match by striking it on the road, adjusted the flame and carefully closed the lantern door again. Then he went round to the other side and did it all again. Polly, guessing that he was moody and depressed, realized that any interference at this juncture would bring on a scene that wouldn't be good for Alix so she said nothing, waiting patiently. Glancing down at her sister, she could see Alix's white face leaning against a seat cushion: she was gripping a handkerchief between her teeth.

Clambering back in at last, Archie too glanced down. 'Oh, God!'

'I'm all right. Just *hurry*.' Alix's voice was faint but distinct.

'She oughtn't to have set out this morning,' Archie whispered.

'I suppose not.'

'D'you know what to do if it comes to the worst?'

'No, of course I don't!' Polly looked aghast.

157

Archie said no more but he looked grimmer than ever. How crazy it is, he was thinking with exasperation, to make higher education available for girls before teaching them to cope with life's crises first! A hundred years ago, the rector's daughters would have been versed in all the household arts as well as knowing how to deal with birth and death. At this moment, Polly stood very low in her twin's estimation. He glanced at her and saw that she was biting her underlip and frowning deeply.

She was in fact wondering whether they might not stop at the Barmbys' farm over there. The Barmbys would take Alix in, especially as the baby's birth seemed imminent. Things like hot water would be needed, she thought vaguely; she couldn't think what for but it always said so in books.

The last gleam of light had vanished behind the low line of moorland. Moths fluttered against their faces and a white owl flew low towards some scrub oak. There was a faint smell of ferns and damp moss as the road unrolled in the faint beams of the lanterns. Alix, huddled in her cloak at their feet, was silent now: with one hand she held on to Polly's skirt. She had taken off her tam and her bright hair had tumbled to her shoulders.

At last, the turning to Eskton lay before them. Pinky broke into a brisk trot, her little hooves ringing in the stillness, her breath clouding the air as she sensed home and oats.

'We must stop at Doctor Mallory's,' Archie said, pulling the pony up as they reached the doctor's house and the first row of cottages leading into the village. 'I'll ask him to come up at once.'

Polly watched him running up the path to hammer on the dark green door with its shining knocker: an oblong of light showed as old Maggie, the maid, opened the door. She breathed a sigh of relief: no need now to think

158

of carrying Alix into Barmbys' farm and putting the kettles on to boil. They were almost home.

Suddenly, Alix's voice startled her. 'Do you remember that last picnic before war broke out? At the Druid's Stone? Ned was with us. Poor Doctor Mallory. Such a long time ago – not two years really. We were just children then. I hadn't met Kit – ' Her voice trailed away as a contraction seized her.

Taking out her handkerchief, Polly leaned down and wiped the sweat off her sister's face. 'Hold on – we're nearly home.'

Archie jumped in beside her and shouted: 'Walk on,' to the pony in so peremptory a voice that for once Pinky walked on as briskly as needed for them to cross the packhorse bridge and to come in sight of the rectory gates.

The front door opened as they drew up and the rector's tall stooping figure emerged. 'Alix, my child!' He put his arm round her and helped her down. 'We've been getting anxious. Was the train late?' He stopped, looking down at her. 'Are you all right, child?'

Polly hurried after them. 'Oh, Dad, it's awful! The baby started at York and I thought it would be born any moment! Where's Katy?'

But it was Nell who came hurrying across the hall to them, quite in her old manner. Taking in the situation at a glance, she wasted no time in questions. Beyond saying, 'Alix, what foolishness to travel with your time so near!' she took her daughter's arm and helped her up the stairs.

The rector exchanged a glance with the twins. They were all too taken aback by the sight of Nell Paget in charge again to say anything for a few moments. Then Nell called down from the landing. 'Arthur, I can hear the doctor's motor. Can you send him up at once?'

But Mrs Linsey, who had come out of her domain to take in the situation, now brushed them aside and lumbered down the front steps calling out: 'Eh, doctor, here's a to-do! Poor Miss Alix's time has come and t'poor lass only lost her husband yesterday and we haven't a stitch to put on t'bairn – '

The doctor looked at her appreciatively. 'Trust you to give it to me in a nutshell, Martha Linsey. You're wasted here, d'you know that? I believe Whitby is looking for a new Town Crier.' Shrugging off his Burberry, he rallied his old friend, the rector, who was hovering in the background. 'No need to look like that, man, Alix is like her mother, a real little moorland pony. We'll be drinking the baby's health in no time.' With similar insults and encouragements Doctor Mallory always rallied his patients and their relatives.

As he mounted the stairs and disappeared round the corner, the rector shook his head with a sigh. 'That's what he always says,' he observed, unimpressed.

Archie took his father's arm and led him into the dining-room. 'It's rotten management on her part but that's Alix all over,' Polly heard him say.

She sat down heavily on a hall chair, reaction setting in. Archie's forgotten we haven't unharnessed Pinky, she thought. For a moment, she felt too weary to move and had to drag herself out to take the pony to her loose box and give her her supper.

Going upstairs to wash her hands afterwards, she was electrified by a strangled scream of pain from behind the closed door of the spare bedroom where they had taken Alix. There it was again; just as if she were being tortured. Turning round, she fled downstairs and burst into the dining-room with a white, scared face. 'Oh, Father, I think Alix is going to die! She's crying out dreadfully!'

The rector was carving ham at the sideboard but he paused to put a comforting arm round his daughter. 'Come and have your supper, Polly. Your sister is not going to die: your mother and Katy and Doctor Mallory are with her. It's perfectly natural for women in labour to cry out, you know. It sounds much worse than it really is.' He handed her a plate of ham. 'Come now, my dear, you'll feel better when you've eaten.' Sitting down in the big chair at the head of the table, he helped himself to the small pat of butter that was supposed to be shared by them all. Wartime scarcities meant little to the rector. When the food was there he ate it, but its absence didn't trouble him at all.

A cry from upstairs, prolonged and agonized, made them put down their knives and forks and look at each other.

'Why can't Doctor Mallory give her something?' Polly demanded hotly. 'Why should she suffer like this?'

The rector broke open his baked potato and inserted the pat of butter. 'I told you: a woman in labour always cries out. It's perfectly natural.'

'Natural! Men wouldn't endure it for five minutes!' Polly said passionately. 'If they had to have the children, they would long ago have found something to make birth bearable. It's typical!'

'But birth is a perfectly natural process, child. Later on, perhaps, Mallory will give her a little chloroform and soon she'll be sitting up as right as rain,' the rector said with forced cheerfulness: he hated suffering in anyone and his daughter's cries of pain were making it difficult for him to eat. But with the twins' eyes on him, he made valiant efforts to swallow his food and to appear reassuring. 'After all, your mother had five of you without mishap,' he pointed out. He couldn't remember Nell making the sort of noise that came now from upstairs, he was thinking. If only one of them would come down and give them a progress report!

The meal, such as it was, was quickly over and the

161

rector looked round the room. 'Where is my good William? Pussy, pussy, pussy? Don't throw those bits away, Archie, William might like them. Where is he? I want to brush him.'

Archie pushed back his chair. 'He's in the morning-room in front of the fire. I'll fetch him for you.'

William, a large spoilt cat with a coat the colour of a fox's, objected with growls and clinging claws to being removed from in front of the fire. Archie bore him to the dining-room hanging limply under his arm. 'He weighs a ton,' he observed, putting him down with relief. 'If things get really bad we'll be able to eat him.'

'That's not funny, my boy. Come, William, come, good cat,' crooned the rector, producing a brush from behind his back: in times of stress he found grooming William calmed his nerves. William, for his part, hated such attentions on his master's part and with a purposeful expression stalked to the closed door where he sat, wearing a vilely cross expression. Undeterred by throaty growls from his pampered pet, the rector pounced, plying the brush vigorously as he kept William imprisoned between his legs.

The door opened and Katy came in slowly, her face very sober, and went to her place at the table. They all looked at her expectantly but she said nothing.

Polly asked apprehensively, 'How is Alix?'

'Everything's slowed up,' Katy admitted. 'The doctor thought she was going to give birth at once but now it looks like being a long affair. She's getting a lot of pain but making no progress at all.'

A cold gloom settled on her listeners. Hiding her apprehension as best she could, Polly went into the kitchen. 'There's no more butter, I suppose?'

Mrs Linsey was sitting rocking comfortably in front of the stove. 'There is not and that's a fact. You can have some of that marga stuff if you like – they say it's made of candlegrease or worse. Smells like it. I never touch the stuff meself. How's dear Miss Alix? Suffering by t'sound of it. Aye, it'll be a long job I'm thinking. She's that small. Just like my niece Beatie. Now she was in labour three whole days with her first and then the bairn was born dead.'

Polly looked frightened. 'Oh, but Alix couldn't endure it for *three days*! She'd die. I do wish Doctor Mallory could help her.'

The cook shook her head knowingly. 'Women just have to put up with it, Miss Polly. They do say putting a knife under t'bed cuts the pain.'

Polly brushed aside the piece of folklore. 'He'll *have* to give her something for the pain! It's cruel not to help her!'

'I tell you there's nowt he can do, miss. We're in God's hands. Live or die, it's up to the Almighty, that's what Mother used to say.'

'Well, all I can say is He hasn't made a very good job of birth!' Polly retorted angrily.

'Nay, Miss Polly, don't let rector hear you speak so!' Mrs Linsey was sitting bolt upright in horror. 'I don't know what's got into you at that college – the awful things you say sometimes!'

'Well, some things need saying and very loudly, too. Is that Mother's tray? I'll take it up.'

She carried the tray of supper up the narrow, dark back stairs leading from the kitchen and down the long landing to the spare room. The lamps had been lit now and cast pools of light on the oak floor. Putting the tray down on a chest, Polly knocked gently on the door. 'How is she?' she whispered when her mother opened the door.

'Things aren't too good.' Wearily, Nell pushed the hair back from her face. 'I'll eat in my bedroom. Alix will be all right, the doctor's still with her. What's happened?

Well, the contractions have almost stopped.' She sat down in a basket chair and Polly placed the meal on her knees. 'The baby's weaker too, Doctor Mallory told me. Now, don't worry, she's in good hands and you've all your packing to finish – '

'But I can't go back tomorrow now! Not if the baby's not been born. Oh, Mother, don't ask me to do it. Alix might *die*. I'll telegraph Miss Conway in the morning – '

'Certainly not! Of course you must go tomorrow. What can you do anyway, Polly? Now don't argue but go and finish the trunk and then go straight to bed. You and Archie must get up early tomorrow to catch that nine o'clock train. Now, run along. Good night, darling,' Nell said, attacking her food with appetite.

Closing the door behind her, Polly went thoughtfully upstairs to her bedroom. Her mother was . . . different . . . restored and invigorated. She looked as she hadn't looked for a year and a half. Indeed she sounded almost herself again.

Polly's room was up a half-staircase from the main landing: a square room with two windows and a walk-in cupboard for her clothes. Going to one of the windows she saw that drifting rain clouds had obscured the moon. There was a sudden dash of rain against the glass and she hurriedly drew both sets of curtains before lighting the lamp. Then she contemplated the pile of clothes she had never got round to packing that morning. With a deep sigh, she set to work to fill and lock the trunk. As she worked she was aware of activity below her, of a sense of unease filling the house and her own head. She heard the knocker on the front door rattling loudly; voices on the stairs; feet going up and down. Someone had evidently fetched Nurse Barnes from Whitby.

She undressed and lay unable to sleep, aware of a low

164

murmur of voices. She turned and tossed, feeling hot and miserable. How long would it be before the baby was born? Eventually, about one o'clock, unable to bear it any longer she gathered up her eiderdown and pillow and stumbled downstairs to her twin's room.

He was still awake and reading. 'Hullo, what's up with you?'

'I can't sleep I'm so worried about Alix. Can I camp out on your sofa?'

Archie could see that she was on the verge of tears. 'Of course you can, Poll. Want another blanket?'

She shook her head, snuggling thankfully under her eiderdown. She was no longer alone; warm comfort flooded her. 'Just like the old days, Archie,' she murmured and was soon asleep.

Archie blew out his lamp and tried to settle to sleep himself. But whether it was the sound of light snoring from the sofa or the subdued activity downstairs, he found it difficult to relax. He always hated not going off to sleep at once for it was when lying in the dark that his hidden fears came to the surface. He was a cripple who now had to change direction in life. What if he didn't get up to Oxford? He didn't possess a brain like Polly's and books had always been a struggle. All his life had been bent on action and from the age of fourteen he had found it in the navy as a 'middy'. Now that life was gone for ever, blown up like his shipmates on HMS *Cobra*. It was vital that he earned a living and became independent as soon as possible because all he had was a tiny pension from the navy. He had been glad for his father to make the decision for him and decree that a career in the church was the most suitable for him: now he wasn't so sure.

He sighed, lying on his right side facing the wall: he still couldn't bear any pressure on his stump. Although the whole arm up to the shoulder was gone he could swear he felt it sometimes, could even move fingers that were no longer there.

He sat up suddenly for there was renewed activity in the house: doors were opening, footsteps echoed. Looking at the clock he saw it was four o'clock. He scrambled out of bed, shrugging on his dressing-gown, and cautiously opened his door. Looking over the well of the stairs he saw a little group outside the spare room door: his mother, Doctor Mallory and the nurse. He called softly: 'Has the baby been born? Is she all right?'

They turned their fatigued faces up to him.

'She's weaker,' Nell said. There was a hopeless look on her face: fate hadn't finished with her yet, it seemed, and she was going to lose another child. Weary tears ran down her face. 'It's the shock of hearing about Kit. She's exhausted – I really believe she wants to die.'

'No, no, my dear, I'm sure that's not so.' The doctor had put a hand on her arm. 'I fear we may lose the baby, though.'

'If only we had news of Kit to tell her! Good news that would make her rally and take an interest in giving birth – '

'Then of course we must tell her just that!' Archie interrupted. 'Mother, don't you see? Alix must be made to believe that Kit has been found. You can say Uncle Dolly found out for us and telegraphed the good news. It will give her the strength she needs, don't you see?'

They all stared at him, their eyes dulled by weariness.

'But think of tomorrow when we have to tell her it's false news,' Doctor Mallory pointed out doubtfully.

'Let tomorrow take care of itself. By tomorrow – unless we do something – Alix and her child may both be dead,' Archie retorted impatiently. 'Who can do it convincingly enough? Mother, will you?'

'Oh, I couldn't – she would only guess it was a falsehood if I attempted to do it,' Nell said quickly.

They were all staring at him, he noticed. 'Very well, I'll do it. It's my idea, after all. Don't worry; she'll believe me,' he added. Without waiting for permission he pushed open the spare room door and went in very quietly. A lamp burned on a chest and a case of instruments was open on a chair. A fire had been lit and on the guard waited the unborn infant's clothes, clothes used by Little Dick at his birth. It was the family Moses basket that stood in its stand by the bed, a cot used by each of them in turn.

It smelt hot and unaired with the window closed and the fire a dull red glow. He went across and opened the heavy velvet curtains and the window itself. She would need every scrap of oxygen she could draw into her lungs to expel the baby, he told himself grimly. Then he turned to the bed where Alix lay silently, her head limply turned away.

Help me to lie well, God, he said in his head and realized how incongruous the prayer was. But the God he believed in so hazily would understand, he felt sure. He bent over her and was instantly shocked by the change in her face: she looked old and wizened and there was a dark shadow round her mouth. Poor little devil, he thought with anger, they've been badgering her for hours, exhorting her to 'get on with it'. Now she had had enough and her whole face was tightly closed against them.

'Alix, it's me, Archie. I've got news for you. Listen to me, please, Alix.'

The lamp cast grotesque shadows as she moved her head and reluctantly half-opened her eyes. 'Archie?'

'Yes, it's me, dear. I've got good news for you about Kit – Alix, open your eyes, please, and look at me.'

Her glazed eyes met his. 'News? Kit?' she mumbled.

'We've just heard. Uncle Dolly telegraphed. Kit is safe. Can you hear me? *Kit is safe.*'

Suddenly she seemed to come alive: her eyes were full of the lamplight as her head came up. 'Kit? You're sure? He's – he's all right?'

'Yes. Wounded and coming home.'

She struggled to sit up, her dry hot hands clutching at him. 'Oh, Archie! Oh, God, I can't believe it – ' She fell back against the pillow and he rushed to the door.

'Come on, quick! She needs you,' he gasped.

Nurse Barnes pushed past him first. 'Now, Mrs Gromont, just you leave everything to nurse and do what I say – '

The door shut on them all and he stood dazedly outside. *What have I done?* Tomorrow – ah, yes, tomorrow (or rather this morning) after the baby had been born would come the reckoning. His pyjamas were soaked with sweat and, remembering that Polly was in his room, he stripped in the bathroom and rubbed himself down. He felt terribly tired as he crept back to bed. Well, God owed him something, he thought as he drifted into uneasy sleep.

It was several hours later that he was woken up by Polly leaning over him saying his name. 'Wake up! The baby's come! It's a girl. I've just seen it – hideous, poor little thing, exactly like a frog. Can't you hear it yelling its head off? Oh, and the most wonderful thing has happened! Kit's been found in hospital in the rear.'

'That's what I told her,' Archie groaned, sitting up and rumpling his hair, thinking of the cruel deception he was going to have to explain to poor Alix. Would she ever forgive him? But the baby had been born, and alive too. 'It isn't true,' he tried to explain. 'I made it up to help things along.'

Polly stared. 'What are you talking about? Do wake up! The telegram has only just come.'

Archie felt the hair on the back of his neck rising. 'You've seen it?'

'What? The telegram? Yes, of course. I've *told* you. It's enormously long and that's the gist of it. Kit's been identified in hospital. He'd been labelled and sent to the rear and the ambulance carrying him was blown up and all the men inside were burned – oh, it's horrible to think of but that's why they thought he was dead too. He had no identification and was unconscious. Uncle Dolly's friend at the War Office found it all out.' She broke off to stare at her brother who was laughing silently, holding the sheet to his mouth.

'It's the last time I play God!' he gasped when he could get his breath. 'It can only happen once and I've used it up already!'

'I don't know what you're driving at but I've got to go up to London. I'm half-dead from lack of sleep and I haven't packed yet.'

He sat silently in his bed after she had gone. Warmth was spreading slowly through his body, bringing comfort and hope. He was convinced now that God had touched him last night. Now he wouldn't be going into the church for the sake of a meal ticket. Was this what was meant by 'a call'? He was filled with an immense gratitude to the nebulous God he had been brought up to believe in, yet had never quite done so. Now . . . yes, now he could believe. Last night God had nudged him. He felt sure of it.

CHAPTER ELEVEN

The Hand of Fate

Polly reached London at six o'clock. She got a cab without difficulty and by six-thirty was greeting Robson who opened the shining black door of thirty-six Leander Gardens with a beaming face. 'We're all delighted to hear of Mrs Kit's safe delivery, miss. Oh, yes, the telegram came just before luncheon and we were able to drink her health and that of the little girl. It's a blessing, miss, to have news of the captain and we hope he's not too badly injured.'

'Rather a day, isn't it, Robson? I too hope Captain Gromont isn't too badly wounded. I wish we could hear something.'

Robson was directing the cabby to put the trunk in the hall and over his shoulder said: 'Mrs Emerson would appreciate a word from you after dinner, miss. We're all grieved about the captain but he's a strong young man and we're sure he'll pull through.'

'Tell Mrs Emerson I'll come down later. The baby is very healthy, tell her.'

'Polly!' a voice called out and there was Celia Gromont, her cousin, running down the stairs. 'Polly! I'm so happy you're back! Oh, Polly, I've bought a new teddy in Scotland. You must come up and see him!' Celia, the Gromonts' only child, was twenty but her mental age was eight: sometimes, sucking her thumb and murmuring to her family of teddy bears, she could seem even younger than that. Lovely to look at, being willowy with a pale oval face and a cloud of dark hair, she had had a very successful Season two years ago, the last before the outbreak of war. It was only as she became better known that word got about that Miss Gromont was not quite what she seemed. The fact that she had been born retarded was steadfastly ignored by her mother. In her heart, Nora Gromont was bitterly envious of her sister's brood with their good looks and intelligence. They hadn't a penny to bless themselves with but somehow it didn't seem to matter: they got on despite this liability. Really, it wasn't fair! Her envy sometimes made her tongue bark more sharply than was kind.

From under her arm, Celia now produced a small and shabby bear with one eye. 'This is Theo. Do you remember how Kit mended his ears for me? I'm going to send him to Kit now that he's ill. Poor Kit, will he get well soon?'

'Celia, for heaven's sake! There's twenty minutes before dinner so please hurry, both of you. You know how the judge hates to be kept waiting.' Retired though he was, Nora still referred to Sir D'Oyly as 'the judge'. She had found it carried more weight than 'my husband' or 'your uncle'.

'Come on, Celia.' Polly took her cousin's arm. 'You can show me your bears while I'm changing. Am I in the blue room again?'

Celia slipped her slim hand in her cousin's, smiling happily. 'Come and see the teddy I bought in Scotland.' Together they went upstairs to the small bedroom on the second floor that Lady Gromont thought good enough for her nieces to 'thrash around in', as she put it. Here Polly unlocked her case and hurriedly withdrew her best dress. She had long ago learned not to give her aunt's maid, Louise, her keys to unpack her case. Louise had once inspected everything with a disdainful eye and pronounced *mademoiselle*'s possessions to be unfit to wear. So now the best dress hadn't been pressed and was very

171

much creased. Aunt Nora was sure to notice and to click her tongue at her, she thought impatiently as she hurriedly poured water into the washing bowl. Celia helped button the dress up the back quite successfully and together they ran downstairs.

Her uncle greeted her affectionately. Sir D'Oyly Gromont was many years older than his wife. With no son of his own, he had brought up his orphaned nephew from the age of nine and now his hooded eyes were sombre as he talked about Kit's wound.

'At the moment, he's partially paralysed – '

'*Paralysed*, Uncle Dolly?' Polly's face went white. 'But that's terrible! Poor Alix is so relieved and happy that he's been found so quickly, how can one possibly tell her this?'

'We may not have to. He's being brought home – I've arranged a private ambulance – and then he'll be examined by Sir William Varley, the neuro-surgeon. Apparently a piece of shell is lodged somewhere in his spine, causing paralysis. If it can be safely removed, the prognosis is good. A long time in hospital perhaps, but eventually he could be as good as new. But as we shan't know the extent of the damage until Varley examines him we must say nothing to Alix.'

She nodded, unable to speak, the delicious food like ashes in her mouth. It was all too horrible to contemplate. Kit had a brilliant future predicted for him at the Bar – if this war ever came to an end. It was just as well that Alix hadn't been told.

Robson came in bearing a cream and rum pudding. How on earth did the cook contrive such concoctions with everything so scarce, Polly wondered as she ate it raptly. She had as yet no knowledge of the expensive black market that was presently flourishing in London and which her aunt enthusiastically supported, unknown to the judge, who always preached patriotic economy. Robson, before handing round the pudding, had bent over Sir D'Oyly and murmured into his ear. The judge pushed back his chair. 'I'm sorry, my dear, but I have to go on duty. A Zeppelin has come in over the Thames estuary.' He was a special constable in the Knightsbridge area, his duties filling the vacuum left by retirement. Certainly he had brightened considerably as he hurried from the room leaving his wife wailing: 'Oh, not another raid! I can't – I won't stand another raid! My nerves are too fragile. It's obvious we're losing this war and we'll have that horrible Kaiser sitting in Buckingham Palace – '

'*Nora*.' Sir D'Oyly had come back into the room and his voice was low and icy. *His Black Cap voice*, his nephew Kit called it feelingly. 'I will not have you spreading alarm and despondency in this reprehensible manner.'

'Oh, Dolly, how can you! No one has put more into the war effort than I – *no one*! The Duchess was only saying yesterday – Celia, stop fiddling with that spoon! You're getting on my nerves.'

'Poor Mama's worried.' Celia stroked her mother's hand. 'So I won't do it again, I promise.'

The judge's face melted and he bent to kiss his daughter tenderly. 'That's my good child,' he said huskily, his hand touching her dark head. His eyes went to his niece. 'Look after her,' he said. Then he shrugged into the dark navy-blue mackintosh held by Robson and hurriedly left just as the long wail of the newly introduced sirens split the air.

'Oh, that noise! So stupid of them to have such a bloodcurdling screech.' Nora Gromont held her head. 'I feel quite dizzy – Celia, you've spilled the water now! Robson, mop up Miss Celia. Don't dither, Polly: you can finish your pudding later. We must go down into the cellar.' Over her shoulder, she added: 'I was only saying to Imogen yesterday afternoon – '

'To Imogen? Is she on leave? We haven't seen her for a year.'

Nora Gromont was seating herself on a comfortable chair in the clean dry cellar that was well-lit and equipped for any emergency. 'I shouldn't have told you. She asked me not to but of course I've a very frank nature. You can't blame Imogen, like all girls her age she's bent on a good time in London. Yorkshire's no place to spend your leave! I came across her quite by chance at the Stores. She had a charming officer with her. I shouldn't have blurted it out but it's entirely due to my nerves. They're all to pieces.'

Even after a month's holiday in Scotland? Polly thought scornfully. Really, Aunt Nora took the bun! And how could Imogen behave as if her own family didn't exist any longer? Hospital service in France had certainly changed her eldest sister. But her aunt ought not to encourage her in this deceit and it hurt to remember how her parents longed to see Imogen on one of her leaves. 'You'll hear from the powers-that-be soon enough if anything happens to me,' she had told them airily before going abroad.

Robson came down the cellar stairs carrying the coffee tray. 'I hope you don't mind, madam, but the kitchen staff are staying upstairs to finish their work. If we hear a bomb, I'll send them down at once. Everything's quiet at present.'

'I think I'll go back upstairs myself.' Polly sprang up with relief. 'There hasn't been a sound – '

'Sit down, Polly! I forbid it. If you go, Celia will want to follow you – you know how silly she is.' She was opening a box of chocolates, a gorgeous round box of what were called *matinée* chocolates. 'Hugh Worth brought me these yesterday. Such a sweet boy in the Guards.' She bent over the box, a frown of concentration on her face as she helped herself first. She was affecting a

174

very young style of dress. Gone were the days when she wore last Season's dresses for dinner at home. The beaded chiffon she wore tonight would have looked more suitable on her daughter but war fever had seized Nora Gromont as it had seized so many women and the cold hard fact that she was over fifty was forgotten. She would refer pityingly to 'poor Joan' or 'poor old Sylvia' as getting very shaky, poor things, as if they belonged to another and older generation. After dinner, if the All Clear sounded she would no doubt telephone some young officers to escort her and the two girls to late supper and dancing into the small hours. Polly dreaded these occasions for she knew her home-made dresses were conspicuous and the young officers, brainless youths in wonderfully cut breeches and with neighing laughs, treated her as the country cousin who had never seen London before.

'I'll ring Hugh when we go upstairs,' her aunt said, reading her thoughts without knowing it. 'We'll go dancing to that new place – what's it called?'

'I'm awfully tired, Aunt Nora. Do you think I could be excused?'

Her aunt's cold eyes swept over her. 'I suppose you want to go to bed with a book as usual? Really, what a little blue stocking you are!'

'Oh, Aunt Nora, what a *passé* expression!' Polly murmured, getting her own back. 'It's Victorian, isn't it?'

At that moment, a resounding crash shook the house.

'There! What did I say? Oh, my poor old Dolly out in this – he'll be killed – I know he will!'

Celia began to cry, her slim body shaking with fear. Polly jumped up and hugged her. 'Buck up, Celia, old thing. It's nothing really. Let's play ludo. Have you forgotten how you beat me last time we played?' Her aunt, she saw with distaste, was comforting herself from the second row of chocolates in a rapidly emptying box.

She stayed until after lunch next day. There had been no more bombs dropped and the raiders had gone back down the Thames estuary and out to sea. Her mother always insisted on Polly breaking the journey back to Cambridge by staying with her sister in London. Although she said it was because she didn't want her daughter arriving very late in Cambridge after such an early start from Whitby, Polly suspected that her mother enjoyed getting news of her sister Nora at first hand. Tomorrow, Polly knew, she would have to write a long account home. It was all very well for Alix, who docilely fitted in with Aunt Nora's whims, Polly told herself, but for herself it was an endurance test. It was no pleasure to her to breakfast in bed and then to go on the morning round of shopping for a hat for Celia or wait patiently in Swan and Edgar while her aunt was measured for stays. The only pleasure lay in the food, which was amazing for wartime.

'Last night there was quite a lot of damage down by the docks,' Sir D'Oyly said over lunch of lamb and mint sauce followed by hot chocolate soufflé. 'Aeroplanes this time. I fear we can expect a lot more raids this summer. Unlike the Zepps, they can raid us at any time and I'm sure they will. Our anti-aircraft guns don't seem to frighten them.'

Robson began to remove the pudding plates and Polly sat back replete from what by rectory standards was a feast.

'No cheese for me,' said the judge and so they all went upstairs for coffee. 'What time is your train, my dear? Five o'clock? Then Robson must get you a cab in good time.' He drained his cup and got up. 'Nora, I'll be in to dinner but I'm going round to the club for a round of bridge this afternoon.' He went across to his niece and kissed her, pressing a wad of notes into her hand. 'A few Bradburys for next term,' he whispered in her ear and went out before she could thank him.

'Your uncle's too generous,' Nora Gromont said. 'I don't know where you Paget girls would be without him. I suppose your father's stipend is still not much more than three hundred a year?'

Polly's quick temper threatened to burst its bounds for she recognized this as her aunt's usual taunt about her father. *Poor Arthur, all those children and unable to provide properly for them.* With an effort, she swallowed a quick retort and said instead: 'I must go and fasten my case. I have enjoyed myself and especially the food, Aunt Nora. Mrs Emerson is a marvellous cook.'

'Yes, it will be vastly different to what you're used to, I'm afraid. Is your mother still employing that terribly plain cook she's had for too long?'

It was her Parthian shot and Polly let it be so. But as she went upstairs she reflected it must be sad to be Aunt Nora who seemed to have everything and yet was so discontented that her sharp tongue frightened people away. Her mother's naïvety about people blinded her to Nora's venomous nature: all she felt was pity for a sister whose child was not whole. But Nora didn't want her younger sister's pity: she wanted her envy and Nell (who often felt envious) never showed it. And – worst of all – the rectory children seemed to get on despite all the drawbacks. It wasn't fair, Nora would tell herself, and her tongue would utter something sharp and hurtful.

Money's not everything, Polly told herself, cramming her dowdy best dress into the valise. All the same it was comforting to have those notes of Uncle Dolly's in her pocket.

* * *

177

She left earlier even than Sir D'Oyly had advised and felt relief as the cab swung out into Knightsbridge leaving Celia waving with tears in her eyes. Celia hated to see her cousins leave. What sort of life could the poor girl have, Polly wondered, with a mother who would not recognize her daughter's mental state? It was only too true that one could pick one's friends but God gave you your relations! Remembering Uncle Dolly's kindness, she fished the banknotes out of her pocket and stuffed them away in the bronze nappa handbag that the squire had given her for Christmas. She drew out the silver-backed mirror from its silk pocket and examined her reflection. The new street outfit was nice: even Aunt Nora had said so, albeit grudgingly. Polly had used the whole of her quarterly allowance on the good Yorkshire facecloth material she had bought at Scarborough. With it went a blue velvet collar and velvet-covered buttons. Nell had been horrified to see that her daughter was to wear this best outfit to travel to Cambridge. She had exclaimed even more loudly when Polly added her best glacé kid shoes to the picture. 'I'm not spoiling the ship for a ha'porth of tar,' she had stated firmly and had been annoyed when her brother went into peals of laughter.

Looking out of the window she saw that there were few people in sight. Then as they drove down the Mall, the AA guns in St James's Park came into action, causing her to drop her handbag.

The cabby opened the glass partition. 'Must be a raid somewhere, miss. There's been no warning. Want me to stop?'

Polly hesitated. She was scared of air raids but even more scared of Miss Conway's displeasure if she were late returning to Girton. 'If you don't mind going on, I'd like to get to Liverpool Street to catch my train.'

'I don't mind, miss. Hang on to your hat!' the man said cheerfully.

A few people were running down to the tube station at Charing Cross and as they emerged on the Embankment, the man pointed across the river where puffs of smoke indicated a fire. There was no sign of any aeroplanes, Polly thought uneasily, straining her eyes into the sky, but they must be about.

They got to the station without incident and she tipped the man well.

Her train was waiting on a side line. Looking round the compartment at her fellow travellers, Polly groaned to herself. Her father always insisted on her travelling first-class when she was alone and this always ensured the dullest of travelling companions. This evening she was to be accompanied by a dean in gaiters, an old lady in black whom he addressed as Mother-dear, and two oldish men buried in evening papers. *Speak to no one*, her mother had always emphasized. It wouldn't be hard to achieve, Polly thought as she took out a battered copy of *Silas Marner*. It wasn't easy to see under the darkened roof of the station and one of the men snapped on the light. In the silence, the insistent sound of running feet suddenly echoed: voices called out urgently and it seemed as if a London bus were passing overhead . . .

'Stanley!' the old lady quavered, clutching the dean. 'Is that an aeroplane?'

'Now, Mother-dear, keep calm, I beg.'

But the plumes in the old lady's hat were beginning to quiver pathetically. 'There! I said all along we ought not to have come up to London!' she wailed tearfully.

Suddenly, the door of their compartment was wrenched open and a young officer got in. One arm was held in a black sling and he looked pale and drawn. He sat down in the vacant place beside Polly and stared morosely ahead

179

until the dean's mother added: 'If only we knew where the aeroplanes were. One is so vulnerable in a railway station.'

'They are overhead,' the officer said suddenly, bringing his melancholy gaze to bear on her.

The old lady gave a subdued shriek. 'Why weren't we told? Come, Stanley, we must find a more durable shelter than this.' Feigning reluctance, the dean rather self-consciously collected their hand luggage and followed his mother, his gaitered legs moving fast.

At that moment, the bark of an AA gun and a shower of shell splinters on the station roof made the rest of the passengers exchange glances. A woman porter's shrill voice was heard calling: 'Take cover! Take cover!'

'It's too late to move. We're as safe here as anywhere,' the soldier observed. Polly saw with surprise that his face was twitching and yet his voice was quite matter-of-fact. With an air of insouciance she was far from feeling she opened her copy of *Silas Marner* and attempted to read. She wished with all her heart that she had taken an earlier train. Her hands were damp and her heart was beating wildly under her outwardly calm appearance. It was no good pretending: she was very frightened. She felt sick and her tongue had stuck to the roof of her mouth.

A huge *c-rump!* shook the whole train. Clamping her jaw, she opened her handbag and pretended to search inside for a handkerchief. Her whole nature was urging her to run screaming from the confinement of this first-class compartment. Only pride held her to her seat.

The young officer turned his twitching face (of which he was totally unaware) and glanced curiously at her. The girl beside him was barely discernible in the half-light but she hadn't displayed any fear, not even giving the high-pitched shriek one expected from females. Game little thing, he thought, easing his wounded arm on the window

180

ledge: he had been holding it tightly against his body as if he feared further injury to it.

Today he had been up before a medical board.

'Of course you'll want to get back as soon as possible?' one officer had said.

'Oh, rather, sir!' he had lied with a ghastly grin.

So they had given him another two months' leave to finish his treatment, and his secret dread of returning to the front had become a living thing again. It gnawed at the centre of his being, affecting his brain and his nervous system so that he had become a different person to the eager boy who had joined up in the autumn of 1914.

He stared out at the dirty platform, at the familiar posters for cocoa and baby carriages, at abandoned barrows and chocolate machines, seeing none of it. Instead his inward eye, like a kinematograph, played over and over again the same scene: a forest of jagged tree stumps near Contalmaison, the rolling coil of black smoke from a 'Jack Johnson' bursting in front of their parapet and his best friend Hugh Isherwood lying face down in a bomb crater on that last raid they were returning from. He had tried to rally him, kneeling in the sucking mud beside him, saying urgently: 'Hugh! Hugh, old boy, are you all right?' Then he had seen the gaping hole at the back of Hugh's head . . . So that was the end of Hugh, who had been at school with him, joined the Territorials with him, kept them all laughing with his irrepressible wit and had been the best and truest of friends. His own wound later hadn't caused him the anguish that he had felt at Hugh's death.

He moved restlessly. God, this filthy war! His only brother was gone, killed in the Dardanelles, and one by one his friends were dying. Why didn't it end *now*, before the entire youth of the world were wiped out? For a bitter moment, he wished the aeroplane overhead would drop a bomb and kill him here and now so that he wouldn't again have to face the terror of returning to the front.

Then it happened. There was a blinding flash and roar as if the station roof were falling in and his nostrils were filled with the sickening and familiar smell of lyddite. The shock of the explosion set the train lights glimmering fitfully and in the sudden dart of light he saw the girl turn to him, her hand gripping his arm in a vice of fear. No sound came from her but her large blue eyes were fixed beseechingly on his face.

He patted the hand on his sleeve (thank goodness, it was his sound arm) and said soothingly: 'It's all right, it's nowhere near us.' But even as he spoke he could hear terrified screams from trapped people and smell fire. Shouts and running feet now added to the sound of panic and, with muffled exclamations, the two other passengers threw open the door and jumped on to the platform, running like hares to the underground.

'S-somebody's hurt – oh, what can we do?'

The soldier put his arm round her shoulders. 'Nothing. Just stay here. Jerry will be miles away by now. They always hop it after throwing the bombs.' He felt wonder that it was he giving reassurance to another human being. Since that last battle in January, the sound of an explosion or any loud noise would set his nerves jangling so that he couldn't think coherently. But now he felt steady and confident. It was very queer. Was it because the girl had turned to him for reassurance and had given him no time to think of the effect on himself? A warm glow of satisfaction irradiated him. Glancing down at the face so near his he saw a pretty profile, an auburn curl and lips that quivered. She was small, this girl, with a fine delicate skin that had gone very white and long lashes that fluttered involuntarily as new and jarring sounds rent the

182

air: klaxons, motor engines, a babble of frightened voices, cries.

Then she turned suddenly, straightening the blue velvet tam that had become lopsided, and gave him a faint grin. A long dimple creased one cheek and her eyes – as blue as the tam – sparkled again. 'Goodness, we're alive! I've never been so frightened. Thank you for being so – so reassuring,' and she drew away for she had suddenly become aware that their shoulders were touching and – oh, how awful! – he had an arm round her! Nell Paget's face floated before her daughter's eyes: *Why can't you remember you're the rector's daughter?*

Glancing shyly at the soldier she saw how young he was: her own age, probably, and very thin and slight with a delicate fair face and a sensitive mouth. He had one arm in a sling and a wound stripe on his sleeve. His lint-fair hair kept falling across his forehead and he kept pushing it back, she noticed. Suddenly, he became aware of her scrutiny and they both smiled; she noticed his smile didn't reach his eyes: they remained haunted-looking. His uniform looked too loose as if he had recently lost a great deal of weight.

Suddenly the train gave a preliminary jolt or two and began to draw out of the station.

'You see? They're sending us off so the raiders must have gone.' He glanced at his wristwatch. 'We're going to be an hour late at Cambridge – you are going to Cambridge?'

'Yes, I'm going back to Girton.'

'My people live there – keep a boys' school on the Madingley Road. My name's Mike Wynne, by the way.'

She shook his proffered hand. 'I'm Polly Paget.'

If Nell could have seen her youngest daughter chattering happily to a strange young officer she had picked up on the train, her worst fears would have been realized. Of all her children, she believed Polly had the least sense of fitness. Those short skirts! The Castle Clip style of hair! If she wasn't very careful she would be dubbed *fast*.

But to Polly, the officer was no longer a stranger. She knew his name and his address and now she was hearing about his wound on the western front in January.

Leaning back in his corner, he began to tell her about his medical board that morning, how he had got two months' grace (he had nearly said *reprieve*) before returning to France.

'Will your wound really have mended by then?' Her eyes were examining his black sling with sympathetic respect.

He reddened. 'Oh, it's nearly all right now.' But the sulky, withdrawn look was back on his face, she noticed. He was seeing in his mind's eye the cool eyes of the three men on the medical board. *Why are you wearing that sling? There is no longer any need for it. The wound has mended completely.* They had made him feel a fraud, a shirker. Damn them!

With an effort he brought himself back to the present and to the girl whose eyes were fixed sympathetically on his face. He warmed to her: she didn't think him a shirker. She had actually turned to him for reassurance and comfort. Only about eight weeks left before he must face the terror again. He must see more of this girl. 'Do you have to be chaperoned if you come to a *thé dansant* at the Dorothy Café? I would like to ask you to come with me one afternoon.'

Her eyes widened in amusement. 'But I would never be given permission to go there! Yes, we're chaperoned everywhere – especially to supervisions at the men's colleges. Our Mistress fears the worst.'

'Miss Jones? She's a friend of my parents. Does she

wear mittens still? When I was a child I didn't believe she possessed hands!'

'I hardly see her so I don't know. It's difficult even to see her from my seat in chapel.'

His face had brightened, was even smiling now. 'There's a story that she once said to a member of the college hockey team: "If you must play hockey, hit the ball *gently*."' He had made her laugh, he saw delightedly.

From then on it was easy and they didn't stop talking the whole journey. As the train slowed on the outskirts of Cambridge, he said eagerly: 'Can we meet again? Please say yes. It will be perfectly in order, you'll see. Miss Jex-Blake who's going to be the new Mistress at Michaelmas was up at Girton with my mother.'

'But Miss Jix isn't my tutor! Miss Conway is a stony person. Will your mother write? I'd have to bring a friend, you know. We're not trusted out on our own.'

He groaned. 'It's too antiquated for words! But I'll get my mother to write to your tutor – Miss Conway, you said?'

He took out a diary and jotted down the name. As the train drew up he glanced out of the window. 'We're later than I predicted. Tell you what, I'll run you up to Girton in my little bus – it's out in the station yard. She goes like the wind, a spiffing Model T Ford I bought from a friend who's gone back to the front.'

'But it won't take a trunk, will it? Mine's huge.'

'That's true. Never mind, tell them to send it up by carrier.' He laughed, his spirits rising as he took her arm. 'And I tell you what – '

'So there you are!'

They leapt apart guiltily. A thin little woman with a disgruntled face under a severe hat was blinking crossly at them. Polly recognized her as Miss Hornby, one of the Girton housekeepers. 'I've been waiting over two hours.

Where have you been, Miss Paget? You're late – very late.' Her eyes snapped in Mike Wynne's direction, drawing their own conclusions. 'Where are Miss Gibbon and Miss Heath? They were supposed to be on this train. And who is this?'

'I didn't see Miss Heath or Miss Gibbon at Liverpool Street. I'm sorry I'm late but the train was held up by an air raid. And this is a friend, Mr Wynne.' Polly added this boldly, nettled by the woman's attitude.

'Miss Paget and I travelled down together because our mothers are such great friends.' Mike Wynne smiled charmingly as he lied. 'As you can see, I've been wounded and Miss Paget was kind enough to help me on the train.' He was drooping slightly. 'So kind of her but then we were brought up together, you know.' He was about to add that he and Miss Paget had shared the same bath as infants and stifled this flowery invention just in time. But Hugh would have said it, he thought with a pang, and would have smiled so innocently and confidingly that this gorgon would have believed him.

As it was, the housekeeper's suspicious expression didn't relax. The young man was certainly pale and thin and his arm was in a sling – on the other hand, she knew modern young people were completely lacking in morals: what about all those war babies? 'Goodnight, Mr Wynne,' she said in a steely tone. 'Come along at once, Miss Paget.'

Mike Wynne stood looking after them: the grim woman was escorting pretty little Polly Paget as if she were an escaped prisoner-of-war. He knew the type: the hospital where he had spent three months had possessed a ward sister cast in the same mould. He noticed that Polly Paget didn't dare risk even a backward glance. What pretty legs she had! He watched until they were out of sight. As he walked to his motor car he thought: I must see her again.

It was ten-thirty when he let himself into the dark house that was his father's preparatory school. It was near the university observatory at the top of Madingley Road and was a large ugly red brick building with bay windows, turrets, cupolas and pebbledash decoration: solid and ugly and sitting in a garden filled with monkey puzzle trees and clumps of fine beech.

It was still the Easter holidays so the house was empty of small boys. As he crossed the creaking oak boards of the wide hall intent on going straight up to bed, the door leading to the kitchens swung open and his mother, Ruth Wynne, emerged. She was wearing a discarded Jaeger dressing-gown of Oliver's, her dead son, with a net on her iron-grey hair and a glistening of cold cream on her wind-roughened skin.

'Hullo, there, old chap! Thought it must be you. I'm just making the cocoa so come and have a cup.' She led the way back into the cavernous kitchen where a dim oil lamp lit up a corner. The stove was still glowing and the room was stuffy with a permanent smell of past meals.

Mike sat on the edge of the big table in the centre watching his mother at the stove. Most mothers, he felt sure, would have met him at the door, anxiety forming staccato words like, 'Well? Quickly, tell me. Is it – must you – how long have you got?' His mother had asked him nothing. Indeed she was now talking over her shoulder to him about the prolonged battle at Verdun that had been slowly bleeding the life out of the French army since February.

'Did you hear any news in London? You saw Jumbo Broadbrook, didn't you? What did he have to say about it?'

'Oh, come on, Mother! You comb *The Times* every morning, don't you? All Colonel Broadbrook said was what we all think: there's got to be a push soon if only to

187

take the pressure off Verdun.' Now, surely she would ask: How did you get on at your medical? Have they passed you as fit? When do you have to go back?

But no; talking about the western front, she was spooning cocoa into their cups and boiling up the milk. He found himself staring at the cups: Indian Tree pattern. He had known them all his life. They meant home to him – like his mother. As he took the tray and stood on one side for her to precede him, he remembered that he and Oliver had never run to her for kisses and comfort when they were small. 'Be a man,' she had always urged when they fell and scuffed their knees. Tears were a sign of weakness and were never allowed. He doubted if she had shed any tears when Ollie was killed. He had seen his father cry. Not his mother, though. He wondered how she would feel when he too was killed.

He had no doubt that this time he would be killed when he returned to the trenches. He had been lucky. The chances of any young officer surviving three or four months were slim, so in another six months he would be dead. His body shrank from it yet his mind burned with this foreboding that was a certainty. He didn't want to die before he had tasted life. Poor Ollie, who had had a girl he wanted to marry, had been snuffed out like a beetle underfoot. Didn't his mother guess what the future held for him – for his whole generation – if this war continued into next year? What use then would be her jingoism, the same jingoism that had gripped the whole country following several defeats and recently published stories of German atrocities.

Fight to the bitter end! Total victory only! Give your sons and all you have to the war machine. Give! Give! Give!

And in Germany there were more women like his mother, mad with the idea of the total sacrifice of all they held dear for the sake of the Fatherland. They were all drunk with it and the war, feeding on these emotions, would go on indefinitely.

He followed her out and across the hall to the study where it smelt stuffy and dusty as if the windows had been shut all day and the sun had burned up everything in its path. The heavy curtains were drawn across each of the windows.

'Is Dad in bed?'

She settled herself in a leather chair and took the cup he proffered. 'Of course. You know how he is, must get his seven hours. I can't understand why he's always so tired nowadays: he does very little. Nothing in the holidays and a few classes in term time.'

'Oh, come on, Ma, the poor chap has the whole caboodle on his shoulders! It's a worry.'

'Nonsense – and don't call me *Ma*. What is wrong with the honourable word *Mother*?'

He sighed. 'Sorry, I forgot.'

'I'm the one who carries the burden of this place: your father does the fretting and I do the work.' She sipped her cocoa in silence. 'Well, did you have a good day?'

She had taken him by surprise. He blinked at her. 'Oh, exhilarating!' he said dryly. 'I went before a medical board.'

'Good news?'

Good news. My God, she meant it, too. For a moment, he hated her. 'Oh, the best,' he retorted and recklessly tipped the remaining sugar into his cocoa. 'They passed me as nearly fit. I'll return to France at the beginning of June, probably.'

'That's splendid, old boy! I know you'll be eager to get another crack at the Hun, eh? Of course you'll get a decoration this time. It would be splendid, Mike.'

He stared at her dispassionately, realizing afresh why

he couldn't love her. They were poles apart in outlook. She refused to acknowledge what the war was like: an obscene carnage, a waste of young life. She was the same breed as those white feather donors who waited outside theatres to pin them on men who weren't in uniform. Draining his cup, he got up and stretched. 'I must go up – I'm half asleep. It's you who deserve the decoration, Mother, you and countless others who have already given your sons.'

If she winced inwardly she gave no sign of it. 'My dear, we're more than willing to give everything in this great cause. I'm thankful I've had sons to offer my country and that one has already made the great sacrifice.'

She was mad, he thought with dull pain as he went wearily upstairs. War frenzy had taken hold of people. Some day, without warning, they would suddenly become sane again and the full horror of what had happened would finish them. By then it would be too late to recall their sons from the dead. Their houses, their lives, the future would be empty.

'That you, Mike?'

His stealthy footsteps were causing the floorboards to creak.

'Yes, Dad.' He pushed open his father's bedroom door and smiled at the man sitting up in bed. Walter Wynne was propped against a mound of pillows in his Jacobean-style oak bedstead. His sparse grey hair was on end and an old-fashioned striped nightshirt was buttoned tightly to the throat. On the mock-Jacobean side table an economical half candle burned in its brass holder. Everything in this room was mock-Jacobean as supplied by Messrs Maples thirty years earlier when the Wynnes were married and setting up the school. It was good and solid, meant to last several lifetimes, but remarkably ugly. 'I thought you'd be asleep, Dad.'

'I'm trying to get some extra rest before the boys return on Friday.' He sighed tiredly at the thought of coping once more with that crowd of restless humanity that gave him his living.

Mike sat down on the foot of the bed. 'You'll enjoy it as you always do once term begins.'

'*Enjoy* it?' Walter was nettled. 'Enjoy teaching classics to ten-year-olds? Rubbish, boy, it's the bane of my life! Well, what transpired in London? What did the board say?'

'I've got till the end of June to get my arm muscles in shape again.' He stretched his left hand, feeling the weak stiffness travelling back up his arm. 'I'm to go daily to the Eastern General for wax treatment. Oh, they expect I'll be fighting fit by June!'

They were both silent. Walter's face was creased with worry. In the silence they could hear Ruth Wynne calling the cat in and the chimes of one of the college clocks floating across the fields on the still air. The distant but even more distinct sound of Ruth treading heavily on the stairs brought Mike to his feet. 'Goodnight, Dad, don't worry about me.' He bent and kissed the top of the grey ruffled head and Walter was touched. He nodded, gripping his son's uninjured hand. 'Goodnight, my boy. Remember you're all we've got left,' he muttered. Unable to communicate their strong affection, they were yet fully aware of their feelings for each other.

After his son had gone back to his room, Walter lay staring at the pool of light flickering on the ceiling. The boy dreads returning, I know, he said to himself. Hadn't he done enough? Eighteen months' service, a bad wound, shattered nerves and he wasn't quite twenty, yet they would send him back again! He had earned a rest, a place in some base camp for a time. Yet all because he and Ruth knew no one who could pull strings for them, they were helpless. They had tried Jumbo Broadbrook and he had been vague and unhelpful. What a failure he was as a father, Walter reproached himself, turning and thumping his pillow frustratedly: there was nothing left that he could do for the boy.

In his room, Mike was undressing quickly. His body burned with fatigue like an old man's. Once, he hadn't known what it was to be tired, but nowadays he had to pace himself or he disintegrated into a hopeless wreck, he thought with self-contempt. If only his nerves would heal and he could be himself again! Shrugging on a dressing-gown, he went into the other wing to take a bath in one of the school tubs: here the gurgling water wouldn't disturb his parents. There were six baths in a row, their enamel scarred by the passage of hundreds of small bodies over the years. There was plenty of hot water supplied by geysers and he lay up to his neck holding his damaged arm above the water. God, what a vivid mark it had made, the passage of that piece of red-hot shell! He stared at the new pink skin growing round the stitching: it was still tender to the touch, the whole arm aching where the muscles had been torn.

He had just two months left.

He threw his sponge into the last bath in the row and rose to towel himself vigorously. Well, he intended packing a lot into that time and tomorrow he would begin by asking his mother to invite Polly Paget to tea and tennis.

In Girton everyone was still awake and visiting each other's rooms with gossip about their activities during the Easter vac. Behind carefully drawn curtains, the lamplight glowed. There was still no electric light anywhere in the red-brick buildings that even in daylight were a bewildering composition of Gothic arches, turret staircases and dark corners. Gas burners flickered in the corridors but there were only oil lamps in the sitting-rooms with candles for the bedrooms. Each student had the luxury of two rooms to herself and the unpacking of the big leather trunks and wicker portmanteaux overflowed from one room to the other. There were books to be placed on shelves, photographs scattered about the rooms, pictures to be pinned up. Musical instruments, tennis racquets and golf clubs filled corners. People ran down corridors, doors were banged, voices called out and at eleven o'clock Miss Conway's gip, Elsie, stumped up the stairs.

'Miss Conway's compliments and I'm to ask you young ladies to please hush up.'

There was a howl of laughter at the idea of Miss Conway telling anyone 'to please hush up'.

'Elsie, you fraud, you're making it up.'

'I never am, miss. And here's a note for you, Miss Paget.'

Polly went back into her room to read the three-cornered chit. Her tutor had written in her Italianate script:

Dear Miss Paget,
               Please call on me at ten o'clock tomorrow morning.
                                                    M. C.

It was five minutes to the hour when she reached her tutor's room next morning. With an eye on her watch she waited for the exact minute before tapping gently on the door.

'Sit down, Miss Paget.' Miss Conway leaned back in her chair and toyed with an amber paper-knife. The usual Russian cigarette had been laid aside on an ashtray. She means to give me just two and a half minutes, Polly thought with relief, for she knew quite well why she had been summoned.

'Miss Paget, here at Girton we regard our students as adults. We have no wish to treat them as silly schoolgirls who cannot be trusted to behave themselves on all occasions. It annoys me when I have a case like yours before me. I've always regarded you as one of the more sensible freshmen – not someone likely to pick up an officer in a train.'

Despite herself, Polly felt an annoying blush spreading across her face. 'I didn't! At least, I didn't mean to. It was because of the air raid. We began to talk when the bomb fell on the station.'

A ghost of a smile touched the tutor's thin lips. 'But I understand from Miss Hornby that the officer actually had you *by the arm* on Cambridge station. Surely you didn't allow such a liberty from a perfect stranger?'

Too late, Polly realized that she ought to have lied, lied good and hearty, as Archie called it. 'I – I don't remember that – no, I'm sure he didn't.'

'Miss Hornby has made it all up?'

'Oh, no. But I simply don't remember him taking my arm . . .' A mental picture came into her mind: *So there you are!*, and they had leapt apart. 'Yes – it's true. I remember now.'

Miss Conway sighed. 'I'm disappointed in you, Miss Paget. It's not your morals I'm concerned with but the good name of Girton. That I passionately care about. The university has never liked us. Can you imagine their glee if it came to their ears that Girton girls were untrustworthy little flirts?'

Something in Polly recoiled from this academic iceberg. 'I'm sorry you consider me that. We would never have spoken if it hadn't been for the air raid. Mr Wynne is a perfectly respectable person. His father runs a boys' private school at The Red House on Madingley Road.'

'Oh, that Wynne. They're odd fish. That explains it.'

194

'Are they?' Polly asked, opening her eyes innocently. 'He said his mother was a great friend of Miss Jex-Blake's.'

A little frown marred the perfect smoothness of Miss Conway's brow. Her pale eyes sharpened. 'That is all, Miss Paget. Please take this as a warning. You may go.'

Polly didn't go back to her room. She wanted to think so she headed for the Honeysuckle Walk, a popular place with most of the girls but empty this morning. She strolled along with her hands deep in the pockets of her knitted jacket. The walk was sheltered by tall hedges and trees and in a month's time pink honeysuckle horns would spread themselves lavishly over the hedges and the sweetest of smells would fill the air. Now on this fine April morning there was a scent of new growth and green leaves were tentatively pushing forth.

Her head was full of Mike Wynne. The memory of his wan, boyish face floated before her eyes. A deep, warm pity for this boy – her exact contemporary – caused her to wonder how she could help him over the next few weeks. It had been so obvious that he dreaded returning to the hell of the western front and was indeed unfit mentally to do so. Even after three months he still seemed to be suffering from battle shock and Archie had once told her that this took longer to heal than a wound.

If he gets his mother to invite me, she thought, I will get round old Conway somehow and go – I'll go without permission if need be.

At that moment her impulsive heart was ready and eager to go to any limits to lift that terrible shadow from Mike Wynne's eyes.

CHAPTER TWELVE

The Pity of Love

It was May and the Ransoms were at last back at Northesk House.

Looking round her old home where as an only child she had been so restlessly unhappy, Elaine realized she was seeing it with new eyes as a safe haven. She was home and they were all safe, except poor Nanny. Reaching Northesk late one night, her heart had leapt at the familiar smell of the place. She was met by the warm Yorkshire voices of the Elliots and she had felt tears springing to her eyes.

'Come you in!' Mrs Elliot said in her comfortable way and then, seeing the tears, had added, 'You'll be that tired, Miss Elaine. Now you go straight up to bed and I'll see to the bairns.'

'It's wonderful to be home,' she said shakily, taking Lizzie Elliot's advice.

This was soon being repeated round the village: Miss Elaine had said it was wonderful to be home! Why, the poor lass had probably been pining for Northesk these past twenty years and all she'd done was to pay two brief visits with Master David. It stood to reason why she was so thankful. That America wasn't *Yorkshire*, was it?

Thus, hardly meaning to do so, Elaine won back the hearts of the simple folk who had been so startled by that awful divorce action that (to their secret shame) had been splashed all over the newspapers.

It was not going to be so easy to win over the county, though. None of the well-known families called to welcome her back to the estate that had been in the North

196

family for two hundred years. As far as they were concerned, the waters had closed over Elaine North's head when she had had the gall to pillory one of her own sort for the vulgar people to mock. No wonder that poor chap Argyle had given up his political career and gone to live in France! She had behaved disgracefully, they told each other, and kept away.

Within a week of her return, Elaine found herself lonely and bewildered, deeply regretting her decision to follow David to England. Reggie was in a private hospital in York; he was paralysed down one side and would need nursing and a great deal of attention for months, perhaps even for the rest of his life. This was the difficulty: private nurses had all but disappeared because they had gone into the services or were with the newly raised hospital units in France and Serbia. So until she could find someone, Elaine had to persuade Reggie to stay in York.

He had aged so much that he was now barely recognizable as the youthful-looking man who had waltzed with her on board ship the night before the disaster, who had still been able to make ardent love to her and whose presence in her bed and life she so sorely missed. His face was badly twisted and he dribbled helplessly from one corner of his mouth. His eyes were the same, though: they were alive with feeling when she took the children in to see him. He had looked eloquently at her. Thank God, those eyes said, our children are safe.

But she knew that she had lost him as a husband and lover and that all that lay before her was his old age. He could never recover fully, the doctors had warned her. She had wept with grief and rage in the long nights, repeating his name over and over to herself. She blamed David and the German navy in equal proportions. After all, if David hadn't been in such an absurd hurry to rush to England none of this would have happened. If only he had waited! David realized the strength of her feelings as she emerged slowly from the shock of her experience and, wisely, didn't attempt to argue with her. But to himself he had to admit that he resented her attitude: hadn't he begged her to stay home in Boston? She had wilfully ignored his wishes and those of his stepfather. Now it was Reggie whom he pitied with all his heart.

A fortnight after their return Elaine found someone permanent to nurse her husband: a middle-aged woman with some experience who had nursed her old mother for years. Miss Matthews was very plain and Elaine understood only too well what Reggie's anguished expression meant. 'I know, darling,' she murmured teasingly, 'but I daren't let you have a pretty nurse – you know what you are!'

The tiny joke was an echo of their past life together and he pulled her hand to his lips. Once, not long ago, he could have crushed her in his arms and tears sprang to her eyes. How cruel life was!

Two days before he left, David came running downstairs whistling under his breath.

'Where are you going?' Elaine asked curiously, just in time preventing herself from saying 'in this benighted hole'.

'I'm going over to Eskton.'

'Eskton? What on earth takes you there?' Another benighted hole. The whole area was dotted with them, she remembered sadly.

'Oh, just to see a chap I met when I was here on my own. He's the rector's son, Archie Paget. He was invalided out of the navy last year – he's only a kid, too.' It was better not to mention the dazzling Miss Polly Paget yet; his mother would be sure to jump to conclusions.

'Very well,' she said indifferently and continued to stare out of the library window. Fuel was rationed so they lived

198

in the library now; when Elaine was alone she even had her meals there on a tray. The landscape was as bleak as she always remembered it. It was now early May but it seemed to her that everything – sky, trees, even the grass – looked greyish. Greyish green. Greyish blue. Greyish brown – yes, even the soil was a uniform pale grey! She closed her eyes to shut it out, longing suddenly for the New England spring, for weekend visits to Newport, for Long Island Sound with the tide running fast and the exhilaration of being on Reggie's new yacht in the opening days of summer . . .

She opened her eyes and stared with hatred at the land that had been the soil she sprang from. Her mother had hated it too and had languished and died in this hateful house. That old devil, Leo, had kept them chained here as surely as if he'd put a padlock on them. No wonder she had been only too ready to marry Gilbert Argyle! Just to get away.

Her head was aching dully as she sat down on a windowseat and re-read Anna's letter.

I cannot describe [Anna wrote] what I went through when I heard of the disaster. Oh, Mother, why did you go to England? I feel so helpless cut off from you all. Sam Murray has been a brick. It was he who brought me the news that you were safe – all except darling Nan. How we shall miss her! I wouldn't want to live through those awful days again. I couldn't have done it without Sam. He has been so thoughtful, such a support and friend . . .

Elaine threw the letter down, an exasperated frown on her face. *Sam Murray*. His name ran through the letter like a litany. It was obvious that David's partner had captured Anna's heart. Did Carl, the fool, realize it? And if he did, didn't he care? Anna hadn't mentioned him once. Well, there was nothing she could do about it. The

Atlantic lay between them and *nothing* would prevail on her to sail back to the States until the war ended. Anna must make her own decisions for good or evil. She couldn't even caution the girl in her letters in case Carl read them. Really, what a kettle of fish it was! It was all David's fault; he need not have volunteered. When she thought how happy and contented they had been until this spring!

She looked round this, her father's favourite room, with distaste. Did she imagine it or could she still get a whiff of his cigars? No doubt the smell would linger on inside his books; a whole line of his favourite authors were beside his big leather chair. They had never got on, she and her father. He had been incapable of love; besides, she was not the son he had hoped for. Only family pride moved him; because of this, he had left everything to her son, his only descendant. She could swear she could smell his ancient spaniels, too. If it weren't for the war and shortage of labour she would have had this room changed while David was away: gutted and rid for ever of her father's ghost.

But the war put paid to all these plans. There were no decorators. Conscription had become law this year and men were being called up in turn, the married men last. Women were taking on men's jobs and leaving domestic service in droves. Mrs Elliot ran Northesk with the indifferent help of two women from the village – Umplebys as usual. The Umplebys were an enormous clan spread over several villages and were not only chars but potato-pickers and turnip-howers in season, milkers, baby minders and errand boys. Most of the men were in the army now, in the horse lines of cavalry regiments. Three had been killed and their women scraped by on widow's pensions of five shillings a week. They had dozens of children between them and several were usually in the

Northesk House kitchen being fed bread and jam while their mothers scrubbed and washed and turned the mangle in the dark scullery.

Her thoughts were broken into by the opening of the library door and Annie Umpleby in a dirty apron said apologetically: 'I were scrubbin' front step and this 'ere gentl'man come and ask for you, mum.' She stood aside and a large man with a heavy, deliberate step pushed past her, switched on an automatic smile of greeting and held out a thick-fingered hand. 'Mrs Ransom?' He was middle-aged, very fat and red. His heavy breathing sounded like a bellows in the short silence that ensued as Elaine wondered who on earth this was.

'Name of Matthew Hoggarth. Don't suppose you remember me?'

She shook her head, trying to place him but without success. He exuded a prosperous and self-satisfied air and wore a good steel-grey suit with a thick watch-chain displayed across his broad chest. A bowler hat dangled from one hand and the fixed smile had broadened, showing two rows of large false teeth.

'I'm sorry but I don't. You must forgive me. I have a wretched memory, I'm afraid.' She dropped his damp hand quickly. Who was this unprepossessing man and what could he possibly want with her?

'Your old dad employed a gamekeeper by t'name of George Hoggarth. I'm his son.'

She stared at him, remembering the well-mannered, knowledgeable gamekeeper who had taught her everything there was to know about the country round North-esk. He had carved her whistles out of birch, cured her pet dog when it fell ill, taught her how to hold a ferret and not to be frightened of it – a hundred things she had learned from him. Could this coarse fellow be George Hoggarth's son? He bore no resemblance to him in any

201

way. George had been a gentleman. 'That's very interesting. Do sit down. So you were brought up on this estate?'

'That's right. The cottage over yonder. Lamb's Cottage, t'were called in them days. It's derelict, isn't it? Had a look before calling in here – just for old times' sake, you know.'

'I haven't seen it since my return. I haven't been here long enough to go round the estate – ' and had no inclination to do so. 'The place belongs to my elder son now.'

Matthew Hoggarth nodded, looking round the shabby library with a contempt he didn't try to hide. 'To think I used to consider this place a little palace – well, well!' He chuckled richly. 'Live at Howton Hall meself – bought it last year and have done it up a treat. The lady wife, y'know, likes things just so. It's twice the size of this place.'

'Oh, it is.' Elaine was smiling involuntarily, for the man's blatant swaggering amused her. 'I hope you have a large family to fill it?'

'Just the one boy, David.'

'My elder son is David.'

'Aye, I know. That's where I got my youngster's name. Thought it had tone. We've got money and a country seat so I reckon there's not much difference between us now, eh? The war's done me a power of good, I can tell you – I manufacture tin plates and mugs for the army over in Middlesbrough – well, it's bound to do someone some good, stands to reason! It's an ill wind.'

Elaine felt a shudder down her spine: did the man only feel that about this horrible war? That it was good for *him*?

'Aye, t'works runs itself. Profits are pouring in.'

She could hardly bear it and waited with growing

impatience for him to stop boasting and begin to tell her why he had come.

He was now clearing his throat as if about to address a meeting and his voice took on a new gentility. 'We were all sorry to hear of your ordeal at the hands of the Hun, Mrs Ransom. A dirty business, this submarine warfare. I trust Mr Ransom is fast recovering.'

'Slowly. He suffered a stroke after being in the cold water so long. We are fortunate to be alive. My husband is still in hospital in York.'

'I'm sorry to hear that. We can only trust all will be well eventually. Believe me, we didn't want to worry you at a time like this – '

'We?' She looked puzzled.

'My committee and me. I'm chairman of the local Red Cross committee.' He wagged his head humorously. 'If they want summat done they put Our Matt at t'head of it!' He appeared to be referring to himself and she smiled as he slipped back into the vernacular.

'And what do you want done, Mr Hoggarth?'

He leaned forward confidentially. 'We'd like you to turn over part of Northesk House to us. We need a convalescent home for officers urgently in this part of the world and I reckon you don't use the whole of the house now, do you?'

'Well, as you say, it's not very big – not as big as Howton, didn't you say? Have you considered making your home into a convalescent hospital?'

He was taken aback. 'Wouldn't be suitable,' he said quickly. 'Too near the manufacturing area. Raids and so on, you know. Now you're in the middle of beautiful country. Good air. Probably plenty of butter and eggs to be had. It's very suitable.'

'Thank you,' she said drily. 'I would have to consult my

son. He owns Northesk. But I doubt if this place would hold many patients.'

'Nay, you misunderstand me, Mrs Ransom. Just you hear me out. We'd be putting beds in big marquees in the park – I reckon on forty to fifty beds when we get going. Your west wing would house the office and the nursing staff. See?'

She nodded. The idea attracted her and she had no doubt that David would agree to it. Besides it would give her something to do – take her mind off Reggie's condition and the war and David's uncertain future. 'It's an interesting idea. How soon would you want our decision?'

The two-seater motor car was covering the ground between Northesk and Eskton at record speed. Great little bus! Bursting into song as the dust rose under his wheels David found himself singing: 'I've got everything I want but you-oo!'

He was happy. At last he was in uniform and his commission had just come through. After a couple of months' intensive training on Salisbury Plain he would be going out to France. He and Sam Murray had both been in the National Guard in the States and this now stood him in good stead by cutting his training by weeks. It was, therefore, imperative that he reached some sort of understanding with Polly Paget. He was, of course, going to be extra careful not to put her back up again with what she had scornfully called his old-fashioned notions but which he considered simply hard common sense. Never mind; it wasn't sensible to argue with the girl. Let her have her way so long as she returned his feelings. Yes, he loved her! Of course he'd been in love many times before but not like this – no, he was sure not like this. He hadn't stopped thinking about her since that day on the moors together. He felt he could conquer the world with a girl like Polly by his side. *Polly – Polly – Polly!* sang the little motor as he double-declutched and pointed it downhill, feeling the excited leap of the heart as he crossed the packhorse bridge and turned in at the rectory gates.

Nell Paget was writing letters in the morning-room when the young officer was shown in by Mrs Linsey who didn't regard answering the doorbell as part of her duties. At first she couldn't place him; in uniform he looked very different and he had also had his hair cut shorter. It said much for the improvement of her spirits that she wasn't put out by his sudden appearance in her sanctuary. She held out her hand. 'I'm so glad to hear the good news about your family. Your mother tells me in her letter that your stepfather is improving. I wrote to her, you know: we knew each other when we were younger.'

'Yes, she told me. She thought it very kind that you should write.'

She sat down by the empty fireplace, filled now with potted plants and ferns, and motioned him to a chair on the other side. He put his brand new cap under it and turned his fresh face with its eager eyes towards her. 'I've called to see Miss Paget – Polly. I'd like her to come driving with me.'

'Oh, I'm so sorry but Polly's gone back to Cambridge.'

'You mean to college? Your terms must be different to ours in the States. I guessed I'd find her here.' Sharp disappointment shadowed his face. It was a blow.

Nell, seeing the disappointment clouding his expression, wondered how she could make up for it. 'Archie's here, though. I'm sure he'd love to have a word with you.'

He concealed his exasperation charmingly: did she really think Archie Paget was compensation for the absence of the other twin? 'I won't disturb him – take him from his books. Not today. Er – what is her address at Cambridge?'

'Just Girton College will find her. She'll be back here at the beginning of June when she's got her exam results.'

He retrieved his cap and rose. 'I'm going to the officers' school on Salisbury Plain in two days' time. I'll write to her.'

He held out his hand, smiling, and Nell was struck again by his good looks and charm. She hoped fervently that Polly wouldn't be foolish and let this obviously interested young man slip through her fingers. One of the girls *must* marry well for the sake of the others. Unfortunately they were all obstinately determined to go their own ways and make hashes of their lives, Nell thought resentfully as she stood on the steps watching him reverse his car out into the road. Turning back into the house she wished that she could talk things over with her husband as of old. She would have gone running to him, bubbling over with the news. But what was the use? Arthur hardly seemed to hear her nowadays. He had become remote from her since Dick's death. Still, there was Alix. Remembering her, Nell hurried upstairs to the large spare room.

Alix's baby was now three weeks old but Alix was still not allowed downstairs. She sat in a basket chair by the window sewing baby clothes, a little frown on her face. As her mother opened the door, she turned to her, eagerly expectant. 'Who was that? Was it news of Kit? A fellow officer?'

'No, darling, nothing to do with Kit. It was David Ransom from Northesk. What do you think? I believe he's really interested in Polly!'

Alix turned back to her sewing, her head drooping. She wasn't interested in young soldiers who came calling on her sister Polly. All she wanted was to get out of this room that had become her prison. But what was the use of telling her mother and Nurse Barnes that she felt

206

perfectly fit and strong and able to resume life? They were always warning her about her milk 'going off' if she attempted anything they didn't sanction. When the baby was five weeks old, she might be allowed downstairs at last.

'When am I to be allowed downstairs?' she asked yet again, for she never gave up trying to change their minds. 'Mother, I must go and see Kit. Southport isn't so very far.'

'Alix, are you mad? You forget you're feeding the baby. I'm sure Kit realizes you must put little Christine first now. She's so helpless and relies on you for her very life.' Patting Alix soothingly (an act Alix found very irritating) she added: 'Father and Uncle Wilfred have been to see him twice. He's getting the best of nursing and sent you his love.' She hoped her tone was convincing. Arthur and Wilfred Filey had come back very shaken from both their visits; perhaps more so the second time. For Kit Gromont lay like a dummy on his hospital bed, his burned head swathed in bandages, his only communication with the outside world a pressure of the hand. He was still partially paralysed and soon to be operated on again. It would have caused Alix's complete collapse if she had seen him. 'You can't expect letters yet, dear, he's too weak.'

Alix's face was flushed with distress. 'But I'm nearly mad with worry! Mother, don't you see? I feel he needs me there – I know he does! I want to put Christine on a bottle and leave her here with you and nurse while I go across to Southport. I could take lodgings there.'

'I wish you'd learn to be calmer!' Nell scolded. 'It's so bad for your milk. Nurse has explained how essential a mother's milk is to a baby. Why, I remember I fed each of you children for nine months – '

'My God!' Alix cried, jumping up and bursting into

207

tears. 'Do you mean to keep me a prisoner here all that time? When Kit might be dying – when I know he needs me!'

Nell opened the door of the adjoining room. 'Nurse! Nurse! Come and help me calm Mrs Gromont! She's hysterical and it's so bad for baby.'

Oh, God, Alix thought despairingly, why was I born a woman? Why have I been so stupid as to have a child now of all times?

And for a few minutes she hated the child that Nurse Barnes hurried to put in her arms.

The note from Mike Wynne's mother had arrived a few days after their first meeting. He had certainly not wasted much time, Polly thought as she read it, but then to him time was of the essence. He had so little of it left before he went back to France.

Miss Conway gave her consent reluctantly. 'You can't afford to waste precious time this term, Miss Paget. Your examinations are only five weeks away. It does seem to me that you're not preparing seriously for them,' and she tapped the note contemptuously. 'I hope you're not in danger of forgetting you hold one of our studentships? We expect to see you do well in return. You are not *free* to waste your time.'

Polly forced a smile of weak acquiescence. Inside she was seething with rage. The Iceberg never lost an opportunity to point out that she was a scholarship girl, here on college charity. How dare they think they had bought her lock, stock and barrel? Would the Iceberg have spoken so to Thelma Lacy of the leather jacket and breeks? No! She had positively simpered over Lacy. Some day, Polly vowed, some day I'm going to be rich – I swear it – and then I shall offer to found a studentship myself. That will make them sit up!

'Are you listening, Miss Paget?' Miss Conway was giving her a basilisk stare.

Polly coloured. 'Yes, Miss Conway, I do realize that my studentship puts me in a special position.'

'Very well, I shall allow you to accept Mrs Wynne's invitation. Who will accompany you?'

'Miss Thomson.'

'And you'll be back in time for Hall – that goes without saying.'

Polly said demurely, 'Yes, Miss Conway. Thank you.' But upstairs in her room she did a jig of pleasure before running into Honor's room to inform her that the expedition was on. Honor hadn't finished unpacking although term was three days old, and she was sitting in a circle of books munching an apple. She knew all about Mike Wynne and Polly's meeting with him on the train.

'Well, did you succeed in breaking the Iceberg down?' she asked lazily and threw her apple core through the window.

'One day that will land on the Mistress – bang in the middle of her best hat and serve you right.' Polly couldn't resist following the arc the apple made: a pity, it had landed on the grass. 'Then you'll get sent down, my girl! Yes, it's all arranged. You're to come with me. Can you bear it? He warned me the tennis wouldn't be up to much.'

'I shan't grumble if there's a good tea.'

'We can bicycle there, can't we?'

'Unless it's raining. We'd look too sweet for words with our panamas limp and all the starch running out of our tennis blouses. Remind me to whiten my shoes tonight.'

Polly went back to her room to write a letter of acceptance. After she had sealed it, she sat back in her chair with a thoughtful look on her face. Never before in her life, as the youngest in a big family, had she felt

209

needed. No one leaned on her, least of all her twin: it was she who had always turned to him for help in sorting out knotty problems. No one took her opinions seriously or even considered she had anything worth contributing to their lives. But she knew that Mike Wynne needed her. With her tales of the family she had amused and enthralled him for the second half of the journey from London. He had even laughed once or twice and had lost that brooding look that had so struck her when she first saw him. Dimly she had sensed something of his misery and despair although he had said little about it. At the end he had said that he must see her again. And now, tomorrow, they would meet and maybe she would get to know what troubled him so deeply.

Their bicycles were not needed after all for he called to collect them himself in a shining black Model T Ford of which he was very proud. Polly and Honor went downstairs together, Polly suddenly feeling very shy, carrying their shoes and racquets.

'I say, he's rather good-looking!' Honor whispered, visibly brightening.

The man who came forward to greet them certainly looked better than the unhappy young officer Polly had met on the train. White flannels, a blue and white blazer and a boater gave him quite a different appearance: here, no longer, was an object for her concern and pity. Consequently she was rather tongue-tied and after she had introduced him to Honor, she left them to do most of the talking. They all sat in front, the dickey at the back being reserved for a gramophone and a pile of records, all borrowed from a friend at Trinity. The car smelt strongly of engine oil and was so noisy that they had to shout at one another. With the hood folded down, a strong breeze blew off their hats as they went at a spanking pace down the road. Mike was blissfully uncon-

210

scious of the discomfort being experienced by his passengers. 'Isn't she a priceless little bus! Everything about her is A1. I've checked her over and under the bonnet it's as good as new.'

'Why is there such a strong smell of oil?' Honor asked.

'Is there? I've not smelled a thing. I got her from my friend John Connor, you know. His leave was up last week and he sold all his possessions to his friends. I shall do the same – sell her to someone else at the end of my leave.' Thrusting an arm out he swung the car to the right and down a Z-shaped road that ran out on to Madingley Road. A few hundred yards up was a sprawling red-brick house, its ugliness partially covered by virginia creeper and ivy. Half-buried in thick laurel bushes a large notice board proclaimed *The Red House Preparatory School for Boys* and in the field adjacent to the house, small boys were playing cricket, their shrill voices echoing in the elms surrounding the whole property.

Turning in at the peeling five-barred gate, Mike parked the Ford in the shade cast by a clump of chestnut trees and helped the girls down. Then he pulled out a large gramophone with a horn and a pile of records in rather torn buff covers. 'We can dance after tea.'

The girls eagerly scanned the red labels on the records. 'Oh, look here's *Destiny*!'

'And *Dreaming*. That's my favourite.'

'*Song of Autumn* – don't know that. And here's *I've Got Everything I Want But You*. Archie whistles that all the time. I'm really rather sick of it now.'

'Did you see the show? Elsie Janis was quite superb – so was Basil Hallam. He brought the house down with *Gilbert the Filbert* – look and see if that's on the record.'

'It's on the back of this one, I think.'

'Look, we'll carry these while you take the gramophone. It would be an awful shame if one fell – they break so easily.'

All restraint had fled. They were laughing and talking together as Mike led them indoors, pushing open the door with a foot to allow the girls to pass inside.

Polly looked round the dark-green hall with a shudder: what an unwelcoming place for homesick little boys coming to school for the first time.

'Oh, Mike, there you are!' A commanding female voice made Polly jump. A tall, well-built woman was coming down the stairs and staring curiously at the two girls.

Mike's expression had become hunted; he looked uncertain and awkward. 'Oh, Mother, these are – are my friends from Girton, Miss Paget and Miss Thomson. This is my mother.'

They shook hands, Mrs Wynne continuing to stare, Polly noticed uneasily: had she a smut on her face or something? Her hand strayed up to her face, colour flooding it.

Up the steps from the garden came a welcome diversion in the shape of the headmaster who shook hands and smiled a shy welcome. Tall and thin, fair hair now dusty grey, he resembled his son in an indefinable way that Polly found puzzling. Perhaps, she thought, Mike will look like this when he's fifty, yet they haven't one feature in common.

'Mike's been up since dawn rolling the tennis court,' Walter Wynne said, laughing. 'So see you do justice to it, young ladies.'

Both girls had warmed to Mike's father at once.

'Will you give us a game?' Honor asked.

'Certainly not! My husband has better things to do.' Mrs Wynne did not believe in mincing words, it would seem. Honor looked warningly at Polly for she had begun to shake with suppressed laughter in the face of this

212

gorgon of a woman who so obviously had the upper hand of her menfolk. 'You're late, Walter. The bell went quite ten minutes ago. Mike, take your friends into the garden. The Grahams are there.'

Two people rose from deckchairs as they went out through the garden door. One was a man in his late thirties with a balding head and a pipe that he began to knock out at once. Major Graham had been invalided out of the army a year ago but it was some time before Polly realized he had only one eye; the other was false. With him was his sister Amy who looked as if she had never been younger than she was now. About twenty-six, she had a pale expressionless face, smooth brown hair under a hat and a flat-chested figure in a high-necked old-fashioned blouse and a white duck skirt down to her ankles. She reminded Polly irresistibly of the good little mouse in a child's book. She even had a long pink nose that twitched at the end.

They spun racquets to decide who should sit out the first set and this fell to Mike who assured them he was so rusty he would be glad to watch them play. The Grahams took on the two Girtonians. Honor was a very good player; Polly was not and after a set she was glad to sit and let Mike play instead.

Tea arrived on the verandah and the Buddha-like form of Mrs Wynne loomed over the tea table as she poured the tea for a maid to take round. Polly and Honor looked hopefully at the table with its lace-edged damask cloth and pretty china: food at Girton was neither good nor plentiful now despite the fact that the lawns had been ploughed up for allotments. Disappointment awaited them. On the three-tiered wooden stand known to everyone as 'the curate' were an assortment of sandwiches curling at the edge and obviously stale, some marie biscuits and a seed cake that tasted of sawdust.

'Dear me, the sandwiches are not in their first youth, I see!' Mrs Wynne said with heavy jocularity that sat uneasily on her. 'But we mustn't waste good food in wartime, must we? Waste not, want not. Can I tempt you, Miss Graham? You've been making valiant efforts on the court, I believe. Miss Thomson, do have one.'

Mike shifted uneasily, wishing that his mother would show some friendliness to Polly Paget. He knew what it was: Polly was too pretty. His mother invariably dubbed a pretty girl 'empty-headed' because she couldn't believe beauty and brains went together. The sort of young woman she admired were the Amy Grahams of Cambridge: earnest, High Church and, of course, plain. She called these girls 'splendid young creatures' and fully expected her son to marry one.

Seeing the lost expression on Polly's face, he took his chair and went to sit beside her. 'Let's go and put on the gramophone,' he suggested as soon as tea was over. 'Excuse us, Mother, please.'

As the strains of *Joshua, Joshua, nicer than lemon squash you are!* floated out to the tea party, Mrs Wynne gave a caustic little laugh. 'So that's the calibre of Girton students nowadays! Very different from when I was up under Miss Emily Davies.'

'Oh, come, Mrs Wynne!' Major Graham rolled his good eye in her direction. 'Don't be hard on those little fillies. It's a long time since my eye lit on a pretty girl – I'm going to join 'em!' and he heaved himself out of his deckchair and disappeared through the glass door.

Walter Wynne put his cup down. 'Come along, Amy, what about taking a twirl as you young people call it?'

Amy Graham, who had never used this expression in her life, feebly acquiesced. 'But I'm not a good dancer, I'm afraid,' floated back to her hostess as they went indoors.

You made me lo-ove you! wailed the gramophone as Polly circled the polished floor of the drawing-room in Mike's arms. He had recklessly thrown the rugs and furniture to one side and with flushed cheeks and glowing eyes looked as if he were enjoying himself. Now, his chin resting on her curly head, he softly sang the words of the song: '*You made me love you . . . I didn't want to do it – I didn't want to do-o it –* '

Her warm pliant body close to his brought him a sort of peaceful comfort and he tightened his grip on her.

When Major Graham cut in and took Polly from him – damn the man! – he was momentarily dazed and uncertain again. Across the room his father was humping a heavy-footed Amy Graham round the room with old-fashioned flourishes. Feeling cold and lost he went across to Honor who was winding up the gramophone again.

'Do you mind if I don't dance?' he said, his face sunk in lines of depression. 'My arm's hurting – probably playing tennis didn't help.'

He drove them back to college half an hour later. Polly was in high spirits, feeling that despite Mike's gorgon of a mother, she had enjoyed herself. On her other side, Honor was wondering how she could extricate poor little Paget from this strange family she had got involved with: didn't the girl *see* what an odd lot they were? She was quite certain herself that she wasn't going to waste another afternoon as chaperon. That terrible tea! Her stomach was rumbling emptily.

When they reached Girton, she jumped down with alacrity and, thanking Mike politely, hurried away: she had a tutorial, she said.

Mike stood looking down at Polly. 'What about tomorrow afternoon? We could go on the river. I'll punt you up to Byron's Pool – oh, do come! There's such a short time left.'

'I don't think I can. Miss Conway will put her foot down. I've *got* to work for Mays.'

'Then sneak out about four o'clock. *Please*, Polly.' He had used her name quite naturally, catching up her hand as he did so and pressing it with his thin cold one that seemed to reflect his unhappiness so vividly. 'There must be lots of ways you can get out unobserved. Who's to know? I'll be in the Ford just down the road under the chestnut tree. When – when I'm with you, everything's different – everything's bearable. I forget France and the filth out there. Life is worth living again. Don't deny me this for such a short time,' and his haunted eyes looked deeply into hers with such a pleading expression that she could not deny him anything. Already he had become her child, the one to whom she brought comfort and peace. This simply amazed her: indeed it made her quite reckless all of a sudden. Her family, who chided her often for her impulsive ways, would have recognized this and warned her against it if they had been there: *Polly, stop and think.* But there was no one to restrain her.

So she sat up until two A.M. finishing an essay that was already two days late and was consequently half-asleep in the Girton bus next morning as they were driven in to a lecture. As promised, she escaped notice and met the Model T Ford under the chestnut tree and they spent an hour on the river getting to know one another.

'Tomorrow?' he murmured eagerly as they parted.

CHAPTER THIRTEEN

The Decision

Most afternoons that term Mike's little Ford waited down the road outside Girton and Polly made her way to it by several discreet routes.

The second occasion she had asked for an exeat, Miss Conway had tartly reminded her that her first year exams were only a month away; that she had been late with her essay that week; that she must set aside time for revision. If Miss Paget still wished to postpone her studentship until the end of the war, Miss Conway pointed out, then much depended on the results. Failure meant she would not get her studentship renewed when she returned.

It was all true and Polly knew it without being told. Yet it seemed quite suddenly utterly irrelevant. Reading in the newspapers about the long-drawn agony of Verdun and of the terrible end to the rising in Ireland, she felt more and more detached from Girton, from the first year exams, from medieval history itself. History was being made daily; it was here and now. Studying the distant past seemed to have no bearing on the agonizing present and the way that death stalked the young. Where once work had absorbed her, she now found a vacuum and could only envy those other students who seemed to be able to distance themselves from the war and plunge with all their hearts and minds into academic work.

That Mike was deriving benefit from her companionship was becoming obvious to his family – or at least to Walter Wynne. If Ruth Wynne noticed it, she said nothing. She hadn't taken to 'the silly little thing with red hair' as she referred to her. But Walter took Polly aside one afternoon at the Red House, saying warmly: 'You've made him forget the war, Miss Paget. God knows, he needed to forget. Your friendship and companionship are just what the boy needs at this time. Mike is plagued by too vivid an imagination, you know.' He gave a melancholy little smile. 'He gets it from me. I know so well what he's feeling. He's done enough and has earned a respite. I've approached a friend at the War Office, Colonel Broadbrook, but he doesn't hold out much hope. Every man is needed for the great push they're talking about for this summer.'

One day, a letter arrived for her from David Ransom. It was a short letter, friendly and open, hoping they could meet on his next leave.

It looks now as if I won't get to France before the fall. I would be back in Yorkshire for short leaves over the summer. Will you be there? Please say you will be! We never finished our conversation, remember? Don't forget me, please. I think of you a lot.

Closing her eyes she recalled him to mind: a healthy glowing face with a pair of frankly admiring eyes. A man who didn't know yet what the war was like. A man full of patriotic enthusiasm. A rich man, someone who had never been denied the good things of life . . . Oh, yes, she liked him a lot; he was attractive and had charm. But he didn't need her as Mike needed her. He was a self-sufficient person whose nerves were sounder than most people's. But Mike's had been almost destroyed by the war and he was still only a boy. Soon he would be recalled to the hell he dreaded with all his heart and mind. She mustn't let him down. He needed her.

She put David's letter in her writing case meaning to reply to it when she had a moment. Then her eyes fell on a pile of books awaiting her perusal. There would be no

218

second chance if she failed her exams this term: there were too many bright girls clamouring for the college studentships of £150 a year.

She glanced at her watch: three o'clock. At four-thirty, the little motor would be waiting to whirl her away. A knock at the door made her jump: it was Elsie, Miss Conway's gip, with one of those familiar triangular notes in Italianate script. Her tutor wished to see her at once.

With a dark sense of pending disaster, Polly tidied her hair and washed her hands. Something was up. There was no doubt about that.

Miss Conway's face and voice were icy as she bade her pupil sit down. 'Miss Paget, I'm gravely disturbed. I have just learned that you have been seeing a young man every day without my permission and without a chaperon. I have seen how your work has been suffering and have wondered at the cause. Now I know and all is clear. You have probably ruined all chances of doing well in your exams. Indeed, I ask myself if you will scrape a pass? But what concerns me even more is your cheap behaviour.' Her lips curled round the last two words and Polly reddened. 'If known outside these walls this same behaviour would disgrace Girton in the eyes of the university and the town. No, don't speak. I haven't finished yet.'

With difficulty Polly remained silent under this verbal lashing. Inside her head, fury mingled with a feeling of disaster. Who had seen them? Who had been so mean as to sneak on her? She felt that she already knew: Mike's mother. Mrs Wynne had shown on that first day that she didn't like her.

'No man is worth sacrificing your career for,' went on the relentless voice. 'I know you will live to regret it. I've seen other girls – not many, thank God! – throw away a brilliant academic future to become some man's slave, to push a pram and manage his house when they could have

219

had careers, been independent beings and not second-class citizens for the rest of their lives. You've got this chance now. Believe me, no man is worth the sacrifice. I *know* what I'm talking about. Root it out – stamp on it! To give up the fruits of the mind for the sake of the promptings of one's body is repugnant to an educated mind.' The hand holding the long cigarette holder trembled suddenly.

Polly stared at her. She had only to look at her tutor to see that unlike most of the other dons she was not a natural celibate: dark rings under the eyes, the ceaseless smoking, the trembling hands, the vehemence of her words showed very plainly the struggle there had been in her life. *No man is worth it. I know* . . .

'I don't think I'm infatuated with Mr Wynne. That's not our relationship at all. We're friends and I've been able to help him a little – he's shellshocked, you know. He's suffered in mind and body in the war and he's only twenty. Of course I want to help him to get over it! Why should I have the right to be selfishly engrossed in my academic future when he probably has none? He had a place at Trinity and was going up like his father and grandfather before him when war broke out and he and his brother volunteered at once. His brother died at Gallipoli last summer. When I remember all he's suffered, of course I want to help him enjoy these last few weeks before he goes back. I'm working late at night to make up –'

'That's enough. I see how defiant you are, Miss Paget, and I fear for your future. Have you no sense of shame at your behaviour? I forbid you to see this young man again – no, don't argue, please. Your arguments are quite spurious and it's my duty to guide you if you refuse to heed my warning. You're gated until the end of term.'

Polly jumped up. 'You couldn't be so cruel!'

It was Miss Conway's turn to go red with anger. 'If you're determined to be defiant then I can only recommend the college authorities to send you down for good. We have no use at Girton for young women who are simply looking for cheap thrills.'

Polly went back to her room and closed the door with a bang. *Cheap thrills!* She was furiously angry. She didn't rush in to Honor to seek her sympathy and advice; this was something she would have to think out for herself now. She found she was trembling with reaction and she slumped on to the windowseat and put her head in her hands.

Presently she looked up, letting her eyes roam wistfully about the room. It was filled with her books and the few treasured possessions she had gathered over the years: a tiny blue and white jug filled with a sprig of lilac that was flooding the room with scent; an early Kate Greenaway book bought from the bookstall in the market; some black and white prints of the town pinned on the wall. She had taken a real delight in this room, her own domain that no one entered unless asked. Was she about to lose it all? But surely Mike was more important than all this? More important than the nebulous success she was told she would find some day when she went down. Perhaps by that time, women would be awarded real degrees and the letters after her name would not simply be honorary . . .

She bit her lip and jumping off the windowseat began to pace to and fro. Only yesterday he had turned to her, saying impulsively: 'I do wish we were married, Polly! You've come to mean so much to me. We could be together all the time then.' He had looked at her wistfully and she knew that it needed only one word of encouragement from her for him to complete this half-uttered proposal of marriage. Instead she had turned it aside and begun to talk about something else: it was, she knew,

221

because she was afraid to face this decision. It meant the burning of all her boats.

They had been strolling together in the orchard at the time and from a distance had come the *thwack* of leather ball on willow as the little boys played cricket under the supervision of one-eyed Major Graham who could be heard bellowing encouragement and criticism. Blossom was beginning to fall off the apple trees and now lay like a sprinkling of snow on the grass. Bees hummed in the branches and clouds of gnats rose in a veil as they were disturbed. May in all its beauty was here at last and the sun was hot on their shoulders. Here and in the town the scent of lilac was suffocating and punts of convalescent soldiers in hospital blue passed up and down the river. It made Polly ache to think that she might have to leave all this after one spring, one experience of Cambridge in springtime. And then she thought with a squeeze of the heart: it might be his last spring here too.

'Listen to that!' He pulled her to a stop.

A blackbird's song, full-throated and mellow, was shaken over them like a benison. Shadows from the leaves mottled their faces as they looked up to catch a glimpse of the bird singing its heart out on a high branch. Polly was wearing a summer dress of blue check Madras cotton with a deep white piqué collar. She had flung her straw hat on the grass and sunlight poured on to her hair, setting it on fire for a few moments.

'Polly, you're beautiful.' He put out his left hand and took one of hers.

'It's better! You can really use it again! Oh, Mike – ' The joy faded from her voice. 'Does this mean – I mean to say – '

'Yes. I was finally discharged by the Eastern General Hospital this morning. I'm passed fit for service again. I

222

shall be back in France the week after next. Mother's pleased,' he added bleakly.

'Oh, Mike!'

'The western front . . . and this.' He was looking round at the scene with longing in his eyes. 'We must all be mad. The world is so lovely – you're so lovely! Oh, Polly, I can't bear to leave you!' He turned to her blindly and she put her arms round him as if he were a child in need of her comfort and reassurance. She could feel him trembling, taste his icy cold skin as she timidly kissed him.

'Mike – Mike, don't! Your leave was bound to come to an end. We've both known it from the beginning.'

He didn't seem to hear her. The bitter, defeated look was back on his face. Vivid memories came flooding back into his mind and for a minute or two he was back in the all-too-familiar world of the trenches. But when he spoke, his voice was strangely calm. 'I reckon I have about two more months of life left. By the law of averages I shall be killed this time. I've been lucky. I got away with just a wound when my best friend Hugh was killed. There was a huge hole in his head . . . Most officers only last about eight weeks at the front. We lead the men, you see – first over the top with a cheery "Come on, lads!"' The bitter irony in his voice sharpened and his mouth twisted into the semblance of a smile. 'They say the gods will only be appeased when the youth of the world are dead.'

She could find no words in the face of such hopeless bitterness. Instinct told her that his mind had been irreparably damaged by his experiences: raw and vulnerable, it was filled with distorted and hideous images that would not fade. This, she knew, was called shellshock. How cruel it was to send him back to face more horror. He was one of a band of men, their nerves destroyed, who sometimes shot off their fingers or toes in order to escape the trenches. Mike would simply gird himself to

223

face the ghastliness again because it was the conduct expected of him. She turned and suddenly drew him close, longing to protect him from the nightmares that haunted him.

He said quietly, his face against her hair: 'I don't want to die – to go out into the dark for ever and leave you and all this.'

She felt a terrible pang, knowing that with these words he touched the fears that always lived inside her. She, the rector's daughter, had no faith in another world, a heaven awaiting her when she died. *Going out into the dark*. She shivered in the hot sun, feeling his fear as if it were her own . . . because it was. 'No one does,' she whispered, the lump in her throat making her hoarse. 'Oh, Mike, if only I could help you in some way!'

He raised her hand and kissed it, his lips dry and burning against her skin. They stood silent and close. By being close to her, he seemed to draw some of her strength into his mind. Sometimes, after she had left him, she would feel weak and limp as if he had drawn off her life-blood into his own arteries. It was the same now. He was suddenly tranquil again, smiling down at her. 'You help me so much, Polly. What am I going to do without you?' And it was then that he said: 'I wish we were married! I'd have something to live for then. You've come to mean so much to me.' He needed her as thirstily as a dried-up plant needed life-giving water: a little every day. She realized this and was afraid; afraid that she couldn't sustain the channelling of her life-energy into his mind, supporting and strengthening him. So she hadn't responded and the moment had passed. He had looked at her with a shy uncertainty and dropped her hand.

Now as she paced her room, her mind was being made up for her: he needed her more than anyone else in the world and it was a heady feeling. Surely it must be love that she felt for him? She thought once more of David Ransom and now she was almost afraid to do so because in her heart she had already committed herself to the man who needed her.

She glanced at the clock. Four twenty-five. He would already be out there waiting under the chestnut tree. And if she didn't go out to him? Sent him instead a note saying goodbye? He would believe that she didn't care what happened to him and all the bitter fears and uncertainty would flood back and engulf him again. She would have failed him.

Seizing her hat, she crammed it on and walked defiantly downstairs and across the courtyard to the front gate where the portress sat in her cubbyhole. There was no longer any need to hide the fact that she was going out with Mike without permission. Her decision had been made and there would be no turning back now or in the future.

'Arthur! Arthur! Where are you?'

His wife's urgent tones brought the rector back to the present. He was in his church, standing before the tablet recently placed on the wall above the rectory pew: a small brass plaque to his dead son. Last Sunday he had dedicated it before the whole congregation and his voice, proud and strong, hadn't faltered. But as he stood today before the shining tablet he was remembering a small boy on the rectory lawn with a bat too large for him, to whom he bowled tirelessly on long summer afternoons. There had been pigeons cooing from the tall elms mingling with the little boy's shrill voice. Long ago now. Almost another world. And as he stood here, motionless in his cassock, his head slightly bowed, he knew that something inside him had broken for ever.

When he turned towards Nell's figure outlined against

the sunlight pouring through the door, his voice was as steady as usual. 'What is it, my dear?' *This is the first time she has been through that door since October 1914*, he thought with wonder.

Nell's agitation was apparent: she had run across to the church without her hat and she was holding a letter in a hand that shook. 'Oh, Arthur, it's Polly.'

Inured to disaster as he thought he was, the rector's knees seemed to fail him and he sat down in the nearest pew. 'What has happened? Is she ill?'

'No, not at all, but mad – quite mad! She is going to marry a perfect stranger!'

The rector smiled with relief. 'Is that all? No doubt he will not be a stranger long to any of us.'

'I mean on Friday – this Friday!'

'This *Friday*? What nonsense is this? Did you know anything about it, Nell?'

'I? Does she tell me anything?' Nell was holding the letter very close to her myopic eyes. 'I'll read you what she says: His name is Michael Wynne and he's a second-lieutenant in the East Suffolks . . . was wounded in France last January . . . his people keep a private school in Cambridge – I can't read this next bit.'

'Let me.' The rector took the letter, read it through rapidly to himself and then looked up at his wife waiting impatiently. 'She's been sent down from Girton because of this young man.'

Nell paled and clutched blindly at a pew to steady herself. 'Oh, Arthur, she's ruined her life! What has she been doing? *Sent down*. What will the parish think?'

The rector gave one of his wry smiles. 'Ah, yes, the parish. My dear, as far as I can make out our daughter hasn't done a stroke of work this term and has been meeting this young man clandestinely. Well, I've always maintained that young women are totally unsuited to

226

university life. I wasn't happy when she won her student-ship – '

'Arthur, how can you? I was so proud that she had the brain to do so – perhaps I've been too proud of that and now it's come to nothing. I thought it would get her out of this awful hole,' Nell said bitterly, 'and that she would make something of her life. She's thrown her only chance to the winds for the sake of this boy who is probably as penniless as she is – a pair of children!' Nell's anger suddenly erupted as she remembered that charming and eligible young man, David Ransom, who had so obviously been attracted to Polly. 'I can hardly bear it,' she said in a low, hard voice. 'I shall never forgive her – never!'

'You say young Wynne's a child, Nell, but he seems to be a seasoned soldier: has been out since 1915 and is now recovering from his wounds. He's due to go out to France for the second time very shortly.' The rector folded the letter and gave one of his wry smiles. 'Well, my dear, the army doesn't seem to consider him *a child*! Things are very different for the young nowadays: the future of the young men is measured in months not years and the young women know it. Don't let's grudge these two their brief happiness. Only God knows what's in store for them. Michael's family are people like ourselves from what Polly says: educated professional people with very little money. I shan't forbid this marriage.'

'But, Arthur, the child's only nineteen!'

'How old were you when you joined your life to mine? Not even nineteen! I was curate to Mr Nolan for £150 a year. We had no private means but remember how happy we were?'

She could feel the foolish tears rising in her eyes and turned hastily away. Yes, they had been blissfully happy, especially when their first baby was born. Richard Arthur Pennington Paget. Dick. The most beautiful child in the

227

world, his young parents had thought. And yet what had it all been for? Dick, a regular soldier, had been killed two months after war was declared and she had lived in darkness since then. For a moment or two, the memory of that early happiness came back and touched her deeply. How wonderful it had been! Involuntarily, shrinking inwardly, she at last turned her head and searched for the memorial tablet on the wall. She had never been able to look at it before – had not been inside the church since it was put up – and, yes, there it was: a simple plaque with his name on and the name of his regiment and underneath just:

Born at Eskton 16 July 1890
Killed Ypres 21 October 1914

What had it all been for? she asked herself again. All that love and care gone in a few seconds and nothing left but the memory of a handsome face and a lazy voice calling her 'mater'.

Arthur Paget took her arm and led her out of the church. They stood on the steps blinking in the bright sunshine. 'Come and break the news to Archie. Remember, Nell, we must wear glad faces at our daughter's wedding. The boy goes back to the front next week.'

They were married with what Nora Gromont described as 'unseemly haste'. The Gromonts had come up from London the night before the Pagets and had taken full charge of the hotel in Trinity Street by the time the bride's parents and twin brother arrived.

'My dear, the food is awful! And the chambermaids are cheeky. Every time I ring my bell they take ten minutes to arrive. Well, Nell, you're looking peakier than ever – and Arthur, I'm sorry to see you've lost so much weight.

228

Celia! Don't bother your uncle! Now, Nell, come and sit down and tell me the reason for this sudden marriage. She's not . . . you know what I mean? You're sure? Well, it's very inconsiderate of her but Polly has always been the difficult one, hasn't she?'

Nell, who always looked forward to meeting her sister again, opened her mouth to defend her youngest child, felt the pressure of her husband's hand on her arm and smiled instead. 'We're very happy she's found such a nice boy, Nora. I'm sure they're going to be happy.'

Really, Nell and Arthur were a pair of unworldly children! Nora thought despairingly. If ever a pair of young people faced an uncertain future, these two did.

It was a lovely morning of June sunshine when they were married the next day. The church of St Benedict's was lit by only one lamp and no sun penetrated the stained glass windows so they emerged to be blinded by sunshine. Nora Gromont had a small bunch of roses from which she theatrically tore the petals to throw over the bridal pair and Celia disgraced herself in her mother's eyes by holding up Theo, her one-eyed teddy bear, to be kissed by the bride.

Archie, hugging his twin before she left, said in her ear: 'Mrs Wynne's face is a study, Poll! Go and kiss her like a dutiful daughter.'

So rather timidly Polly kissed her mother-in-law's whiskery cheek, getting nothing in return but a surprised look: kisses, it seemed, were not much in Ruth Wynne's line. Walter hugged her. 'I've got a daughter at last! Bless you both, my dear.'

Her father, she saw, was delighted. He had taken to Mike at once, but that her mother had doubts was plain to see. However, Nell made an especial effort because not for the world would she let Nora see that she considered this hurried wedding a mistake.

As they drove to the station they saw a news-stand with a large poster: GREAT SEA BATTLE –

'For five days I'm going to forget the war,' Mike said, averting his face and so avoiding learning about the battle off Jutland, the first big naval engagement of the war. 'Happy?' he asked her yet again and again she smiled and assured him she was.

For the brief honeymoon Mike had chosen a large London hotel popular with young officers on leave. He needed its noisy gaiety. A band played every afternoon for a *thé dansant* and there was a new place called an American Bar where he spent his time drinking when Polly was upstairs changing her clothes. Their honeymoon in this noisy Mecca of youth frantically enjoying itself while there was yet time was a strange affair. Mike hadn't married her out of passion but out of his desperate need for comfort. His attempts at intercourse were half-hearted: all he wanted to do was lie in her arms talking, talking and deriving comfort from her warmth and near-ness and the reassurance he so urgently needed.

Sensing how damaged in mind he was she made no demands on him but lay hour after hour through the first couple of nights listening while he poured out the accu-mulated terrors of the last eighteen months. She found she could soothe him into calmness by speaking hopefully of an early end to the war and of their life together afterwards. He had, she realized, never dared think ahead to a life when peace returned because he had been so certain that only death awaited him.

By the third day he looked so much better and brighter that he seemed another person. Now they were able to make love successfully and he stopped being self-absorbed and began to think about her future instead. Though

230

delighted by the change in him, she was nevertheless exhausted mentally: she had put so much of herself into bolstering him up that she was drained. But she didn't dare show this, not while he wanted distraction in the shape of bright lights, loud music and quantities of alcohol. He had discovered in the trenches that alcohol dulled one's worst fears if one drank enough of it, so he kept himself on a high pitch of gaiety with its consumption. He didn't want time to think, every moment must be filled and as he had accumulated pay swelling his bank account, they spent freely, visiting a different smart restaurant every day. She became quite familiar with the Trocadero, Quaglino's, the Hungaria, Rule's, the Café Royal. They lunched at one place and booked a table for late supper at another. In between they went shopping to Harrods, Selfridges or Swan and Edgar and he showered presents of lingerie and trinkets on her. Flowers waited for her on restaurant tables, bottles of scent on her pillow: these were the only ways he had of telling her he loved her for never once during their five days did he say as much. His feverish behaviour didn't escape her and she accepted all his attentions with professions of surprise and delight. But, painfully, she realized she would have responded to a loved child in the same way and she knew then that something in her remained totally untouched. She didn't – and never would – love Mike in the way she wanted to love a man: passionately, with her whole being.

One night he had a nightmare. All the horrors in his haunted mind came tumbling out as with strangled shouts and terrifying staring eyes he threw himself out of bed. She jumped up and tried to pull him back beside her but with a blood-curdling wolf howl he sprang at her, fastened his hands round her throat and nearly strangled her. She couldn't breathe and her eyes bulged in her head when suddenly it was all over. He sank back on the carpet mumbling of trench raids and the Hun. His hands still twitched but now he shivered as if very cold, his face ashen.

Crying incoherently she stumbled to the wash-stand and bathed the purple marks round her neck. Peeping at him over the towel she saw that he had got back into bed and had closed his eyes. He seemed to be asleep.

She crept in beside him and lay not daring to sleep again.

Next morning he was himself again. He seemed to have no memory of what had happened and never referred to a nightmare. She thought it prudent not to mention it herself but the experience had frightened her more than she liked to admit.

Dining at the Connaught Hotel she saw her eldest sister Imogen. Dressed in a slip of a black-and-pink chiffon dress tipped with golden beads that dipped low at the breast and was cut off at mid-calf by a fringe of gold beads, she was at first unrecognizable. Polly stared at this painted girl, her straight fair hair curled into the new short bob, her eyes feverish and blank as she danced the Turkey-trot and the Bunny-hug with an officer on the Staff.

Could it be – was it *Imogen*? She had noticed the dress first; it was so covered in beads and spangles and tassels that it seemed to have a life of its own. Her partner was middle-aged with a dark cadaverous face and Imogen had eyes for no one else as she frenetically moved to the rhythm of the noisy band. But as she passed within a few feet of their table, Polly saw her sister's eyes lift and rest on her for a few seconds then look hastily away again. Polly realized at once that she didn't want to be approached. How sad, she thought. It's two years since I've seen her . . .

'Do you see that girl in the beaded dress, Mike?'

'The fair goddess with the brigadier?'

'A brigadier, is he? Well, she's my eldest sister.'

'Good lord!' He leaned forward, looking more closely. 'She's a stunner but the chap's old enough to be her father. Are you going to have a word with her?'

Polly shook her head. 'No. She's seen me but I don't think she wants me to know her.'

'I'm not surprised,' Mike said.

'Why?'

'Don't you see? She's – she's – ' He stopped, deeply embarrassed by Polly's clear young eyes fixed on him. But it was obvious to him that Polly's sister was a trollop. It was there for all the world to see: the way she dressed, moved, wore rouge and conducted herself. No wonder she didn't want to meet her little sister. 'I thought she was out in France nursing?'

'She is – at least, I think so.' Her eyes followed the pink-and-black spangles as they danced back across the room to a secluded corner. 'Perhaps I ought to have a word with her – '

'No!' His hand enclosed her wrist. 'Don't go, darling. She would hate it, I think.'

She gave him a startled look. She was no fool and she could see what he was thinking. 'Imogen's not – not – ' Confused, she was silent.

'Forget you've seen her,' he advised, 'and don't breathe a word about it to your parents. Promise?'

She nodded, a chill of sadness overcasting her enjoyment. She saw that Imogen now sat with her back to the dance floor and was engaged in animated conversation with her companion. 'Let's go,' Polly said. 'I'm tired, Mike.'

As they drove back to their hotel she saw a news-poster advertising a late extra edition of an evening paper. 'Kitchener what?' she wondered, looking back.

'Yes, it's Kitchener, miss.' The cabby had half-turned round. ''Im with the moustache – 'ee's bin drowned.'

They looked at each other, amazement reflected in their faces. Not Kitchener, the nation's hero, Secretary for War and mythmaker? *Drowned?*

It seemed to them symbolic of the way the war was going for the Allies – inexorably downhill. A little shiver went through Polly.

Their last day came.

They were bright and reassuring to each other. There was last-minute shopping at the Army and Navy Stores where Mike bought the black crêpe armband that the army had been ordered to wear in memory of Kitchener, a new pair of wire-cutters and some leather gloves. 'The wire tears your hands so,' Mike explained almost casually. He also bought a litre bottle of whisky, chicken and tongue in glass containers and a stock of drugs that every officer was required to carry.

They went to lunch at the Trocadero, to tea-dancing at the Connaught and then changed quickly for the Queen's Theatre where they had seats in the stalls for *The Tiger Cub* in which Madge Titheredge was the big draw. They had been to the theatre nearly every night and although he had seen it before, Mike thought he must take his wife to see George Robey and Vi Lorraine in *The Bing Boys* at the Alhambra.

It was here that they saw General Haig and his wife in a box with friends. Polly privately thought he looked rigidly pompous and wondered what plans he carried in his square iron-grey head.

Mike displayed a febrile gaiety that evening. He drank a lot at supper at Rule's and it was one o'clock when they returned to their hotel. With a sinking heart, she realized there were only about six hours left to them. They lay in each other's arms but he was unable to make love.

Switching on the light she saw his face was ghastly. 'Mike – Mike darling, what is it?'

He clung to her. She could feel his violent shaking and realized with anguish that the old terror had got him in its grip. Even his teeth chattered, and sweat stood out on his brow.

'Oh, Polly – oh, darling, help me – help me – ' The cry was wrenched from him. 'I don't want to die – we're so happy – so happy.'

She wept then, knowing that she was powerless to help him as he so urgently begged her. She could only hold him in her arms and try to lead him back from the tunnel of terror down which he floundered. At last he stopped shaking and lay quiet. Gradually he slipped into an uneasy sleep while she stroked his arm. But sleep was far from her. She lay beside him, keeping watch, determined not to miss one of the remaining hours left to them.

It was four o'clock when he woke with a strangled shout, hitting out and struggling, his eyes wild and unseeing. He had the strength of a madman as she tried to wake him. Then it was over: he was conscious and staring at her. 'Oh, God,' he murmured brokenly as he saw that outside the window it was already light.

Suddenly she knew what he reminded her of: a condemned man who was to be shot at dawn. Only then did the full realization come to her of what it was to be a soldier returning to the front after one ghastly experience or long months of gruelling service in the trenches. They were condemned and knew it and because they were young and strong and loved life so much they bitterly resented having the years ahead snatched from them.

He got up at seven-thirty and they breakfasted in their room. She watched him put on his uniform: the new breeches she had admired on their wedding day, the shining buttons on his tunic that she had herself polished.

Then he fastened the Sam Browne round his lean waist, adjusting the holster. He was ready all too quickly, she saw, her heart wincing in terror. He had refused to allow her to see him off at Victoria, but she knew he would be marching at the head of a new draft of men so had made her own plans.

She was still in her white lawn nightdress when he held her close for the last time, covering her face with kisses, pushing her hair back from her face with an unsteady hand. 'I love you so much,' he told her for the first and only time as she clung to him, loath to let him go. But strangely he was now the stronger of the two and with one last crushing embrace, he tore himself away and walked out of the door.

Then with hasty, awkward fingers she washed and dressed, putting on the new white linen dress and jacket she had bought for her marriage. With it went a hat encircled in marigolds: a perfect outfit for a perfect June morning. It was hot outside, smelling of tar melting in the heat and of horse dung and petrol fumes. She hurried along feeling hot and tired, looking for a motor cab: these were now few and far between because of the need to save petrol but presently she found one and drove to Victoria.

'I shan't be getting out,' she told the driver. 'I just want to see – see some soldiers off and then you can drive me back to my hotel.'

The cabby had seen other young ladies do the same thing. Poor young thing, he thought philosophically, and took out the morning paper.

Polly sat in the dark cab looking out on to the brightly lit street. A convoy of ambulances were meeting a train. Three nurses in scarlet capes hurried past. Then family parties came one by one to see their son or husband off to the front. A newsboy was selling papers and she averted her eyes: she didn't want to know that there had been 'Activity on the Western Front'.

Presently there was a steady tramp of feet and a long column of men came into the station square. There at the head as the senior officer was Mike. Behind him were two very young subalterns. Her eyes devoured him but she knew she mustn't let him see her, mustn't put him through the agony of parting once more. He looked strong and composed; as the column broke rank, he turned to one of the officers and said something with a smile. The boy, who looked about eighteen, was grinning back. A burly sergeant came up and saluted. Together, he and Mike scrutinized some papers the sergeant was holding. Then they disappeared inside the station. He had gone.

Archie met her at Whitby and hugged her convulsively. 'Poor old Poll!' They drove home silently. As they neared the village she looked up and said bleakly: 'How long is this war going on for, Archie?'

'I wish I could hazard a guess that would be near the truth. There's a rumour about a big push soon . . .' He broke off apologetically.

'Yes, Mike told me.'

He could see the tense shape her hands were making. 'Sorry, old girl, wish I could be more cheering. But I'd be encouraging you to live in a fool's paradise if I said anything else. I like Mike: we shall make a good trinity!'

She was recovering her spirits. 'Not a quartet? I thought I was going to come home to find you had popped the question to Cass!'

'Shut up!' Archie growled. They clattered over the bridge and were home.

On this hot June day, the family were gathered under the mulberry tree. The tea table was loaded with home-made food: scones and jam, cucumber sandwiches and a war cake with candles stuck in it. It was Katy's birthday and Mrs Linsey had hoarded sugar and fat and dried fruit for the occasion. The old battered silver teapot was full of the special tea kept by Mr Herbert Beddows, the Scarborough grocer, which Nell only used on occasions like this.

They greeted her warmly and soon she was sitting in their midst, comforted by the ebb and flow of family talk. Alix's baby wailed from its pram and she jumped up to rock it, while Little Dick sat on a rug at their feet and pulled a buttered scone to pieces. The war seemed far away and yet each one of them had been altered by it, Polly thought with wonder. Hope began to renew itself within her. Some day, she would bring Mike home. He would sit in one of those chairs. Their children would be running about the lawn and the world would be sane again.

'I've got something to tell you all,' Katy said suddenly. Her face was flushed under the wide straw hat that sheltered it from the sun. She put down her cup and looked round the expectant circle of faces. 'The squire has asked me to marry him and I've accepted.'

There was a stunned silence, then a sharp intake of breath. 'Katy!'

Polly's face was frozen in outraged amazement. Katy, beautiful, lovable Katy was going to marry Uncle Wilfred? But he was *old*. How could she even contemplate such a thing? Now that Polly knew about physical love, she was filled with distaste. And yet hadn't she guessed there was something between them long before this?

Nell jumped up and kissed Dick's widow warmly. 'My dear child, I am delighted for you! Wilfred's the kindest of men. You are truly fond of him?'

'Truly fond,' Katy echoed with conviction. 'There are different sorts of love – I know that now – and with

238

Wilfred I shall be content.' She was smiling tranquilly. She was done for ever with youthful love. It only brought tears and anguish in its wake. 'We thought we would get married in August. There are several alterations to be done first at the Hall.'

'My dear, we shall miss you and little Dick,' the rector said, patting her hand. He had known of this step his old friend Wilfred Filey proposed taking: they had talked it over together last week. But he mustn't let Nell see that Wilfred had taken him into his confidence for she would be deeply offended. However he was not a good actor and Archie watched his father thoughtfully as they all talked and laughed. He had been as astonished as Polly over this announcement and not sure that he appproved until he saw that his father knew and thought it a good thing for Katy. Perhaps the squire wasn't so old as all that, Archie thought, thinking of the small nut-brown man who had so often acted as fairy godfather to the family.

Later, when Polly was unpacking, her mother sat on the windowseat and talked to her.

'Uncle Wilfred's quite old, Mother. How can Katy do it?'

'He is forty-seven. That's not *old*,' Nell said indignantly. 'Katy is a sensible girl to take him. He will give Little Dick a splendid life. He adores the child because he is Dick's son. You know how he loved Dick.' Tears began to fill Nell's eyes and, to divert her, Polly showed her the black silk petticoat and pretty pair of knickers that went with it that Mike had bought her in London. Nell stared in horror. Why the *legs* of those knickers barely measured *four inches*! And covered in lace. And black. Hadn't the boy realized that only a *demi-mondaine* would wear such garments? 'Not in good taste, darling. I hope you will never wear them.'

'Oh, Mother, how old-fashioned you are! Mike couldn't stand my cambric knickers and those dreary petticoats you bought at Marshalls in Scarborough.'

'Polly!'

'Well, he did see me dress and undress for a week, you know! I'm *married*, Mother, have you forgotten?'

Nell buttoned her lips: Polly was such an outspoken girl, heaven knows what she might say in a minute. Not for worlds would Nell have told her daughter that in twenty-five years she had *never* dressed or undressed in front of her husband. 'I won't say that I wished you hadn't done it, child, for we like Mike, but it was a pity it had to be such a rushed affair.'

'Yes, it was a rushed affair but life has changed.' Polly folded the precious garments in tissue paper; they wouldn't be worn again until Mike came on leave. 'There's so little life left for a lot of people – as if they are ninety and not nineteen and know they are measuring what remains to them in weeks and not years. Death is so close. Just round the corner, really. Is there a more apt saying than *Here today and gone tomorrow* for my generation?'

Nell stared at her daughter in anguish. Don't say it, don't say it; she begged her silently. Don't put into words what we dread and know only too well!

'Why doesn't this horrible war stop? It's an obscenity and they all know it. Do we really want the whole world to bleed to death? What will it be like when the young men are all dead? It's the old who are keeping this war going but it's the young who are paying the price.' Tears suddenly ran down Polly's cheeks but her mother knew better than to run to comfort her. Instead they were both silent until Polly had wiped away her tears. Her mother patted her, thinking that the tears were a sign of Polly's

240

love for her new husband, but Polly knew that what she felt for Mike was the fiercest pity that had ever possessed her.

The first David knew of Polly's marriage had been from the announcement put in *The Times*. He opened it in the train, going up to London from Salisbury on forty-eight hours' leave. It was the first free weekend of the ten-week course but too short a time to go up to Yorkshire. He had got a room at the Ritz and he and three other cadet-officers intended seeing a couple of shows and dining and wining well. He was happy and relaxed as the train gathered speed. His friends opposite were discussing Kitchener's death and he listened to them with affectionate tolerance. Leaning over, he lifted *The Times* off Jack Montague's knees.

'I'll borrow this while you two finish your argument. I want to find out what's on in the theatres.'

He still found *The Times* a strange paper: even a disaster was reported in its centre pages. He skipped the headlines as he already knew them and read down the list of theatres. Plenty to see there. Lots of talent, too. He discussed the merits of the plays with his friends who had now tired of their argument and they settled on three: one tonight, a matinée and a music hall tomorrow. Folding the paper, David glanced at the Births, Deaths and Marriages. The ON ACTIVE SERVICE column was dolorously long as usual. Then, suddenly, a name caught his eye.

Paget. Petra Mary Paget

The breath seemed to be leaving his body as he read:

On 2 June 1916 at St Benedict's Church, Cambridge, Michael Robert Wynne, the East Suffolk Regiment, to Petra Mary (Polly), youngest daughter of the Rev. Arthur and Mrs Paget, The Rectory, Eskton, Yorkshire.

She was married. She had married another man. How could she have done such a thing? He loved her! He had fallen in love with her in the overgrown rose garden at Northesk the very first time he saw her. He had written to her, too. She hadn't replied. He saw why now.

'What's the matter, old boy?' Jack Montague leaned over and tapped David on the knee. 'Feeling sick? You've gone a funny colour. I told you not to eat that filthy rissole for breakfast. Rissoles! My God, the evil they do! I remember the dam' things at my private school . . .' He rambled on. He was a compulsive talker and David was glad to be saved the effort of a reply. Yes, he did feel sick – sick at heart, with bitter disappointment, a feeling he had never experienced before in his life.

Part Two

And through some mooned Valhalla there will pass
Battalions and battalions, scarred from hell;
The unreturning army that was youth:
The legions who have suffered and are dust.

Siegfried Sassoon: *The Troops*

CHAPTER FOURTEEN

The Push

The train for the front was packed leaving Boulogne and the evening light shimmered over the sea as they bumped over the level crossings before branching out on to the flat Artois plain. Mike still had the two young officers under his wing.

'No need to call me "sir" when we're together,' he told them for the third time. But they had just left school and it came easily to their lips. He was only two years older but looked more than that and they were treating him like an assistant master.

'Right-ho, sir – I mean, Mike,' Hemmings amended with a grin, continuing to pelt him with questions. Dickens, a stolid-looking boy with glasses, hardly spoke at all and read absorbedly as if he were going on holiday.

Their first-class compartment was packed with officers eager to retail every adventure of their leave; sexual adventures usually. Mike felt sorry for Hemmings who seemed stunned by all he heard, turning his childlike face from one to the other, his early chatter frozen. Dickens remained buried in his book. The fug of pipe smoke thickened into a blue haze. The senior officer present, a major in the Royal Fusiliers, refused to have a window open. 'Sit down, boy!' he roared at Dickens whose hands were on the window. 'You've a thing or two to learn. Keep your hands off the window till your seniors give you permission.'

The authorities did not seem in a hurry to get them to the railhead. After their long sojourn at Boulogne while they awaited orders from the Embarkation Officer, they were now stopping in a siding for the tenth time to allow ammunition trains loaded with shells to scream past.

Mike stared out of the hole he had rubbed on the misted window. Why did French trains have such a mournful whistle?

'A hell of a lot of shells on board those puffers,' someone remarked.

'For the Big Push,' the major explained with gloomy relish. 'Going to pulverize 'em this time, mark my words. I hear it's fixed for this month. They've got us back just in time, blast 'em.' His small, shrewd eyes ran over the new uniforms opposite him. 'You out for the first time? Poor little buggers.'

Hemmings flushed. He had a smooth, girlish skin that coloured easily. Dickens went on reading, deaf to the talk all round him. Mike turned Hemmings's attention back from the tactless major by retailing a game of rugger he had played against their fifteen in 1912.

'I was in the Colts then,' Hemmings said eagerly. 'I say, were you in that team? Then you must have met Geoffrey West, our captain? He was my cousin.' He stopped suddenly but Mike had noticed the past tense.

The train crawled into Amiens at eight o'clock next morning and the cramped soldiers emerged 'more dead than alive', as the major remarked bitterly. Mike gathered up his half-company and went to Brigade Headquarters to report. Then, having seen his men into a church hall that was their reception area and where they would be given a hot meal from a field kitchen, he went thankfully to his own billet that belonged to a captain on the staff who was at HQ for a couple of days. The two new officers shared a room on the floor below. The staff captain's batman prepared him a bath in a canvas bath and supplied him with a towel and soap. Then he fell into bed and slept for several hours.

When he woke, the sun was still high in the sky. He had been dreaming of a holiday he had had when he was small; a holiday by the sea. For a fleeting moment, he could not remember where he was until in the distance he heard the distant rumble of guns.

The dream was over. Harsh reality was knocking at his door.

Giving himself no time to think, he dressed. Collecting Hemmings and Dickens, he took them to the Godbert Restaurant for a meal. Afterwards they strolled back to their quarters to await a movement order. The staff captain had been back for a bath and had left a message with his batman: Mike was very welcome to a sleeping bag on the floor if his orders didn't come through.

And if they did come? Then it was a long trudge up to the front tonight.

His stomach began to churn at the thought. Fear: cold, black and throat-gripping fear came over him again.

Within a few hours he would be marching down that dead straight road to Albert, the road that was all-too-familiar to him from 1915.

He must do something. Too much time to think was dangerous. He would write to Polly. To her, he could pour out his inmost thoughts secure in the knowledge that she would understand because she loved him.

It was his first letter to her and with something of a flourish, he wrote: '*My darling wife* . . .'

When he had finished, he felt different. The black fear had retreated. Something of Polly's optimism had taken its place. He felt calm, even confident now. Some people got this way with religion, he thought, with a queer little smile twisting his lips. Polly is my religion. If I can hold on to her, I shall get through and not make an ass of myself.

Her face floated before him. He smiled contentedly.

He had a strong feeling he would survive and return to her. For the first time, hope in the future began to blossom inside him.

It was late the next night that they reached Albert. Most of them staggered in; every man in fighting order and carrying with him a bayonet, water bottle, ammunition pouches and a weighty knapsack that contained a ground-sheet, a change of socks, iron rations and a sewing kit. In addition they carried gas helmets and goggles. Some had the additional weight of digging and entrenching tools, Stokes mortar bombs, Mills grenades and cartridges. With the June sun blazing down, the ten-minute halt in every hour never seemed long enough and although it was only fifteen miles (and the veterans in the platoon had been on longer marches than that), by the time they reached the heap of rubble that was Albert, they were ready for the hour's rest they were given while they waited for their guide to take them up to the firing line.

'I say,' said Hemmings excitedly, pointing to the battered redbrick cathedral, 'she's still there! They say if she falls, we'll lose the war!'

Mike, loosening his Sam Browne belt, squinted up at the golden figure of the Virgin bent at right angles to the tower. 'So they say. But I think you'll find it's been wired there. Jerry used it as an artillery fix so, short of taking it down, the French have bent it over.'

Hemmings was frightfully disappointed. His boy's face clouded. 'I say, I wish you hadn't told me that! Seems a bit of a sell. I wonder if Dickens knows?' and he moved off with a light, elastic step to inform his brother officer.

God, he's young, Mike thought, watching Hemmings gesturing and explaining to the silent Dickens: too young to be in this mess. He ought by rights to be playing cricket at Marlborough.

As he sat on a heap of rubble and drank from his water flask, he was remembering the even grass and sheer singing greenness of his own school pitch. Tall elms to the south and an open vista to the west – one of the loveliest grounds possessed by any school. Who was it said Waterloo had been won on the playing fields of Eton? There was some truth in the statement when you looked at Hemmings and Dickens with their clear eyes and smooth healthy skin, well-developed bodies and sound heart and lungs. Then you looked at the ordinary Tommy and saw years of bad housing, bad food or no food at all. You saw bodies bred in dirty dark slum ghettos with open drains; bodies that now were undersized, with bad teeth and bow legs. He had noticed how some of them had laboured over this march, how Hemmings and Dickens had helped by taking over heavy burdens. Yet it was the Tommy's unquenchable spirit and cheerful cheekiness that counted in the end. The rain could pour down and Jerry send over a barrage of shells, but there always seemed to be a joke and rough humour in the trenches, and someone would be brewing a can of char on a kerosene stove.

My God, they deserve better than they've had in the past, he thought grimly. If this war ever ends, something must be done to share out the better things in life. He had never met an East End boy before the war nor had the East Ender known – really known – 'a toff'. There had been two worlds in England for too long. Now they shared a common danger and they had drawn closer. It no longer mattered if you had a strong, healthy body: a piece of red-hot shell was not selective.

'Mr Wynne, sir.'

He looked up and a sense of relief and gladness filled him for there, saluting him, was Sergeant Thomson who had watched over him and Hugh Isherwood when they first came out. Sergeant Thomson from Ely, a regular who had seen service in India.

'Thomson! What luck!' He leapt to his feet and pumped the man's hand. 'Never thought we should meet again. Are you in these parts?'

'I'm back with the battalion, sir.'

'Oh, I am glad!' Mike's face expressed his feelings. Good old Thomson was a rock he had leaned on often in the past. 'Did your mother tell you I went over to Ely in the spring to see her? She gave me a splendid tea.' The afternoon he had spent in that little cottage in the shadow of the cathedral was vividly before him now. 'She told me you'd been moved to another battalion after your blighty.'

'That's right, sir. Then Captain Armitage asked for me back and I reached them in March. Captain Armitage has gone himself now, sir – '

'Not killed?'

'No, sir. But moved to higher things as you might say,' Thomson grinned. 'We've got Captain Starr now, sir. A bit of a fire-eater but the lads respect him. You'll like him, sir. Is this your pack? I've got Corporal Harris with me. He's our guide but I asked permission to come as well soon as I heard you was back. Things have been pretty quiet in the line, sir. Brewing up, I'd say. There's been talk of the Big Push so long we've almost given up hope!' He shouldered Mike's pack. 'We're due out on Wednesday. We've got decent billets in a spot back there. You'll like it, sir.'

'Where's our bit of country?' Mike shielded a tiny flashlight over a map and Thomson's stubby finger picked out a road heading south-east over a small tributary running into the Ancre. 'It's marshy country, sir. We follow this stream – must have been full of trout once upon a time!' Thomson added wistfully. 'Must have been a very pretty chalk stream. Then we dip into this sunken lane which runs into our support trench. We're four hundred yards in front of Mametz. The line takes a sharp right-angled bend beyond this point to Hardicourt. But *this* line is us.'

Within twenty minutes they were on the road again. It was nearly midnight but so near midsummer that a brightness filled the sky and it was easy to see the fat white sausage shapes of many balloons floating overhead. To the east, magnesium flares came and went on the enemy line but it was eerily quiet once they had threaded their way through the horse limbers and troops at Crucifix Corner. The statue of Christ was plainly silhouetted against the flares.

They fumbled their way across uneven ground with laughs and muffled curses that Mike had to quell, for they had now reached the sunken road. High banks on either side gave them a false sense of security. Mike halted the straggling column and went along the line speaking in an undertone as he did so: 'Absolute silence is essential. Jerry is likely to pitch a shell or two into this lane if he hears activity.' He realized that the men were for the most part young conscripts excited by their nearness to the front line and keeping up their courage with laughter and jokes. When he again moved off, he had Corporal Harris by his side. The man seemed to possess cat's eyes and pointed out hazards in their path with uncanny accuracy. Their progress was slow and the silence queer. To the north, one could see the barrage, but here one was aware of the enemy waiting and listening.

And then, before they realized it, Harris had given the password to a sentry and they were dropping into a support trench and were treading on duckboards.

It was at this precise moment that with a warning howl half a dozen shells came over and burst just behind them. They crouched in the support trench, watching flares sailing over them, lighting up the whole ground. But Harris did not pause. He led the way to a dug-out with a tarpaulin stretched across the entrance and the three officers found themselves confronting the colonel who, by the aid of a couple of candles, was writing busily at a table. Another man lay trying to sleep in a wood and wire frame fixed against one wall. Through the entrance to another hole sat two men wearing earphones who were sending signals. A smell of sweat, whisky and lyddite had been captured in these close quarters, a smell familiar to Mike. Oh, God, I'm back! he thought. But when he shook hands with the commanding officer and spoke, he heard himself being very calm and cheerful. Fifteen minutes later, after a whisky all round, they set out on the last few hundred yards to the front line. The colonel had explained that they were being sent to a company that had been recently badly depleted not by enemy action but by dysentery; that only three more days of the tour of duty in the front line remained; and that, depend on it, this calm state of affairs couldn't go on much longer. They had arrived in time for the summer offensive.

Mike wrote his second letter to Polly while they were in their rest billets in a quiet village on the banks of the Ancre.

Each day in the line has been like a 'first' for me. I had the horrible feeling that I would fail. Thank God, I didn't. I brought out two young officers and everything is a genuine first time for them. The younger one, Hemmings, reminds me of Hugh Isherwood. I've told you about him, haven't I? He keeps us all good humoured despite our natural desire to growl at each other. I like the boy. The post has come up and there's a letter from my wife! Bless you, darling.

But his spirits were low when they returned to the line four days later. The weather had changed to rain and mist. There were gas attacks all along the line and they had to wear their gas masks continuously which was a strain. Captain Starr, who had, as Hemmings put it, a short touch-paper, was in a fury at the condition of the trench. He called the regiment they had relieved 'those filthy hounds'. The trench was not fit to live in. 'Wynne, get your platoon to clear the place up. It won't be dysentery we'll get this time but worse. Bloody fools! They haven't even mended the parapet.'

Two men were shot by a sniper as they mended the gap in the parapet. Mike felt sick as he saw them carried away for he knew it had been his fault. He ought to have waited until dark as Sergeant Thomson had advised, but Starr's peremptory roars of complaint had got on his nerves and he had brushed aside Thomson's doubts. Now the poor devils were dead. His new-found confidence ebbed.

That night he led his platoon out wire-cutting. He was jumpy and could feel cold sweat pouring down his body as they crawled about, wrestling with the rusty barbed wire. They spent four hours out in the open, freezing into immobility at the first sign of activity from the German side. The heavy ground mist helped and they dropped unscathed into their trench at dawn.

On 24 June, the British offensive (the Big Push that had been talked about for so long) opened with the most terrific bombardment ever known. Starr said with glee that there wouldn't be many of the enemy left to trouble them after a week of this barrage.

His jubilation turned to disgust when, instead of being relieved on the twenty-sixth, they were ordered to stay put for three more days. Apparently, the main attack originally scheduled for the twenty-eighth had been postponed. It would now begin on 1 July. The troops who would be leading the assault that day would relieve them on 29 June. Meanwhile, air patrols reported that the wire in front of Mametz had not been cut sufficiently well for the assault troops to get through. The colonel himself appeared in Starr's dug-out: the barrage would be lifted in front of their line from midnight tonight for two hours in order that the work might be done. The bombardment, concentrating on the enemy line, had left a lot of wire untouched.

'So see to it, old chap, will you? Cut a decent lane through as far as you can go. Brigade's frightfully keen about it.'

'Bloody hell!' Starr growled when the colonel had departed. 'As if we haven't sweated our guts out cutting that damned wire! Jerry's been mending it as fast as we destroy it. And we've another two days of this din to endure. Those poor bastards out there must be deafened by now.'

The men had scraped shallow holes in the trench walls and were crouched under their groundsheets, trying to get a little sleep for an hour or so. But under that screaming, howling passage of shells overhead, it was impossible and they were exhausted. Unshaven and hollow-eyed, ten of them heard they were to go on yet another wire-cutting party that night.

Through a spyhole in the parapet, Mike looked out on the scene before him. The village of Mametz on the German side, now almost obliterated, had been built on a slope of chalkland. Shells, tearing into this, seemed to have ripped out white strips of flesh, leaving jagged wounds. Mametz woods were now just splintered tree trunks and Fricourt woods, jutting out beyond the northern part of the village, were in the same condition. Yet HQ insisted that a lot of wire was still intact. It seemed impossible.

Somewhere along the trench he heard someone laugh: the irrepressible Hemmings was sharing a joke with his men. His platoon gave him a doglike devotion, for Hemmings wore his gallant youthfulness like a glamorous cloak and was touchingly unaware of it. He was a reincarnation of Hugh, Mike thought. He used all Hugh's schoolboy expressions. He never groused. The world loves a cavalier and his platoon worshipped him. From them tonight he would demand – and get – the last ounce.

Tonight. He mustn't be allowed to go.

As he turned away from the parapet he saw Dickens come out of the officers' dug-out to relieve Hemmings. Dickens, the stolid reader who had looked unshakeable, was obviously badly affected by the continuous howling, shrieking barrage overhead. His skin was olive-green, his eyes strained. He refused meals and lay on one of the bunks sleeping every moment he was off duty. Mike recognized the signs he knew so well in himself: the man with a highly sensitive nervous system who could not stand up to the hellish din that filled their lives. Men like Dickens and himself were marked down as 'cowards', which was unfair. Their resistance to stress was lower than the others', that was all.

'I'd like to go tonight, sir,' Mike told Starr. 'Instead of Hemmings.'

Starr looked at him sourly. 'Don't be a bloody fool, Wynne. No one would *like* to go tonight unless he was a suicide case. You were out last night. I'm sending Hemmings, an NCO and ten men.'

Hemmings laughed excitedly as they blacked his face, his bright blue eyes sparkling through the corked mask. The thought of the coming task actually seemed to exhilarate him. He was an adventurous youth and now he would have something to write home about at last. This was no ordinary wire-cutting job. Why, they were even going to lift the barrage for a couple of hours! He borrowed Mike's better pair of wire-cutters and downed

255

his rum at a gulp. It was one o'clock when he and his men slipped past the sentry with a last harassed warning from Starr.

'For God's sake, don't be longer than two hours. It'll be light by three and the barrage is due to be lowered.'

Overhead, the sky was a mass of coloured lights like a gigantic firework display. Shells still shrieked over their heads but now they were bursting above Mametz and if one didn't fall short, the wiring party would have a clear two hours to work in. In some ways it would be easier for them because the noise obliterated every sound. But the Germans might be doubly alert, suspecting an attack, at dawn . . .

'Hope Hemmings doesn't overdo things,' Starr muttered. 'The fellow's inclined to be foolhardy at times.' He looked over his shoulder: in a corner of the shadowed dug-out, a figure wrapped in a blanket lay motionless in a bunk. 'Nerves of iron,' the CO said enviously of Dickens.

It was about two o'clock that they heard the rattle of a machine-gun close at hand. Starr and Mike ran along the trench to the spot where a cluster of dark figures huddled.

Sergeant Thomson was there. 'There's been trouble, sir. Hewart and Reed are back and they say Mr Hemmings is lying out there badly wounded. Corporal Black is dead.'

'Damn! How did it happen?'

'We lost our way, sir,' Reed volunteered. He was panting hoarsely. 'Mr Hemmings was ahead of us – we'd managed to cut a lot of wire, working fast-like because of the noise – ' The man gulped and sweat glistened on his blackened face. 'Then Jerry opened up with a machine-gun – almost under our feet. They got Black and then Mr Hemmings as he was crouching over Black. I think he's alive, sir. I heard him moaning as we scrambled back. The others got in further down.'

'I'm going for him,' Mike said. He felt suddenly quite cool and sure of himself, of what he must do. He brushed aside Starr's doubts. 'No, don't stop me, sir. If Hugh's wounded, I must get him in.'

'Hugh? I thought Hemmings's name was Keith?'

'I'd like permission to go with him, sir,' Sergeant Thomson said.

'Very well. For God's sake, *hurry*. It's getting light.'

Mike was already on the fire step and he could feel Thomson close behind him as they crawled out, feeling for the white tape the others had taken with them. In one hand, he carried his revolver. He felt no fear, only a glad relief that he was going to be able to do something for Hugh at last.

Thomson, leaving several yards between them, crawled after him. He could smell the sour acrid earth under his nose. *Hugh*, Mr Wynne had said. A slip of the tongue no doubt. Or maybe he was reliving that time last winter when they were over near Contalmaison in those sodden trenches . . . He stopped, lay very still. What the hell was that? He strained his eyes, trying to see the figure of his officer ahead of him. There were muffled sounds that made his pulses gallop apprehensively. Something *was* happening over there . . .

Suddenly, out of the black ground from which a thin white mist was rising, two figures loomed. As one brought down his rifle butt on Thomson's head, the other seized Mike and bore him back to the German trench undeterred by a burst of firing higher up the line.

Someone brought the news to the CO: a raiding party from the other side had captured or killed Mr Wynne and Sergeant Thomson. 'We think they've taken them prisoner. Difficult to tell but it seems likely. They sprayed the parapet with fire and Hunter's badly wounded, sir.'

'My God, what a night's work!' Starr turned to the

prone figure lying on the bunk and yelled savagely: 'Get up, Dickens! How the hell can you sleep through all this? Get up! You're needed.' To no one in particular he said helplessly: 'Two damn good officers and that decent, reliable Thomson. What a pretty night's work. Whoever has survived will be interrogated about the push, you can bet your life,' he added, turning to Dickens who was slowly getting off the bed. 'Get on to Battalion HQ for me.' He reached for the whisky bottle (this was the last and they had two more days to go) and splashed some into his mug. His face was sombre: that nice lad, Hemmings, who had only been out a fortnight and poor Wynne who was newly married. And Thomson who was the sole support of his mother. 'I'll have to post them Missing Believed Killed,' he said heavily as he gulped down the whisky. 'Even if they're captured, I can't see them surviving long under our bombardment. Listen to it!'

Over at Northesk, David was on leave while he waited to go on a small arms course. Once that was over he expected to be posted to a regiment that was serving in France. It was rumoured that a big battle was planned for the summer, a battle that must finish the Germans and end the war. He secretly hoped that it wouldn't all be over before he got out there and experienced some of the excitement for himself. After all, he had come all this way to go to war and now everyone was saying it would end this summer with the Big Push Haig was planning.

Being at home chafed a bit because he knew Polly was only three or four miles away. He had glimpsed her once as he passed through Eskton in his motor: the rectory gates had been open and he had recognized her bright head against the background of trees and herbaceous border. He had slowed down, hesitated and then resolutely gone on, knowing he must make no effort to contact her again. She had married another man and the wound was still sore. No, he couldn't re-open it.

Reggie was home at last and spent some time in a Bath chair each day as David pushed him about the grounds, keeping up a monologue to which Reggie responded with grunts.

Elaine was fully and happily employed in supervising the changes being made in the west wing for the convalescent home for officers. By autumn they would be getting their first patients. Never happier than when fully occupied, she seemed to have winged feet as she went from one floor to another overseeing the work, having a quick word with David or dropping a kiss on her husband's head in passing. 'All right, darling? Going out with David this morning? That's right!'

There was nothing wrong with Reggie's brain although she seemed unable to understand this. Occasionally Reggie's eyes, warm with humour, met his stepson's: if he could have winked he would have done but only his eyes remained lively in an immobile face.

'Mother, you oughtn't to talk to Dad as if he's a child!' David expostulated. 'He understands everything just as he did before the stroke. He's paralysed, not an imbecile!'

Elaine wrinkled her forehead. 'He just doesn't seem himself, wrapped in that awful silence. You don't realize how awful it is for me when you aren't here, David,' and tears of self-pity clouded her eyes.

'And don't you think it's awful for Dad? Imprisoned in a body that doesn't work, speechless, helpless?' Sudden anger choked him. 'I wish you'd think of him and not yourself for once!' David shouted angrily. 'You're being utterly selfish, Mother!'

'Selfish? *Me?* How can you say such a thing? I'm one of the most unselfish people alive!' Elaine shouted back, believing implicitly in the truth of her statement. Tears now rolled down her cheeks. 'Reggie would never have allowed you to talk to me in this manner – so rude and unkind –'

'I'm sorry, Mother. I beg your pardon, I don't want to make you cry. I just feel we should forget ourselves for once and think of the hell Dad's going through. Our little discomforts can be nothing compared to his misery.' Dad has spoiled her, he told himself, and she can't see anyone's point of view but her own. To soothe his ruffled temper he asked Miss Matthews to get his stepfather ready for an outing round the grounds. Reggie always looked spruce as he was wheeled up and down the mossy paths: his thick white hair was topped by a white panama hat, he wore a silk scarf tucked into a soft shirt and a cream linen jacket that now hung on his fleshlessness. Freshly shaved, a new pink colour in his face, he began to look much improved during the days of David's leave.

'I'm thinking of replanting the woods, Dad. The Ministry of Supply has taken all the mature stuff but Elliot thinks we ought to be able to get hold of boys awaiting call-up to give us a hand with the planting. They could work at weekends too. He says Squire Filey at Eskton has done that for the past couple of years. If we have anything like decent weather this autumn we can get the scheme started. I want to arrange everything now as I may not be home again for months.' Putting on the brake, David went to squat on the ground facing his stepfather. 'You know that I shall be going quite soon, Dad?'

Reggie's eyes were fixed on him with a strange intensity. His face worked as he tried to say something.

'Don't worry, Dad, I intend coming back! But I've got to think of the future. If we let the Ministry skim everything off the place without replanting, my children will have nothing to turn into capital! There must be investment for the future on a place like this. The Ministry have forced us to sell now but the wood at Farley Bottom should have had another eight years. My grandfather has it all written up, you know, and I've been studying it.' He got up and took the handle of the Bath chair again. Reggie's weak hand touched him, his eyes eloquent with words: *You must marry. Must have a son . . .* Slowly, painfully, he nodded his head to emphasize what he was trying to convey.

They were so close in spirit that David understood at once. He gave a queer little laugh. 'All very well, Dad, but I've lost her. She's married someone else.' Suddenly he was pouring it all out to the man who had been more of a real father to him than Gilbert Argyle. How he had met and fallen in love with the Rector of Eskton's red-headed daughter Polly and how she, without a word of warning, had married another man. 'I suppose she didn't realize how I felt about her. But to meet and marry another chap in a month!'

They had reached the lake now and both brooded over the dark sheet of water with bulrushes and flags at its edge. Reggie sighed and David gave a half-hearted laugh. 'You're right, Dad. Women are the devil, all right. Come on, let's go back. It's getting chilly.'

With so little help available, everyone at Eskton Rectory had to turn to and perform allotted tasks. With two babies in the house (for poor Alix had not yet succeeded in escaping) there was much washing of linen and prams to be pushed. The rector undertook to clean everyone's shoes but it was so badly done (brown polish absent-mindedly applied to Polly's cherished black kid slippers) that very soon the family refused to let him handle their footwear. The rector's help worked out expensively, Archie pointed out. This was after he had found his father making home-made polish on the range on Mrs Linsey's afternoon off. He had ruined a saucepan, not to mention the cook's temper on her return to a kitchen full of the smell of beeswax and vinegar.

'We'll get on quicker if rector sticks to his books,' she was heard muttering as she consigned the milk pan to the dustbin. 'One of me best ones and you can't get 'em for love or money now,' she mourned. 'But that's t'master all over – he was only trying to help,' she excused her favourite hastily. 'Bless him! I don't like to hear you talking so about your father, Mr Archie,' she added, most unfairly Archie thought, turning on him as an outlet for her irritation.

Nell seemed to forget that Polly was now a married woman and soon returned to the general assumption that Polly was simply a thoughtless child. Indeed, because they hardly knew him, Mike's name was rarely mentioned in the family circle. After a time she found herself slipping back into being Polly Paget again. No one in the village called her Mrs Wynne and she only had his occasional letters to remind her that she had a husband serving in France.

One perfect morning of blue sky and scudding clouds, she put on her old gingham dress, tied up her hair and made an assault on the loaded gooseberry bushes: Mrs Linsey had been saving sugar for jam. There was a little breeze smelling of the moors and she felt a wave of contentment and hopefulness as she knelt by the bushes. She knew that this was probably due to the change in the weather, nevertheless she wanted to bask in the feeling while she could. She was just sucking a pricked finger when a shadow fell across her and there was the squire looking so exactly himself that she was confused. The man who was about to marry Katy ought to look quite changed, she thought foolishly. Instead in his brown suit and old panama hat he looked exactly as he had done for years.

'Now then, Polly my girl, what d'you mean by getting married in all that hurry? Eh? Eh? I thought you were going to be a Senior Wrangler or something?'

She scrambled off her knees and kissed him. He held her away from him, staring at her with his sharp little eyes. 'All square and above board, eh?'

She laughed, nodding her head, no longer offended by the inquiry for it seemed to her that all older people leapt to this conclusion. War babies. Everybody was having them. 'Absolutely above board, Uncle Wilfred. You see, Mike's leave was nearly over and there was so little time left to be together. Besides, Girton no longer wanted me. I suppose you think I've wasted the studentship?'

They were strolling back towards the lawn. The squire halted. 'Now, have I said a word? Never did think it a good idea, as a matter of fact. Men don't like clever girls, y'know.'

'But if I hadn't gone up I wouldn't have met Mike!'

'You'd have met someone else, m'dear, and thought yourself in love with *him*. Know you gals!' Wilfred Filey gave his bark of a laugh. 'Now what are you going to do with yourself? Stay home and help your mother?'

'Well, I ought to since you are stealing her right hand,' Polly said slyly. 'Congratulations, by the way, Katy's a darling.'

The squire paused to blow his nose emotionally. 'Thank you, my dear. Needless to say, I'm a very lucky man.'

There threatened to be an awkward pause and Polly said quickly: 'Oh, by the way, I'm thinking of joining an all-women hospital unit.'

Wilfred Filey stared at her. 'Are there such things? *All women?*'

'Haven't you heard of Doctor Elsie Inglis and her

263

Scottish Women's Hospital? And Girton has a couple of units, too, in France and Serbia.'

'Women operating on our chaps?' The squire swung his cane violently. 'God bless my soul! What's the world coming to?'

'No, in general they're working for the other Allies. The RAMC won't look at them. The women surgeons have all had their training abroad because they're not allowed to study surgery in this country. It's all such nonsense!'

'I don't blame the War Office – it would never do to have gals operating on our chaps. Good God! Women on their own and using the knife in the operating theatre? Damme, anything might happen!'

She bit her lip, swallowing laughter.

He brought his eyes to bear on her sternly. 'Now, Polly, m'girl, don't let me hear any more nonsense about going into the operating theatre from you. It's farcical.'

'But how could I? I'm not a qualified surgeon – '

'No woman's a *qualified* surgeon if she's not been trained in Britain,' the squire argued. He took a final swish with his cane at the gooseberries and they went through the door in the garden wall and on to the lawn. Suddenly remembering something he stopped and fished first in one pocket and then another, finally bringing out a scrap of paper that he thrust into her hand.

'Wedding present,' he said and marched on.

It was a cheque for a hundred pounds.

'Oh, Uncle Wilfred!' She felt a surge of gratitude. With this in the bank, she could go to London and hunt for a job – and she would be able to buy a food hamper for Mike filled with all the things he liked, like tongue and Stilton cheese – oh, heaps of things!

Running after him she kissed her embarrassed benefactor on the cheek. 'Thank you a thousand times!'

* * *

264

On the first Monday in July she was first down for once. Today she was going to Scarborough to visit the dentist and was armed with a long shopping list for the household. While she put on her straw hat and fetched a couple of baskets, Archie drank a hasty cup of coffee and ate a piece of toast. He had harnessed Pinky and had tied her to the gatepost where she was now trying to tear down the syringa hedge.

'We'll never catch the nine o'clock train!'

'Never, madam, is a word we do not allow!' Archie retorted in a good imitation of Uncle Dolly.

But they were too late for the train and had an hour to wait for the next one. Fortunately, Polly's dental appointment wasn't until midday. 'Tell Mother I shall be late home – meet the six o'clock, Archie!' she called out of the train window. Archie waved his arm nonchalantly as he strolled to the Nestlé chocolate machine to assuage his hunger with penny bars.

The route to Scarborough was over magnificent scenery: the cliff top and the sea (now renamed North Sea instead of German Ocean) one moment and pastoral scenes the next. It was a piece of country Polly never tired of although she had journeyed over it many times in her life. The shipping lanes out at sea were busier than usual and she spotted a naval frigate, some coalers and many small fishing boats snatching a living in dangerous waters. Early in the war German destroyers had emerged out of a sea mist to bombard Whitby and Scarborough. They had caused terrible damage and loss of life. For a time the coastal area was closed to everyone: no more donkeys, no more children building sandcastles, only barbed wire and notices saying *Keep Out*. Some people left their homes to set up new ones inland. Suddenly, the war had come home to the people of Yorkshire. And then, as nothing more happened, people had regained their confidence.

The War Department notices were taken down, the boarding houses reopened, the beaches were peopled again. Now this summer of 1916, the season was in full swing, Polly realized, as she emerged from the station and walked down Westborough to Rowntree's department store where she had to begin her shopping. Arranging with the shop to deliver her parcels to the station before five, she kept her dental appointment from which she emerged with a few fillings. Feeling rather battered she walked down to the chocolate and coffee shop overlooking the harbour on St Nicholas Cliff: she was by now badly in need of sustenance before completing the shopping.

By the town hall she paused to stare down on to the beach, which was packed with people: the fine weather had sent everyone beachwards and from above they looked like ants on an anthill, she was thinking when suddenly the newsboy's shouts penetrated her thoughts. He was at his stand outside the Royal Hotel.

'News extra! News extra!'

She could just see the poster he held. It was flapping in the sea breeze and at first she couldn't make out its scrawled message. There had evidently been an extra edition that morning.

GREAT BATTLE ON WESTERN FRONT

Her mouth was dry as she bought the paper, smiled at the boy and agreed it was a lovely day.

There were seats near the town hall. She sat down quickly and fumbled with the paper, trying to find its centre page.

FORWARD IN THE WEST
START OF A GREAT ATTACK
FIERCE BATTLES ON THE SOMME

266

The bright sun was making her feel sick. She could feel herself shaking. She must go inside somewhere and sit down. The nearby coffee shop smelled reassuringly of coffee and hand-made chocolates; it had always been a place to go as a special treat when she was young. Now she crept into its darkest corner and hurriedly read the account of the attack that had been launched on 1 July. Two whole days ago.

NINETY MILES OF UPROAR
THE GREAT BATTLE

'Your coffee, miss.'

'Oh . . . thank you.'

'It's awful about that battle, miss.'

'You know?'

'Oh, yes, Our manageress bought a paper. Her son's out there, you see.'

Polly glanced across at the neat little woman who was serving a customer with chocolates: the hand wielding the tongs seemed to be quite steady. She was even smiling as she helped the old gentleman to choose his chocolates. But Polly sipped her scalding coffee with trembling lips.

SPECIAL ACCOUNT: 'The biggest British offensive.'

British HQ. Saturday 1 July

At half-past seven this morning a great battle began on a front of about twenty-five miles above and on both banks of the Somme. Perhaps it will be known in history as the Battle of the Somme . . .

She got up, began to stumble towards the door.

'Good morning, miss – oh, thank you.'

'It was lovely coffee but – but I couldn't finish it.'

'I understand.' The girl smiled, pocketing the tip.

Now where's my list? she thought distractedly, bumping

into people in the street. Veiling for Katy's hat. That book for Father. The groceries for Mother – I can't. I can't do any of it. I must go home.

She tried to keep on walking steadily, to glance in shop windows, but all the time her brain was whirling as if it was made of cogs and wheels. A great battle. Mike. A great battle. The Somme. He was there, she knew, because he had written that he was back in familiar country: a place of chalk downs, little woods and sluggish streams, 'Very pretty once but not so now,' he had written. And she felt the same terror that she knew he must be feeling. But her terror was for him.

'Hullo!' Someone was standing in front of her: a young officer in a smart new uniform. Blinking, she recognized David Ransom. They stared at each other.

'What's the matter?' He took her arm. 'Come on, let's go in here.' He was steering her up the steps into the Royal Hotel. 'Coffee as quickly as you can,' he told the old waiter and put her into a comfortable chair in the hotel lounge. Drawing up another, he looked at her searchingly. 'Not going to faint, are you?'

She shook her head and tried to breathe deeply to steady the wild sick beating of her heart. 'No. But I've just seen the poster – read the paper. This battle on the Somme – ' She drew another long breath. 'I believe Mike – my husband – is there. It was on the Somme that he was wounded last time and he'd written to tell me he was back in the same place. Only last week he wrote – ' She shook her head looking down at the twisted hands in her lap. The waiter came and poured the coffee and she waited until he had finished before fixing her eyes with their anxious expression on David's face again. 'He dreaded going back. He really wasn't fit to face another battle so soon – he was badly shellshocked. Oh, why doesn't this terrible war stop!'

He took the cup of coffee from her shaking hands and put it back on the table. 'I saw in the newspaper that you had got married.' He kept reproach out of his voice with an effort. 'Was it a sudden decision or were you engaged when we first met?'

'Oh, no. I wasn't engaged then! I hadn't even met Mike, you know.'

Bafflement was apparent in his eyes. 'You hadn't met him? You mean you met and married him within a month or so?'

'Nearly six weeks,' she corrected him defensively. 'We met on the train when I was going back to Cambridge.'

He was at a loss for words. What on earth could this Wynne be like? He had evidently swept little Polly Paget off her feet and married her out of hand. He felt depressed suddenly. He had thought she liked him. True, they had argued but it had meant nothing. He had been certain she had felt the tug of attraction just as he did. Then Elliot had arrived with the news of the sinking of the *Oceana* and that had been that.

'He had suffered a great deal,' she said, staring out of the lace-curtained windows at the green-blue sea. 'I don't mean his wound but in his head. He dreaded going back, you know. I'm so thankful I was able to help him.' Tears clouded her eyes suddenly. 'Now he's in the middle of this battle – everything he dreaded – and I can't help him. If only he could get a small wound and come home again quickly!'

He was looking at her alertly. She had unwittingly told him everything he wanted to know. This wasn't a sudden great love that had swept her off her feet: it was the man's need for Polly and Polly's capacity for pity that had caused this sudden marriage.

'Why are you staring like that?'

He tore his eyes away and laughed. 'I'm sorry.' But he

could have shouted for joy. She might be another man's wife but her capacity for passion hadn't been touched. He could swear to it from the way she spoke of her new husband. So he tried to comfort her, to explain that the front was a very long one and that her husband could have been sent to quite a different part this time and she might have misread the hints he had given in his letter. And above all, this push was going to hasten the end of the war – everyone was saying so.

He saw before long that he had succeeded in what he had set out to do: she was brightening; she finished her coffee and even smiled at last. Soon she was asking his advice about her search for war work.

'Why not try the Red Cross? We're seeing a lot of their people now that Northesk is being converted into a convalescent home. I'll sound them out myself if you like and let you know. You're going to be at home for the rest of the summer?'

The long dimple in her cheek was beginning to show. 'Not if I can help it! That would be too dull.'

He laughed, offering her a hand to pull her out of the deep chair. 'Come on, I'm going to drive you home. I've saved lots of gasoline for this leave.'

She accepted at once and enjoyed the run back through a string of sleepy villages to Pickering and thence up on to the moors, approaching Eskton from an entirely different direction. The road had been rough, almost a farm track in parts, but she had barely noticed it because they had been borne along on oceans of talk. They had so much to say, to tell each other about their lives, that it was a shock to find the motor turning in at the rectory gates. But they were miraculously back on terms of close friendship.

'No, I won't come in.' He looked closely into her face, holding her hand in both of his. 'Goodbye, Polly, spare a

270

thought for me sometimes. I shall be thinking of you every day.'

Colour ran into her cheeks. 'No – no, please, you mustn't. I'm married. It wouldn't be right.'

'You can't stop me,' he said quietly. 'My thoughts are my own property. Besides, I knew you before Mike did – you can't deny that!' He released her hand and sprang back into his seat. The car had gone before she could think of a retort. But she was smiling as she turned to go in.

The door had opened at her approach and her father stood there. There was a look on his face – apprehensive, full of pity – that caused her heart to jump. Even before he put the opened telegram in her hands she knew bleakly that David Ransom's words of comfort were worthless. She had allowed herself to be lulled, that was all. She unfolded the orange form and saw it was from the Cambridge Territorial Headquarters.

Regret to inform you Second-Lieutenant M. R. Wynne, East Suffolk Regiment, reported missing. This does not necessarily mean he is killed or wounded.
Colonel-in-Charge
Territorial Force Records, Cambridge

Suddenly, the family were pouring through the door, surrounding her, assuring her in a chorus that Mike was only missing. Why, look what had happened to Kit! Uncle Dolly would be contacted at once and would go and see his friends at the War Office. Meanwhile Mike's parents must be telegraphed and no doubt Walter Wynne would go round to Territorial Headquarters to see if there was fresh news.

She said very little, allowing herself to be pulled inside and her hat and gloves removed. She was numbed, unable as yet to feel much. But round and round in her brain went the thought: only three weeks of life had been left to him when he went back and he had known it.

Sir D'Oyly Gromont went at once to see his friends at the War Office. They wanted to be helpful but the greatest battle in history was in progress and there was utter confusion in the Next-of-Kin department. The casualty lists were bloated and those who could have given information about the missing were themselves dead. 'Try Territorial Records,' he was advised.

But Walter Wynne had already done that without success.

The terrifyingly long lists of dead, wounded and missing printed in *The Times* each day made it difficult to hope. How could he be alive, one amongst thousands in this carnage?

Captain Starr wrote to her on his field pad.

Mike and his sergeant went out to fetch in a wounded officer who was lying in a shell-hole. Our sentries reported that they encountered the enemy and were killed instantly or taken prisoner. But we have not found their bodies. It was just before the Big Push and things have been very confused since. I hope you will get good news soon. We miss him very much.

She read and re-read this scrap of paper but without any renewal of hope. Then she folded it forlornly for the tenth time and put it away.

Archie put his arm round her. 'Do cry, Poll. It worries me that you haven't done so.'

'I somehow can't grasp it yet.' Putting her hands over her face she whispered: 'He was so afraid of death.'

'If he's dead he's at peace. He won't feel afraid or even afraid of feeling afraid, which is sometimes worse. And if he's not dead, then he'll be back some day.'

She nodded, hope putting forth new shoots. Yes, if he

272

were dead, he would no longer feel the soul-corroding fear that had made the last few months of his life such hell. Tears began to roll down her cheeks, but as she wiped them away with Archie's handkerchief she remembered Mike saying: 'I don't want to go out into the darkness . . .'

CHAPTER FIFTEEN

We Meet But To Part

Two days later, she got a note from David expressing his regret at her bad news: he had learned of it from Cass Byrne. The second half of his letter was to give her the name and address of a newly formed hospital unit with committee headquarters in London. They were, it appeared, advertising for someone to run the clerical side of the hospital in France.

It was a friendly if slightly formal little note. She was grateful that he had remembered she was looking for a war job. She wrote at once to Doctor Helen Gregory who had formed the unit six months earlier and within a week had been asked to go up to London for an interview. It would, she thought, be an opportunity to visit Mike's parents in Cambridge at the same time.

But first there was the wedding; Katy and the squire had decided to get married quietly and take a much-needed summer holiday as their honeymoon trip. Nell was a great deal put out: not only was Polly planning to leave and take a job but now Katy. And what would she do without Katy who had run the house for eighteen months and looked after them all? Then suddenly Alix announced that she was going across to Southport to be near Kit, taking little Christine and a young girl from the village as a nursemaid. They would take furnished rooms and Aunt Nora was paying for it all.

'How dare Nora do this behind my back!' Nell stormed at her daughter. '*Furnished rooms!* And a delicate little baby – '

'Christine's as tough as a boot,' Alix said shortly,

doggedly packing. 'And Aunt Nora's helped me because I've become your prisoner, Mother. It's nearly three months since Kit was wounded and I haven't seen him once. He needs me as much as Christine does. Besides, Maggie Umpleby's a good little thing and she loves babies so I'll be able to leave Christine with her while I visit the hospital.'

'An Umpleby! Well, I've heard everything now. They're dirty and unreliable. She'll drop the baby or give her gin to stop her crying – '

Alix burst out laughing. 'Gin? Poor little Maggie? No, Mother, that won't wash – nothing will. I've got the money and the rooms are booked and I'm going tomorrow.'

'Before the wedding?'

'Yes, before the wedding. Katy knows and understands.' Folding the last of a pile of clean napkins, Alix looked her mother squarely in the eye. 'Please try and remember that I'm married, that I have a wounded husband and a child, that their welfare comes first with me now and always. Why don't you let us go, Mother? Polly's married – she's not to think of herself as a widow – and has a different future from the one we envisaged for her a few weeks ago. She's going into a job. I heard you nagging her a few minutes ago, telling her it was *her duty* to stay with you and Father. You're wrong: it's your duty to release your grip on us and allow us to lead our own lives. I can't blame Imogen for escaping to do what she wants to do. It's not fair to expect any of your daughters to sacrifice their lives to you. You're comparatively young and you and Dad can still have a good life together without the rest of us. Archie will be going up to Oxford next year and I don't suppose he'll want to spend every vacation at home.'

If a sheep had turned round and bitten her, Nell would

275

not have been more astounded. Alix had always been the most loving of her children and now she coolly stood there and more or less proclaimed that her mother's welfare counted as nothing to her! 'You know how ill I've been,' Nell said tearfully. 'This house is too much for me. How am I going to manage on my own?'

Alix made no reply and, as there was no one else to offer support, Nell adopted a martyr's mien and shut herself up in the morning-room again.

On Saturday morning, Katy walked across to her wedding in the church. She wore a corn-coloured silk dress and a Leghorn hat and carried a small posy of yellow rosebuds picked by Polly in the garden that morning. Archie who was to give her away had her by the arm and could feel the slight tremor of her body. Polly, walking behind them as they went out of the sunshine into the shadow of the elms, wondered what her sister-in-law was thinking. Only two years ago she had arrived unexpectedly in their midst as Dick's bride: they had been manifestly in love and his death in action had been a terrible blow. Now with a little set smile on her face but with tranquil eyes she was walking into church to marry a man old enough to be her father. What she did, she did with all her heart as was her way. There would be no looking back for the girl who had grown up in a home for abandoned children and, by her beauty, had become one of George Edwardes's chorus at the Gaiety Theatre. As she passed the brass tablet put up to Dick, she didn't even glance at it; her eyes were firmly on the small nut-brown man waiting for her at the altar.

The church was full of friends and the squire's tenants while outside pressed a small crowd of wellwishers from the village who couldn't find a pew. They clutched bags of confetti to throw at the happy couple in fine disregard of the rector's detestation of what he termed 'that pagan rite'.

As the beautiful words of the marriage service were spoken by her father, Polly felt she was going to break down. It was only about five weeks ago that she and Mike had stood together at the altar at St Benedict's church and made their responses. Now he was lost to view, maybe dead, maybe not. She bit her lip and glanced at Nell's stony face at this, the first service she had attended in this church since Dick had been killed: her eyes were fixed on the brass tablet to her son. Impulsively, Polly took the hand nearest her and gave it a little squeeze: Nell did not respond and her hand felt cold and dead.

After the service, everyone crowded into the rectory drawing-room or spilled out into the garden eating the buffet lunch Mrs Linsey had triumphantly produced using the hams and chickens sent over from the squire's home farm and salads and peas and new potatoes from their own garden. A cake had been impossible so there was fresh raspberries and cream instead.

'Well, Polly, what news of your husband?' she was constantly asked by well-meaning friends. Or they commiserated with her. 'My dear child! It's too dreadful. Only married for a month, too!' they would add to each other as if she couldn't hear. Her smile became a little fixed until at last she could escape to her bedroom where she sat on her bed, her hands clasped tightly in her lap, a cold sweat drying on her body.

Oh, Mike, where are you? If only I could help you! Oh, Mike, I pray you aren't frightened – aren't in pain – know I'm thinking of you!

Her imagination was suddenly overloaded with horrible and vivid pictures of what might be happening to him and she pressed her icy hands to her eyes, rocking to and fro.

Downstairs the voices and laughter gradually faded as

277

the guests departed. Wilfred Filey's Rolls Royce with Woodcock at the wheel had carried the newly married couple to Whitby to catch a train to London where they would stay one night before going on to Wales. Little Dick, still wailing after the parting from his mother, was being put to bed by his new nannie and Archie, still in his wedding finery, was finishing off the hock cup by himself on the lawn.

Nell collapsed on to one of the deckchairs on the terrace: she looked white and drawn. After so many months' isolation, today had been a real effort on her part. Several times she had nearly turned tail to run to her room and barricade herself against the world. But she had stuck it out and even composedly answered questions about Dick's death in action. People who had not seen her since then had felt bound to mention it, coupling it quickly with references to Katy's new happy future. It had cost her a great deal in nervous effort and now she sat, drained of all thought and feeling, dully aware that her best shoes pinched.

Archie strolled across to her holding a bottle. He looked at her keenly and then smiled. 'Where's your glass, Mater? Drink this down. It's not that vile hock cup but the bubbly sent across by the squire for the toast.' He gave a wicked wink. 'Due to good management on my part there were two bottles hidden behind your chair in the morning-room! Drink up, Mater, you look as if you need it.'

She raised the glass to her trembling lips: he had called her Mater! That had been Dick's name for her. Dick, she thought with a sudden surge of grief, oh, Dick my dearest son, the doors are shutting on your memory one by one. Soon I'll be the only one who remembers you every day. Your child will grow up calling another man *Father*. Yes, the waters are closing over your head.

'Mater?'

She met her younger son's concerned eyes. Making a great effort, she pulled herself to her feet. 'Fill your Father's glass. Arthur, I want to drink a toast . . . to Dick.'

'To Dick,' they said and his name seemed to go echoing round the garden where the evening shadows were already lengthening and a pair of blackbirds hopped about the lawn picking up crumbs from the party.

Two days later Polly went up to London. She was glad to leave the rectory which was now very quiet even though Little Dick was still in residence. She was sorry for Archie who was struggling with his books for his exam in November. Although the rector had set his heart on sending him to Oxford, Archie had consulted Walter Wynne and had decided to try and get in at Magdalene, Cambridge, instead. It was a much smaller college, was sympathetic to wounded officers and he himself had fallen in love with the town when he went there for Polly's wedding. Only when he had completed all the arrangements did he break the news to his father. To his credit, Arthur Paget had hidden his disappointment well. It was, after all, an excellent sign that Archie was taking hold of his life again. Now the hurdle to be taken was college entrance and Archie was no longer wasting his time but working steadily every day.

'You needn't be sorry for me,' he told his twin firmly. 'I'm beginning to enjoy the work.'

Polly's interview had been arranged with Doctor Helen Gregory at the committee room of the unit in Victoria Street. *Please be punctual* had been written in an architectural script unlike any she had ever seen. She sent a telegram to Nora Gromont hoping she could put her up for a couple of nights and had one back saying, *Yes please bring honey*.

'Oh, Dad! Why did you promise Aunt Nora some of your honey? I shall have to carry it – you know there are very few porters!' Polly grumbled, cursing her father's generosity which always cost his family dear; not only several jars of honey but two books for Uncle Dolly were part of Polly's luggage this time.

The committee room of the Gregory Hospital Corps was a dark and dusty-smelling room on the third floor above a tobacconist's shop. Three women sat round a deal table covered with papers. One was tall and elegant with a discreetly painted face under a black velvet hat. The second woman was bare-headed and anxious-looking and proved to be the secretary whose daily life was spent in this room. The third woman was Doctor Helen Gregory herself: half-Scots and half-Norwegian with the face of Brünhilde and a rich warm laugh that filled the little room. She smoked non-stop during the interview and alarmed and then amused Polly with her questions and comments. She wore a squashed felt hat and when she was exasperated by the irrelevant questions of the elegant Lady Murray, she would pull out a hat-pin and drive it into a fresh place. 'Really, Alverna, what has religion to do with Mrs Wynne's suitability? I'm an agnostic myself.'

'I don't think we should give the post to a Roman Catholic, Helen – '

'But I'm Church of England,' Polly interposed.

'I don't give a damn if the girl's a Buddhist,' roared Dr Gregory, 'so long as she's as strong as a horse and can talk decent French! Good God, woman, forget John Knox and all his works.' In went the hat-pin again, and Polly wondered if this time she would stab herself, but her aim was faultless.

'Mrs Wynne is very small – quite slight, really. You did say, Helen, that you wanted a strong lass.'

'I may be small,' Polly said boldly. 'I'm only just over five foot tall but I'm strong. Indeed, I'm never ill.'

'Conditions are fairly primitive at Compiègne,' warned the secretary, Miss Lock.

Doctor Gregory jumped to her feet and her frail kitchen chair fell over. Leaning across the table, she addressed her fellow committee members in threatening tones. 'Why are you bent on putting the girl off? I'm not taking that putty-faced niece of yours, Alverna, so you needn't try to make me. You've wasted my afternoon by interviewing six girls who are useless – useless! Soft dainty hands and accompanied by clinging anxious mothers – that's all they've got to recommend them. No! I will have my say. It's *my* hospital, may I remind you? Oh, I know full well that you and the rest of the committee raise the money but I run the hospital and I know the sort of girl I want. The last lass you sent out to me was no damn good. This girl – ' her large index finger pointed at Polly ' – knows what the war's all about. She has a husband who's missing. She's not twenty-one yet but as a married woman she has every right to serve abroad. I'm taking her. She can add up, which is more than Miss Carter could.' With a nod of triumph she plucked her chair off the floor and sat down. Leaning across the table she began to describe the hospital unit that was housed in a former nunnery at Compiègne. It was staffed entirely by women from surgeons and doctors to clerks and cleaners. The French orderlies were the only men in the unit. 'You realize, don't you, that we are on the French front and serve under the Croix Rouge? We can pay you ten shillings a week and you get your keep. You'll have to sign on for six months to begin with. Are you prepared to take the job?'

'Yes,' Polly said quickly, avoiding the chagrined faces of the other two.

A broad grin on the doctor's face revealed two rows of splendid teeth and her toffee-brown eyes were kind. 'Good girl! Get yourself woollen combies and drawers for the winter – you'll need 'em. We'll send you your uniform in a week or two.'

She had got the job! It was difficult to hide her glee as she shook hands all round: Lady Murray was evidently not pleased. She hurried down the two flights of uncarpeted stairs to the street. Crossing the road, she walked towards the Army and Navy Stores that seemed to be thronged with late afternoon shoppers. She had decided that this was a golden opportunity to stock up with woollen garments for a winter in France. As she passed the windows, she saw her reflection; a slight girl with dark red hair escaping from under a brown knitted tam that matched her brown knitted jacket. Her cheeks were flushed with triumph and excitement. She stopped to stare at her mirrored self. *Small. Frail. Not strong.* They had called her all these things, those women in the committee room. Is that how I look to other people? she wondered. To her family she was strong, obstinate, even tough. That was how she thought of herself too.

David standing on the other side of the glass saw the familiar face, serious now, staring at the goods in the window. His heart gave a great bound: Polly! and in London! What luck – indeed it must be fate that their paths were crossing again. Was she coming in? She was looking undecided. He dodged people and hurried to the door, reaching it just as Polly pushed it open, having made up her mind to enquire the price of heavy woollen underwear suitable for active service.

'David!' She looked stunned and she had, he noticed

with glee, used his name. 'How extraordinary to meet here!'

'Is it? It's full of the army and navy like its name! It sells everything one can possibly need in the trenches – '

'You're going?'

'Tomorrow. I thought the day would never come. I've just been buying a few things to take out with me.' He glanced at a counter where an assistant patiently awaited his choice between two pairs of wire-cutters. 'Are you in a hurry? Then can we have tea somewhere? I'm just going to buy these things and then I'll be with you.' He quickly paid for the wire-cutters and some other things, glancing back at her as if to make sure she was still there. Then he steered her through the main door. 'Stay here while I get a taxi,' he directed.

She watched him hailing one. What a good-looking man he is, she thought.

'The Ritz.' He helped her in, intensely aware of her proximity, of the sweet scent she wore that smelled of spring. Polly could have told him it was only the expensive lily-of-the-valley soap provided at Aunt Nora's: to him it seemed her very essence. He realized yet again that he was painfully in love with another man's wife.

The tea room at the Ritz was packed with people who had come in from a charity matinée at Drury Lane. So they went to sit on a gilt and brocade sofa in the hall outside until a table was free. The faint strains of the Destiny Waltz came through the door played by an orchestra hidden behind the palms at the further end of the room. David could see her relaxing in the warm scented atmosphere, her wide eyes following the smartly dressed women who strolled past accompanied by officers in every sort of uniform.

'I'm not really dressed up enough for this place,' she said. 'But if you don't mind, I don't.'

'Mind? Of course not! You look fresh and – ' he stopped, afraid of saying too much. She looked young and vulnerable, yet there was a wisdom in her eyes that belied her looks. She had suffered and it showed in the shadows on her face.

Soon they were seated at a little table near a large window consuming tiny pâté sandwiches and shortbread and then the waiter, with silver tongs, was placing a confection of almond paste and strawberry icing on her plate. She was enjoying herself and was not afraid to show it and this added to his pleasure in her company. Suddenly he longed to have the right to lavish the good things of life on her, and his eyes yearned over her when she wasn't looking. But he knew that the only service he could render was to let her talk about her husband. So he listened, giving his opinion when asked for it, and praying that their hour together wouldn't pass too swiftly.

Suddenly he realized that this might well be the last time he would see her. He was going to France tomorrow and God knew what fate awaited him. If he were badly wounded, became a gross sight, he would not want to meet her again. And he might well be killed during his first tour in the trenches. The lifespan of a young officer going out was now six weeks . . .

'Look,' he said, 'the English are a reserved lot but you called me David back there – '

'It fell out,' she confessed with a laugh. 'It's how I think of you.'

She thought of him! He swallowed, forgetting what he had been about to say. 'W-what I wanted to say was – well – couldn't we make it Polly and David, please? I know I've called you Polly almost from the beginning.'

'Of course. The other's so stodgy,' she agreed. 'Do you know where I've been? To the Gregory Unit committee room!'

He looked puzzled. 'Do I know it?'

'You sent me to that address, remember?'

'You got an interview?' He looked delighted. 'That's wonderful! They accepted you? But I needn't ask: I can see from your face that they did.'

'Not until October, though. Two of us will be going out together and two others coming home. I'm glad it's not until October because I might have heard about Mike by then.' The colour and light died out of her face, leaving it pinched and older. 'Did you know that it takes at least eight months to get news of prisoners in German hands? And one doesn't know if they're injured or how badly.'

'It's too long. Surely they could do better than that if they tried? But you seem hopeful about his prospects. Has anything happened?'

She shook her head. 'No, but I've got this strong feeling he *is* alive.'

He didn't tell her that the feeling she described was shared by many bereaved families. They had not seen the body so part of their mind refused to accept the reality of a soldier's death. They continued to be hopeful that the missing man was alive and would get in touch. She looked so confident suddenly as she poured out more tea that he was careful not to dispel her frail pipe-dream. Poor little Polly! he thought tenderly. How I wish I could do more to help. 'Where is the Gregory Hospital situated?' he asked to turn her mind away from the uncertainty of her husband's fate.

'At Compiègne north of Paris. It's an old nunnery and the wards are marquees in the courtyards and the surrounding parkland. A hundred and twenty beds,' she added impressively.

'Compiègne?' He was suddenly frowning apprehensively. 'But it's on the French front, pretty near the front

285

line. I remember reading it had been overrun by the Germans when they raced for Paris in 1914.'

'Yes, it's near the front line. The French, Doctor Gregory says – and we're working for the Croix Rouge Française, you know – like their hospitals just behind the lines. It's so much better for the wounded. They can get proper attention so much more quickly – '

'But not so good for the staff!' he interrupted. 'Especially not so good for a hospital run only by women. I think it's a stupid idea!' he added violently and cursed himself for getting the Gregory Unit address for her. Run by a pack of suffragists, by the sound of it. This girl could easily lose her life – be injured – raped. He went red with apprehension and anger, cursing himself for being a meddlesome idiot and putting her in touch with this mad woman, Gregory. She looked so small and frail, so young. 'Conditions out there are pretty terrible – ' he began but, laughing, she put a hand on his arm to restrain him.

'Don't try and put me off, *please*. My parents will be sure to do that when they hear about it!' She hesitated, then rushed on. 'You see, I must have something to do – a real job to occupy my mind, otherwise I shall spend my time worrying about Mike. And – and there's another thing. I've not put this into words before but I'm frightened sometimes that I shan't know Mike when he does come back. You see, we knew each other just five weeks and were married for one. I've got his picture but I can't remember his voice . . . or what he thought about things. It worries me terribly. Shall we be strangers?'

He tried to smile reassuringly. 'I'm sure you won't be. It will all come back.' But would it? he wondered. He had been in love – or thought he was – with Beth Evett. They still kept in touch, but already his feelings for her had evaporated. He loved this girl, Polly Wynne, who was another man's wife. And this love was different from the last. He had given Beth a lighthearted boy's love: they had been two children thrown together by the wishes of their mothers. What he felt for Polly was altogether different. He wanted her so powerfully that had she been the sort of girl who would consent to sleep with him, he would have gone out into the hall and engaged a room. The thought of parting from her – perhaps for ever – was making him feel sick.

'I shall have to go,' she said, gathering up her gloves and purse. 'My uncle is taking us to the theatre tonight.'

And he heard his own matter-of-fact voice saying that they would get a taxi at the Arlington Street door.

'Oh, no. I'm going by underground.'

'Certainly not. We're going to get you a taxi. I ought to be taking you back to your uncle's myself but I've got to finish my shopping as I go early tomorrow, and then I'm meeting my mother for dinner.'

She walked rather unwillingly to the door: a taxi cab would cost at least a shilling – perhaps even more – while the underground was only twopence. She waited while he spoke to the doorman, watching him covertly. She hadn't liked any man so much before – except Mike, of course. David was charming and understanding, a man to lean on, she thought wistfully, and pulled herself up sharply. Stupid to think like that.

He had turned back to her. 'Here's your taxi.' He put her in it and she was surprised by the intense look in his eyes. Suddenly, he slipped off her glove and kissed the palm of her hand. 'Bless you always,' he said huskily, longing to take her in his arms.

The last she saw of him was his tall bare-headed figure standing with one hand raised in farewell.

Round the first corner, Polly tapped on the glass partition.

'Put me down here, please.'

287

The man drew to the kerb, turning his astonished face to her. 'This ain't Leander Gardens, miss!'

'I know that. I-I've changed my mind. I want to get out here.' She could see the underground station a few yards away.

'The officer give me five bob to see you 'ome safe and sound,' the cabby said obstinately. 'An' see you 'ome I will – so just you sit tight, miss, and leave it to me.'

Why, how kind David was! she thought gratefully. He must have guessed she hadn't much money to spare and had taken the whole thing out of her hands. She liked him even more for being so quietly thoughtful. I do hope he comes through, she thought, leaning back in her seat. The thought was fervent, almost a prayer.

As the troop train drew out of Victoria Station, Elaine lowered her hand that held a fluttering handkerchief and applied it to her eyes. For a few moments she felt despair: the moment she had dreaded had arrived. David had gone.

The crowds who had been seeing off husbands and lovers to the front were pushing past her, many of the women in tears. She turned and allowed herself to be borne along with them towards the cab rank. Already there was a crowd pouncing on each cab as it drove up. David had begged her not to come to the station; he had warned her she would find it difficult to get away again but she had insisted she would be all right.

Bewilderedly, she looked for a way out. She would walk part of the way and pick up a taxi as she went along – 'Oh!' she gasped as a heavy foot kicked her from behind. Blindly, she put a hand out, biting her lip in pain, and found herself being supported by an officer with red tabs on his collar.

'Are you hurt?' he asked solicitously.

'Thank you, I shall be all right,' she gasped.

He was looking round. 'There's a seat. Let me help you to it.'

She sat down, laughing helplessly but on the verge of tears. 'It's so silly of me. I changed direction and someone walked into me. It was my own fault.'

The general stood in front of her looking uncertain. 'Are you alone? Then I cannot leave you like this.'

'Oh, please! I shall be all right in a few minutes. I was going to walk a little way and pick up a cab.'

'I don't think that would be a good idea. If you wait here, I'll see if my car is near at hand.' He saluted and strode away. While he was gone, Elaine tested her foot and found it painful when placed on the ground. In a few minutes, the general had returned accompanied by a bandy-legged soldier who appeared to be his driver.

'I hope you will allow me to take you to your destination? I am due back at the War Office at midday but I wanted to see my boy off – his second time out, you know. My name is Brewer – General Edward Brewer.'

'It is so kind of you. I'm very grateful. I am Mrs Ransom and I've been seeing off my eldest son. It's his first time. He didn't want me to come as he feared I would have difficulty in getting away again and I'm afraid I have never used the underground and would be in an even worse predicament.' With help from the general and his driver, she reached the staff car. 'I'm staying at Brown's Hotel in Dover Street.'

Beside her, General Brewer leaned back in his seat. He had a dark, rather bitter face, she saw as she glanced at him, with iron-grey hair and moustache. 'What regiment is your son in?' she asked for something to say.

'The Highland Light Infantry. He was at the Scottish Bar before the war.'

The car was turning into Whitehall and then across Trafalgar Square.

'I feel I'm taking you very much out of your way,' she said apologetically.

'I'm glad to be of service.' His melancholy face lit up with a sudden smile that changed his whole aspect. 'I don't often get feminine company! I share a flat with my son while I'm at the War House but my home is in Scotland.'

'You must miss your son very much while he's in France. I know I shall miss David – ' She bit her lip and turned her head away. 'One must just pray that the war is soon over and that they come through safely. Oh, are we here? How can I thank you? You rescued me! It's just gone eleven – do come in for a cup of coffee.'

He hesitated and then said, 'Thank you but I must get on. A lot of things to be seen to before a meeting, you know.'

'Then thank you again. I hope my foot isn't going to play up. I'm only here until Friday when I'm due back in the North Riding.'

'A lovely part of the world. I shot there often before the war.' He helped her down. 'Are you sure you'll be all right? Shall I get someone?'

'Stupidly I came without my maid. But the staff here know me well so I'm in good hands.'

They shook hands solemnly, his rather melancholy eyes fixed on her face. 'Goodbye,' he said quietly and saluted her.

Her foot was red and swollen, she found when she had peeled off her stocking. It really was provoking. She had planned to do a great deal of shopping in the remaining two days of her stay. The two chambermaids brought her cold compresses and helped her into bed where she remained for the rest of the day, taking dinner in her room. To her relief, by next morning the swelling had subsided and she was reasonably comfortable.

Wearing her new blue cloth jacket and matching cap with a feather, she went downstairs at eleven o'clock intending to visit 'her dressmaker. As she reached the foyer, the door opened and an officer with red tabs walked in. In his hand he awkwardly held a bouquet of pink carnations and maidenhair. It was General Brewer.

With a curious inner excitement that she hadn't experienced for years, she went forward to meet him.

'Mrs Ransom!' His face lit up. 'I certainly didn't expect to see you recovered this morning! Are you sure you should be using that foot?'

'I must. I have so much to do. I'm only thankful I can get a shoe on again. Are these for me? How lovely!'

They stared at each other over the flowers, their eyes eager and saying things that their tongues couldn't utter. Mutual attraction held them spellbound for seconds. Then he said clumsily, 'I'm free until three o'clock – I mean to say I'd be so grateful if you would allow me to take you out to luncheon. I thought the Savoy – or – or – would you prefer Claridges?'

She felt breathless with this new excitement that possessed her. 'Oh, yes, I'd like that! But my shopping?'

'You must allow me to accompany you,' and he held out his arm. 'I have a cab outside. Where to first?'

Polly had dreaded going to see Mike's people and she felt quite sick as she travelled in a cab up to the Red House in Madingley Road. It was the Long Vac and the town was emptier than in any Long Vac before: those who might have come back to work after doing badly in their exams had cut their losses and joined up instead. Only long gowns fluttered in Trinity Street as two ancient dons crossed the road to turn in at the Great Gate of Trinity.

She was more thankful than ever that she had taken the course she had. The academic life was gone for ever as far as she was concerned. If Mike – no, *when* Mike returned he would need looking after: of that she was certain. Remembering that she was returning to his home she felt herself shiver, dreading this meeting with people she had never really got to know in the short time she had been Mike's wife.

Paying off the cab, she rang the bell. The place seemed deserted and gloomier than ever without the little boys in residence. No one came to answer the door. Peering through the glass panel she felt her heart stop and then race on for there on the hatstand was Mike's cap, the shabby affair he had been wearing when they met, the cap he had worn for eighteen months of service . . . Then she remembered: of course; he had bought a new one to be married in. Feeling quite weak from reaction, she pressed the bell again and at last a very young girl in cap and apron came through the baize door from the kitchen and opened the front door.

'Mrs Wynne? I'm Mrs Michael Wynne, her daughter-in-law. You're new, aren't you?'

'Yes, 'm.' The girl looked at her without interest, breathing heavily with her mouth open. 'The missus – Mrs Wynne ain't in,' she said in her flat Fen voice.

'But she was expecting me. Perhaps Mr Wynne is here?'

'No, he ain't.'

Polly hid her exasperation: the girl was probably the only labour available and was obviously weak in the head but it was strange that no one was here to welcome her. 'Then I'd better go up to my room and wait for them.' As she moved towards the stairs she felt the housemaid's eyes fixed on her back.

'Missus never said to expect anyone,' the girl said sullenly.

'She must have forgotten. Please tell her I'm upstairs when she returns.' She walked along the creaking landing to Mike's old room and shut the door: the bed was not made up, the striped horsehair mattress rolled up to one side. Polly sat down on the bare bedstead and looked about her at the unprepared room, her heart sinking. This could hardly be termed a friendly welcome, she thought bleakly. She got up and walked about the room, inspecting Mike's possessions: an assortment of books from childhood, a couple of cricket bats and a squash racquet in a corner. The pictures on the walls were of school groups; Mike seemed to have played every game possible, according to these. He had been a very good-looking boy at school, his fair hair crisp, his eyes untroubled by what lay ahead. She stared and stared at these pictured faces, all so different from the strained man she had met on the train. *Oh, darling Mike, you had suffered!* she thought with a renewal of pity. Now she was more thankful than ever that they had had nearly a week together and he had gone away comforted.

A tap on the door made her wheel, expecting Mrs Wynne, but it was Walter Wynne who entered and kissed her affectionately. 'My dear child, what must you think! I had no idea you were coming – Ruth said nothing to me. It's a very great pity she's away . . .'

The tight bands round her heart slackened and she realized she was very thankful she was going to be spared her mother-in-law's company. 'My letter must have gone astray, I'm afraid. Can I stay the night?'

'Of course.' He hesitated and then blurted, 'No, your letter did come and she read it out to me but said nothing about you coming down here.' He looked unhappily at his daughter-in-law. 'Ruth's not herself. This last blow – oh, she shows no emotion but she's very strange. She's hardly ever here, fills her life with war work – she's gone up to London today to some meeting or other. She never mentions him or – or his chances of survival: she's just locked herself away.'

'My arrival here would have forced her to talk about it,' Polly said thoughtfully. 'I think she was bound to pretend I wasn't really coming.' But all the time she was thinking: is that how mothers take these griefs? Yet although her own mother had done very much the same thing, she had also retreated from life and this very evidently Mrs Wynne had not done or she would not now be in London sitting on a committee. She never really accepted me, Polly thought, that's the plain truth.

Lunch was meagre and consisted of some tired corned beef, a tough lettuce from the garden and half a tomato each. This was followed by prunes and a very watery custard. No wonder Walter Wynne looked so thin and the colour of old parchment! Even the war was no excuse for such a repast. By common consent they quitted the bleak dining-room and went to sit on the verandah where, after asking her permission, he lit up his pipe and they sat in comfortable silence for a few minutes.

Polly broke it by asking him boldly: 'Do you believe Mike has survived and is a prisoner?'

He shook his head. 'No, my dear, I don't. He might have survived for a short time but anyone wounded just before the commencement of this last awful battle would have had little chance of survival, you know.'

She nodded, a lump in her throat, remembering Mike's fear of 'the darkness'.

'We shan't know, I daresay, until the end of the war what really happened. If then. Thousands have disappeared in just the same way. I think it leaves you in a very difficult position: married and not officially a widow. You're very young and you'll have to be very patient but that's the position.'

'I have no thought of marrying again,' she said quickly. 'Not until I'm sure that Mike's not coming back and not then unless I meet someone I can care for.' Unbidden, the thought of David came into her mind and she felt ashamed. How could she be thinking of another man so soon? Her head dropped.

Because you have always thought of him from the day you met him, a tiny voice reminded her.

But she had married Mike. Mike was her husband now and until the day they told her he was dead.

Looking up again, she met Walter's eyes. 'I've got a war job,' and she began to tell him about the Gregory Unit.

After tea she telephoned for a taxi, despite his protests. 'I know I came for the night but I think it would be better if I returned to London instead.'

Reluctantly but with the innate honesty that she had come to expect of him, he agreed. Taking her by the arms he looked at her searchingly. 'Promise me one thing, my dear: always remember that your life matters. Don't sacrifice yourself because of what has happened. If Mike returns – and I doubt it very much – then you can be his wife again. But never forget that the chances are you are his widow already. I've faced it and soon I shall pick up the threads of life again. Both my boys are gone but there is still work to do. And you're little more than a child yourself, remember, with all your life before you. Make a life for *yourself*.'

It was a generous gift he gave her, urging her to go free and forget his son. *Both my boys are gone*. As she travelled back to London she was aware at last of a loosening of the tight bonds that had been making a prisoner of her. She was Polly Paget again and not Mike Wynne's wife. She *would* try and make something of life without Mike.

* * *

'Are you sure you don't have some work waiting for you?' Elaine asked as she and General Brewer emerged from Claridges after an excellent luncheon despite it being a 'meatless day' as decreed by the Food Controller. She glanced up at the man standing beside her. He was really very good-looking, she thought approvingly. Their friendship had advanced by leaps and bounds over the meal: she had told him about her family, about the torpedoing of the SS *Oceana* and Reggie's resultant stroke and he had told her about the death of his wife ten years previously while he was stationed in India.

'My son and I are closer to each other now than we would otherwise be,' he explained. 'He's a good fellow, George. One can only hope he gets through this business safely.'

'Your only child?'

'Yes. He's twenty-six now and he's been in from the beginning with a spell on the Staff after a bad wound eighteen months ago. But he's back in the line now,' he added and the melancholy look returned to his face.

What a lonely man he must be, she thought, as she began to tell him about David who was almost George's age and had gone out for the first time yesterday. She found herself going on to tell him about her unhappy first marriage and how she had lost her little boy after the divorce. Then she had stopped abruptly, biting her lip. She hadn't spoken about this bitter episode to anyone for years yet here she was pouring it out to Edward Brewer whom she had only met yesterday for the first time.

He had put his hand on hers. 'My dear, you must have been only a child yourself when it happened and I dread to think what you must have suffered.'

His gentle words had touched a spring inside her and tears had rushed to her eyes. So he had turned the conversation very tactfully. But this small episode had advanced their acquaintanceship to friendship in one short bound.

Now as they stood watching the commissionaire summoning a cab for them he said suddenly: 'I could get tickets for the theatre tonight. Would you come?'

She felt her breath quicken: so he felt as she did and didn't want this new friendship to end yet! Meeting his eyes, she nodded. 'I think that would be lovely.'

He was smiling now. 'Then I'll call for you at seven-thirty and we'll go on to the Hungaria for supper.'

And at seven-thirty she found his tall figure waiting for her as she came downstairs wearing a dinner dress of sea-green chiffon through which her shoulders and arms gleamed. Over one arm she carried her white ermine cape and a silver band bound her hair. Her mirror had told her that she was looking her best and his eyes confirmed this impression.

Holding out her hands she went to greet him.

'My dear, how lovely you look!' he said in a low voice. 'I shall be a proud man tonight.'

She laughed but she knew that her cheeks glowed and her eyes were sparkling with excitement. She felt young and full of energy, a girl again and not a staid woman with a household to be organized.

'You look like a girl!'

'Edward! That's going too far!'

They both noticed she had called him by his first name. Releasing her hands, he said: 'Please tell me what your name is.'

'Elaine.'

'Elaine.' He repeated it, looking deeply at her. 'It suits you. Come, I have a cab waiting. I've got tickets for *Chu-Chin-Chow* but of course if you've already seen it – '

'I've seen very few plays, I'm afraid. This will be a great treat.'

Afterwards she remembered very little of the show except one catchy tune that ever afterwards recalled the feel of his shoulder touching hers and the expression in his eyes as he turned to look down at her. It was while sitting staring at the lighted stage that she realized how deeply attracted she had become to this man beside her. But there's Reggie, she thought. Reggie. The children. I'm not free to allow this thing to happen . . .

They had gone on to the Hungaria and danced to a very good band. He had held her lightly as they spun round and round and as they returned to their table he had said laughingly: 'I haven't danced since India! But at least I didn't step on your toes!'

'You dance very well.'

'That's because you're such a wonderful partner.'

Too soon it was one-thirty and they stepped into a cab, their day together at an end.

'Where to, sir?' the cabby called.

Brewer hesitated, glancing down at his companion. 'It's late, I know, but will you come back to the flat for a drink? You're going north again in a few hours – please come, Elaine.' As she hesitated, he added: 'We're not children!'

She had the feeling that she was burning her boats as she said: 'Yes, I'd like to.'

It was his son's flat; George Brewer had taken it when he was on the Staff for six months. When he went out to France again his father had left a rather unsatisfactory hotel and moved in. 'I have my batman and a woman who comes in to clean,' he explained as he poured her a soft drink. It was not very well furnished she noticed as she looked round, but the leather chairs were comfortable and there were books and magazines scattered about. But what an unhomely place for a man of his age, she thought, feeling pity as he walked to and fro trying to make her comfortable.

Suddenly, he dropped to his knees before her, taking her hands and holding them tightly. 'Elaine, you must know how I feel?'

She nodded. 'Yes,' she said hoarsely. 'But should we? We're not young people – '

'Thank God, no! The young and callow couldn't feel as I do!' He drew her into his arms and kissed her with frightening intensity. 'I've waited for years to meet someone like you and now that I have, I won't let you go! Don't you realize how lucky we are?' He held her from him and she saw that his eyes were alight with feeling. 'I know you're married and have responsibilities. I know about your husband but need this hurt him? Would he ever know – *need* he ever know? Elaine, I need you. Don't go out of my life, darling.'

For answer, she put her hands up to his face and drew him down to her. 'I feel the same,' she whispered. 'All day I've fought it but it's no good. I've fallen in love with you, too. Absurd, isn't it?'

'No,' he said stoutly, 'not absurd at all. Oh, darling, you've made me so happy – I haven't felt like this for years! I didn't bring you back here to ravish you, you know, but I had to tell you before you went home tomorrow.'

'I'm so glad you did.' She looked round the bleak room. 'You're right. We can't become lovers *here*. I'll come back soon and we'll go away together – somewhere nice and comfortable for three whole days!' She got up and he put her cape round her shoulders, holding her tightly for a moment or two.

'It's very late and I must see you back to your hotel,' he said at last. 'When you've gone I shall believe I've dreamed this, you know.'

'Next time the dream will become a reality,' she promised as he reluctantly released her.

CHAPTER SIXTEEN

Destination France

Standing under the clock at Waterloo at nine o'clock on a cold wet morning in November, Polly began to have misgivings. What was she doing here in this outlandish uniform that made her look absurd? The grey tunic and skirt of the Gregory Hospital were a sore point. Obviously the well-built Doctor Gregory had ordered the uniforms in one size only: her own. Despite Miss Bonner's efforts, it was still too big everywhere. But the sorest point of all was the horrible cap: a tea-cosy on a hatband, Archie called it. When she had tried it on, it had descended over her eyes and proved too much for Archie, who had bellowed with laughter.

'She's done it on purpose, the clever old thing,' he said, wiping his eyes. 'She's determined the French *poilus* shan't look at her girls twice – you know what the French are, my dear!' he added in a high falsetto voice that was meant to be Doctor Gregory's.

'You're miles out, you ass! Doctor Gregory has a deep voice – '

'You're sure she's not a man in disguise? A White Slaver whose hospital is really a bordello?'

'Ssh! Don't let Mother hear you! I'm in enough trouble with her without suggestions of that sort.'

Nell had been thrown into a panic when the uniform, money for the ticket and a letter from Doctor Gregory had arrived a week ago. 'The weather's appalling. Do wait for spring, darling,' she had urged tearfully.

But Polly had stood firm. 'I can't possibly let them down. Don't worry, Mother. The war will be over soon.'

But to Archie she had said: 'Will the war ever end? Do you think we shall go on and on until the youth of every nation is dead?' Depression came only too frequently nowadays. 'Promise me you will telegraph the instant there is any news of Mike?' she begged her twin: after the talk with her father-in-law she was no longer very hopeful.

Her feet were wet and cold, she realized, glancing up at the clock once more. Nine-fifteen. She had been told to wait for her travelling companion until that time. Obviously, the girl was not coming. She had probably changed her mind. Well, she had better make her way to the train. But as she stooped to collect her kitbag, she saw two people coming towards her: a girl dressed as hideously as herself and an older woman.

'Are *you* Mrs Wynne? But I expected someone much older to take care of my girl!' The woman, tall, elegant and dressed in furs looked very annoyed. By her side, the daughter, equally tall and fair, said nothing. She wore a meek look, her eyes quite blank. 'Really, Helen Gregory is a wily-tongued serpent!' stormed the mother to the silent girl. 'She knew I would never allow you to travel alone – two young girls on their own! Anything might happen.'

'I think our train is almost ready to start,' Polly said. 'My porter has my haversack. Would you like to put yours on the barrow, too?' she suggested to the girl, preparing to move off.

'Kathryn, I order you to come home at once! The whole thing is preposterous – no, leave that haversack, my man. Kathryn!'

The girl only smiled and kissed her mother dutifully. 'Goodbye, Mother dear, I'll write. Look after my darling Rascal, won't you?' She climbed into the compartment with Polly. The door was slammed and the whistle blew. The train moved away, leaving the agitated mother talking to herself. Sinking on to her seat, the girl tore off the ugly cap and ran her fingers through cropped hair. 'Thank God! Another minute and my mother would have created a scene!' She grinned at her companion and pulling out a battered pack of cigarettes offered it. 'You don't? Mind if I do? For a whole week it's been touch and go at home. Mother called in the family and uncles and aunts have all preached to me of my duty as an only daughter. They cling, don't they, the older generation?' She puffed inexpertly. 'What a glorious feeling! I'm free at last and I'm going to savour every minute of it, I warn you.'

Polly began to laugh. 'How wrong first impressions are! I thought you were a frightened mouse when you first appeared.'

'Oh, no! I was just a bottle of soda water with the top screwed on very tight. Why don't you cut your hair – what a glorious colour it is, too! I can't tell you what a strange experience it is to have a light head.'

'That's obvious. Yes, I'm thinking about it. Long hair even when pinned up in the neck is a nuisance and under this tea-cosy of a cap it's quite intolerable.'

'You'd look priceless with it short! I say, I've got a scissors in my bag – '

But Polly laughingly shook her head. 'Thank you! I prefer to wait for Paris. I'll find a shop there if there's time.'

There were a good many of the women's services on board the boat at Southampton where they embarked at midday. Life jackets were issued to everyone and they set out on a murky and wet afternoon that was depressing in the extreme. Unable to stand the stifling atmosphere of the saloons, Polly and Kathryn Graham sat on their packs on the upper deck sharing a rug. Tired by her long overnight journey from the north, Polly dozed and woke up with seasalt on her lips, feeling fresh and very hungry.

Of Kathryn there was now no sign but the sound of her high-pitched laugh could be heard occasionally so she had obviously found a kindred spirit.

They disembarked at Le Havre at ten-thirty that night. A severe-looking Landing Sister was meeting a party of VADs and Polly felt relief that she was not in one of the services. Doctor Gregory obviously treated her staff as adults who must look after themselves. She and Kathryn shouldered their packs and pushed their way into a waiting room that came straight out of the Belle Epoque: red velvet padded banquettes, gold and crystal mirrors and lights. The smell of French coffee and garlic-flavoured pâté met their nostrils and Polly's spirits rose. She was really in France! She had done the right thing to get away from England and felt a new person already.

Kathryn had no doubts on the matter. As they ate, she related how she had been spending her time at home. 'Mother had me by her side every hour of the day; if I wasn't there she had to know exactly where I was. When I walked Rascal, my Pom, in the park her maid Amy accompanied me. I'm twenty-two years old and she treats me like a baby. But, believe me, I'm now going to have the time of my life! This child is going to paint the town red before she's finished!'

Polly finished her pâté. 'That was simply gorgeous. Why don't things taste like that in England? I shall be interested to see how you set out to paint Compiègne even a shade of pink – it's a very proper place, you know! Girls who gain their freedom from a strict home always act like idiots at first, so beware. We had a girl like that at Girton – ' She stopped, biting her lip: wasn't that how she had behaved in the end? She writhed inwardly as she remembered some of the things Miss Conway had said to her . . .

'You're not going to be a dull old thing just because

you're married?' Kathryn stretched her eyes saucily at her.

'I hope not! But we are in a country where women are still very much protected. Perhaps we shouldn't shock them too much.'

But Kathryn only laughed.

They queued up for permits to Paris only to be told by harassed officials that there was no knowing when there would be a train to take them there. They had better go and rest in the ladies' waiting room until they were called.

The waiting room was already very full but they managed to squeeze in and sit on their haversacks with their rugs over their knees. A large fire had been built in the grate and was being recklessly stoked up with coke by a girl in a FANY uniform who was attempting to dry her soaked possessions: outside, the rain had been pouring down for an hour or more. By the time dawn broke most people had headaches from the coke fumes and were generally feeling the worse for wear. Polly and Kathryn stumbled sleepily to the buffet to queue for coffee and hot croissants. Service men and women in every sort of uniform were milling round them and out on the platform they had to step over prone bodies patiently awaiting their trains by sleeping or playing cards. On the heights above Le Havre they could see the tents of a British hospital where those soldiers too badly wounded to be shipped across the Channel were being nursed.

'Do you think our hospital will be in tents?' Kathryn asked.

'Isn't it housed in a former nunnery? I'm sure Doctor Gregory said so. We shall at least be sheltered – just look how those tents are billowing! They look about to fall into the sea – ugh!'

At last, when they had almost given up hope of ever moving out of Le Havre they were called to a train scheduled to leave at two P.M. Twenty minutes after that time the train, crammed to the roof, set off. They travelled in fits and starts, stopping at every small station, being shunted on to sidings to allow urgent troop trains or wagons loaded with mysterious goods under tarpaulins to rush past. It was dark when they reached Paris and there was a long queue for taxis but at last they reached the small pension in Place Ste Sulpice where rooms had been booked for them by the Gregory Committee.

It was here that the first real difficulty of the journey arose: Kathryn had no intention of going to bed. She was going to see Paris and Polly must accompany her.

'Don't worry, I know it well,' she said airily. 'I was at school here in 1911.'

'That was different. You went about chaperoned by an older person and I don't suppose you went out much at night!'

'Of course not; I was only seventeen. I'm an adult now and it's completely different. Oh, don't be such a slow old thing! Our uniforms will protect us.'

They argued amiably at first and then with acrimony as neither would give way. Polly's one desire was for sleep after a journey of forty-eight hours from the North Riding. Kathryn, with sparkling eyes and cheeks flushed with excitement, looked as if she never intended sleeping again. 'I'm older than you,' she said at last, 'and perfectly capable of looking after myself so I shall go on my own. Toodle-oo, you slow old thing!'

Too fagged to argue further, Polly, who was longing for a bath but discovered there wasn't one in the hotel, sent for a can of hot water, washed herself down and fell into bed. Even the coarseness of the sheets didn't prevent her becoming immediately unconscious. She woke to the loud peals of church bells outside her window. Drawing aside the blind, she found herself looking down into a cobbled square, one side of which was filled by a huge church and the other sides by the hotel and shops where people were already queuing for their *batons* of bread, and other shops where books and religious relics were on sale. Breakfast arrived: two croissants, no butter, and black coffee, so she adopted the French habit of dipping the hard bread into the hot coffee. The Gregory Committee had certainly not wasted money on their choice of hotel, she thought wryly. She wondered if her travelling companion was awake yet and went and tapped on her door opposite.

Kathryn was sitting up in bed toying with her breakfast. She looked woebegone.

'What's the matter? Don't you feel well?'

For answer, Kathryn hurled herself back on the pillows and began to cry noisily. 'I've had all my money stolen! Every penny!'

'Kathryn! How on earth did that happen?'

'Well, I went into a bar – not like an English pub, you know – a nice place where I could get a meal and drink wine. There were young French people at the next table and we began to talk. I agreed to go on with them to another place they knew – well, you wouldn't come with me so what could I do? It was very dark in the streets . . .' A fresh burst of tears interrupted her story. 'The beasts! They robbed me! Took everything, even my watch, and I heard them laughing as they ran away! What am I going to do?'

'Get to Compiègne as fast as you can and wait for your first week's pay. Oh, do dry your eyes! You've been a perfect idiot and you're lucky to escape so lightly. Look: we can't get out of Paris without a movement order. The chambermaid has just told me. Why on earth didn't the Committee tell us this? We have to go to the permit bureau in the rue Chauveau-Lagarde. So get up quickly and come on. We've no time to lose.'

It was a subdued Kathryn who accompanied Polly to the British Permit Office which was crowded with distracted officials and filing cabinets. It had only just been inaugurated and had been designed to exercise surveillance over British citizens in the French service.

They had no luck at all in persuading a fast-talking, gesticulating Frenchman to allow them to travel by train the forty kilometres or so to Compiègne: they had not got the right papers and without these papers they were virtually prisoners in Paris.

They looked at each other in dismay. With only the small amount of money possessed by Polly they would have to spend another night in the hotel and they would be cutting it fine if they ate at all.

'What shall we do?' quavered Kathryn, who had lost all her bravado. 'Oh, I do wish I hadn't come!' Tears rose to her eyes and she sniffed loudly.

'Oh, do buck up!' Polly said crossly. 'I shall telephone the Gregory Hospital. They must help us.'

'But do you know how to get their number?'

'No, but I shall find out.' And with the help of a motherly Frenchwoman who spoke a little English she did succeed in contacting the Gregory Hospital at Compiègne.

'Oh, poor you!' said a cheerful voice. 'We'll get one of our ambulance girls to fetch you. Give me your address. They'll be with you this afternoon.'

A frugal lunch at a workmen's café had to suffice for Polly was scared of being left without any francs at all. What if the ambulance didn't turn up as promised? She and Kathryn sat in the dark little hall of their hotel, uncomfortably aware that the proprietor's wife was watching them with suspicion and curiosity from behind a glass door.

But about three o'clock a covered motor ambulance

307

drew up outside and a young woman wearing a leather coat, whipcord breeches and the same brassard as themselves ran up the steps and into the hall.

'You poor things! I'm afraid you've had a long wait but I drove like Jehu to get here. Lucky for you things are slack at the moment. These your things? Then dump them in the back – hey, what's up with you?' she asked, for Kathryn had dissolved into tears again. 'Not homesick already, are you?'

'I wish I'd never come!'

'She hasn't slept properly for two nights,' Polly explained hurriedly.

The ambulance driver raised her brows. 'I'd better warn you both: when things get really active on our front, no one sleeps for a week! Come on, hop up, Niobe, and do stop moping.'

It was an icy journey with sleet and rain dashing against the windscreen and a keen wind pouring through the canvas flaps. All three sat in front and the driver, Ursula Gower, drove fast and with expertise. Soon they were crossing a temporary bridge over the Aisne ('Blown up by our side in 1914 to stop the Boche,' Ursula explained) and entering what was still a charming little town. To the east of it lay its glorious royal forest, the leaves turning red and yellow, and it was in this direction Ursula drove the ambulance. A pile of grey buildings backed by trees suddenly loomed out of the mist and sleet. 'This is the hospital,' Ursula said.

They jumped down stiffly and found themselves ankle-deep in clinging mud.

'Go through into the cloisters and you'll find a door on the right. I must go.' And with a wave, Ursula Gower drove off, leaving them with their possessions in a muddy yard. Bending against the driving sleet they trudged across the yard and through an archway. It was dark now but a guttering lamp hanging in the cloister showed them the heavy oak door that had once barred the nuns from the outside world. There were no nuns now for they had fled before the German advance in 1914 that had swept through the attractive little town. The *abbaye* had been empty until taken over by the Gregory Hospital Unit. This had, since its inception, been under the auspices of the French Croix Rouge because the British had refused their services. It was only now in late 1916 that the RAMC was at last cautiously recognizing Doctor Flora Murray's hospital in London. However, Doctor Gregory had decided to remain loyal to the French who had placed all their confidence in her. Her unit's excellence was extolled throughout the zone of the Grande Armée du Nord. It lay, like all French hospitals, only a few miles behind the front line. The keen-eyed man who commanded GAN, General Franchet d'Espery (whom the British had nicknamed Frankly Desperate), had paid a visit to this hospital run by *les doctoresses anglaises*. If he was amazed to find that the chief surgeons were pretty young women, he had concealed it while paying them many gallant compliments – quite unlike his brusque treatment of the GAN staff! Now a large signed photograph of the general adorned the hall: the women had been accepted.

Polly found herself looking straight at this likeness as she and Kathryn, pushing open the heavy door, came thankfully into the hall out of the cold.

An old man in a rough blue cotton smock and corduroy trousers got up stiffly from a hooded porter's chair and hobbled towards them. '*Mesdemoiselles?*' He had a pink, kindly face and grey whiskers. From his leather belt hung a bunch of keys.

Polly explained that they were the two new clerks just arrived from Paris. He knew all about them and had begun to fear for them now that darkness had set in. They were soon to learn that Augustin always feared for his young ladies whenever one of them left the hospital precincts for young ladies should not be allowed out, in his opinion, without a male escort. He led them upstairs to a deal door. Obviously there had been many improvisations in the *abbaye* to give them more room and they entered a tiny office cluttered with papers that (with two others) had been carved out of a much larger room.

A girl rose and came towards them. She had dark sparkling eyes, wavy black hair, freckles and a wide, smiling mouth.

'Hullo! I'm Delia Vane. One of you will be joining me here in this cubbyhole and the other will go to Stores. Which of you is Polly Wynne? Then this will be your chair. Kathryn Graham will go to Stores. First of all, I must take you to see the Commandant and then I'll show you your bedrooms. The best of this place is that there are dozens of nuns' cells so we each have our own bedroom. I did so dread facing dormitory life again!' As she talked quickly on with barely a pause, she led them upstairs, along a corridor and round a corner. Coming to an oak door, she tapped and then opened it.

Doctor Gregory was sitting in front of a stove drinking cocoa. She had opened the door of the stove to let out more heat and had folded her skirt back over her knees, exposing grey bloomers and a pair of stout legs. She remained with her skirt back as she greeted them. 'So you are here at last! It's been a long, slow journey for you. Those *bureaucrates* in Paris! Every month a new *bureau* opens to make life more difficult for us. How is your mother, Kathryn? I was very much afraid she would change her mind and not let you go at the last. Splendid! Now go and get supper in the refectory: I have told the cooks to keep back something hot. We'll excuse you all

310

duties tonight but you will be roused at six-thirty tomorrow so please go straight to bed after you have eaten. And remember not to show any lights: we are very near the front and aeroplanes are often over us.'

Polly remembered those words as she stood at the window of her tiny cell later that night. She had put out her candle and drawn aside the thick curtains. As her eyes grew accustomed to the dark she could just discern the outline of the forest silhouetted against the lighter sky. The wind had dropped. Nothing moved. Suddenly her heart leapt as bright lights exploded on the horizon and ran in a long winking line from north to south. Seconds later, a sound like thunder made the room shudder. *The guns*. All those miles away and they sounded like that. *I'm in France. The war is over there*.

She jumped into her hard, cold bed and lay shivering. The blankets were rough and thin, the sheets coarse and the mattress seemed made of damp straw. She knew she could never get to sleep in such discomfort. Jumping out of bed, she fumbled for a jersey and woollen stockings and for her travelling rug to wrap her icy body in, and a large linen handkerchief to lay beneath her cheek. Tomorrow she would find a hot water bag, another blanket . . . perhaps a softer pillow case.

She lay awake for an hour, uneasy in the blackness of the small cell and listening to the moan of the wind under her door. Her thoughts chased round in her brain. The Somme was somewhere to the north . . . was Mike there or was he dead? If only she could remember more about him! Instead, the image of David Ransom seemed much clearer. She could hear his distinctive voice, see the different expressions his face wore. *Mike*, she thought apologetically, *come back into my mind. Don't disappear out of my head*.

Presently she slept.

* * *

There was little time to brood in the days ahead. From the time she stumbled half-asleep to breakfast to the time she fell into bed at night, there was no room in Polly's mind for anything but the life of the hospital. In the office she struggled with the nominal roll demanded by French Army Headquarters. The names of all wounded and dead soldiers who had passed through the hospital had to be kept up to date and despatched three times a week. It involved trudging the wards to get information, a task she dreaded because the sight and sound of badly wounded men horrified her, haunting her dreams at night. She and Delia had to send out orders for food and find a van or ambulance to collect it. Then supplies of medical equipment would arrive at the railway station and transport would be needed urgently to collect it. Everyone's pay had to be ready by Saturday morning each week. In between these duties she and Delia visited the wards to deliver letters and to write letters to the families of those men too badly wounded to write themselves. Polly's dread of the sights and sounds of the wards never slackened and each time she paused at a marquee entrance she had to take a deep breath before she could summon the cheerful smile required for the task.

The marquees were set in rows on the fields between the *abbaye* and the town. Huge red crosses were painted on them but this hadn't saved them from bombs dropped by raiding German aeroplanes.

Sometimes Polly would pause to stare with a shiver at the dripping trees on the outskirts of the dense forest that she had been told stretched right back to the German lines. The forest in this cold autumn was covered in a dark blue light. Sometimes little misty clouds hung over it. She visualized the dreaded figures in *feldgrau* issuing from it and would shiver again. Those trees could conceal so much. Was it out of this forest that the Germans would break through in the next push?

The fields housing the marquees were a quagmire and duckboards connected one marquee with another. If one stepped off a duckboard in the pitch dark one was soon up to the ankles in heavy squelching mud. Polly and many others sent home urgently for rubber boots after one or two accidents like this, but in spite of the boots most people suffered from permanently cold, numb feet. Inside the marquees, wooden floors covered with linoleum gave a sense of permanency but when gales blew the canvas sides of the tents billowed, setting the hurricane lamps swinging violently from the ceilings. With a rather wry smile Polly remembered the hospital tents above Le Havre: she had thought the Gregory Unit would be a much more solid place. How wrong she had been! Trying to keep the patients warm was a full-time task and anyone with a minute to spare spent it filling earthenware bottles with hot water from a big tank. They had to be laid in baskets between blankets and carried back to the wards before they cooled off again.

One day, hurrying back with a fresh load of bottles, Polly bumped into Kathryn Graham. She was shocked by the change in the girl. Her pallor was startling, her eyes blue-ringed and hollow.

'I'm thinking of chucking it,' she said. 'I had no idea it would be as awful as *this*! The food's quite revolting – I can't touch it. Why, I wouldn't give it to my dog Rascal! I hardly close my eyes at night because of the guns. I'm thinking of writing to Mother to ask her to send for me. It's no use looking like that, Wynne. I'm not strong enough for this life.'

'Think how bored you were at home! You said you were almost a prisoner. Do you really want to go back to it? Of course, it's nothing to do with me but if I were you, I'd stick it. One is at least doing something out here.'

'Doing something?' Kathryn echoed. 'We never stop *doing something*! I'm exhausted.'

'I must go or these hot bottles will be cooling off. Don't be an idiot, Graham! You're as tough as the rest of us really.'

Kathryn's pale face flushed. 'I don't expect you to understand!' she said furiously and ran back into the cloisters.

She was still at the *abbaye* a week later, Polly noticed. She was also eating the eternal beans and watery stew at midday dinner. Gradually, as her body responded to the hard life, her face lost its green look and having found a kindred spirit or two, she settled down to the monotonous routine in Stores.

1917, the third weary winter of the war, arrived with a heavy fall of snow. There was little activity on any front as everywhere soldiers dug in and waited for spring and the promised new offensive. The only casualties filtering in to the Gregory Unit were men with pneumonia, trench feet and self-inflicted wounds. These last were cured here only to be marched off to court martials.

It was a bad sign that all was not well in the French army. Underfed, poorly led by officers who had been brought up to think of the *poilu* as an animal, given no leave and infiltrated by a vociferous Bolshevik minority, the army was a time bomb waiting to explode. Now everyone in France seemed to be pinning their hopes on the new Commander-in-Chief, General Robert Nivelle. Even the British were bowled over by his persuasive charm; after all, he had an English mother and spoke to them in their own tongue. Lloyd George, the new premier, was said to be delighted by him: now at last, everyone said, the war would move forward again as soon as spring came.

It was still snowing in late March: wet showers that very quickly turned the hard-packed ground to soft mud that refroze and then was churned again into slush.

Jumping out of the lorry that had brought food and hospital supplies from the station, Polly found herself stuck in the glue-like mud one couldn't escape in northern France and cursed under her breath. She was learning to swear pretty frequently these days, she thought ruefully as she signalled the driver to take the stuff round to Stores. Bending against an icy wind that cut her face, she trudged across the courtyard that divided the road from the Abbaye Ste Catherine. Winter held the whole western front in its frozen grip. Snow; ice; torrents of sleet and a roaring wind were the prevailing weather. Vehicles and horses floundered in the glutinous surface of the churned-up roads. Their own lorry had almost stuck on the way back and she and the driver, a cheerful Lancashire lass, had spent half an hour freeing it with aid of the duck-boards they always carried with them. Now she was tired, dispirited and cold and her frozen fingers had a struggle to open the iron-studded oak door.

She glanced back at the road. So much heavy traffic passing meant only one thing: a big new offensive was building up. The French Commander-in-Chief, Nivelle, was said to have a Plan. Everyone seemed to know about it so doubtless the Germans had also heard. It was whispered that the Germans knew the very date of the offensive and were preparing accordingly. Someone in high places had been indiscreet and talked too much. The enemy had spent two months retreating to their fortified position, the Hindenburg Line as it was called. Now they had come to a halt and were digging in. Between them and the Allies there stretched a waste land. Nothing of any use had been allowed to fall into Allied hands. As the French followed up this retreat and found themselves in liberated villages that had been booby-trapped and brutally destroyed, their anger grew. Someone described the scene 'as if Satan had poured desolation out of a gigantic watering can'. Deliberately, ruthlessly, showing nothing but vindictive savagery, the Germans had destroyed whole villages in the retreat. Châteaux; little houses; reservoirs; bridges; churches: nothing remained. Even the fruit trees had been ringed so that they would never bear again. The French were sick with fury at this wholesale destruction of their land. The Boche were a race of swine!

Noyon, enemy-occupied since 1914, was free again and its stunned old people, young girls and children came out of their cellars to stand silently before the French troops who embraced them with tears.

Polly thought of all that she had heard from the patients as she watched a column of French *poilus* swinging down the road at their quick jog-trot. They were sturdy handsome little men with the rain darkening their round helmets and rubber capes. They knew about this hospital run by the British women and their teeth gleamed in their olive-coloured faces as they waved to the little *mademoiselle* who was watching them go by.

'*Au revoir, mamselle!* A kees, *chèrie!*' they called and she laughed as she blew them several, calling out, '*Bonne chance, messieurs!*' as she did so.

They broke into one of those cheeky little songs so dear to soldiers on the march to the front.

> Elle a quelque chose de blanc, les dents,
> Elle a quelque chose de bleu, les yeux . . .

and so on, naming parts of the body that became more intimate as the song progressed.

316

There were tears in her eyes as she watched them disappear down the road that headed only one way: to the front. How long before they came back here, filling the beds or lying dead on the heights of the Chemin des Dames which was whispered to be the site of the new attack?

The door suddenly swung open without her aid and there was old Augustin beaming a greeting. 'Madame, you are back safe and sound!' he exclaimed in his guttural French she had found so difficult to understand at first. 'The day is dark and I was beginning to fear for you.' Uttering murmurs of relief like a fussy father, he ushered her inside and took off her wet cape.

She reassured him as she gave him the tobacco she had found for him in Compiègne before going up the bare oak staircase to the office. Delia wasn't there but an enamel jug of hot cocoa was steaming on the stove. She fetched a mug and drank it with thankful shudders. The cold seemed to have got into the marrow of her bones and even leaning up against the stove made no difference for a while. What gallons of cocoa they drank nowadays! It was thick with condensed milk and soothed the hungry ache most of them suffered for the food was neither good nor filling at the Gregory Unit.

Taking off her loathed grey cap she shook the moisture off it and propped it up to dry. Then she tidied her hair in the smoky mirror over which hung two tiny flags: the Union Jack and the Tricolour. 'You look like a hungry orphan,' she told her image, attempting to rub colour into her bloodless cheeks. Her hair was escaping from its combs and she drove them impatiently into her head, vowing once again to have it all cut off at the first opportunity. A lot of the girls had cropped theirs off; only the nurses kept their hair wound into buns for it was easier to wear their veils with hair to pin them to.

'Orderly Wynne, stop prinking,' said a false bass voice behind her and she jumped. Delia's face was laughing round the door. 'Caught you!' she said in her normal voice.

'Heavens, I thought you were the Commandant! I was just thinking that there wasn't a soul to care how I looked any more – not even the poor wounded *poilus* would look at me, I think. It's most demoralizing for a female.'

'That's what you think. I've had that nice little soldier from Lisieux asking for you. My nose is out of joint.'

'That's only because I promised to bring him those horrible scented bonbons from Compiègne. He nurtures a passion for them. Thanks for the cocoa, I needed it. The wind is cutting like a knife and blowing sleet straight into the lorry. Those ambulance girls don't feel it, wrapped up as they are in leather coats and helmets and breeches. At the moment, I don't think I shall ever feel my feet again.'

Delia had come in, shutting the door with a foot and dumping her covered basket on a chair. This was the basket they took round the wards in turn. It contained all manner of useful and comforting things for *les blessés*. Cigarettes and sweets, soap and moustache oil (the first sign that a man was better was his desire to oil his moustache again) and a thick writing pad and envelopes, for the girls often had the task of writing letters to wives and sweethearts on behalf of some *poilu* who had lost the use of his right arm or who had never learned to read and write.

Delia sighed as she too propped her cap up to dry. 'That nice corporal in Sister Lyle's ward died this afternoon. He collapsed suddenly. He was doing so well, too. Only a couple of days ago I had the tricky task of composing a letter to his best girl: he was promising to marry her as soon as he got home because a baby was coming. I hate and fear the way death stalks those marquees.' Delia looked down at her hands twisting in her lap. 'One can almost see it sometimes, a figure with a reaping hook. The men feel it too and get low and quiet. Then as soon as the dead man is removed, they go on as if nothing had happened. Even though he might be a friend. Strange. I can't get used to it.' She threw a half-apologetic smile in Polly's direction. 'It's unusual for me but I'm depressed.'

'So am I. Is it to be wondered at? We'd have to be made of wood not to feel miserable at the things that happen here. I think the nurses do too but they're trained to conceal it. Besides, they can use every ounce of their skill to *help*. We're useless really – just an extra pair of hands.'

'But they couldn't function here without us,' Delia pointed out. 'We run the place.'

'Not all that efficiently, I see! Are those today's letters still unsorted?'

'Have a heart! I haven't had a moment since you went off in the lorry.' She slipped the rubber bands off the bundle. 'Give me a hand, there's a dear.'

There were two for her, Polly saw with pleasure. Her mother's weekly epistle and . . . another. Her heart skipped a beat. Across one corner was scribbled *D.N. Ransom*. She slipped it quickly into her pocket.

'What news from home?' Delia always asked this question because she seldom heard from her own people, having walked out one day against their wishes and joined the Gregory Unit. She was rather proud of 'running away from home to join the war' but it wasn't exactly that. She was twenty-four and possessed her own money left to her by her grandmother: she was that enviable person, an independent woman. But she loved to listen to Polly's news of Eskton.

319

'Not much. Archie's got in to Magdalene College at Cambridge and will be going up in October. I'm so thankful the dear old boy's future is settled at last! I must write to him.' But a pang of regret had gone through her as she briefly remembered her own year at Cambridge. She had given up her future for a week's marriage – oh, she mustn't think like that! It was terribly wrong of her! Mike had needed her desperately. She must never regret what she had done.

She was skimming through the rest of the letter when she heard Delia say: 'Oh, sorry. Here's another one for you.'

Polly took the envelope. 'It's from my father.' The rector seldom wrote, contenting himself with scrawled messages at the bottom of his wife's letters. It had been, Polly saw from the postmark, posted a day after her mother's. Breaking the seal, she read it through swiftly. Then she said 'Oh . . .' with a little gasp and read it again. Looking up into Delia's expectant face she said breathlessly: 'Oh, Delia, it's news of Mike! After all this time!'

'Good Lord, has he been found?'

'No, but they've had news at last of the sergeant who was with him when they both disappeared. It appears Sergeant Thomson has written from prison camp to his mother at Ely. After all this time!'

'Oh, do go on!'

'He insists Mike was alive when he saw him last. They were both groggy after being hit with rifle butts but he says he remembers Mike being dragged off for interrogation, remembers Mike calling out "Good luck, Thomson!" That is all he knows. But Mike was alive after capture! He could be in a prison camp himself! He's alive – he must be!' and she burst into tears.

Delia picked up the rector's letter and read it through as Polly mopped her eyes. 'Your father goes on to say there is a strong possibility that he was killed when the bombardment opened again a few hours later. Don't think I'm being cruel, Polly, but your father does advocate cautious hope. It doesn't do to believe that this means that Mike is alive because he was alive when captured. Until you hear from the Red Cross that he is a prisoner you must take all this with a great big pinch of salt. Promise me you will?'

Polly nodded, tears pouring down her cheeks again. She could feel David's letter crackling against her thigh as she turned away to the window, fighting for control. Oh, if it were true that Mike was alive, that he hadn't *gone out into the dark* as he dreaded, how thankful she would be for him! She only wished she could remember him better. A picture of a tall slim fair-haired boy came into her mind. A boy. Very young for his age, despite his ghastly experiences, and bewildered too. Clinging to her because she had seemed to him strong.

But I'm not strong at all, she told herself wretchedly. If I were, I'd tear up David's letter unread. I'm Mike's wife again, not his widow. I've no right to be receiving letters from David Ransom. I've no right to be thinking of him so often. He had kissed her palm in farewell . . . He liked her – perhaps more than liked her – and it was wrong to let him. But she was beginning to like him more each time they met. He had, she believed, changed a great deal since their first meeting.

The door opened suddenly and the Commandant entered.

'Good heavens, this room's icy!' She took the chair Delia hurriedly cleared of files and sat down in front of the stove, pushing open its door with the tip of her stout boot. 'You young things don't feel the cold like an old woman does, though why you should let the fire go down when you've got plenty of wood, I can't think. Put some more on at once, Vane – plenty, girl! Plenty! Is that cocoa? I'll have a cup. Are you sure that window's closed? Then where is the draught coming from? Yes, I'll use your mug, Wynne, I'm not fussy.' Settled at last, she directed her keen gaze at the girls and, involuntarily, they straightened their backs and smiled at her.

Her broad jolly face and twinkling little eyes always brought a feeling of security with them. Strength flowed from her. She was one of a handful of women to whom the war had come as a godsend for she had her own hospital at last. 'You two are quite fit, I presume? You look a bit pale about the gills, Wynne. I've come to talk about the spring offensive.'

They looked at her blankly.

'It's expected any day and when it comes I shall have need of every pair of hands in the wards. We're still short of nurses and can only just manage with our normal quota of filled beds.' She paused and looked full at them. 'We expect double the number of wounded we can take – and we shall take them, of course. The French Headquarters – the Grand Quartier Général as it's called – are moving to Compiègne and they have taken over a château that housed one of their hospitals – turned out the wounded at a moment's notice, if you can believe it. I'd like to see them try it here! There's every sign that they are expecting a spring offensive to begin soon and now they're short of hundreds of beds due to their folly! We'll take all we can and arrange for the rest to be carried by hospital trains to Paris. It means, too, that I have to rely heavily on those of you who aren't nursing staff. Every hand to the pump, understand?'

Polly felt her stomach flutter nervously: *the wards*. It was one thing to carry comforts and hot water bottles to the wards when the wounded were already tidily bandaged, but quite another to do the bandaging oneself.

322

Hadn't she always been sick at the sight of blood? 'I wouldn't be much use as a nurse, Commandant –'

'But there's no question of the clerical staff doing the actual nursing! We fully realize you have not been trained. No, no! I simply intend that you help the nursing staff in any way you're asked. All right? Good! You'll do splendidly,' said Doctor Gregory cheerfully and departed.

'I can't do it!' Polly insisted. 'I wasn't cut out for nursing! Delia, the Commandant must understand if I tell her that I'd be no use –'

'Would she? Besides, how would you feel if you were the only one left in the hospital not giving a helping hand? You've too much imagination, Wynne. Thank heavens, I have none.'

'Yes, you're to be envied,' Polly said drily, trying to swallow her nervous panic and only partially succeeding.

The moment she could escape, she ran upstairs to her room and shut the door. Only then did she take out David's letter and hold it in her hands for a long minute. Part of her longed for him to express his feelings; part of her was ashamed. She was Mike's wife . . . this man should mean nothing to her. She ought to destroy the letter unread. With a firm movement she slit open the letter and read it hurriedly. It was everything she had hoped for and dreaded it would be. His feelings were unmistakable.

. . . Of course the decent side of me hopes you will have good news of your husband. But I'm selfish enough to want you to be in no doubt that I love you. I lost you last summer, Polly, and I won't risk doing so again. Some day when the war is over, there could be a new chance for us – if we both come through . . .

He went on to tell her that he had come through his first winter on the western front unscathed; now he was fitter than he had ever been. Since the Somme battles had petered out in late autumn there had been little action on his front. Now he had been given leave for the first week in April and would be going to Northesk. Could she apply for leave too? He must see her.

She folded the letter, tucking it in her leather writing case. She stood there with her head bowed, supporting herself against the foot of the bed. She felt exhausted suddenly as if she had been running many miles. She let her head fall into her hands and began to shed tears. What was she to do? She wanted to see him too. A week together at home! Spring just beginning to stir. Peace and quiet. No guns. Just the two of them –

No: it was impossible. She was married. She had no right to care for David. Mike, she thought, if only I knew! You need me – if you're alive.

Standing in this cold little cell, she realized at last that she had never loved Mike in the way she loved David and that she had come of age emotionally.

She raised her head and stared through her tears out of the window as if seeking inspiration from the rooftop of the nunnery chapel and the huge oaks beyond it. She must get home somehow, resolve this thing once and for all. They could talk it over, decide what they must do, comfort each other – oh, yes, she must get home. She would go and see the Commandant at once and ask for just five days' leave. It was worth trying.

CHAPTER SEVENTEEN
The Breaking of Bonds

All through the summer following the torpedoing of the SS *Oceana*, Anna Wehner had been falling ever deeper in love with her brother's partner Sam Murray. The fact that he was David's closest friend and his partner had given their relationship its start. He had seemed one of the family, someone to whom she instinctively turned. It had soon deepened into a love affair as Anna's marriage deteriorated. Never one to do things by halves, Anna was now hopelessly, recklessly in love. It gave a new lustre to her eyes, a joyous spring to her step. The music she played was always deeply romantic and it poured through the house in cascades. She was playing Tchaikovsky, Mozart and Chopin with a deeply felt emotion that gave new depth to her performance. It seemed to pour out of her heart through her fingers to the keyboard. She was happier than she had ever been because she was in love for the first time.

But away from the piano she was difficult and brittle. In his calm and stolid way Carl took the only course open to him: he ignored her moods and avoided her company.

Every morning she was expected to join him for breakfast, to watch him eat his way through baked cod with mustard sauce or his favourite 'red-flannel hash', followed by waffles and maple syrup and cup after cup of coffee. He was already a stone heavier than a year ago and although he was only twenty-four, his hair was thinning on top and his neck and waistline were thickening. The Greek god profile that had once captivated Anna was fast disappearing too. Food seemed as essential to him as music was to her.

'And what are you going to do today, my dear?' he invariably asked.

'Do? What is there to do? I'm bored – abominably bored!'

He wiped his lips on a stiffly starched napkin. 'My dear Anna, there is plenty to do if you would but agree to do it. My uncle Henry wants you on his charity committee – '

'It's for the benefit of the German community. I wouldn't lift a finger for it. What? With my brother fighting the Germans in Europe? You're stupid to consider it for me.'

He looked at her helplessly. He didn't know how to manage this wilful girl he had married. He was afraid of her; afraid of offending her in the bedroom and frightened of appearing weak downstairs in front of his mother who still wielded great influence over him. So he made a hash of it altogether and they were strangers living separate lives under the same roof. 'I wash my hands of you!' he declared and had himself driven to his office. Like the Ransoms, there was always a great deal to be done in keeping so many irons in the fire: shipping and railway interests were the main Wehner interests although they also branched sideways into coal and steel. Carl was already an enormously rich man but he had never learned – unlike the Ransoms who had started out earlier – to play; to use his money to enjoy life. He was often shocked – so was his mother – at Anna's lighthearted approach to money and he was thankful that she had her own Ransom income and could meet her own bills. It would have worried him considerably if he had seen the size of her monthly account at R. J. Stearns. What he didn't realize was that Anna had nothing to do except spend money.

326

She took pleasure in selecting and despatching food parcels to her family in England, things that were barely obtainable there because of the war.

While she was downtown she would often call on Sam in the Washington Street office and persuade him to take her to lunch somewhere. Afterwards they would stroll in the newly-laid-out and popular public gardens until – very late for his afternoon appointment – Sam would tear himself away. They were blind with love, forgetting that an unsympathetic world was watching them. People noted and nodded and awaited the inevitable crash of the Wehner marriage.

'Now where do you go?' Mrs Wehner would demand as her son's wife prepared to sally forth in her own little motor. Her suspicious eyes would take note of the girl's new outfit: a black-and-white silk dress with a deep-crowned hat of vivid green; or a pink-and-brown walking costume with a grosgrain tam to match its broad belt: nothing escaped the old woman's jealous eyes. She pointed out that the skirts were too short and she suspected the girl of using pink lipsalve, but there was nothing she could do in the face of the girl's defiance.

However, from time to time, talking to him cosily in German, she would warn her son that no good could possibly come of his wife's habit of 'jaunting round the city with racketty friends'.

Sam would have laughed if he had known that he was counted 'one of Anna's racketty friends'. He took very seriously the task of keeping the law firm going while David was in Europe. Despite being deeply in love with Anna, he remained firmly his own man and not her slave. Some day he guessed she would have to be rescued from this wretched marriage but his immediate concern was the future of his country: war, it seemed to him, would soon be inevitable and when it came he would close the firm for the duration and prepare for active service. For some time he had gone to camp with the National Guard: they would be among the first to go if the United States went to war.

When at last in April 1917 the United States declared war on Germany, Sam left for camp the following day and the affairs of Ransom and Murray, Attorneys-at-law, were put in the hands of another firm 'for the duration'.

Anna's red eyes didn't escape the Wehners.

'What is the matter with you?' Carl demanded. 'Are you ill?'

Anna folded her lips, refusing to tell him. She withdrew into herself, her skin shrinking from his touch, freezing like a statue when he attempted to take her in his arms, for wasn't that the best way to deal with women like Anna? Master her, make her respond to him and do her duty as a wife? When he got no reaction, he told her she should see a doctor for her nerves. Yet, however much she goaded him, he couldn't bring himself to have a showdown with her. He feared it might reveal what he most dreaded, what his mother often hinted at: namely, that someone was making a cuckold of him and that the whole of Boston society knew it and were laughing at him. A deeply proud man, he pretended to remain calmly unaware of what was happening. She was such a child still! She would get over it shortly and it was better to say nothing. But he wished fervently that the Ransoms hadn't gone abroad leaving him with this firebrand in his hands.

As for Sam Murray, the chief object of his life at the moment was getting to the western front. Of course he loved Anna; she was the only woman in his life and they were the greatest of friends, knowing each other's minds in a way that would have amazed Carl had he known. But the army now came first.

It came at last, the day that Pershing's first contingent

sailed for Europe. It was only a token force hastily gathered and despatched so as to keep Allied goodwill until such time as the rest of the army could be fully equipped and despatched. No one guessed that it would be another whole year before this state was reached.

Anna had slept fitfully the night before Sam left for good. Her heart was like lead in her breast and she moaned in her half-awake state, turning and tossing in misery. She woke fully at five o'clock and heard the boom of the foghorn. How would she get to the docks in fog? Terribly afraid of being late, she had to wait until she heard the staff moving about before she rang for tea. She was down before her husband and halfway through her rolls and coffee when he arrived at his usual time. Helping himself at the sideboard, he turned to look at her frowningly for she was wearing a small hat. 'You cannot be going somewhere surely?'

'Why not?' She put down her empty coffee cup with a decided clatter.

'My dear, have you seen the fog outside? It's very thick indeed. Besides you must have forgotten that today is my mother's birthday and her friends will be coming to call this morning.'

Oh, God, she had forgotten! It was usual on her birthday for Mrs Wehner's old friends to call, bringing with them small gifts and prepared to eat the wafer-thin cinnamon biscuits and the fig-flavoured coffee that was invariably offered them. They would fill the large drawing-room talking in their mother tongue for an hour and Anna would be expected to be present: Mrs Carl Wehner III who some day would be the chatelaine of this house on Beacon Hill. There was old Mrs Gebler and her almost-as-old daughter; there was Mrs William T. Goerring, widow of a steel king, who was more incomprehensibly German than any of the others; there were the brothers Harshe and old Judge Greutz. Anna's heart sank.

Carl was still staring at her, pausing in the act of cutting himself a thick slice of ham. 'My dear?'

'No – no, I hadn't forgotten. That's where I'm going now,' she lied brightly. 'To pick up my present at Stearns – '

'But they can surely send it up?'

'Oh, no! You see – I – I've got to make a final choice and I said I'd be in this morning. The fog will be blowing away shortly – it doesn't worry me. I'll be back about eleven.'

He began to protest but she didn't wait to hear what it was. She picked up her purse and fled, calling impatiently for Flanagan to fetch her leather coat.

Her one thought was to get to the docks to see Sam before he sailed. She might never see him again, she thought tearfully, driving too fast down Beacon Hill, the fog eddying round her. In desperation she switched on the lights only to have them reflected back at her making it impossible to see beyond the bonnet's tip. Curbing her natural impatience she slowed down to ten miles an hour and prayed she would be on time.

The troops were already boarding when she got to the ship. Pushing through the milling crowd she searched frantically for Sam's determined-looking face under the khaki hats that hid the soldiers' faces so maddeningly. She found herself peering closely into the faces of perfect strangers until suddenly she saw him waiting patiently by the Customs shed where – she remembered too late – he had told her to look for him.

She threw herself into his arms. 'Oh, Sam, what am I going to do without you? How will I bear it?' she sobbed.

He kissed and hugged her, his face unusually sober. He was aware of uncomfortable emotions making him laugh

330

shakily and finding nothing to say. He had no relatives and had been brought up by an elderly uncle. Anna was the first girl he had ever been really in love with and now she had become a very important part of his life and he didn't know how to part from her. Holding her warm vibrant body close, he whispered: 'Honey, leave Wehner. Follow me to England.'

She gasped and stood back. '*Now* you say it! Oh, Sam, why didn't you ask me before, you great idiot! Of course I'll come – the very next boat I can get passage on. Oh, darling,' she sobbed, and he held her tightly again. For a few minutes they were the only people in the world as they pressed their faces close, whispering endearments, very happy but sick with longing. The whole Atlantic Ocean between them! The thought was unbearable.

'I shan't write and tell Mother and Dad,' said Anna (knowing what they would say). 'It would fuss them no end. I'll just turn up. And, Sam, if we give Carl evidence he will have to divorce me then!'

'It might take time,' Sam, the lawyer, cautioned her. 'Even if we can't marry at once, we can live together. Would you be willing, Anna? It's asking a lot of you.'

Her shining eyes were sufficient answer. 'I'd go to the ends of the earth to be with you,' she said and meant it.

He left her then to go on board and she waited while the slow process of boarding went on. They waved to each other at intervals. All thoughts of Mrs Wehner's birthday had vanished from Anna's head but even if she had remembered she would not have moved an inch until the ship sailed. Paper streamers ran from the soldiers on board to the waving relatives on shore; the Stars and Stripes were waved and a band played a rousing march. Tears ran down the faces of the waving women: mothers, daughters, sisters and friends. Europe seemed so far away

331

and the smiling faces of the doughboys were so young and merry.

Only when these faces became indistinguishable did Anna turn away. It was one o'clock and she realized she was hungry. But she wasn't ready to go home yet to face acrimony. She drove to a drugstore and had hamburgers and coffee and a large dish of ice cream: she had a childish appetite for sweet things and the good digestion that went with it.

The fog had lifted and it was a golden afternoon now as she drove back up the hill, her mind excitedly making plans for the future – the future that she was at last going to share with Sam. She would go down to the shipping offices tomorrow and see if they had a cancelled berth available very soon. Leaving her roadster to be put away by the under-chauffeur she ran up the flight of stone steps and put her key in the lock. It didn't yield. Impatiently, she rang the bell. No one came to the door. She pushed the letter box open and shouted: 'Flanagan, where are you? The lock has jammed – ' She stopped because in the aperture she could see her husband. He stood a yard or two away facing the door; there was an ugly expression on his face. 'Carl? Open the door. It's me, Anna. What's happened?'

He came close to the door and in a voice trembling with rage he said hoarsely: 'You will never enter this house again, you – you Jezebel! Do you understand? Never again! Your belongings are being packed and will be sent to your father's house this evening. Don't put a foot over my doorstep – don't dare – '

For answer, Anna kicked the door with a grand fury that hurt her toes. 'Are you mad?' she shrieked (and darn the servants! Let them hear every word). Again she applied her eye to the letterbox and saw that Mrs Wehner had joined her son. There was an expression of complacent triumph on her small withered face: she had never dreamed of winning so easily.

'Go away!' Carl's menacing voice was still pitched low for even in this crisis he didn't forget the servants. 'Now I understand your eagerness to go out this morning! So you have been seeing your lover off, have you? That upright young lawyer! Fools! You were seen and recognized by friends – kissing and – and – *worse* – in broad daylight, too. I shall divorce you at once – have the marriage annulled. You are no longer my wife. Leave my property and never set foot here again.'

Anna's temper soared dangerously now. It was *she* who was going to leave him and not the other way round! 'You – you Hun!' she yelled and Mrs Wehner clutched at her breast and sank on to a chair: the servants could not help hearing now. 'A pair of Huns! A nest of Huns! I'm thankful – yes, *thankful*, I don't have to share the house with you any longer. As for your mother, I'm not surprised she wants to be rid of me.' Raising her voice another octave she shrieked: 'Because she thinks she's married to you herself!'

Swinging the starting handle of her car, she felt invigorated. She had got it off her chest at last, all that bottled-up resentment against the Wehners that had been soaring inside her for nearly two years. She was free! With a light heart she steered her car out of the big iron gates and down the hill again. Stanley and his wife Matilda were looking after the Ransoms' house; they would welcome her back with open arms. And soon – perhaps even next month – she would be sailing for England to join Sam and her family, the only people she had ever really loved. Her wretched marriage was over.

Coming out on to the terrace at Northesk one afternoon, Elaine searched in vain for daffodils in the grass below the terrace. Daffodils had always grown there but all she could see were a few green shoots. What had happened to the English springs she remembered? Some people said it was due to the guns in France disturbing the atmosphere.

A brisk breeze rocked the tops of the elms in the avenue but there was no sign of the rooks who usually built here. She plunged her hands deep into the pockets of her fur coat and shivered. She had dressed with special care because she was about to receive the Red Cross ambulances bringing several wounded to convalesce at the officers' home that Northesk had now become. She believed they would be cheered by the sight of someone not in uniform for once, so she had donned a blue *panne* velvet frock with a matching hat and there were pearls round her throat and shining softly from her ears. The whole carefully selected outfit made her look younger than her years and, feeling at her best, her face and eyes glowed. She had to admit that the admiration in the eyes of the young men who filled the wards at Northesk was balm to her soul.

The Red Cross Committee had made an excellent job of converting the north wing into staff rooms, stores and offices. Permanent covered ways led through the garden and side doors to well-equipped marquees, each with thirty beds. When the weather was fine, the convalescents had the park to roam about in; later the tennis court would be in use.

As she walked to and fro on the terrace, Elaine realized afresh that the convalescent hospital had proved a blessing in disguise, taking her mind off the many worries that haunted her nowadays. There was Reggie; his condition showed no sign of improvement. There was David on the western front. There was her affair with Edward Brewer. She had been up to London again and they had become lovers. They had occupied a suite at the Connaught: General and Mrs Edward Brewer. It had been a wonderful interlude. But it must be only an interlude, she had told him tearfully. She had felt better about it then. But already she was dreaming of the next time they would meet.

After all, who were they harming? She had no husband in her bed any more and hers was a warm, passionate nature. A woman made for love, Reggie had often told her. Now he was gone from her for good, a frail, remote figure in a Bath chair. Never again would they be lovers. She loved him of course and always would. Sometimes, putting her arms round him she would will him to speak, to reach her somehow. Then he would make a pathetic effort to form a sentence and tears would pour down her cheeks as she held him close to her, more child than husband now. It was an empty husk she held in her arms, she was certain. No; Reggie would not be coming back to her, she realized at last.

Elaine concealed a sigh and tried to pin a smile on her face as she perceived the highly starched figure that was Matron emerging from the house. Like royalty, Matron waited for no one and only took up her position of welcome when her spies informed her that the ambulances were coming down the avenue. She was an oldish woman who had seen service in the South African campaign and she didn't approve of her hostess whom she termed 'flighty'. Shooting her cuffs and straightening an impeccably starched collar she took up her stand beside Elaine as if they were both on a saluting base, determined to display her authority before the new patients got the wrong idea. For the poor fools always succumbed to the melting blue eyes of this useless creature standing beside her exchanging greetings, Matron remembered acidly. 'Yes, very inclement weather, Mrs Ransom,' she said in her minc-

335

ingly genteel voice. 'My patients aren't able to get out as they should – ah, here is the first vehicle! How naice they're on time for once.'

'How many are we expecting today, matron?' Elaine asked as the first ambulance emerged from under the elms and drew up on the gravelled drive.

We, indeed! As if she did anything for them! Matron told herself scornfully. 'I have given orders for ten beds to be prepared, Mrs Ransom. However, I need hardly say that Headquarters can never be wholly relied upon to give me the correct number.' A disapproving row of tucks hardened an already hard mouth. 'Amateurs. Useless at figures but it's what we've been reduced to in this war. Really, they are almost totally inefficient,' and she stepped quickly forward so that she was the first person to be seen as the ambulance doors swung open.

This time five men were helped down: three walking cases and two on stretchers. They saw first of all the huge grey stone house with creeper covering its front; then they saw the starched blue-and-white figure of the receiving matron who was giving unnecessary directions in a no-nonsense voice. It was only as they started up the steps on their new crutches that the walking patients saw the pretty woman in blue velvet and furs smiling at them and offering them a hand. After weeks of being surrounded by uniforms and the smell of antiseptic, Elaine appeared to them as 'a sight for sore eyes', as Major Grantley put it later. He was in a position to know for, having been gassed on the Ypres salient, his were very sore indeed.

Elaine, looking into his scarred face (mustard gas ate into the flesh), concealed her horror and said gaily: 'Welcome to Northesk! I do hope you'll settle happily here. It will be a rest after hospital as we've few regulations, have we, Matron? We want you to get well as quickly as possible and then you'll be going home.' For the army would no longer need these poor wrecks, she thought sadly: not one was over twenty-five by the look of them. 'You'll enjoy the garden when the weather gets warmer.'

Matron tightened her lips: that fool of a woman was giving them *carte blanche* to misbehave. She knew young officers: devils to control even without legs and arms.

'Goodbye. I shall see you all later.' Elaine waved her hand at the three boys on crutches who were insisting they could manage the steps despite hovering nurses. She turned away to conceal her sudden distress: David's age; so young to be limbless. Oh, God, what if that happened to David? But how could he escape?

'I say, what a stunner!' young Ainsley remarked to a brother officer as they watched their hostess walking away down the terrace.

'No talking!' Matron was harrying the stretcher bearers. 'Nurse, show the walking cases to their wards, please. Tell them to sit by their beds – not *on* the bed – until Sister comes.' She shot her cuffs again, a habit of hers to add emphasis to her orders. These young fellows were going to have to learn without delay that they couldn't make rings round *her*. 'No smoking!' she added quickly for the big Australian, Major Grantley, was fumbling with a packet of Players. 'Especially with *your* lungs,' she added, glancing at his medical details on the sheet of paper she held.

He let his hand drop and stared at her. 'Ow, Matron, have a heart! Even in hospital we were allowed gaspers – '

'Don't argue with me, major. There'll be no alcohol consumed either on *my* side of this establishment.'

'Wake me up, somebody! Am I back at school?' whispered irrepressible Captain Ainsley, staggering on his crutches.

But Matron (just like the matron at his private school, he remembered) had the sharpest pair of ears in the convalescent home as many a young VAD knew to her cost. She crushed young Ainsley and the gassed Grantley in no time at all and had bent a warning glance on the young second lieutenant who was allowing the VADs to arm him up the steps but he offered her no resistance as he felt too weak. The two stretcher cases had disappeared inside and the second ambulance was now drawing up. Satisfied that she had made her mark, Matron went to meet it.

Aware that Matron resented her presence, Elaine had quickly faded out of the picture: there would be time later to get to know the young men. She crossed the gravelled drive and walked briskly down a broad laurel-bordered path that led to the river. The cold wind whipped colour into her cheeks and brought a fresh smell of growing things to her nostrils. She paused to look about her: she had been wrong; spring *was* on its way despite the weather of the last weeks. There were buds beginning to show on the trees and catkins swaying in the wind, while the green swords of daffodils were spiking the grass here by the river.

It had been a long, hard winter and it wasn't over yet. A sigh caught her throat. Here, away from the house, she could allow her expression to slip. Oh, the tired ache that a bright smile brought to one's face!

She had reached the river bank. The green depths of the water concealed the life below the surface and nowhere was there a sign of the fish she knew to be there. Pink-stemmed dogwood ran along the further bank and here at last were the snowdrops that had been so long concealed by snow. They were nearly over and very tall. She stared at them with a lift of her heart and was

338

suddenly startled by a heron that rose from under the river bank below her and flapped awkwardly away.

Northesk. Some of the unhappiest years of her youth had been spent here and history was repeating itself. She hated the place, the unluckiest place on earth for her. Closing her eyes she found herself longing for the happy years in Boston to return; the pleasurable routine of their years spent there and in Europe . . . But it was no use wishing to be back there for the war – this vile war! – had changed everything. Remembering those young wrecked bodies who had just arrived she prayed that David would come through safely, that his wound when it came (and she must face the fact that it would come some day) would not mean the loss of his limbs or his handsome face or his mind – she shuddered and tried to regain her optimism. She mustn't think like this or she would be ill. The children would be on holiday in two weeks time and running about the place all day again. That would cheer her up.

But the thought of Edward was the greatest comfort of all, warming her when life seemed particularly bleak. She needed Edward as much as he needed her. She sighed. She couldn't admire herself but she was at least aware of the sexual side of her nature. Perhaps some day this sexual urge would leave her and she would be free at last to spend the rest of life with Reggie in tranquillity. Now because of this primitive clamour inside her, she was powerless to act in the way common sense commended – but thank God it hadn't gone! She felt wonderful: young and wanted by a good-looking man. How lucky she was! And how awful it must be to be old and finished with love!

It was dreadfully easy to deceive those who loved you, she had discovered, because they trusted you and never doubted your word. It was horribly easy to lead this double life.

In a couple of weeks, David had written, he was coming home on leave. She would go up to town to meet him; it would be the perfect opportunity to see Edward once again. The Connaught again. Perhaps the same suite. A glass of champagne when they were in bed. A joyful smile lit up her face as she remembered those three nights at the Connaught. The last of her depression fell away from her and she turned back to the house.

He met her train, saluting her with smiling politeness in front of the porter. But once inside the dark cab he crushed her to him. 'My dear one – my love – ' Laughing shakily, she extricated herself and straightened her hat. 'Darling, the cabby!'

'What about him? He's seen this little scene a thousand times, I'll warrant.' And he defiantly kissed her again. 'It's been an age,' he whispered.

Meeting his eyes she realized that he was in deadly earnest: he loved her. Her heart misgave her a little. He would never let her go. If only he would treat it as an episode in their lives, enjoyable while it lasted but nothing permanent about it. After all, there was Reggie, whom she still cared for. Edward must be made to understand this. Haltingly, she tried to explain this to him.

'Of course you care for him,' he agreed. 'Good heavens, I would expect it of you – I know your nature, darling, and I honour you for it. But what possible harm can it do him by caring for me as well? He may never recover – '

She recoiled and he saw his mistake at once.

'I'm sorry, darling, but isn't it better to face facts? He's an invalid and he's twenty years older than you – '

'He could live for years and I want him to. He – he means a terrible lot to me, Edward. He's part – a large

340

part – of my life. I would hate him to get hurt by my relationship with you.'

'He'll never know about it,' he reassured her. 'I wouldn't add to his troubles for the world. We won't mention it again. Promise?'

'I promise.' He was right, of course; Reggie belonged to the other side of her life.

Once in their suite at the Connaught, Edward became positively boyish. 'Three whole days!' He swung her round and round. 'I shall savour every minute. I've got tickets for *Fishpingle* tonight and I'm told it's very funny. Then supper at Rule's.'

She went into the large, comfortable bedroom to change and bath. It was the same suite as last time, which was imaginative of him, she thought as she stepped into the scented water, because it made it seem like coming home. He came in through the steam and handed her a glass of champagne – just like last time. Now he sat on the edge of the bath trickling water on to her back and saying: 'You're the loveliest thing, Elaine.' He bent and kissed her moist face, his eyes laughing at her. 'My own girl,' he said and went back to get the champagne bottle.

A sense of misgiving gripped her again. If only he weren't so possessive! The trouble was that he was a very serious man: he had never loved often or lightly. He was nearly fifty and had been on his own for years. Now that he had found her (and she couldn't doubt his feelings for her) he had become primitively possessive. What, she wondered uneasily, would happen if she said that she wouldn't see him again? Some day she would have to do this to him. When the war ended she would be going back to Boston with Reggie. A parting was inevitable.

David put his letter to Polly in the battalion postbag and reaching for his Sam Browne fastened it on. He had thought for a long time before writing that letter and now he felt a comforting relief. Whatever happened after this she would know how he felt about her. Their three days of rest at an end, the battalion was going back up the line. By the door a fellow subaltern, Ryder by name, was whistling 'A Broken Doll' under his breath; for the past few days he had nearly driven them mad by playing this one record over and over again on his gramophone. It was this same gramophone he was about to carry downstairs to leave with the old woman who ran the *estaminet* next door. The *estaminet* was also the Company Officers' Mess and Ryder was determined that the next battalion would not find the gramophone: Madame in return for a large *pourboire* had promised to keep the machine under her very own bed.

As he went clattering downstairs with it, David moved to the window and looked down on the square below. The men were already lined up, every one of them burdened not only with their own packs but with extras like boxes of ammunition and stores and canteens of drinking water. They were already singing: whatever the mood they always sang. Now it was 'Good-bye-ee' appropriately enough. Well, it was a change from that infernal 'Broken Doll'.

The colonel on his grey horse, the adjutant by his side, could now be discerned through the rain approaching the square. With a last look round his billet, David hurried down the bare wooden stairs and quickly took up his position at the head of his platoon just as the colonel arrived in the square and the battalion came to attention.

They had experienced six days of the battle of Arras before being taken out for a rest. No one would have admitted it but each man lined up in the square felt a weakness in his bowels, a clamminess of the hands at the thought of returning to the battle. The journey itself was

342

hazardous, especially at the spot they feelingly called Hell's Crossroads. Here, a dozen shells had landed as they crossed it coming out of the trenches. It was obvious that the enemy had it well within their range and that every movement was noted. And it had to be crossed; there was no other way round.

There was a rumour that the battle, planned as a distraction to the main thrust by the French on the Aisne, had failed. Certainly the Canadians had done splendidly by taking Vimy Ridge at great cost; everywhere else the troops, having at last come out of the trenches after many months, were pinned down in shell holes and on open ground by the Germans who had managed to bring up reinforcements in time. When the French had attacked, the Germans had been waiting and ready. A French sergeant-major captured by them two or three weeks earlier had been carrying the plan of attack: every detail down to the time of zero hour. General Nivelle's master-stroke, the Plan, the surprise attack that would finish the war, had failed and the French found themselves up against fresh German divisions who were waiting for them. The last two days had seen the French massacred and losing heart.

It was vague rumours of this that was making the British troops uneasy. The colonel, who had heard the news from Brigade HQ only an hour ago, looked worried and grim as he rode to the head of the column and they set off.

It was a long march over difficult terrain and as they fell out at ten minutes to each hour intervals there seemed to be more and more stragglers panting to keep up. The subalterns would gather in a small group to smoke and crack a few lame jokes but each felt there was little to amuse them. Rain was falling in sheets and the day was darkening rapidly, looking more like November than

April. An evil little wind sent the rain in gusts against their faces as they set off again towards the east. Now the sound of the guns that had been like the rumble of thunder in the distance was sharp and clear. The whine and c-crump of shells was a descant to their singing. Hell's Crossroads was three miles away and the trenches another two, yet on this flat plain the lights from bursting shells could plainly be seen. Both sides were having 'a hate' by the look of things.

A mile from the crossroads the colonel dismounted; the adjutant and his groom would take the horses back to the village and the colonel would be on foot for the rest of the way.

Half a mile from Hell's Crossroads they halted: as usual shells were raining down. It was nine P.M., a moonless night, and the white light from starshells was lighting up the countryside. As they watched, having a last smoke, they saw a line of Red Cross ambulances coming slowly off the battlefield and approaching the crossroads. Immediately shells began to fall again; the ambulances went faster on the rutted, pitted road but one in the middle was blown up by a direct hit and the next two caught fire.

'God Almighty!' The colonel closed his eyes for a moment. 'Poor devils – no! we can't help. Every man jack of you is needed as reinforcements. How the hell are we going to cross *that*?'

Hell's Crossroads had once been the busy square of a pleasant little village. With mounds of rubble and a river on one side there was no way through, only across.

David pulled at the chin-strap of his tin hat, easing it off his chin: it had chafed him for the last hour. His platoon sergeant came up to him, looking expectant, quite confident his officer would have the answer. 'It don't look too good, sir, but we'll manage it somehow.'

'I think we can do it in small parties; say six at a time. I'll see if the colonel has a different plan.'

But the colonel hadn't. Conferring with his officers he had only added: 'For God's sake, *count*. Jerry is as regular as clockwork. Just watch how those shells come over – one – two – three – now a space. Just long enough to sprint into that shell hole – crouch – up again and out into the open leaving space for the next six in the shell hole. Get your chaps spread out over there – understand?'

'Christ!' Ryder muttered, grinning all over his face. 'Never was any good at split-second timing! Like to go in front of me, ol' dear?'

'Sure.' David tried to smile nonchalantly. He called up five men, explaining to them that when he raised his hand he wanted them to cross the road, past the blazing ambulance and into the shell hole that was half full of water on the other side. He would come last. 'Goodbye, sir. See you on the other side!'

'Goodbye, David. Good luck.' The colonel wiped rain out of his eyes watching the five figures, their capes shining in the light from the fire, following their officer and going forward, disappearing into the gloom. He began to count the shell bursts: one . . . two . . . three . . . One . . . two . . . three . . . One . . . two . . . three . . . Had they got over? Impossible to see. It was going to take all night at this pace but there was no other way to get through this hellhole of a place.

David had been counting too. His pulses were hammering in his dry throat. He saw five pairs of eyes looking at him, awaiting the signal. One . . . two . . . three . . . One . . . two . . . three – 'Now!' They were off, scuttling like rabbits, and he followed them. But he heard the shell overhead as he stumbled and fell. There was a blinding flash going off in his head. Searing pain went like a

345

lightning bolt through his legs and something hit him on the side of his face. Then it went dark.

'God Almighty!' The colonel, crouching in a ditch, wiped mud off his face. His skin was tingling with a myriad tiny cuts from sharp stones. 'Have the whole lot been wiped out?'

Ryder gasped: 'Impossible to say, sir – wait! Someone's signalling. Waving his arm.'

'What the hell does he mean by that? Come or stay back? Can you see David?'

Ryder turned half-round to the side, screwing his eyes up. 'No, sir – but there's one of them lying in the open – '

'It's Mr Ransom, sir.' David's platoon sergeant had wriggled on his stomach over to them. 'He's not moving. I'd like your permission to fetch him in, sir.'

'And get yourself killed, too? No. I can't allow it.'

'I'd like to do it, sir. I think he's alive.'

'Very well, Dale. On your head be it.'

The man had gone, stumbling over the churned-up ground.

'Hell!' the colonel said savagely. 'I was fond of Ransom. He was a good officer.'

Ryder said nothing. His eyes were on Sergeant Dale, who was already returning with his burden. 'Good man,' he said softly. 'Look out, sir! More shells coming over!'

Elaine was at Victoria twenty minutes before she needed to be to meet the leave train, her stomach fluttering with excitement. How strange these two sorts of love were! The physical love she felt for Edward and the anxious maternal love she felt for David, returning from the western front at last. As she paced to and fro she knew that of the two the maternal love was the stronger. Queer how nature had made it so. And yet *he* would give his love to another woman before long and she, his mother, would be nothing in his life. One always loved one's children so much more than they loved one. She had learned that the hard way, for had David given a thought to her before he threw up everything to come over to England? True, the United States was in the war herself now and he would have been among the first to volunteer but all these past months of anxiety and trouble need never have happened. That was the hardest thing to bear.

Her attention was caught by a news poster: WESTERN FRONT IN FLAMES. She turned hastily away. Well, thank God, she needn't worry about that for a week or two now he was home.

People pressed round the barriers as a train came puffing slowly in. Standing on tiptoe she examined the faces of the troops as they poured out and were greeted ecstatically by waiting relatives. It was difficult to tell officers from men; all were mud-encrusted and carrying a great deal of baggage.

They melted away like a spring snowstorm. He was not among them.

Bewildered, she approached a porter. 'Is there another troop train due in?'

'About five minutes, mum.'

How silly she had been! There were bound to be two trains carrying the men from the troopship.

It came in and again she strained her neck to catch a glimpse of his familiar face. Was that him? Yes! She raised a hand to attract David's attention and then saw that the man was not David at all. She began to tremble, to feel herself in a nightmare of faceless strangers. Where was he?

Elliot was waiting for her at Whitby. It was almost midnight and she was nearly speechless with fatigue.

'Mr David – has there been a message? He wasn't on

the train . . .' Her voice trailed as she saw Elliot's wooden expression.

'I've heard nothing, Miss Elaine.'

They drove in silence. Under the fur rug he had placed over her knees her hands were tightly clasped and a strange feeling of foreboding was making her feel sick. She stared at Elliot's large ears sticking out from under the chauffeur's cap he adopted now he had learned to drive the Packard. He drove very badly, changing gear noisily and missing the clutch on the hills going out of the town. But he had been determined to tackle motors now that he was no longer coachman to the family and until they could persuade him to retire they must put up with him. Besides there were no other drivers available; the war had swallowed them.

They reached Northesk after a maddeningly slow drive through the darkness. Not waiting for Elliot to help her down, she flung herself out of the car and into the dark house. Running upstairs she hesitated: who to ask? Reggie would know nothing.

A door behind her opened and Reggie's nurse came out. She was wearing a blue dressing-gown and her thick plaits lay on her shoulders; she looked so much younger that Elaine was momentarily distracted into astonishment.

'Mrs Ransom, thank God, you're back! I've had to give Mr Ransom a sedative tonight – '

'A sedative? Is he worse?'

'No, but he saw me open the telegram and then I had to tell him. It upset him.'

Elaine supported herself against the door. 'Telegram? David?'

'I'm afraid so. Wounded three days ago. He's in hospital at Ste Omer. The telegram came the day before yesterday and I rang Brown's Hotel but they said you hadn't taken up your booking. I wanted to stop you

348

meeting his train today – oh, I did hope we could find you! I had to tell Mr Ransom you weren't there . . .' She was biting her lip. 'I had to – he wanted to know.'

'He understood?' Elaine said dully. 'I didn't realize he could – could take such news in.'

'Well, he's come on a lot lately,' said Miss Matthews with professional pride. 'When he's not overtired he understands a good deal.'

'I've been . . . staying with friends. A last-minute decision. I should have told you. I'm sorry.' She had sagged suddenly. The nurse grasped her arm and led her into the little sitting-room off Reggie's bedroom. 'Now you sit down, Mrs Ransom, while I get you a glass of brandy. You've had a nasty shock on top of a long journey. Now please drink this.'

Elaine took the glass and gulped it down; its fierce fire burned her throat and she coughed. But suddenly it was warming and stimulating her; the shivering stopped.

'That's right,' said Nurse Matthews approvingly. 'Now I'll just poke up the fire and go and fetch you a poached egg and some milk. You'll sleep better for something in your stomach.'

Left alone, Elaine looked round the shadowed room. David, her heart cried. Oh, God, is this how you want to punish me? Is this your revenge? My son wounded and perhaps dying while I've been lying in Edward's arms and *enjoying* it. While David – yes, perhaps he's dead by now. He could be. Three days. If only I'd known while I was in London! Edward could have got me a permit to go across and see him – but I can still ask him this favour. He'll do it, I know. I'll telephone as soon as I've eaten and seen Reggie.

Oh, this war! If men had to bear the children, she thought with a new bitterness, they wouldn't throw away young lives, crush them underfoot like the lowest form of beetle and demand more – more – more!

CHAPTER EIGHTEEN

The Hour Has Come

Polly's haversack had been packed, her movement papers signed and a lift to the station promised by one of the ambulance drivers when Delia came running upstairs to her room. She looked round on Polly's preparations with a rueful shake of the head. 'Awfully sorry, old thing, to be the bearer of bad news but all leave's been cancelled. Sickening for you, I'm afraid. It's just been posted on the board downstairs. Felt I had to tell you.'

'Oh, no! Oh, Delia, I've simply got to go home! There's someone I've arranged to meet, you see. Someone I care for very much.'

'Well, my child, that's life in wartime. You never know what tomorrow brings.' Then seeing Polly's distress, she tactfully turned to other things. 'Have you a clean pinny? Then get Kathryn to give you one out of Stores. And a clean table napkin for your head. We're to work on the wards.'

With leaden hands and fury in her heart, Polly began to unpack. David would be home by tomorrow evening. He would wonder why she hadn't arrived home, too. Perhaps he would think she had had second thoughts and had decided not to come. If she could find a free minute to do so she would dash off a few lines to explain and hope against hope that her letter arrived before his leave was up. She was tired and had been longing for this leave and on top of everything to be disappointed at the last minute was just too much. She shed angry tears into the pile of clean underwear she was halfheartedly putting back in her locker.

She scribbled her hasty note explaining that if her movement papers had been for the day before, she would have got away. There were, she wrote, remembering the censor, pressing reasons why she couldn't get home after all. She sent a letter in the same vein to her parents.

Running upstairs, she asked Augustin to post them for her in the town when he went in later. Even so, she calculated that David would only get the letter (with luck) just before he returned to France; it was Easter at the weekend and there would be postal delays in England. It was sad but there was nothing more she could do, she decided, and went across to Stores to collect her overall and head napkin.

In a flurry of hailstones and icy winds, the people of Compiègne had gone to church to the sound of loud and continuous gunfire. It was Good Friday and the bombardment had started at dawn. The familiar sound of the French seventy-fives was heartening to the praying congregation: the French army was on the offensive at last.

'Did you know?' they whispered across the pews, 'our President has been here – yes, yes, to Compiègne for an urgent conference. And – would you believe it? – it was held in a *railway carriage* at the station! But yes, it's true. Ask Jean Valois over there. He saw Monsieur Poincaré with his own eyes!'

Standing at the window of her office, Polly could see a huge bunch of German observation balloons against the pale cold sky. They seemed to be over Choisy-au-Bac, three kilometres away. They were the enemy but one had to admire the brave men who manned them, armed only with binoculars – suddenly, a puff of smoke and then a sheet of fire enveloped a balloon. She caught her breath as she watched the basket and observer plunge earthwards. Sickened, she turned away. She had just seen a

351

man die. A German soldier, one of the enemy but a human being too. It was strange and horrible to be so near the front, to be almost part of it. She felt sorry for the French wounded lying in the marquees beyond the *abbaye*. Some were dying, others appallingly wounded, but they were not free of the war which raged a few kilometres away. Yesterday Compiègne had been bombed from the air: the wounded, pinned down in their beds, had been as helpless as flies in amber. Everyone but a skeleton staff had been herded into the cellars beneath the *abbaye* and the Commandant and a few of the medical staff had stayed with the men, soothing them and spreading confidence as they walked through the wards. Two bombs had fallen behind a garden wall; another two had fallen into trees, splitting them in two and leaving a gap like a drawn tooth in the neat row of plane trees. No one had been hurt but as Doctor Gregory remarked grimly, this was only the beginning.

The noise of running feet along the stone corridor made her turn back to the room: who could be rushing along the corridor at such a pace? She hadn't long to wonder. The door burst open.

'What to you think?' Kathryn Graham cried breathlessly. 'The Americans are in! America's declared war!' She flopped into a chair. 'It will make all the difference! We can't fail to win now.'

'Are you sure?'

'The Commandant herself told me. She was posting the news on the notice board. Even she was excited. Isn't it wonderful?'

'But – '

'Oh, please don't start talking cautious Yorkshire common sense at a moment like this! I couldn't bear it. It's the greatest news we've had in three years!'

'I was only going to say it will be months before they

arrive, I'm afraid. They will have to be transported across the Atlantic *and* trained *and* supplied with weapons. If only they had come in last year! I wonder if they've come in time? France is pretty well bled white after Verdun and so are our troops on the Somme. This Russian revolution hasn't done much good. They say a lot of German troops have been withdrawn from the eastern front and sent here. Oh, Kathryn, if only it isn't too late!'

A lot of other people were wondering the same thing.

On Easter Sunday morning, Doctor Chester held a simple service in the refectory. As they knelt on the cold, polished floor, the sound of the guns made the earth beneath the *abbaye* shudder unceasingly. After the final prayer, the Commandant came in and asked them to sit down again.

'As you know, the bombardment we have been hearing for the last few days is said to be the prelude to a big new offensive any day now. We are holding ourselves in readiness for the first call. Those of you who are not nursing staff may be called upon too. I know I can rely on each one of you to give of her best.'

It was a gloriously crisp and cold day. As if a magician had wiped the skies clean and allowed the sun to shine through, Polly thought, looking upwards as she walked towards the marquees with her basket of comforts for the *poilus*. The snow was rapidly melting underfoot and she was thankful for the new pair of rubber boots she wore as she crossed the squelchy ground to the duckboard. Round her head, she had wound a scarf and over everything she wore Archie's naval duffle coat. I look like a gipsy with a basket of clothes pegs, she told herself. A year ago, the thought of being seen in such an outfit would have horrified her. Now, there was no room for vanity.

She stooped under the flap of Ward B only to discover that most of the wounded had disappeared. They had been despatched to Paris on a hospital train last night. Oh, lord, that meant a new nominal roll again today!

'We're only keeping those too ill to move,' Sister Lyle said. She and Nurse Hayward were moving these last few to the outer perimeter of the marquee and were busy making up beds for new patients.

'Can I help?' Polly put down her basket and unwound her scarf.

'Well, another pair of hands would be a relief, I can tell you!' Sister Lyle paused to straighten her organdie veil with the red cross on the front. 'You'll be coming in to lend a hand on one of the wards when we get busy anyway – now, don't look like that. You're a sensible young woman, I'm sure.'

'But can you be sure of that, Sister? What if I faint at a crucial moment?'

'You won't. No one dares faint in my ward.'

Polly hoped she was right. But the fear of failing continued to haunt her and was beginning to outpace the bitter disappointment of her cancelled leave.

All that week they waited. They were like hostesses preparing for a party, going a hundred times to count the glasses and polish the spoons. Only it was forceps and scalpels that were polished and sterilized and lying in neat rows to await the guests . . .

A sense of expectancy hung in the air; everyone was restless. Rows of clean, empty beds waited in the marquees. The last and worst cases had gone on the hospital train to Paris. Sterilization drums stood in position and all time off for the staff had ceased. There were no more walks into Compiègne for hot chocolate at the little cafés. Now all exercise was taken inside the grounds. Time passed slowly.

Then, early on the morning of 16 April, Polly was

jerked out of sleep by new sounds. It was pouring with rain, spattering against the windows and hissing in the gutters. The far-off guns still rocked the *abbaye* but now other earsplitting sounds added to the din: lorries, guns on limbers, and the newest weapon, tanks, rumbled heavily down the road. Battalions of reserve troops were moving up to the front line.

Cautiously, she drew aside the curtains and stood shivering in the half-dark as she watched the procession passing. Suddenly, the whole misty sky seemed to burst into flames in the east and a tremendous thunder rocked the building to its foundations. She reached for her watch, peering at its white dial: five o'clock. All the other cannon fire and bombings had only been an overture. There was no mistake this time: this was the real thing.

Now the sky had become a terrible awe-inspiring spectacle. A sort of devilish firework display filled the misty expanse. Overhead, she could hear French aircraft going to keep their dawn rendezvous with the enemy.

With a blanket over her shoulders, she remained at the window, watching with frightened fascination. The outline of the dark forest grew clearer as dawn broke. In this strange light, the forest seemed to have crept nearer the *abbaye*. Little mists rose from it. She shivered, remembering that over on the other side lay Soissons, held by the enemy. A sick fear possessed her and she felt her heart jump nervously at the old recurring thought: what if they should get through the forest? Descend on Compiègne through that dark shelter of trees? The enemy had overrun the town once before, in 1914. And if they came again, broke the French line and flooded into the town – well, there would be no question of deserting their patients and fleeing before them. The Commandant had told them so: the women's hospital must stay.

* * *

At midnight on the same day, it was still raining in torrents. The drum-fire of the French guns was drowned now by the roaring, howling shells that could be plainly heard at the hospital. The forty kilometres of front was on fire.

Polly and Delia, wearing their rubber rain capes, stumbled over duckboards to the marquees. Ambulances choked the yard and queued in the road. The 'Fall-in' followed by 'At the double' had sounded.

Polly's mouth was dry with terror. She knew she would faint and make a fool of herself. She envied Delia who showed no sign of nerves. Both wore clean overalls under their capes and they had been given clean dinner napkins to tie round their heads. They wore rubber boots and carried shoes in the covered basket carried by Delia.

They paused and looked ahead to the beckoning lamplight. They could see stretcher-bearers passing with monotonous regularity into the tents. Swamped by the enormous numbers of the wounded, Doctor Gregory had had to call on the aid of elderly Frenchmen from the town to act as stretcher-bearers. Watching these old gentlemen struggling valiantly through the rain, Polly's eyes stung: what the French had to bear! What if this were England and that grey-haired man, panting with his efforts, was her father?

'Come on,' Delia urged, thinking her companion had halted through reluctance. 'You'll be all right, Polly, when we get going. Just don't think.'

'Yes. Yes, of course.' But, looking at the wounded and dying covering every inch of space, she wondered if *this* could be the victory they had all expected.

General Nivelle's confident message to his troops before the attack had been: '*L'heure est venue! Confiance! Courage! Vive la France!*'

But his messsage to the officers had sounded a more

sober note. 'We are playing our last cards. A higher courage than ever is demanded by all.'

He had known that the stakes were high.

With typical élan and courage, the long blue line of the French had attempted to scale the treacherous heights to the Chemin des Dames, the road built along a ridge in the eighteenth century so that the daughters of Louis XV could reach their château. Wave after wave of men were cut down by the German machine-guns entrenched above.

Those able to speak were bitter and despairing. 'It's all up,' they whispered across the stretchers to each other. '*C'est impossible*.'

Such hopelessness from the usually cheerful and coura-geous *poilus* was so strange and depressing that the nurses looked uneasily into each other's eyes. This mood of despondency seemed to affect all the wounded: they had lost their belief in victory. Their spirits were broken.

Now serried ranks of stretchers lay under the tarpaulin shelter of the receiving area. The Commandant stood like a rock among the chaos and gave her orders in a steady voice. Her hospital, equipped for about a hundred and twenty cases, was being asked to take more. Every extra bed had been put up but still they poured in until there was nowhere left but the floor.

'Orderly Wynne, please go along to Ward F. Sister Pitt is expecting you. German wounded are being taken in there.'

The enemy. Polly shivered. Was she at last going to see the dreaded enemy? She had not set eyes on even a prisoner of war since she arrived in France.

Ward F had been divided down one side by a canvas screen: five German officers lay behind it. The main marquee was lit by hurricane lamps hanging from the roof and by this light, Polly saw the stretchers on the floor and the still forms on them covered in the dreaded *feldgrau* uniforms. The enemy. Here, in this tent. She could smell them. She would have to touch them . . .

'There you are, Wynne! Do hurry up and stop dawdling over there!' Sister Pitt was a small bad-tempered woman. Using the torch she kept hooked to her belt, she was bending over the patients and reading the labels pinned on them at CCS.

Hurried messages had been scrawled: *26th Bavarian Reserve*. Sometimes a name: *Helmut Schneider*. *Kurt Luden*. Then the nature of the wound. Directing a beam on these labels, Sister Pitt passed down the ward in a stooping position, scrawling *Theatre* in red chalk on some. When she came to the end, the men would be lifted on to the clean beds over which a protective blue blanket had been thrown. Only after they had been undressed would they be put between clean sheets.

Polly followed her, looking without pity but with fierce loathing and some fear on the dreaded enemy. Even as she recoiled, she was stooping over one of them; he was young – very young – and his face was untouched. Glancing down, she saw that the bandages round his legs were dark red. The boy, his face glistening and waxen, had ceased to moan.

She straightened. The enemy. A boy her own age. Somewhere, his family was praying for his safety. 'Sister,' she asked, pursuing Sister Pitt across the marquee, 'that man over there is very bad. He's soaked in blood. Can't we get him to the theatre quickly?' For Sister Pitt, she had noticed, had passed him by.

'He's done for,' Sister said dispassionately. 'It's not worth the trouble of getting him to the theatre. Miss Lovell wouldn't be able to do much for him.'

'But he's so young. Please put *Theatre* on his label.'

Looking exasperated, Sister Pitt chalked *Theatre* in red on the boy's label. 'The only good German's a dead one,' she said grimly. 'I hope you're not going to be sentimental and silly, Wynne. It won't do, you know.'

I've done my best for you, Polly said silently to the wounded boy.

It was now necessary to get the mud-splattered wounded on to the beds. In order to do this, Polly had to kneel at the head of the bed and take the patient's full weight as the orderlies lifted the heavy body off the stretcher. Everyone was panting by the time this work was finished, the wounded who were conscious crying out in agony however carefully it was done. Their uniforms had to be cut off, then they were washed and those who were not to be operated on had their wounds dressed and a cup of Bovril given them.

By dawn, the ward was crowded and filled with groans and cries and the smell of blood. Half-dazed with fatigue, Polly followed Sister Pitt with the dressing tray. The sister, a wiry little northerner, showed no signs of tiredness although her apron was stiff with blood. The smell and look of the wounds nauseated Polly but she kept upright somehow, forcing herself to concentrate as Sister Pitt showed her how to sterilize the dressing bowls by pouring methylated spirits in each one and setting fire to it. 'Iodine,' she snapped. 'Peroxide – where's the lysol? And don't forget to bring the soiled dressing bucket with you.'

'No, Sister.'

'Good. Then come along.'

Her stomach heavy with terror and apprehension, she followed the indefatigable figure of the nurse to the first bed. The blankets were rolled back and a bloodstained bandaged torso exposed to view. 'Bayonet wounds. I'll need the peroxide to soften the gauze. Pour it into the bowl – quickly. There! You've spilt it. Now put a piece of cotton wool to soak in it – no, much bigger than that! Use your sense, girl.'

The patient, a bearded Bavarian, had stricken eyes that fastened first on one face and then the other. He looks like an animal caught in a trap, Polly thought, her hands shaking as Sister finished uncovering the wounds. Oh, God! she thought, biting her lip hard. The flesh was green and foul smelling.

'Gas gangrene,' Sister said over her shoulder. 'Nothing to do with gas. It comes from the filthy soil they lie on. Keep still!' she said sharply to the man, 'or you'll start bleeding again.'

But the man didn't understand and jerked his body in pain away from Sister's probing fingers. 'Keep still, I say! He'll have to have tubes in – it won't drain any other way and I don't want any silly fainting from you, Wynne, when I do it.'

Polly leaned towards the German. 'Lie still,' she said in halting German. 'We shall try not to hurt you.'

'So you speak their filthy language?' Sister's voice was sharp with suspicion. 'You've not got German blood, I hope?'

Polly looked up, startled, and met a pair of cold eyes that were hard with hate. Perhaps that's how I looked when I first came into the ward, she thought. She's stupid with hate. She ought not to be working in this ward at all. 'No, I'm not German but I know a little.'

'I wondered.' Sister's hands went on moving efficiently over the deep, oozing wounds. 'You seemed very anxious about that boy earlier on. I want no German-lovers in my ward.'

'*Danke. Danke schön, gnädiges Fräuleins,*' the man gasped.

'He's thanking you, Sister,' Polly said dryly.

'He can keep his thanks for his Kaiser,' Sister Pitt snorted.

It was at the next bed that Polly nearly fainted: a gaping thigh wound alive with maggots. For a moment, bathed in icy sweat, gorge rising in her throat, she had to hang on to the bedrail. Then she met Sister's small contemptuous eyes. She ungritted her teeth, wiped the perspiration away with an arm and composedly held out the bowl for the blood and pus to flow into as Sister pulled yards of gauze out of the hole. The smell was suffocating.

All the time they worked, orderlies passed in and out of the marquee carrying stretchers to and from the operating theatres where the four women surgeons were working at full stretch. As the men came round, they had to be restrained from tearing off their dressings. Their agonies exhausted Polly. Her head ached and her mind became dulled. Four o'clock passed. Five. Six. The boy with the terrible leg wounds whom she had persuaded Sister to send to the theatre had been put in the centre of the marquee where all the worst cases were. He rolled his head monotonously, crying weakly, fainting from the pain and coming back to consciousness again. Polly put down the soiled dressing bucket that she had been emptying once again, and bent over him.

'You're going to be all right.' She spoke softly in German. 'You are safe here.'

Safe. The boy, only six months a soldier, saw through a mist a girl's face. It was white and strained but the eyes smiled at him and the voice was kind. His lips moved stiffly but no words came out.

'Wynne, hurry up with that bucket! What are you saying to that man? Please remember we can't waste time on the enemy.'

Polly emptied the bucket, straightened her aching back

and rejoined Sister Pitt. 'I was only reassuring him, Sister. He's in terrible pain. Is he going to be all right?'

'All right? Don't be a fool, Wynne, they've taken off both his legs. He won't last the night. I told you there was nothing to be done for him, didn't I?'

For a moment, Polly couldn't see. With trembling hands, she held out a bottle of peroxide instead of iodine.

The hideousness of this war.

Perhaps it all became routine after this for she lost a lot of her apprehension. Roused from sleep, she would throw on her clothes, dash cold water in her face, and tie a napkin over her hair. Then she would collect Delia and together they would stumble out into the dark.

Sister Pitt, preparing to snatch some sleep herself, was short-tempered. 'For heaven's sake, Wynne, wake up! You're like a sleepwalker. Go and help Nurse Hayward sterilize the instruments. There's a scissors missing. Find it.'

Half-suffocated as always by the smell of the German ward, Polly obeyed. As soon as Sister left, she and Hayward would make cocoa on the stove. Like herself, Nurse Hayward was young and desperately in need of sleep after a week when everyone had had too little.

'I'm always nervous when Sister leaves me in charge,' she confided in a low voice, glancing over her shoulder. 'They wake up and watch me. I can feel them doing it.'

Polly shivered, watching the acetylene lamps swinging to and fro. There was a gale blowing tonight and the canvas walls billowed and flapped. Grotesque shadows were cast on the walls and looked like moving figures. It was easy to be jumpy at night.

'It's because they're the enemy. We can feel their animosity.'

'These men aren't so bad. They thank one quite

decently. It's the officers through there, especially the one Sister calls Little Willy. Haven't you noticed how he hates us touching him?'

Polly nodded. Little Willy not only bore a strong resemblance to the Crown Prince of Prussia but was a particularly haughty specimen of the Prussian officer class. He never thanked them, called them imperiously if he needed anything and watched them with hard eyes when they came into the ward.

The two girls finished sterilizing bowls and instruments and put out sterilized drums of dressing for the morning. They made cocoa and talked in whispers, breaking off now and again for Hayward to attend to a restless patient. These men suffered from wounds inflicted by the preliminary French bombardment. A lot had lain unattended on the battlefield for days: most of these had died from gas gangrene; one or two were dying from it tonight. Jaws had been blown off, legs and arms amputated. Several had buttock wounds inflicted as they lay face downwards to avoid shells. All had great gaping wounds that made the human body a sick joke.

Polly watched Hayward with admiration. She felt so helpless beside this girl who was a professional. She watched as she replaced a continuous irrigation tube that had fallen out of a man's shoulder as he stirred restlessly. Pushing the tube back into the body was a skilled job. Lotion, in a douche-can suspended from the canvas roof, dripped through a length of rubber tubing into the wound and from there into a bucket on the floor. Then she prepared a hot fomentation for another man. 'It will relieve the pain until Sister comes back. Go and see if Bed Two is still alive, Wynne. He's stopped plucking at the blankets.'

Polly cautiously shone her torch on the man. He was a typical German private with a long face and ears like jug

363

handles. A heavy growth of beard covered his face like a dark shadow. His eyes, pale blue and small, stared sightlessly, and his mouth was open. The suffocating smell of gas gangrene nearly made her sick. With a gentle hand, she drew the sheet over the lifeless face.

'He's gone? Then one of us had better indent for a shroud. Do you mind if I go? There are one or two things we need and I shall have to bully Stores into letting me have them. Don't let the rats worry you. Just throw something at them.'

Left alone, Polly looked uneasily into the shadows of the floor. Rats and mice swarmed here at quiet times. The rats, particularly, had a horrible predilection for the waste bucket outside the operating theatre.

At half past one, she heard orderlies carrying out patients from the wards to waiting ambulances. Anybody well enough to be moved would be sent by the night train to Paris. It meant one thing only: another convoy was expected. She went to the door of the tent to watch them; thinking again how shortsighted the French army had been. The Grand Quartier Général had descended on Compiègne last month and had taken over a château housing an army hospital, scattering the patients to whatever hospital could take them in. Those extra beds were being sorely missed now in Compiègne.

A sudden thud behind her made her jump. She let the canvas flap drop back into place and stood with her back to it, peering into the dimly lit ward. *Rats!* The thought made her cringe. They were horrible grey and brown creatures as big as small dogs . . . there it was again!

It came, she thought, from the officers' ward behind the canvas screen. She plucked a torch off the table and shone it before her as she cautiously stepped round the screen. 'Oh!' she gasped.

The man they called Little Willy was out of bed,

balancing himself on his remaining leg. With one hand, he grasped the iron bedstead; in the other he held Sister Pitt's missing scissors. The torch light picked up the staring eyes of the other patients, the menacing expression on Little Willy's face and the razor-sharp scissors in his hand.

Polly's knees were weak. Oh, God, if only someone would come! 'What – what are you doing? Get back into bed at once,' she said in her halting German.

The man ignored her, edging his way from bed to bed.

'I will fetch the Commandant if you do not obey.' Even as she uttered this useless threat she heard the squire's warning words echoing in her head: *A pack of women on their own. Anything might happen.* 'Do you hear me? Get back into your bed at once!'

It looked as if his stump of thigh was haemorrhaging, she thought, for in the arc light she could see the bandages were bright with arterial blood. He had reached a corner bed and was clawing at the blankets above a cowering body, shouting incoherently in furious German ' – to talk of the Fatherland so! I will kill you for my Kaiser – '

There was a scream of terror from his victim and Polly launched herself on the assailant. The other prisoners were shouting feebly as, with every ounce of strength, she tugged at the man's body. He was, despite his terrible wounds, immensely strong and tough. Again and again, his hand holding the scissors flashed in the air. Then suddenly his strength ebbed and he fell to the floor, choking feebly. Polly, the napkin torn off her head, her hair over her eyes, scrabbled on the ground for the torch. With its aid, she looked at the man on the bed: he was covered with blood and very still. It was obvious he was dead. At her feet, his murderer was silent, his life's blood flowing out of the severed artery on his thigh.

'Wynne? Where are you?' Hayward called softly.

Polly staggered out from behind the screen. She looked ghastly, her overall covered in blood. Hayward sprang forward to support her. 'My God, what's happened?'

'It's – it's Little Willy.' Her teeth chattered so much, she could hardly form words. 'He's killed another man – the stomach wound in Bed 4. He's dead himself, I think.' She stared down at herself and nausea overcame her as she remembered the carnage behind the screen where Hayward had now run. A minute or two later, she emerged with a grim face. 'The place is swimming in blood. Wait here. I'm going for Doctor Chester.'

In silence, Polly and the remaining three German officers regarded each other. In the main ward, men roused from sleep were whispering and calling out: '*Was ist das?*'

'You did your best, Nurse,' one of the officers said. 'You must know that we regarded von Koenitz as quite mad. He had threatened Nehammer many times. He spoke against the war, poor Nehammer. He had a beautiful wife and two children in Dresden. He wished to go back to them. It is most sad.'

Polly didn't reply. Her head was pounding with nervous pain, her underlip sore where she had bitten into it. The whole place smelled of blood. As if the battlefield was not enough, they must kill each other . . .

'Good girl,' said a calm voice and Doctor Sarah Chester took the torch out of her hand. 'Bring the lantern, Hayward.'

There were other people swarming into the ward now. Stretcher-bearers for the dead; the Commandant; Miss Lovell, one of the surgeons. Someone led Polly away. Someone else held a bowl for her to vomit into. She was aware of a dull shame that she could collapse so completely. For there was Hayward, the trained nurse, coolly clearing up the mess and preparing to lay out the murderer and murdered.

Sister Pitt, roused from bed, praised Hayward lavishly for once. Her glance in Polly's direction was withering.

The Commandant said she could go back to the *abbaye* and be excused duty that night but she pleaded to stay on. Here, there would be no time to remember that horrible scene in the officers' ward. The thought of being alone in her room filled her with repugnance. So she washed and changed her overall and when the new convoy came in at dawn and French wounded filled every remaining space on the floor, she went to join Delia and Kathryn Graham in the receiving bay.

They held feeding cups for all those who were conscious and not suffering from stomach wounds. Those who were, called piteously for water which they couldn't have. A nurse went from one to the other giving tetanus injections and marking their foreheads with a large T. Doctor Chester stooped over each stretcher and Polly wrote *Theatre* in red on the labels pinned to each man. She was glad to be kept busy. It was difficult, even so, to keep pity and sorrow at bay as the professionals did. These men were so young, so gay, so handsome a short time ago! Now, they were cutting away bloodsoaked blue uniforms from bodies that were grievously wounded. For many, life was nearly over.

The line of ambulances waiting outside seemed to stretch endlessly. They were still hard at it at eight o'clock and the four surgeons in the huts that housed the operating theatres had barely paused in their work. No, this could not be the victory that General Nivelle had promised France.

CHAPTER NINETEEN

The Unknown Soldier

For a whole month Polly felt herself living in a nightmare
world. Men died daily and were carried out at the slow
pace the orderlies reserved for the dead. Men came round
after surgery to scream with pain, vomiting and tearing at
their bandages. They were tortured beings but there was
little the medical staff could do to alleviate the agony.
Three times a day they had to have their dressings
changed and she saw the terror in their eyes as she
followed Sister Lyle with the dressing tray in her shaking
hands. Yet she stood stoically with a patient digging his
fingers into her arm while a painful dressing took place.
His screams went on echoing in her ears when she walked
back through the cloister to the *abbaye*. Those who had
to endure the most painful dressings were revived a little
by a small glass of champagne afterwards. But each
dressing left them weaker and if they couldn't put up a
fight, they died. She was haunted by the fear that Mike
had endured such agonies; that David might be called
upon to face the same. The only blessing was that she was
too busy to have much time to brood.

She was thankful to be done with the German ward. So
many beds were now needed that every prisoner had been
sent on to hospitals in the rear and every bed now
contained a French soldier. On Sister Lyle's ward Polly
was happier and made fewer mistakes. Sister was young,
brisk and cheerful and made allowances for her amateur
helpers.

As the days passed, Polly found herself growing hardened to the sights and sounds on the wards. The office

work piled up but could only be accomplished in snatches when the girls were too tired to be either sensible or accurate. Still, orders for food and medical supplies had to be sent out somehow; much worse was the constant demand of the army for its nominal rolls. Woe betide the girls if they were late with that. There were afternoons when she and Delia got up after only a couple of hours sleep and dragged themselves to the office to try and put some order into chaos. They sometimes fell asleep at their desks and woke dry-mouthed and heavy-eyed to get some supper before going back on the wards.

It was May, the loveliest time of the year when the lilac trees bloomed, filling the air with their heavy perfume. The great oaks in the Forest of Compiègne were unfurled, ruffling in the warm breeze. The girls would snatch a walk in the fragrant air and then go into a marquee filled with the smell of gas gangrene, burns and picric: even with the sides of the tents rolled up, the stench was hardly bearable.

It couldn't last. The offensive petered out, the earth ceased to shudder, the long queues of ambulances stopped. It was then that whole divisions of the French army mutinied.

It sent a shock wave through the country. The *poilus*, deadbeat and ill-fed in the trenches, with little or no leave for months, were refusing to fight.

The first Polly knew of this was the day she saw a wounded man being carried away by the military police despite vehement protests from Doctor Gregory.

All the *blessés* were depressed and showed it. 'We shall never do it,' they said. '*They* have thousands of men. More and more come to take the place of the fallen. *They* are bleeding us dry. We cannot go on.'

It was a dangerous situation for here were men

369

acknowledging defeat, almost welcoming it because it meant the end of a prolonged agony.

'But the Americans are coming!' Polly reminded them as she washed them. 'We have only got to hold on until the Americans come.'

But the *poilus* shook their heads. It was too late. They were weary and disillusioned, sick of the war and longing to go home.

This was the beginning of 'the crisis of morale' as it was called, the direct result of the ill-conceived Nivelle offensive that had been so costly in lives and had gained nothing. When the news came that Nivelle had gone and been replaced as Commander-in-Chief by General Pétain, the mutiny began to peter out. More liberal methods and improved living conditions were promised, for Pétain was determined to nurse the army back to mental health. Until it was pronounced fit, there would be no more offensives.

'Now, *mademoiselle*, we shall go forward,' a *poilu* assured Polly. 'Now we need no longer be ashamed. Pétain will see to that.'

'And the Americans are coming! We *must* hold on.'

'And you, *mademoiselle*, what of you?' He had noticed her wedding ring. 'Where is your man?'

She met his liquid brown eyes, so full of sympathy that she had to turn away. 'I don't know. I think he may be a prisoner. It's ten months since he was reported missing.'

It seemed much, much longer.

By July, the hospital was back to normal and the orderlies could return to their own work. So at last there was time to sleep, to go to the bathhouse (a tent in the cloisters) and scrub off the accumulated grime.

Polly lay blissfully soaking as she planned the free day that lay ahead: the first for weeks. She longed for fresh air, longed to get the smell of putrefying flesh and picric out of her nostrils. The French front from St Quentin to Soissons was comparatively quiet now and there were no signs of a new offensive. Rumour said that only a few of the mutineers had faced a firing squad but that hundreds more had been pardoned. Sporadic gunfire still rocked the *abbaye* but even the enemy seemed content to get his breath back.

The sun shone warmly down on her bare head as she crossed the cloister and went up to her little cell to dry her wet hair by the window. In a strange way she felt at peace. It had been a near thing but she hadn't broken down in a panic during her time on the wards. Now she knew she could face it all again because now she wasn't up against the unknown. It was the unknown horror that terrified. She had gained something during those last terrible weeks. She was stronger.

She and Delia decided to spend their free day in Compiègne. There was accumulated pay to be spent on hot chocolate and amazingly good pastries in a favourite café and afterwards they raided the shops. These shops never ceased to astonish them. The front was not many miles away but here they could still buy silk and scent and there were restaurants and a hotel where one could get a good dinner with wine.

Later they found a hospital lorry at the station and were given a lift home by Ursula Gower. 'Mind, we're not supposed to do this so don't let anyone see you or we'll all be in hot water. I'll put you down fifty yards before the gates.'

'I'm not in the mood to tolerate petty restrictions,' Delia announced, waving airily to passers-by. 'Drive on, Gower, and if we meet the good doctor herself, I shall bow like royalty.'

371

'Oh, no, you don't – not in my lorry! Here we are so down you get. Ta-ta, old things!'

'Those ambulance girls are getting above themselves,' Delia said solemnly. 'That chit is particularly cheeky.'

'Know something?' Polly murmured dreamily. 'That bottle of wine has gone to our heads. I feel quite wobbly. After our prison diet our constitutions can't take high living. To tell you the truth – ' she paused, solemnly wagging a finger – 'I believe I'm going to float right up-up-up to the German balloons at Choisy-au-Bac.'

'A blissful feeling,' Delia agreed. Clutching her purchases, she was trudging ahead. 'Why can't we use bicycles? A bicycle apiece would make such a difference.'

'Have you forgotten? No one is allowed bicycles in the war zone. Spies used them a lot at one time so now they're forbidden.'

A glorious sunset, purple, gold and vermilion, was spreading across the western sky. Both girls turned to stare at it.

'I wonder if that's how it looks at home?' Polly said. 'Setting behind the church spire and pouring in at the bedroom windows?' Home seemed very remote all of a sudden, a place of the past.

On their way to bed, they looked in on the office, Delia groaning at the size of the post awaiting them. 'I'm not going to look at a thing tonight. Let it wait. It's our day off.'

But Polly had pounced on her own letters and was already reading one from her mother. Why didn't she write? Nell asked plaintively. It was over a month since they had heard from her. They hoped she wasn't going to be like Imogen and neglect them. *It's very sad about that nice David Ransom. Do you remember him? He was badly wounded near Arras –*

Polly suddenly couldn't see. She staggered, blindly,

372

reaching for a chair and hearing again in her ears the tortured clamour from the wards. Not David – oh, God, not David! – *His leg has been shattered, I hear, and there is a great deal of damage to his face.*

His face. That good-looking face had always been confident and smiling. Except once. That time outside the Ritz when they had said goodbye. She closed her eyes, seeing every detail of his face in her memory. He had walked into her life that day of Cass Byrne's bazaar, walked through the overgrown rose garden at Northesk to take her by surprise. He had known nothing of war then, had no foreboding of what lay ahead. Nor had she. They had been like a pair of carefree children, the future hidden.

Delia looked up, glancing across at her silent companion. There was something about the bent head, the stillness of the figure that worried her. 'What's up, old thing?'

'It's news of a friend of mine. He's been badly wounded. His . . . face. Do you remember that *poilu* in Ward B?' Polly looked up, her eyes holding hurt and horror. 'Sister said a piece of shell had turned him into a grotesque gargoyle under the bandage. He was married and had a family. The children wouldn't know him. They might even be frightened of him, refuse to come near. That's what Sister said.' Her voice shook and she crushed the letter in her hand.

Delia made sympathetic noises. She knew that Polly's husband was still missing after a year: who was this other man whose wounds affected her so deeply? She knew it would be no use probing: there was a reserve in Polly that couldn't be broached. But Delia wished fervently she would make a clean breast of her feelings instead of bottling them up and carrying that tortured look in her eyes.

As the days passed and no one wrote to tell her David had died, her hopes rose. If he lived, what did it matter what he looked like? He would still be David under the mask of a stranger and she would go on loving him just the same. But as another man's wife, she couldn't write what was in her heart; she had no right to.

Summer had come reluctantly but now it was here the marquees were stiflingly hot, despite having the canvas sides rolled up.

As Polly went on her rounds with the comfort basket, she found the men's spirits reawakening too. Except in the ward housing the gassed cases. Here a sense of despair lingered. The smell of burnt flesh hung in the air. Sightless, they lay like figures on medieval tombs, clothed not in armour but in the lint dressings cut to fit their bodies. These had been soaked in pure picric and castor oil: the combination of these smells was sickening. The men lay propped high against pillows, panting for breath as their lungs slowly and inexorably filled with water. For although their burns were grievous, the most dangerous aspect of being gassed was the form of pneumonia that followed. Yet they seemed frightened of only one thing: blindness.

'Sister, I can't see! My eyes – please bathe my eyes!' they beseeched several times a day.

So although it did no real good, nurses patiently bathed the gummed-up eyes with bicarbonate of soda and wiped the blackened lips before offering a cooling drink.

They lay motionless for an hour or two after these ministrations. Then the whispering, anxious cries began again: '*Mes yeux, s'il vous plaît!*'

Dreading the task, Polly forced herself to take her turn bathing sightless eyes, soothing anxious questions with the stock reply: 'You're doing very well. Don't worry.'

Relatives came from remote corners of France to cry noisily by the sides of the mummified figures. Afterwards, when they had gone, the men would be depressed. One said wryly to Polly: 'Marie-Josephe doesn't think I am a man any more under these dressings. But I shall soon change those words on her lips – see if I don't!'

Then, one day in August, the last patient had gone: buried in the graveyard near the forest or sent to a convalescent home on the coast. Because the front was quiet, no one came to replace them and everyone had time to realize how very tired they were.

'Well, Doctor Gregory warned me at my interview that she was looking for women as strong as horses,' Polly remarked, leaning back from her desk and stretching her arms wide. 'All I can say is that after the last few months *I* am now weaker than a kitten.'

The door burst open suddenly and an excited Kathryn thrust her face round it. 'Guess what? We've got leave! You and I, Vane, are to go on Saturday! There, what do you think of that? Home! Real beds! Food!'

But Delia was looking aghast. 'I can't possibly go on leave! Mother would think up a way of keeping me at home if I as much as showed my nose in Wales. Don't forget: I'm absent without leave from *my* home!'

'You don't want to go? You must be dotty. I'm going to pack.' The door slammed.

Delia looked glumly across the desk. 'It's true: I can't go. You take my turn, Polly. You look as if you need it. D'you know, your face is the most unappetizing shade of green – a sort of *eau de nil*, this year's smartest colour but not meant to be worn on the skin! No, I mean it. Honestly. Take my turn with pleasure.'

Polly didn't hesitate for long. 'Home! And my own bed for a week! Do you mean it, Delia? You're a saint!'

'I've wondered for weeks why I was sprouting knobs on

375

my back and ruining the cut of my blouse! Brand-new wings!' Delia grinned and went back to the accounts.

After her long and exhausting journey home, Polly got out wearily at Whitby and spotted her twin busily putting pennies in the chocolate machine. 'Archie!'

He ambled over and hugged her affectionately. 'I say, old girl, you do look cheap,' he told her comfortingly. 'Had a rotten journey? Here, let me take that.'

'Rotten,' she confirmed, shivering in the gentle rain that was falling like a thick mist over everything. 'Ugh! A sea-fret! Now I know I'm home. Have you got Pinky outside? I hope you've remembered to bring the carriage brolly?'

'Stop bustling me, madam! We're going to bear you home in style so pipe down.'

A familiar dark green motor was waiting in the station yard: the squire's Rolls, no less, with Woodcock holding open a door and grinning widely with pleasure. 'Welcome home, miss. We'll put the rucksack in the trunk, sir. Let me.'

Polly cried: 'How wonderful! I'm going to ride home in style.' Then she climbed in to find Katy, looking plump and prosperous, holding out her arms.

'Well, Polly love!'

'Oh, Katy, you've brought the squire's motor!'

Katy chuckled. 'It's mine too, remember?'

Polly sighed with bliss as she leaned back against the grey leather seat and Archie got in beside Woodcock. 'There's a lot to be said for being rich! Tell me, how's everyone at home?'

'Your mother's almost herself again. Your father's just the same, never complains and just soldiers on.'

'And . . . have you heard how David Ransom is? Mother wrote that he'd been badly wounded.'

If Katy noticed the tension in her companion, she pretended not to. 'He's home at Northesk, being nursed in the convalescent home so he must be mending. He was a friend of yours, wasn't he?'

'Yes.' But gladness was choking her. She would be seeing him before long! Seeing for herself how bad he was.

They were turning in at the rectory gates. Everything looked so dear and familiar and unchanged that Polly gave a huge sigh of relief. Suddenly she felt safe. And there standing in the porch was her mother holding Little Dick by the hand. And Little Dick was wearing a sailor suit with trousers!

'Oh, Mother, how lovely to be home. And Dick in trousers! He looks a real boy at last. Is it one of Archie's?'

'My darling girl, you look terrible!' Nell kissed her. 'Yes, it's a little suit that was Archie's when he was *three*. Dick is so much bigger – see how it fits him. Look, Dick, it's your Aunt Polly!'

The child stood his ground firmly as the stranger bent over him. He looked more like his father than ever, Polly realized. 'He's forgotten me, Mother. You've been over-feeding him, stuffing the poor boy with too much oats. Or was Archie really such a weed? Goodness, I'm hungry. Is there any tea?'

'You look half-starved. Thank you, Woodcock, put the luggage there. Katy, you're sure you won't stay? Then we'll see you and Wilfred at dinner tonight.'

'Dinner?' Polly raised her eyebrows as she followed her mother indoors. 'Eating what, may one ask? Have you been saving William against my return?'

'Polly! That old joke. Don't let your father hear you. You know how he loves that cat. Salmon from the Esk – that's what we're having. We've been given a beauty just when we needed it. The squire's bringing the wine. Now, darling, into the scullery with you. Mrs Linsey wants you to leave all your clothes there for her to deal with.'

'But, Mother – '

'Lice,' Nell said firmly.

'I haven't been in the trenches, you know.'

'We're not taking chances. Then after your bath you can come down in your robe. Father will be home soon. Archie, go and stoke the boiler again. I want plenty of hot water available for Mrs Linsey to wash Polly's clothes.'

'You've only just escaped being boiled yourself,' Archie murmured. 'It was quite on the cards this morning.'

Polly submitted meekly to seeing her clothes disappearing into a galvanized tub smelling strongly of Jeyes Fluid. It was bliss to soak in a hot bath and dry oneself on soft towels again.

A small log fire had been lit in the drawing-room to cheer the dismal summer afternoon and Polly curled up on the sofa in front of it and ate a hearty tea of boiled eggs, scones and strawberry jam. 'You people at home don't know how filthy our food is out there,' she said, her mouth full. 'Can I have another egg? I'm simply starving.'

The rector got up and fumbled through some letters on a table. 'My dear, we have some news. Nothing very definite but news of a sort about your husband.'

She braced herself. 'Oh, Father, is he alive?'

'I've been in correspondence several times with the Red Cross in Carlton House Terrace – that is the section dealing with the missing, you know. The Central Prisoners of War Committee at the War Office haven't been able to help at all. Walter Wynne has been up to Carlton House Terrace once or twice himself but, of late, the poor fellow hasn't felt up to it. I've taken over on behalf of you both.'

'Is – is Mike alive?'

'That we don't know but his mother thinks this piece of

news is hopeful. I wouldn't put it as strongly as that. The Red Cross Committee under Lord Robert Cecil have been splendid. The wounded in German hospitals have been questioned and gradually the prisoners' camps have been covered. It has taken time as you can understand.' He paused and looked at his daughter over his glasses. 'There is a man who is suffering from loss of memory in a prison camp. He had no identification, only his uniform half torn off him and a watch he still wore on his wrist. Walter Wynne's almost certain it is Mike's, one he had for his nineteenth birthday with initials on the back.'

'Yes. I remember it.' Polly was shaking, unable to keep her voice steady. 'Oh, Dad, it must be Mike – it must be!'

'We aren't certain, Polly. The man's head has been shaved for a head operation – '

'A head operation?' Her horror was making her sick.

'Apparently he was badly wounded after capture on the Somme. He has spent a long time in hospital. One has to be grateful that under the Geneva Convention the Germans have done their best for him. He has had a world-renowned surgeon, according to the Red Cross. We must remember that this man could be a stranger, someone to whom Mike gave his watch for safe-keeping when he went out on that raid – '

'But you said he was badly wounded after capture!'

The rector sighed. 'It's a jig-saw puzzle, my dear child. We're all trying to put the pieces together. This man is about Mike's age; he has blue eyes; he is the same height. That's all we know. We are doing our best to get him repatriated. A prisoner of war hospital is no place for him any longer.' As he put the letter in his daughter's hands he added gently: 'The evidence is very slender so don't build up your hopes.'

Polly read the long letter quickly. Then she looked across at her twin. 'Archie, what do you think?'

'The same as Father. We mustn't be too optimistic, old thing.' He patted her arm comfortingly.

She could feel their troubled eyes on her. For a minute or two, she was acutely aware of the scene in which they were all fixed like actors on a stage: her father was standing in front of the crackling apple logs; her mother sat very still, one hand on the battered silver teapot; Archie's hand still rested on her arm. She could sense their acute embarrassment as she said: 'We must just hope for the best, I suppose . . .'

She realized it sounded lukewarm even as she said it. Perhaps they expected her to burst into sobs. 'It's difficult to take it in yet. I've thought of him as dead lately. You must see that!'

'Yes, of course,' her father said hastily. 'It's been a shock. The last thing I want to do is to raise false hopes.'

She read the letter again as she dressed for dinner. Were they really talking about *Mike*? Or a stranger, someone else's husband?

She put the letter down and stared at herself in the glass. Her old silk dress, made by Miss Bonner for Girton, was hanging on her; she had lost a great deal of weight evidently. She and Mike would both have changed – he grievously so. She thought of herself as Polly Paget again, not Polly Wynne. Now it seemed she was Mrs Mike Wynne again; it was wicked not to feel glad, to be jumping for joy. That's what the family had spotted: her lack of spontaneous joy at the news of his resurrection.

Clenching her fists she laid her head on them. If only she could feel more! She had become used to his loss; she didn't belong to him any more. It was cruelly true but the whole war was cruel and millions were suffering because of it. Mike's image had faded so much; his face was hidden, his voice was silent. He had become like a dead man. And now he was coming back to life.

There was something else too: she had allowed another man to take his place in her life. She cared for David. Her feelings when she heard he had been wounded had been confirmed for her. He cared deeply for her too; he had written frankly to tell her so. Now she wasn't free to think about him at all, nor should she seek him out at the convalescent home. Mike was alive and back in her life.

'Mike,' she said in the empty room. But now there was only pity where she thought there had been love. Or had there always been pity and a desire to comfort a man whose nerves had been shattered by the war?

I was very young last year, she thought.

How quiet it was! In the world she had left, north of Paris, the guns would be sounding their evening 'hate'. The floors of the *abbaye* would be rocking, the windows shuddering. Queer how one missed them . . .

Part Three

'How can such a thing be endured by women? We have all been caught up into a Greek tragedy and are but gradually beginning to realize it.'

Entry 27 May 1915 in *Lady Cynthia Asquith's Diary*

CHAPTER TWENTY

The Healing Time

Breakfast was a noisy affair at Northesk now that Dan and Laurie were reunited for the summer holidays. Laurie had been going daily to the village school and she had grown up amazingly by mixing with the other children. She was seven and seemed at last to have forgotten her experiences of last year. Dan, on the other hand, was a dreamy, girlish boy, backward at his lessons and inclined to be tearful over trifles. He had been sent to a preparatory school near Harrogate and hated it. According to his reports, he excelled at only one thing: art. Apparently, he showed outstanding ability for his age and the headmaster wrote that as Dan showed no interest or aptitude in any of the other subjects, he doubted whether the boy would ever get to public school.

Reading this, Elaine sighed, tucking the letter into the pocket of her linen dress. How was the boy to be groomed to take his place some day on the boards of the various Ransom companies? Why on earth were her Ransom children inclined that way? Anna with her music and now Dan with his painting. Useless talents! If only Reggie were well enough to be consulted . . . David was certainly in no shape to give her well-considered advice. Perhaps Edward Brewer – no, this was a family matter and must be kept that way.

'Mother, can I go and visit David this morning?' Dan's large dark eyes looked anxiously into her face. He was small for his age and his head with its shock of dark brown hair looked too heavy for the thin white stem of his neck.

'Mother, I forgot to say my prayers last night!' Laurie

whispered urgently on her other side. 'D'you think God will mind?' She had a frightening vision of an old man with a beard sitting in his nightshirt on a cloud and pointing a stern finger down to the earth below. 'That girl Laurie Ransom has forgotten Me again!' She pressed closer to her mother. 'Nanny wouldn't let me say them this morning. She said there wasn't time. But I must pray for Daddy and David – oh, Mother, can I?'

Elaine groaned as she glanced at the clock. 'Oh, Laurie, those prayers of yours!' Laurie's prayers were long and loud with sleepy pauses between sentences. Anyone passing her door at seven o'clock in the evening was called upon to give theological advice. *Can I pray for the guinea pigs? Have they souls?*

'Can I go up and say them now?'

Elaine looked at Nanny, who was pouring out Dan's milk. They nodded at each other. 'Very well but only five minutes, Laurie!'

'David says Laurie is in danger of boring God,' Dan remarked in his precise voice.

'I'm not too!'

Laurie's passions were easily roused. Elaine said hastily: 'Go on, Laurie, and clean your teeth at the same time. Dan, when you're tidy and have been to the bathroom you can go next door and ask Matron's permission to see David for a short time. But don't tire him with a lot of questions, remember – oh, Mitchem, we're late but you can clear now,' and she smiled winningly at the elderly new parlourmaid it had taken her months to find.

'It's ever such a lovely day, mum. I said to cook this morning the young-gentlemen-next-door will be able to get out and sit in the sun today. It breaks one's heart to see them, mum, doesn't it?' She passed a window and stopped, the tray balanced on one hip. 'Well, I never! There's that poor Major Grantley and the new gentleman playing tennis – only two arms between them! Enjoying themselves like children they are – it does you good to see them.'

'Their spirit is wonderful,' Elaine said dully. It was a phrase much bandied about nowadays. *Their spirit is wonderful.* Remembering her son's scarred face, she shuddered: thank God, they had saved his left eye! Nevertheless that piece of shell had damaged him so thoroughly he would never again look like the handsome boy she had always taken so much pride in. The doctors had tried to reassure her: young flesh healed well. Later on they would operate to release the scar tissue puckering one corner of his mouth.

How she had wept when first she beheld him, bandaged round the head and face so thoroughly she hadn't recognized him. The memory of her bleak visit to that hospital near Boulogne would remain with her always. She had gone there convinced that he would not survive. They told her he had lost a great deal of blood from his smashed leg. But if gas gangrene didn't set in, he would have a chance.

It had filled her with sick rage to see that hospital filled with dying young men who should have been enjoying life like their fathers at the same age. Bed after bed was filled with grotesquely wounded bodies: the horror of modern warfare struck her to the heart.

She sighed as she stared unseeingly out of the window and down the rose garden. The second crop of roses, not so strong as the first, was now out. Perhaps she could spare the time later to dead-head the flower beds: it would help Elliot who had too much to do and who now performed six jobs instead of one. David's wounds, she thought, were not just those one could see. He was suffering from hidden scars. Aware of the change in his face, he was refusing to meet anyone outside the hospital.

387

Not even Cass Byrne had succeeded in running him to earth and, goodness, she had tried hard enough!

Oh, God, I'm depressed, she thought as she pressed both hands to her temples. It was an added complication to care so deeply for Edward Brewer. Was she suffering from a middle-aged wish to remain young and desirable? Most of her contemporaries were sinking back comfortably into the horrid prospect of old age. Why couldn't she?

Depression, never far away, had sprung at her and seized her by the throat. She uttered a muted strangled cry: without Edward she would have nothing to look forward to – *nothing*.

She couldn't give him up.

David had a favourite spot down by the lake where he liked to sit on fine days reading a book or simply drinking in the scene before him. He used a wheelchair to reach his hidden corner and had to be propelled back up the slope by any of his fellow convalescents who could walk and had lungs that worked. They would curse him mildly as they did so; they themselves preferred the brighter flower garden near the house or the tennis courts.

It was indeed a glorious morning with a blue sky filled with small puffs of cloud sailing to the north. The water glinted and broke into ripples as he threw crusts for the mallards crowding against the bank at his feet. Sometimes he caught a glimpse of the carp as they leapt for the bread. There were few brown trout although in his day his grandfather had caught them; there was a notebook in his desk to prove it. The day and the hour were recorded, the type of fly and how it was taken, all in old Leo North's fastidious classical writing. David smiled to himself: some day *his* grandson would be studying his fishing records in this same spot – that is, if he survived the war and married. Otherwise the estate was left to his half-brother Dan.

Overhead, birds rustled in the big chestnuts behind him; dancing shadows slanted across his face as he looked up into the leaves. This huge chestnut, the king of the group, must have been here for generations. That's what was beginning to fascinate him about his English inheritance; there were long lines of his forebears stretching back into the past and all had left a mark on this landscape. He would feel a traitor to leave this and go back to the States when war was over. He hadn't told his mother yet but he doubted if he would ever again live there permanently.

His head nodded and he dozed. The smell of the grass, the sound of insects and birds combined to soothe his unquiet spirit as no medicine could. This was a healing time for him; a respite to think and to develop new ideas. He was often amazingly content. This place where he had been born was weaving strong bonds round him.

'David!' Dan's shrill shout woke him with a jerk. He was running down the slope from the house with his arms full of painting materials. Suddenly he caught his foot in a tussock and rolled over, his precious paintbox spilling its contents over the grass. David could hear the little boy's lamentations as he crawled about collecting his possessions and examining the damage. His face was flushed and worried when at last he reached David's chair and poured everything into his lap.

'I've lost my red one and that tube of white Mother brought me from London.'

'Dan, old boy, what was the hurry this time?'

'I wanted to ask your advice. D'you think I should paint the lake or the woods over there? It's a question of light, you see,' Dan explained very seriously.

David bit back a laugh. What an old-fashioned little chap he was! Studying his brother's small anxious face he put a hand on Dan's head and stroked it. 'Will you be a painter when you grow up, d'you think? Or would you like to live here and look after Northesk?'

Dan's eyes examined him. 'But Northesk's yours. Nanny told me. You'll have to look after it, Davy.'

'But if I'm not here, Dan? Would you look after it if I gave it to you?'

The child thought in silence. 'I don't think so. You see, I'm going back to Boston some day with Dad and Mother. Much better if you looked after it yourself.' Then, in case this sounded too rejecting he added hastily: 'But I'll come over from time to time to visit you, Davy. You won't be lonely.'

'I'm sure I won't be.' He squinted at the lake. 'Better paint the woods behind me. The light's too bright on the water. It might hurt your eyes. Prop your board against my chair and sit in the shade. How's that?'

Dan nodded and stooped to fill his tin with water from the lake. Then he retired behind the chair and set to work. There was silence for several minutes and David was nearly dozing off again when Dan said: 'There's Miss Byrne from the vicarage and I'm afraid she's seen us.'

Hell! David thought, looking for a way of escape. There was none: Cass was advancing fast down the slope. Well, let her see his damaged face in the full light of day – oh, God, there was someone else with her. Another girl, walking more slowly but following in Cass's footsteps nonetheless. There was something familiar about the second girl's figure, though.

Suddenly he could recognize her. With a quick instinctive gesture, his hand covered one side of his face while his heart leaped in his chest and nearly choked him.

'Hullo, old boy!' Cass bent over him, solicitude in every curve of her large body. 'Caught you at last! Well, I usually run my quarry to earth given time!' She drew her breath in. 'I say! Tst-tst-tst. What a mess they've made of your face. I would hardly have known you. Will you always look like that?'

''Course he won't!' Dan had emerged from behind the chair. He looked at Cass Byrne with such open dislike that David could have laughed. 'You should have seen the piece of shell they took out of him. He's given it me. Would you like to see it?'

'Certainly not.' She brushed Dan aside for she had no time for small boys. In her view they were grubby and a nuisance. She indicated the figure slowly approaching them. 'You remember Polly Paget – sorry, I mean Wynne, don't you? We're going to play tennis.'

Polly's eyes had met David's. Hers that had held dread were clearing. She smiled as she held out a hand. 'Hullo!'

He took her hand, searching her face for the shocked horror he felt sure would be there. Then he forgot his own feelings in concern for her: she looked both older and thinner and there were blue shadows surrounding her large, expressive eyes. The hat she wore, a pale straw with a circlet of yellow-hearted daisies, looked incongruous above so worn a face. Beside Polly's face, the face of Cass Byrne seemed to him a mockery; round, pink and jolly, it was the face of an inexperienced girl who had not grown up. Her conversation matched her face, David thought caustically.

'I'm off to play tennis with that poor boy Grantley – the Australian,' Cass announced. 'Coming, Polly?'

'I'll join you later.' She was now sitting on the grass, her skirt spread out round her, her face in the shadow of her hat. Her head suddenly turned and her eyes met David's.

'God, it's been a long time!' he said softly. 'I've been hoping you'd get leave while I was here. Do you realize I've been here since my mother kidnapped me from Ste

391

Omer in April? She seems to have pulled some strings with someone in the War Office and I was borne home in a private ambulance and here I've been ever since.'

Her eyes, large and bright, were fixed on his face but she was silent and his own rush of words dried up. Involuntarily his hand went defensively to the scarred side of his face. 'Is it a shock? *This*, I mean?'

She was shaking her head and laughing tremulously. 'No – oh, no! I did so dread what it might have done to you – I've seen some terrible wounds in France – but you're still you. Oh, David, I'm so thankful!'

He fingered his scarred skin doubtfully. 'You mean that? It's not so bad as you expected?'

'Not nearly so bad. When the scars fade, you'll just look a bit tougher and more forbidding than before. You'll have to learn to smile more to make up for it.'

He grinned and then stopped abruptly because it still hurt him to smile. But his relief was immense.

'A few more smiles like that and you'll be as good as new,' Polly teased him.

'Will he?' Dan came round from behind David's chair and touched the scars very gently.

They had forgotten him and were startled.

'Do it again, Davy!'

David leered and then clapped his hand to his face in agony. 'Ouch, that hurt!'

'Well, no wonder,' Polly retorted bracingly. 'I daresay your face hasn't attempted a smile for months, has it? Is this your brother? Well, Dan, you know what you've got to do now, don't you?'

The boy nodded. 'Tickle him or tell funny stories. D'you know this one? There was a Scotchman, an Irishman and an Englishman in a train once –'

'That's enough, Dan. I'm not sure that's a very proper story you're about to tell,' David said solemnly.

Polly broke into helpless chuckles and David, holding his cheek in agony, joined in.

Dan regarded them scornfully. 'You're both silly. I'm going to play with Laurie,' he informed them and ran off, leaving his painting materials scattered on the grass.

'Oh dear, I hope we haven't hurt his feelings. He's a nice little boy.' Polly's eyes still sparkled with laughter. Taking off her hat she threw it on the grass among the paint tubes.

He could see her face clearly now that her hat had been discarded and there wasn't a trace of embarrassed distaste on it. It was true, then. His scars didn't sicken her as he had feared. A great wave of thankfulness washed away the last traces of self-pity and he longed to be able to jump up and swing her round in abandoned joy. Instead, he heard himself saying staidly: 'How much leave have you got, Polly?'

'Six days.'

'I want to see you every day.' She had been constantly in his thoughts for months: in the trenches; during bouts of pain in hospital. *Polly*, he had said to himself, the name a talisman to cling to. He felt the need to remind her of his disabilities. 'I'm an awful crock, you know. Do you think you can bear to come over to talk to me every day? I do so want to see you,' he added longingly.

'Of course I'll come,' she said warmly and put her hand on his arm. He snatched it and pressed it to his lips. She felt the puckered scar on one side of his mouth and felt a surge of love and pity that astonished her with its strength. She tried to take her hand away but he held on to it, saying something in a low voice. Was it *I love you*? It had sounded very much like *I love you*.

'Don't . . .' Her voice was muffled as his. 'Don't make it harder for us, David.'

Coming towards them across the grass, Elaine saw her

393

son holding the girl's hand. They were so deeply absorbed that neither saw or heard her approach. Oh dear, what a complication! she thought. This girl is married. He *can't* get involved with a married woman!

Someone near the tennis court had wound up the gramophone and strains of *Roses in Picardy* came floating tinnily across to them. Startled, they looked up and saw her approaching them and she saw by the expression on their faces that they loved each other.

Polly came over every day after that. Once she brought Archie whose one-armed state seemed to make him an honorary member of the Cripples Club as its inmates cheerfully dubbed the convalescent home. Soon he was playing one-armed tennis (service strictly underarm) with the Australians who were the noisiest and most irrepressible group at Northesk. It was during this week that David attempted to walk again but never when Polly was there. He exercised his damaged leg with ferocious determination; the muscles had become very weak and although the bones had mended he was unable to take a step even with crutches. So Polly (who was not allowed to suspect this weakness) wheeled him in his chair down through the park to their favourite place by the lake.

From the window of her sitting-room Elaine watched them with troubled eyes. Absorbed in talk, their closeness was evident. David's face as he twisted round to exchange laughter with the girl looked as it used to look before he went to the western front, his mother thought. Instead of being glad she was deeply apprehensive: what was going to happen when this camaraderie had to come to an end? The girl was married and there was no getting away from that fact. David had told her that the husband was missing and that a man answering his description had been found in a prison camp. So didn't he see how outrageous their behaviour was? What sort of young woman was this who was already getting involved with another man? Elaine asked herself with indignation.

Then, like a clap of thunder, it occurred to her: *her* sort of woman, for wasn't it exactly what she herself was doing? Had done?

Nonsense! she told herself briskly. It's entirely different.

But she knew in her heart that it wasn't.

Nevertheless, she decided she must talk to him as soon as the girl went back to her job in France.

On that last day of Polly's leave, David asked his mother if her cook could supply them with a picnic basket. They were going up on to the moors, he explained, in the rectory dogcart.

Polly drove and their progress was slow and filled with laughter at Pinky's antics. Never before had David come across such a wilful little pony with a cunning will of her own and he exhorted Polly to be firm as Pinky stopped dead and began to crop a hedgerow.

'Would you like to try?' Polly handed the reins to him.

'Right. A firm voice and a touch of the whip – where's the whip?'

'The whip?' Polly repeated in a shocked voice. 'Why, we're not allowed a whip! Father owns the creature and she's supposed to respond wonderfully to a kind word or two. Do try,' she invited, sitting back.

After two minutes David admitted defeat. 'At this rate we'll never get there.'

'When she's had enough we'll move off. You'll see.'

David looked at the rounded figure of the pony. Her mouth full of grass, Pinky turned her head and returned the look. Throwing back his head, David roared with laughter, as usual clapping one hand to his scarred cheek.

'Well, I'm glad you find it funny,' Polly observed. 'If Archie were here, he'd be simmering madly now.'

'But what's the hurry after all? Come on, Polly, we'll take the day at Pinky's pace. It's a beautiful morning and we've the whole day before us.' He put an arm round her and kissed her daringly. 'Oh, darling, our last day! Let's make the most of it.'

As if agreeing, Pinky moved on again. Down the winding roads into another riverside village. Then over a stone bridge and away into the rolling wilderness of the moors, purple with heather and smelling freshly of bracken and sheep. The road climbed like a long grey ribbon unwinding under their wheels and soon they could see the Hambleton Hills on one side and the Cleveland Hills on the other stretching into the blue distance. A brown beck accompanied them, running shrilly over brown stones and down into the valley to join the Esk. An occasional white puff of cloud sailed overhead and there was not another living soul to be seen. The war and the killing grounds of France seemed very far away.

Polly spread a rug under the shade of some ancient scrub oak and David looked round in a puzzled way as she helped him down and on to the rug. 'I've been here before. It's familiar.'

She nodded, smiling. 'On our very first picnic together. A year ago last Easter. The day you heard about the sinking of the *Oceana*. Remember?'

He nodded, his face grim. 'I remember. If that hadn't happened, we would have got to know each other then and you wouldn't have married Mike Wynne.'

'I don't know that that is true – '

'I wouldn't have let you marry him! I would have pursued you quite ruthlessly.' He leaned over and thrust a bottle of white wine into the beck to cool. 'Last time we were here I proposed a toast. "To us"! I said and you said – '

' "To our generation".'

' "Because our generation is going down the drain faster than flood water",' he quoted back at her. 'Darling, I didn't believe it then – I was so ignorant! Now I know how true it is. We shall be lucky to survive ourselves,' he ended, his voice low.

Pain burned dully in her at these words. She turned her head away. She wouldn't want to survive if David was killed when he went out next time. At his rate of progress he would be back on the western front in late autumn. She had fought against her feelings for this man for months and all in vain: they were growing stronger every day. How could she feel happy about their growing love when Mike – if Mike – She swallowed and said: 'Don't. I can't bear it.'

He turned her to him, his face alight. 'Polly, you feel as I do! Oh, darling, that's what I wanted to know!'

'David, we mustn't. Don't call me "darling". I'm married. Please, please help me to remember that,' she said with a sob.

He rocked her to him, feeling her slightness through the thin muslin blouse she wore. He could smell her scented warmth and the faint echo of her fast-beating heart. 'How can I? I love you too much. There's so little time left.'

Again she felt the twist of pain and, turning, pressed herself against him. Neither said a word for a minute or two. He was the first to recover. With a shaky laugh, he raised her head and said teasingly: 'What a stiff-necked New Englander I was the last time you and I picnicked here! Just over a year ago – it seems another life to me.

What did I say? I think I called girls who worked for the women's suffrage battleaxes, didn't I?'

She was recovering her spirits. '"We men like to think of our womenfolk safe at home. It's what we're fighting for."'

'You're making that up! I don't believe I was such a prig!'

'I'm not making it up, I assure you. Those words were graven on my heart after that day! I nearly hit you with the wine bottle! You were a little – er – self-satisfied.'

'Self-satisfied, was I?' He looked at her narrowly and then a smile began to break through. 'You're right! I was a blinkered fool.'

'I'm so glad you admit it,' she murmured demurely and began to unpack the picnic hamper. The dangerous moment was over. They had put emotion behind them and were teasing each other again. But they were closer to each other now – much, much closer. It was as if they had stepped across an abyss and landed safely on the other side.

'What is Mrs Wynne to you?' Elaine's voice was more strained than she intended.

David didn't seem to hear her. He was walking round the library with the aid of two sticks; he had made enormous progress lately and had moved back into his own room at Northesk House. 'See how I'm getting on, Mother? By November I ought to be quite fit again and able to have a medical board.'

'I know you don't want to answer me, David. You think it isn't my business, I suppose? But you're my son and I think I have a right to know what's going on between you and Polly Wynne.'

He looked at her levelly and slowly shook his head.

'You've no rights over me at all. I'm not a child. I shall be twenty-seven next spring. I'm old now compared to a lot of my fellow officers. My life is my own business, Mother, please understand that.'

'All I'm saying is the girl is married. The whole world can see you have some sort of relationship with her. It's not right!' Elaine added vehemently, hating her own shrill voice.

A little nerve twitched near the wound on his face. 'I think Polly and I must be the judges of our own conduct. Yes, she is still Mike Wynne's wife although he's been missing for over a year. Personally, I think the poor chap is dead; shells don't leave much of a human body lying around, you know. Someone like him has been found in a German prison camp and Polly is convinced it is her husband.'

'But can't the man himself speak?'

David looked out of a window. 'He's a cabbage. Better if he were dead.'

'Oh, David!' She felt sick.

'They removed a shell splinter from near the brain but terrible damage has been done. Perhaps it will heal – I don't know. I hope to God it isn't Wynne for Polly's sake. She only heard just before she went back to France. Poor kid!'

'I'm very sorry of course but she is still married and you ought to remember that.'

'Why?' He turned and looked at her coldly. 'It never made any difference to you, did it?'

She felt the blood recede from her face. Did he know – could he know about Edward Brewer? 'What do you mean?'

'Your early life wasn't exactly *comme il faut*, would you say? It's a bit rich preaching at me, Mother! You see, I've read all the old papers I found in here when I first arrived.' He limped across to a cupboard built into the bookshelves lining the room. There were two of these cupboards painted with bookspines to look like part of the library shelves, a device dear to eighteenth-century architects. Pulling open one of these, a heap of dusty newspapers tumbled out.

She stared at them aghast: newspapers, a quarter of a century old. She knew them as she knew the shape of her own hands. 'I – I didn't know they were there,' she said in a small voice.

'I never mentioned them because I didn't want the past to hurt you,' he said and pushed the papers back in the cupboard. 'Believe me, I would never have mentioned them if you hadn't been so hypocritical about my relationship with Polly Wynne.'

'Those papers – that case – they have nothing to do with you any more!' she cried. 'You ought to have burned them. You don't know the real story! That suit brought by – by Gilbert Argyle was a lie from start to finish! He won because he was powerful.'

'Then what was the truth? Can't you tell me? I'm a man, not a small child, Mother, and I'd like to know the truth.'

She bit her lip, colour flooding her face. 'I can't,' she said in a strangled voice. 'For God's sake, don't ask me!'

He looked at her steadily for a moment or two. 'Perhaps you'll tell me some day,' he said in a flat voice.

The pulses in her head were beating painfully. What was happening to them as a family? Never before had she and David quarrelled in such a fashion. 'I'm only concerned for your happiness.' But she knew as she said it that he wouldn't believe this. It sounded hollow to herself.

'Don't you like Polly?'

'I hardly know her. What I've seen of her is pleasant enough but I can't approve of her attitude. She has no business to have an affair with you when she is a married woman. One wonders what her people think. Her father is a parson after all.'

He could hear Polly's voice and her laughter: 'As the rector's children we're supposed to be sub-human! Thank goodness, Father doesn't expect it of us,' and his mouth curved in a smile. They had been up on the moors . . .

'Oh, you can smile, David, but facts are facts and if she's not careful that girl will get herself talked about. You too.'

'She was only married a week.'

'And regrets it bitterly, it appears.'

'She was only nineteen and immature. Young and headstrong and very much aware what was expected of her as the rector's daughter. So she didn't go up to London for an illicit weekend with Mike Wynne: she married him and now you want her to pay for her folly for the rest of her life! God, you *good* women sicken me!' He limped to the door and went out, slamming it behind him.

She sat slumped at her desk, feeling tears stinging her eyes. She had always so adored this son – Johnny Saxon's son. David said he had read those newspapers . . . then did he realize he wasn't Gilbert Argyle's son? He hadn't mentioned it. If only she could be sure about the girl! Did she really care for David or was it just that he was a rich young man who could give her a good time? Girls were so hard and calculating these days. It was all the fault of the war. Everyone wanted 'a good time' and all that this meant. As soon as one man died they attached themselves to another. If only she knew a little bit more about Polly Wynne! If only Reggie were fit and strong and she could run to him with this story and lean on his judgement and not bother her head any more – oh, how her head ached!

She was lonely and miserable without him and he was never going to be a husband to her in any sense again.

She wept into her handkerchief, her shoulders bowed, her face suddenly looking her true age. How horribly wrong everything had gone in the last two years! Oh, this war, this war!

Looking out of the window she saw that the weather was in tune with her spirits. A monsoon-type rain was descending in a dark pall over the garden, mercilessly destroying the remains of the herbaceous border. It was the worst autumn for years and the news from the front was in tune with it. The terrible battle of Passchendaele (as the third battle of Ypres was now being called) was being waged in a deep quagmire where men were sucked into the mud where they fell. She prayed vehemently that David's medical board would be put off as long as possible.

Mitchem came into the room. 'There's a lady to see you, madam, but she won't give me her name. She says it's urgent.'

'Who can it be, Mitchem? What sort of lady?'

'Young, madam. Very pretty but ever so wet, poor thing.'

'Show her in.' Elaine got up wearily, smoothing her hair. Collecting for a war charity, no doubt. She willed her face into a tentative smile of welcome.

The door opened again and a young woman was ushered in. She was dressed in royal blue and had just handed Mitchem her soaking Burberry. One damp black curl was pressed against a pale cheek, the rest was hidden under a close-fitting blue cap.

'Mother.'

Elaine gasped with shock '*Anna!* Good God, what on earth are you doing here?'

They ran into each other's arms, kissing and crying.

'Darling, how wonderful to see you!'

'Oh, Mother, thank God I'm home at last!' Sobbing

loudly like a child, Anna allowed herself to be put in a chair. She rocked to and fro, her hands covering her face. Incoherent words drifted from behind her hands as she struggled to control herself. 'Such a journey! Never will I forget it – oh, I'm home at last!' She raised a wet face. 'It said Red Cross Convalescent Home outside and I thought you'd left – gone away – ' Sobs shook her.

'But, Anna, I wrote you about turning Northesk into a hospital.'

'I never got the letters. I haven't been at the Wehners for quite a time. Oh, Mother, the only conveyance I could get at the junction was a farm cart! The boy was so kind and gave me a lift – not much older than Dan, y'know!' She was laughing and crying as she opened her arms wide to the fire. 'I don't feel I shall ever be warm again. What a terrible place – so damp and miserable. I don't think I like England much but I had to come.'

'Anna, what's happened? Something's wrong.' Looking back on the summer, Elaine realized that there had been no letters from her daughter. She had been so busy and time had flown so but she ought to have paused to worry and wonder at Anna's silence. *I haven't been at the Wehners for quite a time.* Never did she call it *home*, Elaine remembered uneasily. Now joining her family again she cried: *Thank God I'm home!* Elaine sighed with foreboding as she looked at the damp refugee sitting by the fire avoiding her mother's eyes. 'Dad is better. He'll know you but he can't speak coherently,' she added, giving Anna time. 'David is here. He's been nursed on the other side of the house since April but he's so much better that he's been discharged. Actually, I think he discharged himself! Matron can't do a thing with him.'

Anna raised her huge haunted eyes to her mother's face. 'That's really when I decided to come home. That and – and someone else. I was so unhappy with Carl and his mother. They said the Germans were winning and it would be best for the world if they did. They said the States had no business to get into the war. I wanted to kill them!' said Anna darkly.

'Why do you keep saying "they"? You are married to Carl, my dear, not his mother as well.'

'Much you know, Mother! I was married to them both. I hated them.'

'*Was* married? Where is Carl? Does he know you've come to England?'

'I've left Carl for good.'

Elaine groaned. 'Oh, Anna, no!'

Anna began to cry again. All trace of the vibrant headstrong girl had vanished and in her place was a frightened young woman.

'Don't cry, darling. Tell me about it later – '

'No, I must tell you now. Carl locked the house door against me. He shouted through the letter-box that I wasn't to enter his house again – he was going to sue for divorce.'

'But why? He can't do that – '

'He said I was a bad woman – he called me a Jezebel – '

'Oh, Anna, this is dreadful! Has he gone mad?'

'My clothes were being sent home so I went there too. Stanley and Mathilda looked after me until I got a passage on a ship to England. There were none to be had on the American ships so I came on an Italian liner to Genoa – oh, I thought I would never get home and my money was running out – oh, Mother, it's been a nightmare!'

Elaine got up and walked up and down the room, a frown on her face. 'I don't understand any of this. Carl goes mad, turns you out of the house and your money runs out. But you have your own money – Dad's settlement on you – '

'I couldn't get hold of any more so – so someone lent me enough for my passage to England. He's in England himself – Sam Murray.'

Elaine turned and stared at her daughter. 'Sam Murray! Of course! So that's what this is about. Oh, Anna, I do hope you know what you're doing!'

Anna twisted her hands, her mouth quivering. 'Yes, it's Sam. We love each other. He's come over here with Pershing's troops. Some busybody saw us saying goodbye at the docks and that's why Carl turned me out. But I'm glad about it – I can't bear Carl and his mother.'

'Are you lovers? Has Carl evidence?'

'Oh, no, we've never been lovers. But we shall be now,' Anna ended on a note of triumph. Her confession over, her spirits began to revive. 'We love each other. I ought never to have married Carl. You and Dad did push me, you know. I'm not going back to him – not ever! I want a divorce and Sam and I will get married.'

'Divorce is a horrible business. I know for I've been through it.'

'But, Mother, that was in the dark ages! People aren't such hypocrites now. Besides, look how happy you've been since you got rid of David's father! You will let me stay? You won't send me away?'

'Of course not. This is as much your home as mine and David will say the same thing. I hope you realize you will have to supply evidence for this divorce?'

'Yes, of course. I shall tell Sam and as soon as he gets leave we'll go away together. He's in barracks in the south of England – I forget the name. Then Carl will have to act. He says I'm a bad woman so I'll prove it to him!' Anna had quite recovered her spirits. She was in the bosom of her family and she felt safe.

Later, she will realize what the future holds, Elaine thought sadly as she rang for food to be brought for the traveller. She will be 'the guilty party' and will lose all her friends, be branded a bad woman and avoided by those who once sought her out, an embarrassment to everyone. I know all this too well. I only hope she is strong enough to make a fresh start in life/ – she's only twenty-one, poor child.

CHAPTER TWENTY-ONE

Someday When This Is Over

They had crossed the Channel at midnight as usual. A moderate gale was blowing and the passengers, a depressed bunch returning from leave, sat in close discomfort wearing their life jackets.

Polly felt herself to be a veteran, returning to France after nine months' service. She remembered vividly how bewildered and lonely she had been that first time. Now there was a warm glow of happiness inside her because she had found real love at last. She had asked her father to let her know at once when he got news of the man in the prison camp who could be Mike. She hoped for his own sake that it was Mike: whatever his injuries she would devote herself to his recovery but nothing could take away the feeling she had for David Ransom. Beyond that, she was not prepared to think. Remembering that hour on the moor was enough. And the little glow was stoked up to a fire inside her, causing her to smile to herself.

As she stood in the dark station yard at Compiègne hunting for an ambulance from the Abbaye Ste Catherine, she felt a sense of homecoming that was totally unexpected. The flashing lights on the black horizon, the figures splashing about in the dark muddy yard in the subdued lantern light, the mournfully hooting trains – these were the realities of life, not England and the rectory, the moors and David. They were only a lovely dream, totally unreal here on the French front.

She at last found a lorry loaded with medical supplies leaving the station. 'Hullo!' called the girl at the wheel.

'Wynne! Over here! Vane told us to look out for you tonight or tomorrow. Hop up.'

They drove out on to the rutted road, travelling slowly in the darkness with only a thread of light from their hooded lamps. 'It's still pretty quiet on this front,' the girl said. 'The *abbaye*'s half-empty. Just one or two wards given over to bronchial cases and trench fever. What's the weather like at home? I've never seen such rain as we've had here.'

'We had three or four decent days. But it's pretty wet and autumnal now after the gale.' Getting down into the ankle-deep mud, she thanked the driver and, hauling out her haversack, trudged to the huge oak front door. Shivering in the cold and wet she tugged hard on the bell. Presently it creaked open and Augustin's head appeared as he welcomed her back with beaming eyes and familiar hoarse voice.

'Ah, *madame*, you have reached us safely! God be thanked. It is a long way for you over all that water. *Mademoiselle* Vane wishes to see you in her room: she has refreshment for you.'

Delia had been sent a pound of tea from England and in her dressing-gown, her hair ruffled, was bending over a small camping stove balanced on her bed table. 'I heard you tramping across the yard and guessed you'd need nourishment. How are things at home? I rather thought you'd follow Kathryn's example and develop a convenient illness. No, Miss K is not returning. I guessed she'd skulk ages ago. Fair weather soldiers.'

'Well, her mother will be pleased. Oh, I'm thankful for this. I'm frozen to the bone.' Polly put down her cup and rummaged in her bag, producing a sticky parcel. '*Voilà!* Mrs Linsey's famed gingerbread. What can we cut it with?'

Delia produced scissors and hacked off two slices of the

gingerbread which, her mouth full, she pronounced 'absolutely yummy'.

'Yummy? What's that?'

'Ah, I have something to divulge. The Yankees are here – a whole American ambulanceful! Over the other side of the town. I've got to know one or two at Madame Luc's restaurant. Lovely boys with wonderful manners,' Delia said. 'This is delicious stuff. I'll have a trifle more if you can spare it. I've been longing for something sweet for days. Well, you've lost that horrid green colour, Wynne, and your hair is red again. It had gone quite a sad brown, my child. Wonderful what a couple of weeks can do.'

Polly, under scrutiny from a sharp pair of eyes, felt colour heating her cheeks. 'Yes, I had a lovely time. I slept and ate and slept and slept. Wonderful! I can't believe we took eight hours' sleep for granted once, can you? My leave was a sort of convalescence: as if I'd been ill and was just recovering. And yet soldiers on leave don't behave like that. They throw themselves into enjoyment as if for the last time – which it is sometimes. I suppose that's the difference. *Our* life is monotonous drudgery: theirs is lived as if every hour counts, which it does. Delia, when is this war going to end? *Three years.* It's horrible. And I've had news of Mike.'

'He's dead?' Delia said and put her hand on Polly's arm.

'No. We've heard that he might be alive and a prisoner. There's a man wearing his watch in a German prison camp – a man who's forgotten everything and everybody.'

Delia frowned, staring hard at her. 'But you don't believe it, do you?'

Polly took up her cup. 'Sometimes. Other times, no. The Red Cross are arranging an exchange of very sick prisoners of war. We shall know definitely then. I spent a day with Mike's parents at the end of my leave. They believe it's Mike. I long for it to be Mike, too. He did so dread dying. He called it *going out into the dark*. Yet it would be terribly cruel to bring him back to us with his mind gone, living in the sort of darkness he dreaded so much. He'd have nothing to live for.'

'Nor would you,' Delia said tersely. 'You'd be tied to a dummy. Do you realize what life will be like then?'

'Yes. But I'm his wife. I owe it to him.'

'Oh, Wynne, this war will have wasted your life!'

Polly didn't reply. Getting off the bed, she stretched. 'I must go to bed. It's nearly two o'clock and we're on duty in five hours' time and I feel I could sleep for ten! Just listen to the rain! Someday when this is over I shall remember this terrible rain and my perpetually wet feet and the chilblains on my heels. I think we shall have forgotten the guns and the shells.'

Delia broke off a last piece of gingerbread and sighed as she popped it in her mouth. 'I'll remember feeling hungry all the time,' she said indistinctly.

'Darling Anna,' David's voice said behind her.

Anna, who was unpacking, whirled round and into his arms. 'Oh, Davy darling, how wonderful to see you again!' She pulled her half-brother over to the window-seat. Her gentle fingers traced his still-sensitive scar, barely touching it. 'What have they done to you, Davy, those vile Huns!'

'We've done some pretty vile things to them too, my child!' He held her hands, regarding her searchingly. 'How have things been with you, Anna?' For the beautiful wilful girl seemed to have vanished. Gone were the smouldering, arrogant dark eyes, the spoilt mouth that could harden in determination. Anna's face was older and thinner with uncertain eyes and a hurt look to the mouth.

410

'We've both suffered,' he said gently. 'I'm not sure that your suffering hasn't been the worse. You must never go back to him, Anna – never!'

'Oh, Davy, you are a comfort!' The careworn expression lifted and Anna sparkled again. 'I'm going to marry Sam when I'm free. He's been so good to me. He wouldn't – wouldn't do anything to force the issue, to harm my name, but now that he's here with the first American troops – '

'No! Not old Sam? Here in England? Well, I'll be darned. So Ransom and Murray, Attorneys, are closed for the duration, are they? I hope I see him. Ask him up here, Anna.'

'Not on his first leave. We're going away together to provide Carl with evidence – besides we want to!' She chuckled, her old deep laugh of pure happiness. 'I adore the man and I'd never forgive myself if he went to France and I hadn't made him happy.' She stretched her arms wide. 'And it's much, much more fun than marriage!'

'You're a pagan, my girl. Have you seen Dad yet?'

'No, he was sleeping, the nurse said. I'll go now. David, will I find him greatly changed?'

'I'm afraid so.'

She tilted her chin, but her eyes held panic. 'I won't let him see that.' Tears flooded her large dark eyes. 'Just a short time ago we were whole and happy – all of us. Now . . .' She shook her head helplessly.

David limped to the door and held it open. 'It's no good thinking back to the past. It can do no good. Pick up the bits, Anna, and make the best of things. It's the only way to survive. What will you do over here while Sam's in France?'

She walked out on to the landing. 'I'm going to nurse in the convalescent hospital next door. As soon as Mother explained about it, I knew it was right for me. Then I'll

411

be on hand if I'm needed to look after Dad from time to time. We must persuade Mother to go away occasionally.'

David looked at her cynically. Poor little Anna! What a lot of shocks she was in for! He had suspected for some time that somebody drew his mother to London from time to time and had known for certain he was right when he saw that she received letters in a strong scrawling hand when she returned. She always put them in her pocket to read later but it was a man's handwriting all right. And she had the nerve to lecture him about Polly! He could have taxed her this morning when they were having their row but it hadn't seemed fair. Even if she considered his life was her business, he didn't believe he had a right to interfere in hers. But Anna would. Daughters were like that.

In December, David heard he had passed his medical and was fit for light duties. He had been bored and restless for three months, occupying his time writing to Polly and exercising his leg with dedicated fanaticism.

Elaine heard the news with a tightening of the nerves round her heart. So he was going back into the furnace. Well, she had known it couldn't last for ever, this respite from anxiety about her son, but she sometimes wondered if she would find the strength to bear it this time.

'Light duties means something behind the lines, Mother, so don't look so miserable!' He laughed cheerfully, delighted to be on the move again. 'While I'm limping they're hardly likely to send me into the front line – unless they're desperately short of men! But by the spring I should be fit for anything.' He stretched his legs before the fire. 'Thank goodness for the trees that came down in the gales! We don't have to worry about coal rationing here.'

She agreed mechanically, her thoughts far away. If only

she could pull strings through Edward for her son! Get him on the Staff perhaps –

'Mother?'

'I'm sorry, darling?'

'I said Anna's a new woman since she had that leave with Sam.'

'She's ruined herself, of course,' Elaine said with a sigh. 'But love certainly suits a woman and Anna looks like the happy girl she used to be. There's been no word from Carl, though.'

'Not to be expected yet. He's licking his wounds. Wait until his mother gets to work on him,' David said sagely. 'He'll divorce her all right. By the way,' he added casually, 'if I get the chance to go to Paris this time out I'd like to call on my father. Will you give me his address?'

She was horribly startled and her face went white. Giving her time to collect herself, he pretended to hunt for his diary.

So he hadn't tumbled to the fact that he wasn't Gilbert Argyle's son! Dear heaven! If he really knew the truth about his so-called father! 'But why do you want to see him? He's never done anything for you.'

'That doesn't matter. I need to see him. He *is* my father, after all!'

'Think twice before you do this, David. You might not find the person you expect.' Seeing him smile, she was sorely tempted to tell him the truth. The words were on her lips. Then she met his eyes: young, cynical eyes fixed on her; cool, young eyes ready to condemn, she thought, because he had not yet learned tolerance. Some day she would tell him but not yet, not now. 'I have no address to give you and if I had, I wouldn't,' she said in a quiet decided tone.

Anger flared suddenly in his eyes. 'But, Mother, I'm not a boy any longer! It's right that I should see him. He

413

is my father. Everyone has a right to know their own father, surely?'

She held her head high and met his eyes without wavering. 'You will never know him through me,' she said.

CHAPTER TWENTY-TWO
A Slow Relentless Slaughter

The hospital was only half full as winter slowly gave way to spring, and the French front remained comparatively quiet. It was believed that Pétain had at last succeeded in nursing the army back to health and sanity. Of all the mutineers condemned to death in the summer, only a handful had faced a firing squad. Now, after two successful minor engagements, the army's morale was restored; they had faith and pride in themselves again. Now the whole front was girding itself for a German spring offensive which everyone knew must come before the Americans arrived in force to join the Allies. Three divisions were on their way and another was about to set out. All their equipment had to be made in France or England and the factories were all working at breakneck speed to fulfil contracts.

Most of the patients in the Gregory Hospital were Senegalese units who were fighting alongside the French. They were particularly prone to sudden collapse in the prevailing cold and wet conditions. Their black skins became grey, their spirits apathetic and they died easily as snow and then drenching rain sapped their bodies and spirits. When they were first brought in, paralysed by the cold, their misery was pathetic and their large eyes looked up at the nursing staff without a gleam of hope. Most of them would have welcomed death as an escape from their unremitting suffering. Nothing in the comforts basket brought round by Delia and Polly fulfilled any need of theirs. All they wanted was to go home. But as soon as they recovered from pleurisy or pneumonia, back they went into the line to endure the icy rain that continued to fall in torrents.

In the tiny monastic cells, the hospital staff were also enduring the winter as well as they could. Newspapers and rags were poked into the cracks round the windows and under doors, and cardboard was fixed over the broken panes of glass; after years of bombardment there were few left intact. The black linoleum that spread from room to room was covered permanently with a damp bloom. Soon, the only sensible place to undress for bed was in bed itself. Discarded clothes were placed between the blankets otherwise they would have been too damp to put on by the morning for there were no wood stoves upstairs. The blankets were hairy army issue and contained no warmth. Everyone queued at night for hot water bottles but the cold was so intense that these were icy within a couple of hours.

The wind whined and whistled through the cracked window panes and so got on Polly's nerves that she always stuffed her ears with cotton wool. The cold she could endure but not that forlorn whining wind that only served to remind her that her happy-go-lucky youth had gone almost before it had begun. When the war ended – if it ever ended – she would be too old in spirit to be lighthearted again. And who would there be left with whom she could be lighthearted? No; her generation had been robbed of their birthright. But she didn't want to think about it yet. So she blotted out the sound of the wind while she searched for uneasy sleep and rose at seven heavy-eyed and still tired.

One by one, the staff themselves went sick and a marquee was set aside as their ward. It was bliss, Polly found when it came to her turn to succumb to a heavy cold, to lie in a warm bed, resting her aching head on a pillow and to feel a faint warmth from the wood stove in the centre of the tent. Here sat an enamel jug of cocoa, watery and dark brown until a spoonful of condensed milk was plunged into each mug. Several times a day the jug went round; it left most people with a distaste for the cocoa bean that lasted for the rest of their lives.

A week later, feeling restored, Polly went back into the *abbaye*.

Delia, who had gone sick and recovered the week before her, accompanied her to the wretched evening meal for which Polly had no appetite.

It was as they were finishing that Augustin came into the refectory and, on creaking tiptoe, approached Polly's chair. 'Pardon, *madame*, but there is an English officer to see you,' he said in her ear.

An English officer. Polly felt her face freeze. 'Thank you, Augustin. Please ask him to wait.' She waited with a pounding heart for the meal to finish. It was absurd to think it could be – Mike? Mike returned from the dead – seeking her out. It couldn't be David – not here on the French front even if he were back in France . . . What was she going to do if it was Mike? Her thoughts were muddled as she hurried down the corridor to the bare little room where visitors were received. Basket chairs and a few chintz cushions had been added to the austere furniture and helped to brighten the place but it was a dark little room all the same.

She felt her breath suspended as she pushed open the door. A tall figure in khaki rose to face her.

David had taken off his British warm and his cap. On his face was an eager look of anticipation.

She stared at him stupidly for a moment then with a little cry she ran into his arms. They stood wordlessly holding each other tightly: her face was crushed to his chest and his cheek was pressed to her hair.

417

'Darling, you're trembling.' I ought not to have surprised you like this.'

'It's not that. It's just – well, Augustin said an English officer and I thought – I thought – ' Her voice died away.

He put her from him and drew a chair forward for her. 'You thought it was your husband.' His voice was flatly matter-of-fact.

She nodded, biting her lip. 'I thought that Mike – I thought by some miracle Mike had come back from the dead and heard I was here. It was stupid of me.'

'It means he's never far from your thoughts. You still love him, I think.'

Dismay was creeping over her. His eyes were so stern, his voice so clipped. 'I don't know. How can I know until I see him? I believe he's alive . . . somewhere. I do wonder about him sometimes. I don't love him as I love you. I never did. But I shall never feel free to love you, David, until I know what happened to Mike. I wish you could understand, darling. He was so young. *I want* him to be alive – to have more of life than those few years.'

'I'm not such a brute as to wish him dead!' he exclaimed hotly. 'What d'you take me for? God! I know how precious life is! To be taken from happiness – you – everything – ' He turned away.

'I'm sorry,' she offered in a small voice. 'I didn't mean that.'

He turned back to her. With an effort he smiled. 'I'm sorry. I'm being a fool. I'll wait, darling. Some day this war will end and we shall know for certain then. However long I have to wait, I'll be there.'

If the war hasn't destroyed you first, she thought. There were tears in her eyes. Seeing them he took her hand and kissed it.

'I can't believe you're here,' she said, squeezing the

hand that still held hers. 'You didn't write, so I couldn't know you were in France.'

'I didn't write on purpose. I wanted to turn up – like this – and surprise you. It was a stupid idea.'

'It wasn't! If I'd known you were coming I would never have stayed in bed last week. I had a bad cold – we've all had it and the Commandant ordered us to bed one after the other. But if I'd known you were liable to turn up – ' Her eyes were eloquent. 'Can you imagine how I would have watched the door?'

He grinned happily, his confidence in her feelings restored. 'They've made me a junior liaison officer to the French. After next week I'll be at the GAN Headquarters in Clermont. That's quite near, isn't it? We'll be able to see one another sometimes.'

He wasn't back in the trenches! Her face lit up with relief and any lingering doubts he harboured about her feelings were dispersed for good. She looked at him as if she could never look away. How changed he was from the boy who had smiled at her that first time in the rose garden at Northesk, she was thinking. His face had craggy outlines now and a grimness of eye that had not been there then. The jagged scar from his wound last year ran like a pink tape across his cheek, from eye to mouth: that side of his face could never be the same again even if the expression in the eyes returned to gentleness one day. But would either of them be the same again? All her wounds were inside her and sometimes she felt they bled. She too was very different from the girl in the rose garden. How carefree, how young she had been!

She put out a hand and touched the scar very gently. 'How well you mend! It's faded beautifully.'

'The scar will never fade, I'm afraid. My leg's a miracle of wires underneath – '

'Don't!' she winced.

'Well, it's better than having an artificial one!' he pointed out. 'I'm absolutely fit, you know,' he added defensively.

'I know you are.'

To his eyes, she looked drained; much older. Her spontaneous smile was the one familiar thing in her small white face. Her eyes were bigger than ever and haunted.

'I wish you weren't here – so near the front,' he told her worriedly. 'I had no idea until I looked at my map that you're only a few miles from enemy lines. It's wrong. English hospitals are never placed within striking distance of Jerry. The French must be crazy to allow it. This is the war zone, fit only for casualty clearing stations.'

'This is not unlike a CCS, only larger, and we have two splendid operating theatres in the huts outside. We move patients on to Paris as soon as it's humanly possible but they would die in the train if we didn't keep them for a week or two.'

'But our trains are equipped like hospitals now! Why can't the French do the same?'

She shrugged. 'This is what they're used to: their hospitals are on French soil. Does it matter how near the enemy they are? We've been bombed several times and we're used to the sound of shells falling near. The Commandant says we shan't move. Must you go?' For she saw that he was glancing at his watch.

'I must. I'm dining in the mess at the French HQ tonight and daren't be late.'

They clung together. He held her so tightly that she felt her bones must break. 'I need you – need you so much. Don't stop loving me.'

'Never,' she promised, sick with longing.

He broke away with a groan, loathing having to leave her in this bleak place so near the front. As he drove back into the town he felt as if he had been visiting a prisoner

420

condemned to a long sentence. The smell of disinfectant, the bare whitewashed walls and the high, barred windows were reminiscent of a prison. It was no place for her, his love, his darling.

Rage filled him as he drove too fast and the motor protested. But he also carried with him the memory of her softness and the faint familiar scent of her skin.

As Elaine arrived downstairs dressed for the train, Anna came through the connecting door that led to the convalescent wing. She worked there now and was wearing the blue overall and cap that the unqualified helpers wore. It suited her admirably, her mother thought as she stood in front of the hall mirror adjusting her small fashionable hat made of feathers. Since going away with Sam Murray in the autumn, Anna's beauty had been restored and she looked vital and glowing again: love suited her as it did most women, Elaine told herself contentedly.

But at the moment there was a strange expression on Anna's face as her gaze went from her mother to the leather suitcase Mitchem was taking through the front door to the waiting motor car. 'Where are you going, Mother?'

Elaine drew on her mushroom-coloured suede gloves that wrinkled so satisfactorily round her wrists. 'To London. I must have forgotten to tell you before you went on duty last night, I've a list of things needed by Matron and several things to see to on my own account – ' She broke off: Anna, her face very serious, had gripped her by the arm and was firmly propelling her through the library door.

Closing the door behind them, she faced her mother. 'Why are you lying to me, Mother? It's a man, isn't it? I've guessed it for some time. After all, I'm not a fool or a child!'

'Anna! How can you suggest such a thing?' But guilty colour was darkening Elaine's skin. Their eyes met.

'I suppose it's because poor Dad's an invalid now.' Anna's voice was hard and steady. 'And, of course, you need a man. It's the way you're made.'

'How dare you talk to me like this!' Elaine blazed defensively.

'It's pretty cheap, Mother, you must admit. Besides, you ought to be done with that sort of thing at your age –'

'At my age!' Elaine gasped. 'Why, you little fool, I'm still young and – yes – I love admiration and affection and all that goes with it!'

'It's just bed you like and you know it!' Anna snapped. 'You wouldn't like to give up being Mrs Ransom, would you, Mother? If Dad divorced you you wouldn't have a penny. You've been eager to trap me into a loveless marriage with these rich Germans. It's what comes first with you, isn't it? Or perhaps I should say after the pleasures of the flesh?'

They were two women – not mother and daughter now – shouting unforgivable things at each other.

'You're an impossible little fool! I'm not surprised your marriage failed. How Carl put up with you at all astonishes me. He has all my sympathy!'

'That I was always aware of. You've never loved me. It's been David – David – David all the time! And I've known it.'

'Anna!' Elaine was weak with astonishment and horror. She sat down heavily in her father's old leather chair and stared at her daughter. There was contempt and anger on Anna's face as she stood over her mother saying these hateful things. 'You're a wicked girl to talk to me like this. It's so unfair – don't smile like that. Very well, it's true, there is a man in my life and I'm going to meet him

422

in London but only – only to go to the theatre and out to supper at the Connaught afterwards. What possible harm is there in that? Dad, poor darling, is in no condition to be worried by your feverish imaginings so don't attempt to bother him or I shall be angry and you would have to leave.'

'No, I wouldn't. *You* would have to leave, Mother. This is David's house and he wants me to stay.'

'You're talking rubbish!' Taking out a handkerchief she mopped her eyes, glancing at her wristwatch as she did so. Good heavens, at this rate she'd lose the train. 'Don't you think I deserve a break after all I've gone through?'

Anna's eyes were still smouldering. 'A break. Is that what it's called now? Not a dirty weekend? And before you throw Sam's leave in my face, let me tell you at once that I've been perfectly open about it and sent all the evidence to Carl. *I'm* not trying to hide dubious moral actions under the guise of a well-deserved *break*! You embarrass me, Mother. You see, I know.'

'Your mind's disgusting! What do you *know*?' Elaine was suddenly frightened. How on earth could the girl know? She had been utterly discreet – hadn't even gone up to London as often as she had longed to go.

'He telephoned last night. Oh, he was very discreet and pretended it was a business call. But he thought I was you at first and said "Elaine" in a confident and familiar manner that told me everything. He was confirming your arrangements if you want to know.'

Elaine felt a little glow lighting up inside her. Poor darling! He hadn't been able to control his impatience after all. She had warned him not to telephone but despite the fact that it sometimes took hours to get through he had done so. She ought to have sent him a note to reassure him that she was coming.

'You're not listening, Mother!'

'No – no, I'm not. But I am wondering what business it is of yours, Anna. I know you're unhappy and have had a hard time but there's no need to be jealous of me – '

'Jealous! I'm thinking of poor Dad!'

'Rubbish,' Elaine said crisply. 'You simply can't bear for me to be happy – you're just like your grandmother Otile Ransom. She was dog-in-the-manger about everyone. Her mouth ran down like this – ' and Elaine pulled at the corners of her mouth ' – until she grew two pouches of discontent on either side of it. *Very* ugly.'

With a smothered exclamation, Anna ran out of the library and crashed the door. Elaine straightened her shoulders and went to the waiting car where Mitchem was placing her crocodile dressing case on the floor.

'Your other case is in the boot, madam.'

'Thank you, Mitchem.' In a low voice she said: 'I want you to do something for me. Here is my telephone number in London. Don't show it to anyone. Keep it safe and use it only if there is an emergency. You understand?'

Mitchem looked scared as she put the piece of paper in her cuff. 'Like what, m'am?'

'Like any grave change in Mr Ransom's condition or – or – an accident or – '

'I understand.' Mitchem nodded her head so vigorously that her pinned lawn cap nearly came adrift. 'You can trust me, m'am.'

'I know I can.' As she drove off behind Elliot she felt a vast relief flooding her veins: for three or four days she was free of this vast responsibility – and Edward was waiting for her.

Anna went back into the study and shut the door, leaning against the cool wood with an aching head and heart. She ought not to have turned on her mother like that, she thought forlornly, but seeing her running downstairs to

424

prink in the mirror like a young girl had suddenly made her terribly jealous. What right had her mother to snatch this illicit happiness when other people were so unhappy? She had had her life! It was her duty now to stay home and nurse poor Dad, not to go gallivanting up to town to meet her lover. Hot anger made the girl clench her hands, seeing the garden outside the window through a curtain of tears. It wasn't fair! The old had had everything handed them on a plate: like the long years of peace when they were able to play like carefree children who need never grow up but who lived only to enjoy life. Anna remembered how her parents had set out for months in Europe every spring. 'Some day I'll take you, darling,' her mother had promised as she supervised the packing of her new season's clothes into several trunks. Instead, Anna had been persuaded into a 'safe' marriage with Carl Wehner while still only twenty. Her youth had been eroded by bewilderment and unhappiness and now the war looked like robbing her of the one man she had ever loved. No, it wasn't fair!

A terrible depression caused her to hide her eyes in her hands. Sam and she had been deliriously happy on their illicit honeymoon but then he had left for the front, part of the token force of American troops sent to keep French opinion quiet. Pershing, Sam had told her, was refusing to use his troops as a relief force to prop up weak parts of the line held by the Allies. They would have to be absolutely ready and fully equipped before he would agree to sending them in and even then it would have to be a piece of front given over entirely to the Americans to defend. No amount of bitterly worded reproaches from the French moved him from this all-or-nothing stance. The token advance force was his only concession.

So far, her darling Sam was safe and writing cheerful letters. If she should lose him – oh, God, she wouldn't want to go on living if Sam was killed! She scrubbed at her wet eyes. They had sent Carl all the evidence he needed to sue for divorce but they had heard nothing. Surely he wouldn't be so cruel as to refuse her a divorce after all? She wanted to marry Sam as soon as possible so why didn't Carl make a move? It meant she was living in limbo and this was an uncomfortable place to be.

'I think this must be the last time, Edward.'

He laughed under his breath and turned her to him. 'This is what you said *last* time, remember? That conscience of yours needs to be smothered – like this!' and he began to kiss her passionately once again.

But Elaine pushed him away. 'No, darling, *please*. I can't think straight when you make love to me. Can we talk?' It was two A.M., the bleakest time in the whole twenty-four hours when bogeys manifested themselves and regret took over, giving her nightmares. She had been dreaming of Reggie, had woken expecting to find him there beside her . . . 'We must talk.' She propped herself on one elbow, trying to make out his face in the dark. 'I can't go on coming up to London for nights with you. Anna knows. You shouldn't have telephoned, dearest, because you only confirmed her suspicions. We had a horrid scene before I left home.'

'Oh, darling, I'm sorry. Actually, it was your voice I needed to hear. D'you know, she sounds like you? I thought it was. But she's a woman not a child so why should she expect you to live like a nun? Elaine, Reggie could go on for years in his present condition. Surely you're entitled to some life of your own?'

'But the children, Edward! The children would never understand! David is twenty-six and I know already what his reaction would be if he knew I had a lover. If Anna tells him – oh, God, if Anna tells him, what am I to do?

They will hate me for ever. You see, it's different for women.'

'Yes, I'm afraid it is.' He reached over and took a cigarette from the box on the table. She winced as the smoke reached her: she had never allowed Reggie to smoke in their bedroom but Edward did it without thinking: he had slept alone for so long that he had got into bachelor habits. As she remembered this, she felt a twinge of remorse: how could she abandon him when he loved her so much? The change in him since the beginning of their love affair had been phenomenal. Gone was the melancholy reserve, the lost look in his eyes: he now looked ten years younger, an ardent man in love at last.

But there was Anna. And David.

He had taken her gently in his arms. 'I love you but you know that, don't you? I can honestly say I've never felt like this about a woman before. If you leave me now – well, life's finished for me.'

She kissed him. 'Wasn't that the chance we took? But I can't shatter my home, my whole background for you. Perhaps it's not brave of me but I have the two smaller children who need me – and there's Reggie. I shall always love Reggie and I must give him the best that is in me: he deserves that.'

Beside her, he was silent but she could feel the weight of his sorrow. They lay with their arms round each other, both bitterly unhappy, caught in the web life had woven round them.

With the lengthening days, an intense activity gripped the Gregory Hospital.

As the staff returned from their enforced sojourn in the ward, still woebegone and snuffling from the infection, the Commandant dragooned them into preparation for the spring offensive. Rumours were thick in the air. Some said the Allies intended to take a leap forward and finish the war at the beginning of March but most people favoured April. The weather remained vile. Rain poured remorselessly down and mud clogged the wheels of the ambulances and lorries.

As Polly and Delia splashed through the rain into Compiègne on a free morning, they walked without pleasure, just doggedly going in pursuit of an omelette lunch at a small café they knew. Passing vehicles spattered mud over their capes and Delia said grimly: 'We're mad to tramp like this but the thought of staying indoors is really too much. Perhaps it's being Scottish but the Commandant doesn't notice the miserable conditions. *Good girl – get a breath of air!* she told me as I opened the front door.'

'She's made of granite,' Polly agreed. 'We'll never be like her. Not after a youth spent in these conditions. The thought of Mère Baudouin's herb omelettes and wartime coffee is the only thing filling my horizon and making life worth living at the moment.'

They had reached the little town, once a charming little place set where the Oise and the Aisne met and became one broad river. Now the buildings were battered with windows boarded up; the main square was a sea of mud and the streets were choked with vehicles.

They darted across roads and down a side street to Mère Baudouin's. Pushing open a door, they saw that it was full of soldiers and a few nurses. Mère Baudouin and her niece Natalie, a pretty girl with roguish eyes, were doing a roaring trade. Heaven alone knew where Madame got her supplies, the Commandant had said, for she too was fond of the omelettes and pancakes turned out in full view of the customers.

The girls looked about them in dismay for there was not a free table.

Then a man in a strange olive green uniform rose and said: 'Excuse me, *mademoiselle*, but my friend and I are just leaving. Swallow that up, Charlie boy, and we'll be off.'

They were Americans, among the first to be seen in Compiègne apart from the American Ambulance Unit. They had ruddy faces and tranquil eyes; their movements unhurried and loose-limbed. It was impossible not to contrast their healthy faces with the hard-bitten, disillusioned faces of the Frenchmen at the other tables. Thin and drawn, their movements jerky, cigarettes held in not-quite-steady hands, these French soldiers were probably only a day or two out of the line. By contrast, the smiling doughboys were like creatures from another planet . . . and with a pang, Polly remembered that David had once looked like that. She thanked them, accepting the chairs they held, but was aware all the time of the bitter, dark eyes fixed on the Americans from all corners of the room.

'Well, if you're sure you've finished?'

'Sure, sure. You're English?' one said in surprise. 'Gee, I didn't know the English were here. Did you, Charlie?'

'We're at the Gregory Unit – the hospital run entirely by women.'

'Well, how about that!' Charlie seemed stunned as all males did at first.

'Look,' Polly said quickly, 'don't rush off because of us.'

'Thanks a lot.' They sat down promptly on the spare chairs. They both looked too well-nourished to be true and had left part of their precious omelettes on their plates to which they now added (first asking permission before lighting up) used matches and cigarette ash.

Charlie and Frank came from New Jersey and were soon pouring out their life stories over fresh cups of what they called 'cawfee'. 'It stinks but it's wet,' said Frank, draining his cup.

At the end of the meal it became apparent that neither man intended losing sight of their new friends. Putting on their Boy Scout hats, they pretended not to see the outstretched hands of farewell. 'We'll just walk around awhile with you ladies,' they said with friendly grins. 'Gee, but it's nice to be talking to a girl again!'

Polly shot a warning glance at Delia which Delia chose to ignore. She was enjoying herself and even if they bumped into the Commandant herself, she was in no mood to care: she had taken a liking to Frank and proceeded down the road at his side, chattering gaily about her friends in the American Ambulance Unit.

Polly and Charlie followed, Polly trying to keep up with the pair in front, Charlie deliberately dawdling. They came out into the main square and there, drawn up on the opposite side, was a khaki-coloured automobile with an English officer having difficulty starting it. As he straightened up with the starting handle in his hand, Polly saw that it was David.

'Oh, will you excuse me? I see a friend – ' and she darted across the square, springing over the puddles and calling out breathlessly: 'David! David!'

His face lit up. 'Well, what luck! I was going to call in to see you when I got this darned engine going. Who's the Yankee waiting with such a possessive air?'

'He's called Charlie from New Jersey. That's his friend Frank walking ahead with Delia. They're awfully nice boys and just landed I should think. Anyway they're determined not to lose sight of us and I hardly like to be unfriendly.'

'Hardly,' David grinned. 'They're lonely, poor devils. I'll have a word with him in my best Boston voice – the nasal one you think so funny!' He crossed the road and spoke to the American as they saluted each other. They smiled, Charlie laughed and presently they parted, Charlie throwing a farewell salute in Polly's direction.

David returned. 'It's fine. He understood. Get into the car, Polly, it's raining and I want to talk to you.'

Inside, under the hood on which rain pattered, it felt like a world of their own. They kissed, a long kiss of the thanksgiving and joy that was always in their embrace now.

'If only you were free to marry me.' There was a world of longing in his voice.

'Oh, David, I wish it too! You know I do.'

'I was coming to see you, to ask if we could get a couple of nights together somewhere.'

She sighed. 'How I wish we could. But it's impossible.'

'Is it, d'you think?'

In the silence that followed he fumbled for his cigarette and lit one with his trench lighter. She could see his grim profile outlined against the yellow-shaded mica window. The raindrops on the canvas hood became suddenly louder and she pressed close to him. All hope seemed to die out of her. Life was hell. You couldn't call your soul your own without movement papers, couldn't go away with the man you loved without officialdom poking its nose in and making everything ugly. 'Oh, hell!' she said savagely and he broke into a laugh for he had never heard her swear before.

'What is it, love?'

'Oh, David, *us*! Where can we go? I get so little time off.'

'Would you come away with me if it could be arranged?' he asked tentatively.

'You know I would.'

'Then ask for a couple of days' leave – no, make it three – and a pass for Paris. I'm due to go there next week. We can have two nights and three days in a good hotel. Think of the baths! Think of the food! Think of *you* . . .' He kissed her longingly.

She drew a long breath. 'Oh, do you think we could? Oh, David, it would be something to look back on – three days – three whole days!' Tears had sprung to her eyes: if he's killed, if I have to go back to Mike, she was thinking. Three whole days to last the rest of her life.

For answer he bent his head and let his firm, warm lips travel over her face and eyes to the hollow of her throat. She could feel herself dissolving under his touch, murmuring his name under her breath.

His last kiss was one of rough despair. 'I must go, love. So must you.' He hated leaving her more each time. Putting her from him he jumped down and savagely turned the starting handle. This time the motor burst into life and she roused herself, preparing to jump down. 'No, stay there. I'm going to run you back to the hospital. I'm not having you walking down that road alone.'

Ten minutes later they drew up outside the main gate.

'If you were married to me, I wouldn't let you stay in France,' he warned her. 'I hate to think of you in this bleak spot. Besides you're far too near the front.'

'I wish you wouldn't worry about me. I'm a veteran now. Can any of us be safe? I don't think so.' Flinging her arms round his neck she whispered: 'I love you, I think.'

They clung silently together then he pushed her from him and opened the door. He could see her small figure reflected in the mirror as he turned and drove away. She looked very vulnerable. This bloody war! His eyes were blurred with the pain of parting from her. To think that only a couple of years back he had been eager to join in the 'adventure' of this war! It was no adventure. It was just the slow relentless slaughter of the youth of the

432

world. When it ended, and if they survived, they would have forgotten how to be young and carefree. There would be no place for them.

He was glad he hadn't told her of his plans; that he had asked to rejoin his regiment before the spring offensive. His leg had healed completely and every man was needed if this war was ever to end. So he would be leaving the French front and moving north again before the end of the month. Time enough to tell her when she joined him in Paris.

CHAPTER TWENTY-THREE

A New Plague

Mitchem's voice down the telephone was agitated. 'Is that you, madam? I've had ever such a bad time getting through. Quite half an hour I've been – '

'What is it, Mitchem? What's wrong?' Elaine was struggling into her wrapper as she spoke.

'It's Miss Laurie.' The voice faded.

'Hullo? Mitchem?'

Mitchem's voice suddenly came back strongly. ' – sent all the children home because of this influenza. Nanny took her temperature and put her to bed.'

'Well, I shall be home tomorrow. Tell Nanny to – '

'Excuse me, 'm, she's worsened overnight. We think you ought to come.'

Elaine rumpled her hair distractedly. 'But how ill is she? Is Mrs Wehner there? Ask her to come and speak to me.'

'She's with Mr Ransom. He's poorly-like. Nurse Matthews has the weekend off, mum, if you remember, so Mrs Wehner's seeing to him. Oh, mum, I think you ought to come! The little girl's asking for you,' and Mitchem drew a long agitated breath clearly audible down the phone.

'I'll come on the next available train. Tell Elliot to meet me at the junction from five o'clock onwards.'

But how slow the train seemed when at last she was on it! Why did fate make her the special target for its darts? Elaine asked herself resentfully. As if the very act of love had to be punished! Edward too had been resentful at her sudden departure but her concern was now simply for Laurie.

There were lights shining from all the windows on their side of the house, Elaine noticed as they drove up the drive. No one had given a thought to the black-out obviously and this spoke volumes to the anxious woman in the motor car.

Mitchem swung wide the door. 'Oh, madam, thank heavens you're here! She's been asking for you.'

Elaine let her draw the heavy sable coat off her shoulders. 'How is the child? Has the doctor been?'

'Bad. Nanny's not left her side today and Doctor Mallory is coming back last thing tonight. Run off his feet he is. They say Stan Hodges came back on leave with it and gave it to the Umplebys – he's courting Sue Umpleby – and they all got it. Little Alf has died of it, cook heard.'

Elaine's heart quailed. With leaden feet she mounted the oak stairs. 'Where's Mrs Wehner?'

Panting behind her carrying the dressing case, Mitchem said: 'Oh, she's asleep, madam – '

'*Asleep?*' Elaine whirled round. 'How could she be asleep with her sister so ill?'

'But, madam, she was up with the little girl all night to give Nanny a chance of sleep. Then she had Mr Ransom to see to – he's not been at all well today – and we persuaded her to lie down before dinner and she's slept right through it.'

'I see,' Elaine said dully. Last night she had been lying in Edward's arms while here at home Laurie called for her in her mounting fever. She was filled with remorse.

Nanny sat by the bed in Laurie's room where a shaded lamp burned. Nodding at her, Elaine went to the bed and knelt by it. Laurie turned heavy eyes towards her. 'Mother . . .' she managed through cracked lips.

'Yes, I'm here, darling. Go to sleep. I shan't leave you.'

435

The child's skin was dry and burning, her eyes half-closed as if the lids were too heavy. Elaine held her and felt the unnatural temperature of the little body against her own. Turning to the nurse, there was naked fear in her eyes. 'What does the doctor think? Does he give it a name?'

'Flanders fever – although some call it Spanish flu,' Nanny whispered. 'It's been brought home by the soldiers. They say it's raging on both sides of the western front.'

'My God.' Elaine felt black despair seizing her. They had all read rather fearfully of this horrible fever that was spreading in France and now in England. No one knew how it had started and it killed the very old, the very young and the under-nourished. Was that fever raging in her child's body? Icy hands seemed to be gripping her throat; she could hardly breathe. Fear. She had felt the same fear as the *Oceana* went down. They had nearly lost Laurie then. She swallowed, struggling to be calm. Gently putting Laurie's head back on the pillow, she got off her knees. 'I must go to my husband. He will know I'm back – yes, I'll eat soon but not just yet.' Eat? She would choke if they brought her anything.

In his bedroom, Reggie was propped up on a mountain of pillows watching the door fixedly. As she came through it he gave a little cry of welcome, the noise he made instead of the smile he could no longer execute. No one had been in to switch on the lights or draw the curtains against the cold night and it was only by the burned-down embers of the fire that she could see him.

She kissed him as he murmured, 'Lau – ie?'

'Laurie's sleeping, darling. A nasty bout of flu. What have they been about to leave you alone like this? The fire's nearly out and your hands are cold.' She swung the handle of the bell and Mitchem came in hurriedly, her

436

lawn cap askew, her apron still yesterday's, Elaine now noticed.

'You need a fresh apron, Mitchem, and please pin up your hair and straighten your cap. Do you realize your master's been left sitting in the dark? Put more coal on the fire and draw the curtains. I'm going to have dinner here with Mr Ransom. Bring some veal broth and a cutlet and the egg custard Mr Ransom has every day. Ask cook to lace it with rum tonight. Oh, and open a bottle of that white wine Mr David gave us. See that it's well chilled, please.'

Mitchem was looking scared. 'I'm ever so sorry, mum, but there's no veal broth made today. Nor the egg custard. Cook's been that upset and we've all been at sixes and sevens. I don't know what cook has available for dinner.'

Elaine restrained herself with difficulty. 'I see. Well, I don't know what's been going on while I've been in London but my staff seem to have lost their heads. Bring us what's available and tell cook I shall expect her explanation tomorrow morning. Bring up the wine as soon as it's chilled, please.'

As the door closed behind a chastened Mitchem, Elaine sat down on her husband's bed and took his veined hand in hers. 'Darling, I'm not going away again. I'll send to London in future for all that's needed in the convalescent home.'

He was looking at her with an anxiously searching gaze that smote her afresh. She was bitterly ashamed. She was a cheat – an out-and-out cheat! Red colour swept her face and neck and she leaned forward and held him in her arms. How thin he was! How white his hair had gone! Oh, Reggie, Reggie, if only we could go back to 1915 before our world collapsed! she cried wordlessly.

He bent his head and laid it against her breast. As she stroked his cheek, she felt moisture: he knew. Oh, God, *he knew!* With a strangled cry she hugged him again and again. For a long time they remained like that. Perhaps he was trying to convey his understanding and forgiveness. She had no means of knowing. But it had made her feel better towards herself.

Anna in a dressing gown, her cloud of dark hair lying round her shoulders, came into her father's room as they were finishing a makeshift dinner hurriedly put together by the cook. Her eyes were still heavy from lack of sleep.

'Oh, you're back! No one woke me.'

'We wanted you to get some sleep. Go back to bed. I'll put your father to bed tonight and I'll take the night watch with Laurie – no, I'm not tired. In fact, I feel at the moment as if I'll never sleep again. Have a tray brought to your bed and get a night's rest then you'll be fresh to take over tomorrow. Nanny needs a night's sleep too.' She broke off to listen. 'I think that's the doctor's car. I must go.'

Anna slipped into her mother's chair as the door closed. She took a sip of wine from the glass on the table and sighed heavily. Then she looked directly at her father.

'Dad, I'm sorry. Please forgive me. I shouldn't have said those unkind things about Mother to you. It was unforgivable.' She bit her lip. It was frightening to have to confront that rigid face. 'I was wrong. Of course she hadn't gone to London to meet a man – I think I must have been a little mad.' Did he believe her? His eyes were unblinking. 'I – I'm in a very nervous state. It's all the worry about Carl and the divorce – and Sam on the western front. Oh, Dad, please understand!' She waited anxiously, watching his face for a sign. She wished to God she could control her unruly tongue. He had seemed to collapse when she poured it all out yesterday: for a terrifying moment she thought she had killed him.

Suddenly she got a sign. With a great effort, the corner

438

of his lip rose. It would have been a leer in anyone else but it was Reggie's attempt at a smile.

'Oh, Dad!' she sighed and kissed him as generously as she had done in childhood. 'You're a darling not to hate me.' Then she whisked off to the door. 'I'm hungry. I must get some dinner.' She blew him a kiss and was gone.

He watched the door close and the light died out of his eyes. He knew for certain now that Elaine was being unfaithful to him, had indeed just been to London to meet her lover. He knew her so well. The poor darling was so transparent in her contrition. And Anna's vehement denial of the story she had recounted so angrily yesterday was added confirmation. She regretted telling him the truth now that her mother was home and Laurie so ill.

He didn't grudge Elaine her love affair. She needed love and he could only give her the gentle affection of a spent force. For someone like Elaine this would never be enough. Well, for twenty-three years they had been wonderfully happy and he had never felt the need to wander. They had both gone through divorces in their youth and no one had expected them to make a success of their marriage, least of all his father, he remembered. The old man had been suspicious of his son's English bride for years; but even he had succumbed to her before he died. For nearly every night of those twenty-three years, they had slept locked in each other's arms: one flesh, one mind. It was now all over. If he had the means and the courage, he would put an end to his life. But they kept his sleeping pills well away from him. If he couldn't die, he would retreat into his shell and leave her to her lover. He would pretend not to see or hear what was going on. His heart quailed at the thought of giving her to another man but he mustn't be a dog-in-the-manger and force her to share his misery. He must let her go free.

* * *

As always in difficult situations Elaine became a bundle of raw energy, imperious in her demands on her staff and helpers. With Laurie so desperately ill she spared no one.

That night Laurie's temperature reached 104° and Doctor Mallory's face was tight and grim. 'There's no more we can do. We must just wait and pray. Give her cool drinks and sponge her all over every hour with a sponge wrung out in cool water. I would try and find a nurse but there's no one left in the district. Mr Ransom's nurse is on holiday? Recall her – but leave it till tomorrow.'

Elaine winced, seeing the implication in these words: by tomorrow Laurie might not need a nurse . . .

'Have you asked Matron Higgs if she can spare someone for a couple of days? Don't worry. I'll ask her myself. I have to visit one or two patients there after I've washed.'

He was back in twenty minutes, saying bleakly, 'I'm sorry but Matron can't – er – see her way clear to spare anyone. She's shorthanded, I believe. Just carry on and I'll be back tomorrow morning about eight.'

'That bitch of a woman!' Elaine exploded when he had left. 'I could kill her! Of course she could spare someone – the place is half full now. I'll not forget this,' she added, wondering how she could punish the plump, pale-faced woman who was always such a thorn in her side.

'Oh, Mother, don't let's waste our energy thinking about her!' Anna begged. 'Let's arrange a rota for you, me and Nanny. It will only be for a few days anyway.'

It will only be for a few days. Elaine's heart twisted with anguish as she hung over the semi-conscious child who was still drenched in sweat. She knew the crisis must come soon.

All night she sat, hardly moving, by the child's bed watching the shallow rise and fall of the narrow chest. Now Laurie looked much younger than her eight years; a

440

baby again with a baby's faint whine to attract attention. Elaine soothed her with the same words she had used long ago: a gentle humming, a light patting, stroking the hair back from the cold, wet forehead. 'Go to sleep, darling, Mother's here.' As she stroked she remembered that the red-gold hair was the colour Reggie's had been when she first met him.

She got up and went to the window. How frighteningly bleak it was outside! A dark purple sky was swollen with rain clouds and the surrounding bare trees looked like imprisoning iron bars. God is punishing me, she thought resentfully. All those nights with Edward were to be paid for in the death of a beloved child. Leaning her head against the icy pane of glass, she let the tears fall down her face. Incoherently she tried to pray: *Not Laurie. Please don't take Laurie!* She knew that she had sinned but God knew that she was too weak to resist what her body craved. Oh, how bitterly He was punishing her! He had given her back David and then, heedlessly, she had carried on in her own selfish way and now she must pay.

Confused, faint and dizzy she turned back to the bed. *But this time I mean it – oh, God, believe me, I do mean it! I'll be good and never see Edward again. I promise.*

All that night she watched, never dropping into sleep for an instant. She was going to fight every inch of the way to keep Laurie alive and if it meant pouring her own life's energy into the child, she would do it.

'Mother, you look on the verge of collapse,' Anna said, leading her away at seven o'clock.

'She's still – alive. Watch her – please, please, Anna, don't let her slip away!'

'Lie down, Mother, or you'll be ill next.' Anna went away and returned bearing a tray of breakfast followed by Mitchem carrying extra pillows and a basket of logs for the fire.

'*They*'ve cut down our coal ration again, madam. We should be at the top of the scale with all these rooms – eight hundredweight, Elliot says, but the man – he's that cheeky, too – said we had only to cut down some more trees if we wanted to be warm. They do say he takes the rest home for himself, the scamp, but Elliot's cut down the old apple trees and here they are, smelling ever so nice.'

Elaine hardly heard her. 'Run after Mrs Wehner and give her a message, Mitchem. Tell her to let me know at once of any change in Miss Laurie – she's to tell Nanny that, too. They must wake me at once. Has Mrs Wehner got Mr Ransom up yet? I ought to go across and see for myself but I can't . . . take . . . another step . . .' was her last waking thought as her head fell back against the pillows.

She didn't know how long she slept but she was almost at once, she thought, aware of Anna's voice. 'Mother! Mother, wake up! There's been a change, Nanny says. Her temperature has dropped quite a lot – that's good, isn't it?' Anna's troubled face swam before her mother's eyes as she jerked awake.

'*No*. Get the doctor on the telephone. Run – ' Elaine ran in her nightdress across the landing and up a flight of stairs to Laurie's room. Thrusting Nanny aside, she gathered the child in her arms; she felt icy. *Let her live. Let her live. Let her live*. In rhythm with the words she was rolling Laurie in a blanket, applying a hot bottle to her feet, rubbing her unresponsive body through which the life force was ebbing.

Afterwards she remembered this hour as the exact moment she left the youthful Elaine behind for ever; that wilful, ridiculously youthful, silly woman whom she suddenly hated. In that February dawn of 1918, that woman vanished for good; grey hairs began to sprinkle the thick,

442

glowing hair. Age laid its tentative finger on her, withering something inside.

Suddenly, the doctor was there, taking Laurie from her.

'Is she dead?'

He shook his head. He had put his thermometer under Laurie's tongue and was holding her wrist. 'She's collapsed. The temperature went down too suddenly.' He reached into his bag for a syringe. 'Can you fetch Nanny?' he said casually. 'I want to show her how to do this – '

'Let me.'

'No, Mrs Ransom, I want Nanny.'

Obediently Elaine stumbled from the room and so didn't see the violent effect of the injection on Laurie. Nanny was crying loudly on the landing, convinced her charge had died. Anna sat stony-eyed on the stairs.

'Hot bottles, Nanny. As many as you've got.' The doctor didn't look up.

For half an hour they worked on the child; somehow they kept her breathing.

Mitchem appeared at the door with hot tea and Elaine realized it was only nine o'clock and she was still wearing her nightdress.

The whole house waited, holding its breath.

Six of them set off from the Abbaye Ste Catherine on a cold, dark February morning: Doctor Sarah Chester and four nurses going to England on leave and Polly with movement papers for Paris. She had been nervous asking for three days' leave but, as it happened, Doctor Gregory had decided to give everyone a short break in turn before the push that was expected at the end of March.

As her train jerked and rattled the thirty miles to Paris she leaned back against the hard seats, realizing for the

443

first time that she was dog-tired. She hoped fervently that this fact could be concealed from David.

He was waiting for her at the station, a tall figure in breeches and a British warm, with a red flash on his cap. As he spotted her a delighted grin lit up his face, causing the long jagged scar to look like a crease in his cheek. Swooping on her, he lifted her in his arms and swung her round. 'Darling! You look like a funny little mouse in that cap!'

They clung together. It felt like coming home to her.

'I know I look frightful but I've nothing else to wear except this beastly uniform,' she told him as they walked to the barrier.

'It's priceless!' He burst out laughing. 'Who was the genius who designed such a fascinating disguise for a beautiful girl? It's better than false whiskers and spectacles! No *poilu* would give you a second glance!' and he went on laughing immoderately so that morose Frenchmen turned round to stare.

'Ssh – ssh!' She pinched him indignantly.

He wiped his eyes. '*And* two sizes too big for you, love! Oh, darling, it's the cruellest thing I've seen in this war!'

'Doctor Gregory knew what she was about when she designed this,' she told him primly, caught his dancing eyes and broke into laughter, telling him what Archie had said when he first beheld it. He was in tremendous spirits and she felt her erstwhile tiredness falling away like an unwanted cloak. Hailing a taxi, he directed it to the rue de Rivoli.

'We're staying on the rue de Rivoli? Me in these clothes?'

'Nearby. But we're going shopping first.' He turned and took her in his arms, pulling off the tea-cosy cap and bringing her red hair tumbling down. Then he kissed her all over her face. 'Love's a glorious thing,' he whispered.

'It mended my wounds last summer. Oh, darling, I love you, love you!'

She was breathless, crushed in his arms. 'Oh . . . David . . .'

The cab driver watched complacently in his mirror. Ah, love was a glorious thing, indeed!

'We're going to get rid of these prison garments. I've made enquiries and I know the very *modiste* to take you to.'

'I really *am* a kept woman now,' she murmured.

Paris, she could see at once, was in tremendous fettle. The soldiers were decked out in scarlet and blue with swinging capes and white plumes. They swaggered along like conquerors with fascinating little fashion plates on their arms. Polly found herself gaping with amazement at the long kid boots and short full skirts, the kiss-curls and kepi hats worn by the girls. There was an air of extravagance about: almost one could smell it on the breeze that came through the cab window. It was quite different from London, Polly thought with excitement: they were only forty miles from the enemy but the Parisians were displaying the *élan* for which they had always been famous.

David took her from shop to shop buying everything she would need for their few days together: delicious underwear frothing with lace, kid boots and an outfit that took her breath away; a mistletoe green velvet coat and skirt collared and edged in sable with a sable cap to match. Her red curls sprang up round the cap to frame her excited face. I'm shameless, she said silently to her reflection. This makes me a kept woman; a mistress with her lover – and I love it! I love it!

'Darling, you look wonderful!' His eyes met hers in the mirror. 'I wish we could burn those other hideous things but it would get you court martialled or something.'

All her tiredness and depression had vanished: she felt

alive and pretty and full of life again. I'm costing an awful lot, she thought, but was wise enough not to say so aloud. He wanted to shower things on her and both of them knew that this might be the last time he would be able to do it. If Mike returned . . . or if he were killed . . . No, she loved him too well to stop him. His pleasure in her new appearance delighted her.

They got to the hotel in time for lunch and while he waited, she went up to their room to change out of her uniform. 'I'll be quick,' she promised.

He waited on a banquette opposite an ornate mirror. Now and again he inspected his scarred face. She hadn't mentioned it but it still looked pretty horrible; his mouth would never recover its normal shape on one side. He turned away with a rueful smile. Christ! what a fool he was being! As if a few outer scars mattered. She loves me as much as I love her. I'm a lucky beggar to have found such a woman and I refuse to think beyond this week.

He turned back to the mirror again and saw her reflection coming down the stairs; she was in the green outfit. He caught his breath: she was much more beautiful than he had remembered. Her face was thinner, and had interesting hollows, it had matured since the summer. Her blue eyes caught the light from the chandeliers as she looked for him, one hand on the banister, and he saw other men looking at her. But she didn't notice; she was searching for him and when she found him she smiled with happiness, and came across the foyer.

He stood up, waiting for her, a little smile on his lips. *Even if this is the last time, this is a last goodbye, we shall have known what it is to love.*

As she walked between people to reach him she felt so full of love for him that she thought she would brim over with it. *Never did I feel like this about Mike. What a child I was to mistake pity for love.*

446

She put her hand in his.

'I've ordered champagne,' he said.

'Perfect. I've never felt more like champagne than at this moment,' she said softly.

How they had spent each of the three days she could recall afterwards only as the scraps of torn photographs viewed through a kaleidoscope. She could only remember him: the feel of him; the clean smell of his skin; the little snores he was guilty of when he went to sleep with her arms round him. *The last time*, she told herself, wide awake, *this is the last time*. She believed he didn't know this himself; he appeared to her to be living only in the present and to be happy. But she slept very little, savouring their closeness and dreading the coming of each dawn. So they lay in each other's arms, talking, making love, waking for two mornings with the joyful knowledge that they could spend every minute together. These were the things she was never to forget. To be adored so wholeheartedly put a new sheen on her beauty. Those three days in Paris with her lover changed Polly. She knew that they had no future but whatever happened she would always have this memory of their time together as her armour-plating throughout her life. It wasn't enough but it was something and she was grateful.

The intoxicating feel of her body in his arms brought David a healing comfort that would take him through to the end of his life, whether he died next month or lived into old age. He would never really be unhappy again because he had possessed Polly and nothing could take this away from him. They loved each other. If he survived the war, he would fight to take her from the husband she didn't love. Their love mustn't be wasted despite her scruples. But he didn't tell her that.

All too soon it was the last day.

All night it had been one long goodbye. Neither slept much. They talked quietly together, giving each other strength for the inevitable parting. They had a late breakfast brought up and then they strolled in the Tuileries Gardens where the nannies sat on benches keeping an alert eye over the children playing under the bare trees. Here they lingered, watching the Punch and Judy show, and the old man who sat calling, *'Viens! Viens!'* to the birds to come and eat the breadcrumbs he held out to them. A thin sunlight had come out; it was the first week in March and there was a smell of spring in the air. But instead of bringing hope, this first sign of spring brought dread to Polly's heart. He had told her yesterday that his job in liaison was over and he was going back to the regiment in time for the spring offensive. They walked under the trees, their feet kicking up the remains of last autumn's leaves, their voices matter-of-fact but their hands tightly clasped. Now and again Polly would say: 'What time is it now?'

She didn't have to comfort him as once she had comforted Mike before he left for the front. It was David who comforted her, who dried her tears and told her the war would be over soon – perhaps with this last big offensive. And when it was over they would straighten everything out. They would be together, never to be parted again.

He put her on the train and gave her a last prolonged kiss. 'Goodbye, my love. Don't forget I love you.'

'And I you,' she whispered, clinging to him. 'Always. Whatever happens.'

Then the train went out swiftly and as he walked back alone he stumbled into a luggage barrow because – quite suddenly and stupidly – he couldn't see at all clearly.

* * *

She was back in Compiègne by the evening and sleet had begun to fall. Augustin's eyes were worried as he opened the heavy oak door to her. 'Oh, *madame*, it's so sad that you are to leave me! All – all to go. What shall I do then?'

'*Leave*, Augustin? Are you sure?'

'Very sure. Today – tomorrow perhaps – the hospital goes to Paris leaving poor old Augustin on his own to guard the abbey against the Boches!'

So, Polly thought depressedly, it had come at last: the Germans were considered to be too near for safety and the hospital was retreating to the rear.

Delia confirmed this; she was already hard at work packing up the office. The drawers of the filing safes were open and she was in a fine muddle. 'Yes, it's true. The Commandant wants to stay but General Franchet d'Espery himself has ordered us back. I think we've found an empty mansion on the outskirts of Paris. Talking of which, what was it like in the fair city? Did you have a wonderful time?'

Polly smiled. 'Blissful. It's gone too soon.'

Delia was looking at the cardboard box at Polly's feet. 'Hm. Ill-gotten gains by the look of it. Generous fellow.'

'Wait till you see it! It's delicious velvet and fur and – '

Delia closed the lowest drawer with her heel and snorted. 'My God, Wynne, you're living in a fool's paradise! Velvet and fur forsooth! It's going to be sack-cloth and ashes from this day forward so get started, my girl. There are all the nominal rolls to do.' Dumping files in a large box, she dusted her hands. 'The Germans are expected to try and break through on this front, you know. Not a pretty prospect if all we hear about them is true. Rape and pillage are just everyday fare to them, so Doctor Gregory has agreed to retreat. She feels it, poor darling, having sworn to stay put, but her interview with

449

the general appears to have unnerved her at last and she's scuttling.'

All next day they worked at packing up the office. The Germans were rumoured to be making a move at the end of the month when the ground would have dried up after six weeks of snow, sleet and torrential rain.

'Do you realize it's spring?' Delia said one evening at the end of the month. 'Listen to the birds!' A distinct twittering was to be heard as they leaned out of Delia's cell window.

'This has been the longest winter of my life,' Polly said under her breath. 'I've been expecting to get news of Mike but my father says there's a hold-up. The Germans are demanding too many conditions before they repatriate.'

'They're an arrogant people,' Delia snorted. 'When I think they might conquer us – ' She left the sentence unfinished.

The Commandant rose from her seat at the end of supper one evening and told the assembled staff her plans. The move would begin soon with the despatch of the marquees to the château south of Paris now commandeered as their hospital. 'French Headquarters are obviously expecting a thrust directly through Compiègne towards Paris and under the circumstances I have had to obey and retreat. You will, I'm afraid, have to make do with bell tents for sleeping accommodation but with the coming of summer that should be no hardship.'

Someone muttered loudly and Doctor Gregory looked sharply round the tables. The muttering subsided. But the grumbles were louder as they repaired upstairs to start packing.

'Bell tents! They're ovens in summer!'

'Nowhere to hang a mirror!'

'But no windows to get shattered,' someone suggested. 'I've been sleeping with my head under the blankets for months and it will be a relief to breathe the air again. I've had awful dreams.'

It wasn't fashionable to be philosophical about the move. Everyone was discovering how attached they were to their bare cells, to the little town itself. It was terrible to think it was going to be shattered by the coming offensive. Already, someone said, most of the citizens had left.

Three days later, on the morning of Thursday 21 March, at first light, Polly was shaken by Delia. 'Wake up, Polly! It's started! Do wake up and look!'

Polly struggled to a sitting position. 'What is it?'

Delia, clad only in pyjamas, was hopping from the window to the bed. 'Oh, Polly, just come and look! It's a stupendous sight! Can't you feel it shaking this place to its foundations?'

Polly joined her at the half-boarded-up window and stared eastwards. Then she looked at Delia. 'That's not our front – it's much further north.'

Against a sky that was mistily green, the fires of a deadly furnace were licking upwards like the tongues of a hundred dragons. Starshells of burning white were lighting up the horizon from east to west. Polly was right: the guns were pounding the British front from Amiens to Ypres. It was not yet their turn.

Three weeks after his short leave with Polly in Paris, David was back in the line five miles from Villers Bretonneux. Here, General Gough, C-in-C of the Fifth Army, had recently set up new headquarters. Villers Bretonneux was a small town only a few miles from where the river Ancre joined the Somme. A British army hospital was being hurriedly dismantled and sent to Abbeville and

David hoped devoutly that Doctor Gregory was dismantling her hospital too; the thought of Polly's dangerous position worried him every day.

Lying on the floor of a wrecked farmhouse in his sleeping bag he was unable to sleep. The night was uneasily quiet, the moon obscured by thick fog. Everyone was in battle order and waiting for the enemy to make the first move. As he turned over he was aware of pain in his old wounds; his leg was stiff and aching dully. If he had been alone he would have got out of his sleeping bag and moved about a bit. But nearby Lieutenant Chisholm was fast asleep and snoring loudly and it would have been a pity to wake the poor devil from his snatched sleep.

A rat was scuffling near his head and he cautiously sat up, looking for something to throw at it. He hated the hump-backed creatures although they were such familiar denizens of trench life.

As he rumpled his hair he was aware once again of the heavy feeling of depression that always gripped him on first waking up. It was hell to dwell on such sweet dreams with Polly flitting through them only to wake to the foul reality of war. Had he ever really considered it an adventure? He must have been mad to think of it in such a way. It was a daily hell of fear and discomfort and misery.

Downstairs he heard the platoon sergeant rousing the men. Today they were going back into the trenches to relieve the Hampshires who had been having a quiet time of it this last week. Hardly any activity from the enemy side; it was as if a giant was holding his breath.

Chisholm was snoring louder than ever: what a noisy beggar he was! 'Chiz! Chizzy! Shut up, there's a good fellow.'

But Chisholm didn't hear a word, no doubt dreaming of the girl he had married on his last leave. He had bored

452

the mess to distraction with his talk of Marjory, the sweetest girl in the world, producing photographs daily like rabbits out of a hat.

There was that rat again. Looking for their rations no doubt. The little wretches were now so bold that they were often found foraging in one's pack.

Suddenly a tremendous barrage opened. Chisholm sat up with a bounce. 'What the hell?'

'Come on, it's started!' David yelled and was out of his sleeping bag in a flash and looking out of the glassless window. The sky was scarlet as if the universe were on fire; the noise was so paralysing that he couldn't move from the window for a long minute, fascinated by the terrible sight. Surely there had never before been a bombardment as fierce as this one?

A series of thunderous crashes that shook the flimsy remains of the farmhouse suddenly galvanized both men. They finished buttoning their uniforms and the rat dived for cover on an overhanging beam.

A loud whine filled the air. And another. There was a flash of blue and white and in a cloud of rubble the remains of the farmhouse blew up and subsided.

The German barrage was not being directed on the front line trenches but was systematically raking the communication area. Through the noise and cries of the wounded, David could hear the fierce roar of a fire gaining hold on the dry timbers. He tried to move but something heavy was pinning him down. The suffocating smell of cordite was nearly choking him and he gasped as he pushed at the heavy weight on top of him, pushed with a demonic strength he didn't know he possessed.

Rolling it off him he struggled to get to his feet. Then he saw the body of Lieutenant Chisholm. He was headless.

'Oh, God.' Turning away, he was sick. Poor Chiz – poor little devil –

There was blood all over him; Chisholm's blood, for he himself seemed miraculously unscathed except for a minor scratch or two.

'Mr Ransom! Here, sir!' His platoon sergeant was pulling him over the rubble. 'No, leave him, sir. We'll fetch him out – Lewis is seeing to it with the other men. Yes, six dead, sir. And a couple more wounded.'

Seven dead before they had even started to man the trenches. It was a fiendishly clever plan, David told himself as he leaned against a stone wall and tried to pull himself together. The enemy were going to wipe out the reserve force before they attacked the front line. Nothing like this terrible bombardment had been seen before. Perhaps it was the beginning of the end. He felt so tired that he could hardly summon up the energy to care.

Within a day or two it became clear that the main strike was against the British front: the Germans were attempting to blow open a gap between the British and French. Advancing quickly, they were punching the British right flank, causing it to wheel back. The Great Retreat had begun.

From Compiègne, a fearsome red glow could be seen lighting the north-west sky. By a superhuman effort, the French were managing to close the gap on their front, but nothing was managing to halt the retreat that was turning into a rout.

A notice went up in the *abbaye* written in the Commandant's hand.

The battle that commenced on 21 March is so far confined to the British front. I have therefore decided that our hospital under the Croix Rouge will remain at the Abbaye Ste Catherine. All plans to retreat to Paris have been cancelled.

Vive la France!

They weren't to go! Delighted, everyone began to unpack, to prepare the wards to receive the wounded. Little did they know that Doctor Gregory had made the decision to stay in the face of a warning from General Franchet d'Espery that the French still expected the main blow to fall on the French and American lines in a German bid to reach Paris. She was Scottish and obstinate and knew the whole hospital wanted to stay. Besides, the roads and railways were blocked with refugees and reinforcements. It was too late to move.

Turning from the notice board, Polly saw that Augustin was openly weeping. With his kepi pressed against his stomach he did not attempt to conceal the tears that rolled down his wrinkled face into the white whiskers. She took his gnarled hand. 'Augustin! What is it? It's not your son, is it?'

'No, *madame*. Louis is safe so far.' He struggled for words. 'I weep for France – for *la belle France*, my country. The barbarians are taking it from us. Soon they will be in Paris!'

'No, they won't. You must remember we have the Americans with us. They are on the Marne. They stand between the enemy and Paris. And they're fresh strong troops, Augustin, not tired out like us. They won't let the Boche reach Paris!'

Augustin looked sceptical: who knew if the Americans were real soldiers? Some said they hadn't had a war in years! 'You feel sure, *madame*?'

'Yes, I'm sure,' Polly lied, smiling reassuringly. 'That's why we are staying, you see.'

'My old woman and I – well, we shall not leave even if

455

the enemy come right here to Compiègne. We shall die in our home rather than give an inch to the Boche!' Augustin's eyes kindled with a martial light and he briskly removed the tears from his face with a large bandanna which usually lived round his throat. 'I shall kill at least one before I go!'

Turning away, Polly went back upstairs with a heart that seemed made of lead. She could pretend to be cheerful but in reality she was filled with a deadly fear. She reached the top of the stairs feeling sick and dizzy. *It's too much. How can we all go on?*

By the beginning of the following week, the Abbaye Ste Catherine was flooded with wounded. The 'Fall-in' was now heard with frightening regularity.

Polly and Delia felt like veterans as they went to give a hand in the wards. Even so, as Polly entered Sister Torrance's marquee on her first night on duty to find Sister and her nurse busy draining a shoulder wound, she felt a throb of instinctive revulsion. It was always a sight she shrank from. To see the nurse's relentless hand pushing a red tube into the body of a shrieking patient while the other nurse held him down, was more than she could bear to witness. She was turning away, intent on finding work out of sight and sound of the scene, when Sister Torrance looked up and spotted her.

'Wynne, have you scrubbed up? Then help Vickers with this drip-can. I must go and look at Number Eighteen: he's sinking.'

Despite possessing a tongue like a whiplash, Sister Torrance was a good person to work for. She was a tall, cool woman with prematurely grey hair who never expected too much from her amateur helpers and who encouraged where she could not in all honesty praise. So

Polly congratulated herself on being on her ward tonight: at least Torrance didn't frighten her like Sister Pitt.

A steady stream of orderlies were still bringing in men from the theatre as she went to help Vickers, a slight girl with a gentle voice who never seemed to tire. She watched as Vickers's steady hands capably inserted a tube into a great gaping wound in a man's side. The man screamed, clutching Polly's arm in a grip like iron. Somehow, she managed to hold the enamel bowl for the pus and blood to run into, somehow she continued to murmur soothingly in French. 'Not long now, old fellow. Just hold on to me –'

Suddenly, his grip relaxed as he fainted.

'Thank goodness.' Vickers pushed harder. 'Get him a little champagne from the cupboard when he comes round, Wynne. It helps to lift their spirits. Then follow me to the next bed as quickly as possible.'

At midnight, Number Eighteen died, unable to hear the last rites being muttered over him by the old *curé* who seemed to live at the hospital now, and Polly went to indent for a shroud. As she came out of the marquee she could see the black forest fringed with a scarlet glare to the north-east. She shivered, hurrying towards the *abbaye* with Sister's torch in her hand: in the day, she tended to forget that the enemy were the other side of that sinister forest. The noise of the guns was very close tonight, too. For the first time she felt terror mounting in her: if the advance continued at the same pace, they must surely lose the war.

She reached the yard and paused: a sound that was somehow reminiscent of a beehive reached her ears and she saw that more wounded had arrived and were lying in serried ranks on stretchers. The low hum was the sound of their moans. She wondered dizzily where they would find room for them all.

When they had time to notice, the girls realized that spring had come with a rush of colour and heat. The country round Compiègne basked under a hot sun. The great oaks in the forest were in leaf. The valleys were softly green and wild roses wreathed the hedges. The landscape here was so untouched by war that it was unthinkable that it could be destroyed by the holocaust any day. Winter is a harsh enemy but a war waged among the scent of flowers makes it somehow more terrifying and unreal.

Polly had been sent to help in the gas marquee. Here were men blinded by gas, whose every breath was drawn painfully from gas-filled lungs. The gas had burned them horribly where their clothes clung and she spent her free time cutting large rolls of lint into shoulder or leg shapes that could be put on in one piece. Delia and she did the sewing in their spare time and between them they turned out garments that could be soaked in picric and castor oil and put on the wounded men with the minimum pain.

Now, under the blazing sun, the sides of the marquees were kept rolled back allowing the air to circulate. Despite this, the heat and foetid smell of burns and wounds were horrible.

And still the retreat went on until the bulge in the front line was said to be only ten miles away.

For those on night duty, it now became impossible to get any sleep during the day for ferocious air battles were taking place overhead. Bombs fell indiscriminately; one in the *abbaye*'s yard killing wounded men as they lay helplessly awaiting the orderlies. Polly was kept too busy to feel fear except at odd moments, when it became an icy hand clamped round her throat and she wanted to run. Displaying the red cross on sheets, the hospital stubbornly held on.

Delia seemed untouched by fear. Her intrepidity

shamed Polly who felt that icy hand several times a day now and knew she was no heroine. The feeding, nursing and washing of the hundreds of men occupied each nurse and helper for the whole time she was on duty. Often, nurses stayed on long after the two girls from the office had staggered to their rest. Women from the town came to help with the daily chores and this brought relief but the huge numbers of wounded added to the crushing sense of defeat that secretly gripped them all.

Doggedly, pushing themselves to the limit of endurance, everyone worked round the clock. Each morning at ten, the *curé* read the burial service over the dead who lay under the Tricolour in the cemetery near the forest. Many were dying from terrible shrapnel wounds. Never before had the world seen such a curtain of red-hot steel; the curtain that blotted out everything in its path: whole villages; soldiers; horses; machines.

'We shall not retreat. It is too late for that,' Doctor Gregory told her hospital. Her face was grim and drawn and she had lost so much weight that the familiar grey jacket and skirt she wore winter and summer hung shapelessly on her. 'There is nowhere we can go without killing off these gravely wounded men. There is no transport available. The roads are choked. Our duty is to remain here giving of our best to the men in our charge.'

The gassed cases were double what they had been in last year's offensive. Strychnine by hypodermic had to be given every four hours and Polly followed Sister Torrance with a bowl of boracic solution with which to bathe the gummed-up eyes. Over and over again she heard the old cry that had distressed her so much last spring. 'My eyes, nurse! My eyes! Am I blind? Shall I be able to see again?'

She began to recognize the signs of a dying man: he stopped asking these anxious questions and lay drowning from his water-logged lungs. Soon the screens were put up.

And they were so young. Her own age and younger.

We are doomed, she thought as she swabbed and soothed. There's no future, only this struggle for life in Dante's Inferno.

CHAPTER TWENTY-FOUR

Holding On

The thinly held British front line had taken a terrible pounding under the weight of the German bombardment and the whole one hundred and twenty miles of front was being pushed back. By 25 March the Germans had captured Bapaume. General Gough then abandoned his headquarters at Villers Bretonneux and David's battalion fell back on the village. Soon they found themselves being pushed back to Amiens. By the twenty-seventh, the enemy was less than twelve miles from the city. Once it fell, the way to the sea was wide open and the war would be over, the Germans the victors.

But two things happened. As the Germans poured troops and guns into the Bois de Moreuil for a final onslaught on Amiens, a Canadian cavalry brigade, Strathcona's Horse, swept up the ridge and through the woods, dying in large numbers but killing as many of the enemy. Amiens had been saved.

The other thing that happened was the rain; torrents of it in twenty-four hours turning the battleground into a quagmire, bogging down the enemy in his rush to Amiens.

It was Easter and David's battalion had been in trenches and then retreating for ten days. Their will to resist was nearly at an end when suddenly, by Foch's orders, the British troops in this part of the line were lifted out of the battle and sent to 'recuperate' in the Aisne sector where there was little activity as yet. No major action had taken place here for a year. The French soldiers, who had been holding this quiet sector, exchanged places with them in the front line before Amiens.

The British soldiers thought they had been transported to paradise. It was quiet. Here was real grass; wild flowers; singing birds to remind them it was spring. Leaves were coming out on the trees and there was the sparkling river to cleanse the battle filth off them. In a year of inactivity nature had stubbornly reclaimed the torn land.

Above stretched the long ridge of the Chemin des Dames running from Craonne to Neuville, a matter of twenty miles. Behind, the river Vesle ran down to meet the Aisne. There was much work to be done digging deeper trenches and reinforcing the wire and after a couple of days' rest, they were all ready for it and enjoyed working in this pleasant bit of country. There was time to sleep, to bathe in the river and to write and receive letters. They felt they had become human again.

The rain had cleared and the sun was warm on David's back as he read his mail, the first for a month. He searched feverishly through the pile for one from Polly, but she hadn't written. Was it February or March they had been together in Paris? Dates were confused in his mind. It was now April, but what day was it? Probably the seventh or eighth. He said casually to a fellow officer unwrapping out-of-date newspapers, 'You haven't heard that Compiègne has been overrun, have you?'

'Compiègne? French HQ, wasn't it? Don't think so. Have a look through these papers if you like.'

In the centre of *The Times* there was a smudged map showing the extent of the German push. David bent over it anxiously, tracing the line with his finger. Then he read the text and his face tightened: Pétain had moved his headquarters from Compiègne a month ago. He and his staff were now at Chantilly. Surely that fool of a Doctor Gregory hadn't stayed behind? He thought of Polly, small and fragile, in a hospital only a few miles from the Boche – Good God, what madness! It's against all the odds that we both survive, he thought with a new terrible clarity. That three days in Paris had been their farewell.

A touch on his hand made him look down: a small honey bee had landed on his knuckles and was resting there. How extraordinary, he thought. In the year that had passed since the last big battle in this area, the wild honey bees had come back, had made their nest in a grassy bank and were collecting nectar. Would they harvest the honey? Or would this quiet landscape be torn into a reeking hell before another week had gone? What fools human beings were and how patient and persistent was nature!

He stared at the sunlit slope of the Chemin des Dames ridge. Concealed in the woods and ravines were the German batteries already trained on the defenders below. Perhaps the enemy would come racing down that slope in their bid to reach Paris. Remembering the blinding barrage of exploding shells near Villers Bretonneux last month, he felt his stomach nerves knot. It will be just as well if I'm killed, he thought, depression sour in his throat. It would solve much.

For his life seemed to him a confused muddle. He loved a girl who was another man's wife. Where was the future in that?

He began to open his letters. Two from his mother. Opening the first he learned of Laurie's illness and gradual recovery. That kid has nine lives! he told himself and a shiver went through him: she could so easily have died. The thin partition between life and death was one he ought to be used to by now, and yet it still struck terror in him. Not for himself so much but for those he loved. *Polly*, he thought again with a twist of the heart.

How long is this war going on for? his mother asked in

her letter. *No one seems to think we can endure much longer.*

Stuffing the letters into his knapsack he wished he knew the answer. If they'd reached that stage back home what hope was there for them?

He was not alone in thinking in these terms. A depressed hopelessness was flowing through France and Britain. How much longer? people asked as the casualty lists lengthened.

Then on 27 May the German bombardment on the Chemin des Dames began. Soon both the British and French lines were involved and falling back under a murderous barrage, rapid and obliterating in its effect. Gas was being used and a mass of choking humanity was being driven out of the trenches and made to retreat rapidly. By midnight, eleven hours after the first assault, the Germans had advanced twelve miles on a wide front.

The pleasant valley where the bees had been gathering nectar had disappeared under the wheels of the advancing German guns.

One night in early June, Polly and Delia slipped outside the ward they were working in to get a breath of air. There was a strong smell of lyddite in the air which was anything but fresh but it was a relief from the smell of pus in the marquee.

'I smell too,' Polly said with distaste. 'We haven't washed or changed our clothes for a week – what was that?' she added, her voice sharpening.

'What?' Delia struggled with weariness, biting off another yawn. 'I only hear the gunfire in the distance – '

'Look!'

They could hear the whine and crump of bursting shells quite clearly for the enemy had attacked on the Chemin des Dames a few days ago, had advanced with terrifying speed and were now said to be only eight miles away. The whole sky was scratched with arcs of bright and hideous light. But over there, in the darkest corner by the cemetery, there were unfamiliar sounds and Polly's sharpened senses had heard them. She gripped Delia's arm, her fingers biting into the flesh. There was the tramp of feet. Guttural voices.

'It's – it's the Boche!' Delia whispered shakily.

'I knew it – I knew they'd come through the forest – '

'Ssh – '

They slid back into the marquee.

'Sister – '

'Oh, Wynne, do watch what you're doing – '

'Sister, the Germans – they're outside.'

Sister went on changing a dressing. 'Go on working. Do as I do and leave the talking to me.'

Suddenly, a man was inside the marquee. His face was dark with oil and dust. His eyes darted round the ward and a sardonic grin split his face. His *feldgrau* uniform was begrimed with dirt and sweat but he carried himself with the swagger of the conqueror. He had a rifle slung over one shoulder and a bottle of wine in the other. He took a swig from this and grinned horribly at them.

They had heard that the advancing Germans had been holding up the headlong advance by getting drunk as the captured cellars of the Champagne country fell into their hands. Soissons thronged with unmanageable troops and the *Feldpolizei* had their work cut out pushing them back into the line. This man was not drunk but incensed by wine. The face of hatred he displayed caused them to huddle in a group.

Sister Torrance completed her dressing but her hands trembled. Straightening, she said coldly: '*Bitte?*'

He spoke roughly in German.

465

'I don't speak German. Please go.' She pointed out into the night.

'*Englische!*' the soldier growled and, turning, seized Polly by the arm. With the other hand, his bottle thrown on to a bed, he pulled her veil and tore it. Her abundant red hair tumbled to her shoulders and she looked very young and vulnerable. He gave a crow of laughter and began to tear at her uniform. Sister Torrance and Delia leaped towards Polly trying to add their strength to hers and push his hands away but he was too strong for them. With an oath, he seized his rifle and raised it as if to club them down.

Suddenly, an icy voice barked out an order. The man immediately stood to attention, a foolish expression of frowning obedience on his face.

A German officer, dusty and with red-rimmed eyes, had entered the marquee. He looked hard at the little group: one girl trying to pull her torn uniform together, two other young women ranged protectively round her. Then he looked at the soldier and spat out a word. Thin and tall and disdainful, he watched as two men ran in, seized the drunken corporal and bore him away. Then he turned back to them. 'Are there only *women* in this hospital?' he demanded in French with a German accent.

Polly stood up, the only one whose French was fluent. She tried to stop trembling, to face him boldly, but her voice wobbled. 'Yes. It is run entirely by English and American women for the French Red Cross.'

He looked closely at her. 'You are English, I think?' He now spoke English with an excellent accent. 'All of you?'

'Three of us,' Sister Torrance said. Her face was white. 'That man – like a beast! Here, in my ward – ' Angry tears filled her eyes. She shuddered again at the recollection.

The officer shrugged. 'Alas, yes. My men are tasting wine for the first time in years. I am sorry he hurt you,' he added, bowing towards Polly. 'He is now under arrest.' His light-blue eyes examined them in some astonishment. 'You realize you are very near the front line now?'

'Of course. But we shall not abandon our patients. They are all very sick men in this tent and to move them would be to kill them. Please go now.'

'One moment, Sister. You are running a grave risk by staying.' He looked round on the wounded. 'It is ridiculous! Most of these men will die anyway.'

'Then it is fortunate that they do not understand English,' Sister retorted. 'From the way you speak it, I suppose you have been a visitor to my country?'

'But of course. I have known well the Cornwallis-Wests. Their daughter is Princess Daisy of Pless, a very good friend of mine. You have heard of her?'

'*No*,' Sister said scornfully. 'I'm a hospital nurse not a society woman in disguise.'

Astonished, he laughed. 'I like your spirit. *Good God! A hospital of Amazons!*' He clicked his heels, saluted and left, stooping under the canvas flap. They heard his voice, sharper now, giving orders. They began to breathe again.

'Now, get on with your work, please. Whether we are prisoners of these people or not, our patients need us.' Sister pinned Polly's torn veil back on her head. 'By remaining calm and continuing to work, we have the best chance of being left in peace – '

'If you can call it peace,' Delia murmured as a shell burst in the vicinity.

'We are in God's hands,' Sister said austerely as she went to attend to a patient.

At eight o'clock, wrapped in their cloaks, the night shift walked across to the hospital, keeping very close together. It was drizzling with rain and the thunderous sound of the

467

guns made speech impossible. In the stone-flagged hall of the *abbaye*, Doctor Gregory sat at a table and checked each girl as she came in.

'No one is to go upstairs. We have brought blankets down here and you will sleep anywhere you can find space. Breakfast is being served now.' Her uniform was crushed, her face pale, but she gave her orders in her usual steady tone. Those who had looked frightened seemed suddenly to gain strength from her and began to chat and laugh as they fetched bread and tea and made up beds on the floor.

The Commandant followed them in to the refectory and called for silence. 'The Germans are hiding in the woods beyond the cemetery. I believe there are not many – just a platoon – and I suspect that they have pushed ahead of the main body of the enemy by mistake. They are probably waiting until nightfall to extricate themselves, and withdraw to their own company. They have cut our telephone wires and so I am unable to warn Headquarters at Chantilly. But even if I could, I would not do so. The officer told me that at the first sign of French soldiers approaching, he would give orders for hand grenades to be thrown into every ward.'

A horrified silence was broken by a buzz of anger.

Doctor Gregory held up her hand. 'That is war. Do not let us pretend otherwise. By acting quietly and sensibly we can emerge from this unpleasant situation without a casualty. I have asked the officer to inform his Headquarters of our position on this side of the forest in the hope they will not shell us if they advance further south. We must all pray that the tide will turn any day now and the enemy advance be stopped. Remain steady and calm.'

It was that evening that she pinned on the notice board a copy of Sir Douglas Haig's order of the day that had been issued in early April to all ranks of the British army.

One of the patients was a British despatch rider caught up with the French in the retreat and he had given it her. It was stained and crumpled but in groups they paused to read it.

It ended:

. . . With our backs to the wall and believing in the justice of our cause each one of us must fight on to the end. The safety of our homes and the freedom of mankind alike depend upon the conduct of each one of us at this critical moment.

D. Haig. FM

This quietly worded message from a square-headed unimaginative Scotsman had a far greater effect than any amount of flowery rhetoric. The British women, isolated from their fellow countrymen, and only a few miles from the advancing enemy, responded as if to a trumpet call. No one talked about it but a new spirit entered them. They were tired, unwashed and dirty. There was little to eat but no one had an appetite anyway. The noise of the guns had dulled their hearing. They were frightened. But no one mentioned giving up, of joining the retreating civilians on the roads. They would stay and die here with their patients. There would be no heroics. It was all that was left to them to do and they were going to do it.

By 10 June the Germans were reported to be only seven miles from Compiègne: the shells were now landing on the town.

On this day, the Commandant ordered the evacuation of every patient who could be moved. The railway station had been bombed so the ambulance drivers drove their lorries five miles down the road to another station for Paris. Here the stretchers were loaded on to hospital trains which shunted up the line day and night collecting and delivering their loads.

469

But as fast as the wards were emptied, more wounded were brought in. Fires raged in the town and dark acrid smoke covered the sun, turning day into night.

The women surgeons, their overalls soaked in blood, did what they could to the mutilated bodies lying on the operating tables. But eventually they had to start making the heart-breaking decision as to who was to live and who to die. Beyond giving them large doses of morphine, there was nothing to be done for many men who lay under a hot sun waiting for death. Those not so badly wounded were hastily patched up and loaded on to the train. A good many died on the way.

And, as they worked feverishly, everyone in the hospital was aware that the Germans were pouring down the valley of the Aisne in an attempt to reach the railway line that passed through Compiègne and led to Paris.

In those few moments before sleep came after a night on the wards, Polly would compose a letter in her head to David. How easily the words came! She could share with him then all the fears that haunted her mind: fears that were for him as much as for herself.

Halfway through she would drop into an exhausted sleep, being woken at five o'clock for supper and an hour or two spent catching up with the office work, sending a messenger for urgent supplies, filling in the nominal roll forms still demanded by the French authorities. There was time only for a cup of cocoa before the long and weary night began again. She was now so tired that she wondered how she – all the staff – could carry on.

The letters she wrote him in her head never got put on paper and it would not have been much use if she had written them for all postal services had ceased in the surrounding chaos.

But by mid-July, some order began to come back into

their lives as the tide of battle receded: the German army had been halted thirty-seven miles from Paris and the French army had gone on to the offensive once more. Still the ambulances rolled down the road to the hospital and the wards were choked with wounded. But there was at last hope. Hope that the tide was turning now that the Allies had taken the initiative. It was only a question of holding on a little longer, they told each other wearily. This was a turning point.

Then, a lorry coming through from Paris with essential supplies of morphine and other much-needed drugs brought a huge postbag. Letters were distributed, the first letters for nearly eight weeks.

Polly looked eagerly through hers but there were none from David. Not one letter in all that time. Had something happened?

One morning, as they made their way back to the *abbaye* from the wards, Delia stumbled and fell just as she reached the courtyard. She lay very still for a minute or two.

Polly fell on her knees beside her. 'Are you all right? Did you trip on something?'

She shook her head. 'I feel odd.'

'Put your head down. You nearly fainted, that's all. If you put your arm round my neck – Delia!' Delia, losing all colour, had now fainted in earnest. Her face was grazed by the paving stones; the pins fell out of her hair and little moans came from between her half-open lips.

Panic, never far from the surface nowadays, ripped through Polly. She rushed across the yard, calling for Augustin. With the old man's help, Delia was carried into the refectory and laid on a mattress.

To Polly's relief, two of the nurses from the night shift came in to go to bed. They examined Delia cursorily. 'I think she's gone down with that new fever,' one said. 'Several of us have got it; it started in Sister Lyle's ward. You'd better fetch the Commandant.'

Fetched from her room, the Commandant arrived looking grey-faced and worn. In the past month, driving herself relentlessly, she seemed to have shrunk; her clothes hung on her and there were purple smudges round her eyes. She was over fifty and for the past three years had worked like a woman twenty years her junior: it was beginning to tell.

She looked grim as she read the thermometer that one of the nurses had put under Delia's tongue. 'Mm. Not too good. I'd better have a look at you, too, Wynne. You've been together all the time and I don't see you escaping it.'

'What is it, Commandant?'

'A virus of some sort. Yes, just as I thought. You'll both have to stay in your rooms. Is your throat sore? I think you're beginning a fever.' She looked round the refectory where the mattresses lay in serried ranks. 'I'm afraid you'll have to go back upstairs. It's a risk but I can't let you stay here. I'll get someone to carry Vane upstairs. Where are the orderlies?'

'In the yard. I'll go – I'm not feeling all that ill.' She hurried out into the yard. Two of the men were having a hasty cigarette, their weary backs propped against a wall. They hadn't had their clothes off for hours and their faces were streaked with strain and dust. But they listened to her request and carried Delia and her mattress upstairs to her room. While one was fetching Polly's mattress, the older one asked her what the illness was.

'A fever. There are many cases.'

'Fever. *Mon dieu!*' The man drew back in horror. 'It is the Flanders fever – that's what the Boche call it. Already it has killed many.' He crossed himself and hurried off.

472

Evidently he transmitted the news to his friend for the second mattress got no further than the top of the stairs and she had to drag it the rest of the way. Not having the strength to heave it on her own bed, she pulled it into Delia's room and left it on the floor.

The Commandant had said she was doing her utmost to find a hospital in Paris to take them in but apparently the civilian population had filled all the isolation wards. They must just stay in their rooms.

Delia had come round, Polly found. 'What happened?' she asked faintly.

'You've got flu.'

'I'm cold – so cold.'

'I'll get some blankets.' The sun was blazing outside, Polly saw, as she trudged back upstairs with their blankets. But Delia was shivering violently. She covered her with two blankets and soon the girl was sweating.

'I must get my clothes off. I'm horribly uncomfortable. Water,' she pleaded. 'I'm dry. My mouth is dry. Oh, Polly, please get me water . . .'

But when Polly returned with the jug, she had lost consciousness and was muttering feverishly as she tossed under the blankets. Polly searched the drawers for a clean nightdress but there were none, for the laundry had ceased to function a month ago. Rummaging through her own drawers, she at last found the ridiculously frivolous petticoat that had been bought in Paris – oh, so long ago now it seemed. It was composed of drawn-thread work and blue ribbons but would do nicely as a nightdress. She undressed Delia with difficulty and with some of the water in the jug, she sponged down the flaccid form of the sick girl as she had seen the nurses do in the wards. Then she dragged the lawn petticoat over her head and turned the pillow to its fresh side. For the time being she could do no more for her than to wet her lips occasionally.

Many times that day she walked between the window and the bed, resting sometimes on her mattress on the floor. Through the open window came the sound of the receding battle. About five o'clock, two aeroplanes flew over and bombs rocked the *abbaye*. Another piece of glass fell out of the window but Polly hardly noticed it. She was feeling ill herself now with all the sensations Delia had been experiencing. She was terribly hot and threw off the blankets she had been shivering under. Now she was cold. She drank from the water jug, her head throbbing so painfully that she uttered little moans as she moved. Flanders fever. It was known as Spanish flu by the British and had been decimating their army for a month. Horrific tales of the new fever that was sweeping Western Europe had been circulating as uneasy gossip for some time. Now it was here. She and Delia had caught it.

Outside the sun was still blazing on the battle that was raging a few miles away but now it seemed to be here, in her head and body, burning her up, consuming her mercilessly. She tried to scream, to summon help. Had they all forgotten about her and Delia? Whether any sound came out she never knew for she lost consciousness.

It was Nurse Hayward who came upstairs when it was dark. Quietly and methodically, by the light of a candle, the girl sponged them and dried the sticky sweat off their fevered bodies. Then she wrapped each one in the scratchy, hairy blankets and sought out the Commandant in her office.

Doctor Gregory raised weary eyes. 'I'm still trying to get beds for them in a hospital. There's an American unit with an isolation ward that's being equipped. They're going to telephone me by midnight. How many cases are there now?'

'Seven. Nurse Campbell has died.'

The Commandant closed her eyes a moment. 'Poor

474

Mary Campbell. Her father is a minister at home, you know.' She sighed. 'There will be more, I fear. There's very little I can do for them and we're so shorthanded I've asked the authorities to send extra trains as soon as possible. We shall have to get the wounded evacuated at once.'

Hayward was desperately tired, but not so tired as this woman, she told herself looking at the purple rings under Helen Gregory's eyes. 'Are you all right, Commandant? Shall I get you a cup of Bovril?'

'No, no, don't worry about me. I'm tougher than I look. See to yourself, girl. You've been a brick.'

At midnight, an American voice on the telephone from Paris told them that an ambulance was on its way to pick up the sick members of the Gregory Hospital staff.

At three o'clock in the morning, as the pre-dawn sky lightened in the east, two cheerful young women in olive-green smocks and breeches rolled Polly on to a stretcher.

'There's not much to this one. She's as light as a feather,' Polly heard one of them remark. Lightheadedly, she laughed. A feather. That's what she was. A feather drifting on the wind . . .

Polly had a vague memory afterwards of being carried through an immense and echoing hall; of passing white plaster statues set against green damask walls; of being taken up a wide staircase and of a huge crystal chandelier that dazzled and hurt her eyes.

There were French and American voices over her head. Someone bent over her: a plump male face with rimless glasses and a white coat. Hands lifted and pushed her. She fought them off, crying for 'Water! Delia! Oh, Mother, my head's hurting . . .' She could hear herself whimpering childishly and was ashamed but unable to stop. Nell didn't come in answer to her pleas, as so often she had in the past to soothe and murmur loving words. 'Mother! Mother, where are you?' sobbed the child inside Polly.

An American voice cajoled her to be a good girl while she was given something very nasty to swallow. She was being put between cool linen sheets with a light fluffy blanket for cover. She drifted away from it all, feeling blank and sad and very tired.

She remembered being woken, being bathed and powdered, being given more nauseous draughts.

Then, one day, she woke up naturally and felt herself stretch between the smooth sheets. What a marvellous sleep she had had! She felt so strong and well that she thought she would sit up and examine the place she found herself in.

But when she tried to lift her head nothing happened. Someone had tied her down. She must be tied down for why couldn't she move? But there seemed to be no bonds over her arms and legs. It was strange.

She stared at the ceiling: angels and cherubs, clouds, flowers and fruit floated above her head. She blinked. She was dead. In her grave and looking up at the sky. But she didn't want to be dead! A huge sob welled in her throat and she fell asleep again.

The next time she woke up, it was evening. Pink shafts from a sunset wavered up and down the ceiling. Her brain felt shaken into place again and she knew she was recovering.

Where was she? What was this place? Feebly, she raised her head. A museum? A church, perhaps. It had been turned into a hospital, that was clear, for there were other beds in this room and a white-capped nurse was bending over one.

The nurse turned round at that moment and, seeing Polly's eyes fixed on her, came across to her bed. 'Well, honey, so you're back among us! That's a good girl. Just you wait and I'll fix you a nice drink. You need feeding up. D'you know, you're just skin and bone – sk-i-in and bone.' She laughed, a jolly pink-faced girl with a small nose and twinkling eyes.

Memory was flooding back. 'Is my friend all right? Her name is Delia Vane and we came in together.'

The nurse looked puzzled. 'We haven't a Delia Vane as far as I know.'

'We were both from the Gregory Hospital at Compiègne.'

'Now you lie back and let me do the worrying. I'm Nurse Mary Parsons and you can call me Mamie – everybody else here does! I'll just ring down and order your egg-nog –'

'No, please!' Polly clutched a corner of her apron. 'Please find Delia for me, Mamie. I feel responsible for her. She was awfully ill.' A terrible fear gripped her. Spanish flu was a killer. Those orderlies had said so. 'Please find her. I must know. She's my friend.'

'Now, you'll be running a temperature if you get yourself in a state,' Mamie chided. But she was a kind-hearted girl and went at once to the office to find out if a patient named Vane was still in the hospital.

The ward was very quiet and the other patients seemed to be dozing. No one moved. There was a distant sound of traffic and the sunset had changed and was now flooding the room with a pale yellow light.

Delia couldn't be dead, Polly kept repeating within herself. She was strong. She had always been the stronger of the two of them. But they had been exhausted and undernourished and in no state to fight Spanish flu.

She ran a hand over her body, astonished to find that she had become a skeleton with ribs that jutted and breasts that had shrunk.

477

'Nurse,' said a voice. Someone two beds away was trying to call out. 'Nurse!' Now the girl's voice, thin and hoarse, was childishly angry as if back in the nursery. 'Where the hell's that girl!' the voice shouted, fully adult now.

'Delia!' Polly grasped the iron bedrail and tried to pull herself up. 'Delia, is it you? It's me – Polly!'

'Polly?' Wearily, Delia rolled her head. 'Oh, God, I feel terrible!' she wailed.

'Now what's all this?' Mamie bustled through the door followed by a young nurse. She held an open book in her hand. 'There's been a mistake. Are you Delia Vane? Some idiot – ' She glanced witheringly at the young nurse, ' – some idiot has entered you as Deborah Vaughan.'

'What a terrible name . . .' Delia's eyelids were drooping. 'I'm so thirsty. Is there lemonade?'

'Plenty, my dear, and you shall have it in a moment. Now, Irma, just you scuttle off and fetch everyone drinks from the cold fountain. And next time put your glasses on when you read the patients' labels or you'll be getting us into trouble!' Mamie chuckled good-humouredly as she shook up the pillows.

It wasn't like a hospital really, Polly told herself thankfully. No one remotely like Sister Pitt stalked the wards, scolding and harrying everyone in sight. There were few if any rules except commonsense ones. Instead, they were made to feel as if they were being nursed in a friendly American home with everyone interested in their welfare.

Soon they were free of infection and were moved to a pleasant small room overlooking a formal garden. There were three beds in the room, the third being occupied by a tough-looking Cockney girl with cropped hair who was an ambulance driver.

From the windows, the doughboys could be seen taking the air and a good deal of laughter and teasing of the

478

nurses was heard. The hospital had been the town house of the Marquis de Chavignon who had been in the French cavalry and had been killed in 1914. The Marquise had offered the huge house in the Bois de Boulogne as soon as America entered the war. Scarcely a day passed that a beautiful woman in well-cut clothes with exquisite jewellery and a perfectly coiffed head of fair hair didn't come to the hospital bearing fruit and flowers for the wounded.

One morning there was a knock on the door of the convalescents' room and the same dazzling vision appeared, her arms full of roses.

'*Vraiment*, you are nicely recovered, my dears!' the Marquise said gaily. 'Clementine, bring in the gifts. My daughter, ladies.'

A pretty little girl, her arms full of parcels, sketched a curtsey. '*Maman*, my arms are aching so,' she complained in French. 'Albert says he cannot manage the stairs at his age, not with all that fruit.'

'What nonsense!' retorted the Marquise crisply. 'And speak English, if you please, Clementine. *Mesdemoiselles*, Albert, my chauffeur, is very old, he has to be humoured, I think. He will come in his own time if not ours!' With a lavish hand she tossed packets wrapped in gold and silver paper and tied with white ribbons on each bed. 'This is for you – and this, I think.'

'But it isn't Christmas!' Polly exclaimed, catching a packet wrapped in harlequin paper.

'Christmas, child? But of course not. These are just a few *cadeaux* – how you say? Presents. Ah, yes. A few presents from my friends and myself. You have done much for my countrymen. In return we wish to give you pleasure. I know the good Doctor Gregory – but yes! Well? Open – open!'

Shyly, completely taken aback, they opened the parcels, gasping at the gifts that tumbled out. There were swansdown trimmed chiffon bedjackets; quilted satin mules; sachets of pot-pourri for their lockers; wicker flasks of eau-de-cologne; talcum powder in heart-shaped boxes with puffs attached; covers for their hot-water bags; chiffon scarves; satin ribbons for their hair – all the luxurious objects that rich Frenchwomen gave each other when one of them was ill.

The Marquise looked quizzically at the English girls' astonishment and pleasure. 'You are happy? Then I am glad. Ah! Here is Albert!'

A grumbling voice outside evidently belonged to Albert who, shocked at the idea of seeing young females in bed, cautiously opened the door and shoved in a large basket containing a bottle of champagne, fruit and flowers.

'You are happy?' the Marquise asked again. '*Bon!* Soon you will be well again. Come, Clementine!'

The door closed. An exquisite scent hovered in the air.

Kitty Wilkins recovered first. 'Well, I never did! Mum will never believe it when I tell her. Did you ever see the like? Dressed to kill and all that perfume too. These Frenchies. They don't know there's a war on and that's a fact.' She shook her cropped head in puritanical disgust.

Delia looked at her menacingly. 'Wilkins, you're a bigger killjoy than John Knox! What part of France have you been serving in? Then you ought to know that the French have been bled dry. I think that's a brave and kind woman. The first really feminine woman I've met in France. Hurrah I say for her scent and jewels and pretty hair! She's made me feel a woman again. I had almost forgotten I was.'

'Just think of the effort of keeping yourself pretty and gay and a pleasure to be seen through all this!' Polly said wonderingly. 'She is still in black although her husband was killed nearly four years ago. Somebody has spent hours making this jacket. Just look at the exquisite stitches!' After living so drably for the last few years, Polly was delighting in the *cadeaux* so liberally strewn on her bed.

Kitty Wilkins snorted. 'And I'll bet she's got a lover or two. I know these French!'

'No, Wilkins, I'm afraid you don't,' Polly retorted. 'And you'll go back to England after the war no wiser.'

'A drab wench if ever there was one,' Delia muttered across the beds.

As Polly's strength came back – a little more every day now – so did her worried fears for David. It must be nearly four weeks since she had left Compiègne, she calculated. Anything could have happened in the months since she had heard from him. No letters had been sent on from the Gregory Unit; they had been in complete isolation in more ways than one. She began to chafe at this confinement, counting the days until she could leave this most comfortable hospital and return to the miserable conditions of the Abbaye Ste Catherine. Delia, enjoying herself and putting on weight daily, told her tersely that she was mad – and all for the sake of a few letters.

But their convalescence came to an end at last and one day Ursula Gower brought her ambulance to pick them up and take them back to Compiègne. Delia at least left the de Chavignon hospital with profound regret.

'Back into the cold, cold world!' she groaned. 'I'm not looking forward to work, I warn you. I've been pampered and spoilt and my hands have gone quite soft and ladylike again.'

'Your language has gone soft and ladylike too,' Polly murmured. 'Especially since Wilkins left.'

The ambulance turned out of the gates. Gower, the girls noticed, was unusually silent for someone who had a reputation for chatter.

'What's up, Gower?'

'I don't suppose you will have heard. The Commandant is dead.'

If Gower had told them the war was lost, they would not have felt a greater sense of disaster. That rocklike figure *gone*? It seemed impossible.

'She caught Spanish flu just after you and was dead in twenty-four hours. Hers was the virulent kind. There was nothing anyone could do for her. We've buried her in the soldiers' cemetery by the forest. She would have wanted that, we thought.'

'What's going to happen to the hospital?'

'Doctor Chester has taken over. We're dreadfully short-staffed and have had to close some of the wards. Of course, we aren't getting the same numbers of wounded now. The war has moved away. Some people say it will be over soon. The Germans are in full retreat.'

An hour later, they were turning in at the familiar gates again. Nothing seemed changed, they thought as they climbed down with their paper parcels under their arms. It seemed incongruous to be carrying their presents of chiffon jackets and satin slippers back to *this*. They looked at each other and saw reflected on each other's faces the same war weariness. Enthusiasm for their work had gone for good. They were heartily sick of it.

And although neither mentioned it, they each felt the gap left by the plain, hearty woman who had infused every one of her workers with the spirit of victory.

They went slowly up to the office. Both desks were piled high with paper. Whoever had been lending a hand in their absence had not coped.

Polly looked at her desk, feeling disheartened and weary. Everything was muddled together and would have to be sorted before she could find her own letters.

'Come on, let's go to supper,' Delia said. 'We'll feel

more like tackling these two mounds after we've eaten. The thing that worries me is whether I have the stomach to cope with horsemeat and beans after those dainty repasts Mamie put in front of us.'

They did feel more like it later. Lighting the lamps they settled down at their desks. Augustin had got the stove going again and the musty dampness in the little office was evaporating.

'The clothes in my room are covered in green moss,' Polly said, rapidly sorting papers. 'If there's any sun tomorrow we can air them in the cloisters. I've asked Augustin to fix up something for us – ' She broke off. A letter in a vaguely familiar hand had come to light. It was, she saw as she broke the seal, from Walter Wynne.

CHAPTER TWENTY-FIVE

And All Our Friends Are Dead

Elaine stood at a window watching Anna walking up and down the river path. Hunched in her Burberry, her dark hair soaked by the rain that fell steadily, Anna had been there all day, refusing to come indoors to eat, her face ravaged and her eyes wild and haunted. She hadn't cried out or fainted when the telegram had arrived that morning. She had crushed it in her hands and, throwing on her Burberry, had gone out into the garden and thence to the river path.

Retrieving the orange form from the floor, Elaine had read of Sam Murray's death in action two days earlier: he had given Anna's name as his next of kin. Elaine had gone to the window, sick at heart, to watch her daughter fighting out her grief by herself. Sam, that nice freckle-faced boy, the only person who made Anna happy, gone. Her whole life had depended on him, Elaine thought as she put the crumpled telegram on the desk and tried to smooth it out. That old uncle of Sam's would have to be cabled without delay. He must have loved Sam like his own child. If only the boy had survived the war! Now God alone knew what future Anna had.

Going back again to the window she saw that the girl was still walking up and down, up and down, her arms folded over her body as if nursing a bad pain. Perhaps the pain inside her could only be dulled by movement, Elaine thought with pity.

As the day wore on, she began to worry. Left alone, Anna would walk up and down the river path all night. So for the second time she timidly approached her daughter, carrying another waterproof coat. 'Won't you put this on, darling? Your own is quite soaked. You'll get a bad chill if you stay out here.' Anna, she saw, seemed to have aged since morning. Her face was pinched, the skin mottled, and her dark eyes had lost their lustre.

'I haven't the courage to do it.'

'Do what, darling?'

'Drown myself. Throw myself in the water.' She gestured with one hand. 'It looks deep and cold and it would be easy – wearing this heavy coat I'd sink quickly like a stone. Somehow I'm afraid to do it. Cowardly, isn't it? I don't want to go on, Mother. There's too much pain. I never was any good at enduring pain. So why do I hang back in this – this craven fashion?' She turned to the water as she spoke and Elaine grasped her arm in terror, tears running down her face.

'Oh, Anna, don't! Darling, think of us – the rest of us! We love you so much. It's hurting too much for you to think normally at the moment. Come inside. Let me ring Doctor Mallory and he'll give you something to take the worst of the pain away. Tomorrow – '

'I don't want tomorrow to come.' Anna looked down into the water almost yearningly.

'But, Anna, given time – '

'Time?' Anna turned and for the first time looked full at her mother. 'Time heals, you mean? Not for me it won't. There was only one Sam and he's dead. Finished. He no longer exists. I find that so strange. I had a letter from him yesterday and now he no longer *is*. I shall never see him again. Time won't make things better. Nothing will. I shall just miss him more for every year of my life that remains. That's why there's no point going on – '

'Anna, I beg you not to do anything!' Elaine's voice rose in panic. 'There's been such trouble in this house:

Dad not himself, Laurie so ill. And how do I know whether I shall see David again?'

Anna shook her head. 'No, you won't. They're none of them coming home any more. We're all going to be alone for ever now. Just the women on their own and the old. The young men have gone, thrown into the furnace,' and she began to laugh on a high note as if she had just told a very funny joke.

'Do you need help, Mrs Ransom?' a voice said quietly behind her and there was Major Grantley, the Australian, whose terrible wounds had kept him in the convalescent home longer than anyone else yet.

'Thank God you've come. My daughter's had bad news. The man she hoped to marry has been killed,' Elaine whispered. 'I can't persuade her to come indoors, but she's cold and ill with grief. Please help me.'

For answer, the young officer took Anna's arm in his and said: 'I'm being discharged at last. Heard today. So it's a boat home for me.' Firmly, he led her away. Anna was looking up at him. 'Oh, Phil, I'm glad. I'm glad – ' and she burst into tears. Grantley led her on, up the steps past some staring convalescents and through the glass door into the hall.

Elaine summoned up what remaining strength she had and walked slowly after them. But how can such things be endured by women? she asked herself bewilderedly. It's too much. When will the fires of hell be put out?

But it was only September.

Quite suddenly in August the ferocious onslaught of the enemy in the Champagne area petered out.

David sat on the fire-step of his trench, his head on his arms. He was utterly exhausted. His company had been decimated during the past week and the dead lay in rotting heaps on the parapet: there had been no respite in

486

which to bury them. Only half an hour ago, a shell had landed on the parados and killed and wounded five more men. It had been the last shell and the silence was unearthly. He tried to wipe the stench of the rotting corpses and the choking smell of lyddite from his face and eyes as if it were possible to remove them physically. All will to move had left him.

Raising his head his eyes met the anxious eyes of a little wounded soldier spreadeagled at his side. 'You all right, Smith?'

'Dunno, sir. I can't move. Funny, ain't it?'

'The stretcher-bearers are coming down the trench – they'll be here any minute.' He tried to sound reassuring. The boy, from his own platoon, was very young. Only yesterday he had earned praise from Garforth, the CO, for 'sticking it out like a good 'un'. 'Don't worry. We'll soon have you back in Blighty,' David added, bending over the boy. It was then he saw with horror that the boy's lower body had been badly smashed and his legs were nearly severed. As so often in cases like this, Smith felt no pain but shivered with shock. His life's blood was pouring out of him into the soured earth at the bottom of the trench. David put his hand on the boy's head. 'You've done well, Jack. I'm proud of you and so will your best girl be when you get home.'

The boy gave a ghost of a smile, tried to say something and died. Aware of a bitter anger that had been growing in him lately, David closed the staring eyes. Poor little devil! Had he known what he was fighting for? He had been an errand boy until he'd volunteered, giving a false age no doubt: recruiting sergeants at this stage of the war were apt to turn a blind eye when under-age boys volunteered. Well, the grocer would have to find another errand boy now; for Jack Smith there would be a grave in

France and the remote glory of his name on the Roll of Honour.

Stepping over more bodies, David made his way to the hole in the trench wall that led down to the officers' dug-out. Here he found Garforth, only two years his senior and commanding the company. He was an ambitious man, a traveller in tea before the war who had no intention of returning to civilian life when 'this little show' as he called it ended. He had tasted what being an officer-and-a-gentleman felt like. David detested him – most of the others did too. He held his men's lives too lightly and was out for a medal before the end of the hostilities. He was leaning over the wooden bully-beef box that served as a table, a map spread out before him.

'Christ, you look awful!' he greeted David. 'Has the relieving company shown up yet? Well, where the hell are they? We've been here ten days and it ought to have been only six. If Jerry attacks again we won't be able to throw him back this time. I must have some reinforcements.' He jerked his thumb towards another hole in the dug-out leading through to the telephonist's 'nest'. 'They've been trying to get through for an hour – the lines must be broken.'

David took off his tin hat and rubbed the red mark on his forehead. 'Matthews thinks Jerry's retreating – '

'Retreating? Don't be a fool! They're just drawing breath for a new assault.' He fingered his toothbrush moustache and looked sideways at his junior officer. 'Matthews, eh? He's quite a downy fellow. Experienced. Maybe he's right.' He was silent and David guessed he was wondering how to turn the enemy's retreat to advantage for himself. *The commanding officer, gathering about him the remnants of his company, attacked once more and put the Hun to flight.* It would make the Military Cross he was after a certainty, David thought sourly and unbuttoned his jacket.

'Any whisky left?'

Garforth shook his head. 'Finished the last drop ten minutes ago.'

Selfish devil, David thought bitterly. Trust him to finish off the whisky if he had a chance! He rubbed his aching head with both hands and Garforth's eyes became alert: he was always on the look-out for 'lack of moral fibre' in his officers. 'You ill?'

'No, just dead beat.' It was the noise that did it: the infernal eternal scream and whine of shells passing overhead.

'I'm not going to waste much time handing over to Rowe when he comes. He knows the line as well as we do. The list of trench stores is lower than it's ever been. Some rusty rifle grenades from the year dot and a few Mills bombs. Brigade needn't start asking where the entrenching tools are – they're under the rubble somewhere.' He broke into tuneless whistling as he pushed his belongings into a knapsack.

'Aren't you going to ask who caught that last shell?'

Garforth stopped whistling and again looked narrowly at his companion. 'No. You can tell me when we get to our rest camp – but not tonight. Tonight I want a good dinner and to get drunk – if we ever get out.'

'Pity about Barr, though.'

'Barr?' For a moment Garforth's expression slipped. Barr, the company sergeant-major, had been a tower of strength all through this last show. He had kept the young soldiers steady. They had believed in Barr, leaned on him and gained strength from his rough brand of humour. And now Barr had copped it – hell!

'Yes. Well . . . it's a pity of course, but *c'est la guerre* and all that,' Garforth said and bent to rewind his puttees.

They were stiff with trench dirt and he had to scrape the encrusted mud off with a knife before he could rewind them.

David directed an angry look at the back of the CO's head but was saved from speaking the hot words by a head round the sacking over the doorway. An arm sketched a salute. 'Beg pardon, sir, the new company's just droppin' into the trench. Mr Weston said to tell you.'

With their freshly shaven faces and the dried mud long since brushed off their uniforms, the relieving company looked beings from another planet to the survivors of the battle. They had four extra days in rest camp because it had been impossible to relieve Garforth's company in the heat of a week-long battle. To the deafened weary survivors, the relieving company appeared to have the movements of a disturbed anthill. They bustled. Their voices weren't hoarse and strained but were loud and strong. And they brought whisky with them which they poured out generously.

'We hear that Jerry's running home to mother,' said the fat little major who had come to take over from Garforth. 'Here's mud in your eye,' and he drained his tin mug.

Garforth grunted. 'He might only be up to his tricks, so keep your eyes open. Look,' he stubbed a finger on the map, 'there's a nasty gap in the line here. Needs mending. And here. And I'm afraid we haven't got round to burying our dead.'

'Oh dear,' said the major, pulling his moustache. 'Oh dear. Oh dear. Nasty.'

'Yes,' Garforth agreed. 'Very.'

'But they are retreating,' the major persisted. 'Started this morning. Their western flank was nearly sliced in half by the Americans. They're pulling back fast. Scout's honour. Don't tell me Ludendorff's got more troops to

490

throw in! The thing's impossible. No, looks like the end of the war to me, old chap. You mark my words.'

'That's the worst of rest camp. You get to reading newspapers again and swallowing all the rubbish they write. Mark *my* words,' Garforth said with relish, 'we'll still be here this time next year.'

David's eyes briefly met the major's and they smiled without moving a muscle of their faces. Then, his haversack on his shoulders, David left them to it and stumbled up the steps to the air.

He was thankful to be leaving the dug-out for four days; its earthy smell reminded him forcibly of a tomb. Gathering his platoon together, sixteen men left out of twenty-five, he led the way in single file down the trench, sharply reminding the exhausted men to keep their heads down: Jerry might be retreating but may well have left a sniper or two behind. They turned the corner into the communication trench that ran back to the reserve trenches and then on to the broken mud path that meandered back for a couple of miles across shell-pitted country, every step taken a painful one for the hungry, exhausted soldiers. They reached the guns and the limbers and knew they had crept back two miles. Then at last they saw a tree. Some grass. A quiet green country that looked like paradise to their bloodshot eyes. David saw them into the barn that was their billet and then stumbled along to his own quarters. He felt lightheaded, quite unreal. He supposed it was exhaustion. The noise of shells screaming overhead for ten days had been well-nigh unendurable. How they had all stuck it, he couldn't think. Now the ringing in his ears was making him stumble dizzily. Ten days and he had only received a scratch on the arm from a red-hot shell splinter. Ten days of unimaginable hell. Ten days of choking fear. *Ten days*.

He let his haversack fall to the ground and then he fell

himself on to the sleeping bag his batman had spread out for him. For five minutes he lay too exhausted to move, unable to believe he was out of the line, his senses still alert. His eyes shut, he thought he would fall into a deep sleep. Instead he felt alarmingly alert, as if he would never sleep again. He kept jerking awake and looking round, his hand feeling for his revolver. Shutting his eyes again he saw the colour red; the blood flowing from young Smith's body. He began to compose the letters that would have to be written tomorrow to the next of kin of the men killed.

Oh, God, if only he could stop thinking!

Wearily, he heaved himself up and began to get out of his uniform that smelt of clay and death. He wondered where his batman was; dead-beat like himself, no doubt, but he must have hot water for suddenly it was imperative that he wash from head to foot to rid himself of trench memories. He wrenched open the door and bawled: 'Crai-ig!'

Craig's sleepy face swam into view at the bottom of the stairs.

'Boil up some water. I want to wash.' He would shave too while he was about it and look for the pyjamas he kept in a box with a few other things like a clean shirt and underpants. He would make himself human again; only then would he be able to sleep.

Craig came stumbling up with the can of water that wasn't really hot but would have to do. Funny how the officer-blokes always had to be a-washing themselves, he thought sourly as he poured the lukewarm water into the enamel bowl and handed a piece of towel two feet square.

'What the hell's this? Isn't there a better towel to be had than this?'

'It's all we've got left, sir,' Craig said woodenly.

'Well, go and make me a cup of tea and then go to bed yourself. And, Craig?'

'Yessir?'

'*Boil* the water. It's not tea unless it's boiled.'

Slightly cleaner at last and with a mug of tea in his hand, David got into his sleeping bag. That felt better! He was about to put his head down when he heard footsteps clattering up the stairs again and Craig put his face round the door. 'Forgot to bring up the letters, sir.'

There was quite a bundle for him: bills, subscriptions and two from Northesk. But he tossed them all aside when he found one in Polly's handwriting. He tore it open and read it quickly. It had been written some time back and told of her illness and convalescence in Paris and the conditions pertaining in Compiègne on her return.

On my desk was a letter from my father-in-law. David, Mike is being repatriated with some other sick prisoners. I've asked to be released. I must go and look after him, you see. You do understand, don't you? Darling, this must be goodbye. I can't live a lie. He's alive and needs to be nursed. We shall live at the Red House in Cambridge for the time being and I'll try to do my best for him. I don't know what to expect but shall soon know. Forgive me and try to understand how I feel. I married him and gave him my allegiance. I've got to stick to that. I love you – always shall, you know that – but you must forget me now and look for someone else to share your life.

Goodbye, darling, I shall love you always although I shall not be able to say so ever again.

Your Polly

He felt completely stunned. This news coming on top of the exhausting days spent in the trenches set the seal on a growing bitterness. For he was bitter now. This war to end war was nothing but an utter waste of young lives. It had gone on for four years and the end was not yet in sight, despite what Matthews thought. The clergy were

493

still asking the Almighty to favour the Allied cause. Hell and damnation! There was no God. How could there be a God who allowed the utter obscenities he had lately witnessed to go on unchecked? Men had become beasts, feasting on each other's carcasses.

And now this. The one light at the end of the tunnel for him had been Polly's love. He knew her more fully and completely than anyone else in the world but she was not his. She belonged to this ghostlike person called Mike to whom she believed she owed a duty.

Suddenly the horror and disappointment seemed to burst in his brain and he began to weep, something he hadn't done since childhood. They were not a child's tears but the destroying tears of manhood that he would never forget. He would return home when the war ended, if he survived, to find all his friends dead or so maimed that they were wrecks. The life he had known would have gone for ever and he would be a ghost from the past. The war had taken his youth and destroyed it. It had taken Polly from him as surely as if it had killed her. There was nothing left.

A week after receiving Walter Wynne's letter, Polly was back in England.

Doctor Chester had been reluctant to release her from her contract at first. Unlike the Commandant, the milk of human kindness didn't flow generously through Sarah Chester's veins and she disliked her own sex. A silly bunch of females who would never be able to stand on equal terms with men comprised the staff of her hospital, she considered, and she took cold pleasure in thwarting them.

'No!' she said, thumping her desk. 'The war's not over yet, Wynne – '

'It is for me,' Polly said firmly and stood up. 'I have to

go home to nurse my sick husband. There's nothing you can do about it, Doctor Chester. I volunteered for this job and now I'm leaving. Please let me have my movement papers.'

For a long half-minute they regarded each other steadily, sufficient time for Sarah Chester to realize there was really nothing she could do to force this girl to go on working in the unit. So Polly went home.

From the moment she had opened Walter Wynne's letter, Polly felt numb. She could feel nothing, neither joy nor relief. She didn't know the man who was coming back to her, repatriated with a group of other sick prisoners through Sweden. Gradually, as the numbness wore off, she began to feel terror. How was she to meet him with an open heart and mind when she had given both these to David?

Delia had said awkwardly: 'It will turn out for the best, you'll see. We've all had these war madnesses.'

How could she explain, Polly wondered, that her love for David was real? That she didn't even know Mike? They had lived together for a week two years ago. How could they be expected to come together after so long?

She had heard nothing of David since the battles of the spring and summer. The French post to the front was terribly disorganized, she knew, and managed much better by the British forces but she wondered if this was the reason for his silence or if he had decided it was better this way. Perhaps he had been wounded or killed – but her mother would have mentioned it in her letters. Whatever happened to him now she would have to pretend he meant nothing to her, even while her heart crumbled to emptiness. They had been lovers and now she had no right to ask for news of him. She was going home to a husband she could barely remember.

Walter Wynne was waiting for her on Cambridge

station. Taking her arm he led her towards the station waiting room where two perspiring women were dispensing a watery coffee to travellers. There were lace curtains at the windows smelling of soot and the light was obscured by two large aspidistras. Walter put her bag down and motioned her to a chair. She looked at him wonderingly: why didn't they find a cab and go to the Red House? How old and grey he had become, she thought. He seemed to have shrunk. Even his spectacles looked too big for his face.

Taking one of her hands, he regarded her very earnestly. 'My dear child, you must be prepared for a shock. Mike is – is – worse than we thought – than we realized.'

She stared uncomprehendingly. 'I know he's lost his memory. The Red Cross told us that. But surely when he sees familiar faces – sees his home again – it will come back. Given time, of course.' The words died away on her lips: Walter Wynne's eyes held too much pity, as if he had something terrible to convey.

'They had him at the Eastern General for a general check. From his papers they had no idea . . .' he swallowed. 'The German surgeon had written all details down in his own language. I got in a friend to translate it yesterday. Loss of memory could have been due to shellshock, to his experiences and there would have been every hope that given time, as you say, he would recover without treatment. Unfortunately, it's not due to that. Mike was hit by one of our shells soon after he was taken prisoner. A shell splinter lodged in the base of his skull near the brain. It's inoperable and Mike is a child again – a very young child.'

She cupped her head in her hands, feeling nausea sweep over her. 'Oh – oh, God.' Her mutter was drowned by the sound of a train's arrival outside the window but Walter heard her and patted her shoulder mutely. There was misery on his own face: rather the boy had died than this, he was thinking. He was aware suddenly that she had raised her head and her very blue eyes, although wet, held determination.

'Take me to him, please. I'll look after him.'

'Think first, Polly. Think hard. There is no need for you to sacrifice yourself – he won't even be aware that you're there! You're young with your life all ahead of you. His mother and I will look after him. Let me put you on the next train back to London. Please, Polly, go home. The marriage can be dissolved. You're too young to give up everything for a man who has become a cabbage.'

'No. No, I can't do that. He's my husband and I want to take care of him. I couldn't live with myself if I ran away.' Suddenly, her breath began to pump normally again; the nausea receded. 'Take me to him. I want to see him.'

It was a sunny day, hot for mid-September and as their cab trundled down Queen's Road she found herself remembering that June day two years ago. They were returning from the short wedding service at St Benedict's church, a boy and a girl who were dazzled by each other. She felt immeasurably old and experienced compared to that naïve girl. She stared at the outline of King's College chapel against the clear blue sky; the grey stone bridges; the sluggish river and the green elms, their leaves just beginning to turn. These things endured for centuries – even the trees. It was only flesh and blood that failed. Lives were so short compared to these inanimate things and made shorter by man's hatred and folly, she thought, her eyes watching men in hospital blue, some accompanied by VADs, who were walking under the shade of the huge trees.

'He looks very much the same.' Walter's gentle voice interrupted her thoughts.

497

He looks . . . the same. She had thought there was no horror left that she hadn't met and overcome in France but soon, in a minute or two, she was going to confront a new one.

'He'll be out in the garden. He likes it there. Go out to him while I pay the cab,' Walter said as they turned in at the Red House gate.

The house looked unchanged in its shabbiness and so like the place she had first beheld two years ago that she stopped in the dark hall, half expecting Mike himself to come through the glass doors from the garden carrying a tennis racquet or the gramophone. She went quietly, her feet making no noise, across the tiled floor and out on to the verandah. Ruth Wynne wasn't in her usual chair but the cushions were dented by her ample form and her spectacles and a book were on the wicker table by the chair. Polly stopped, looking round cautiously: the last thing she wanted was her meeting with her husband to be under his mother's eyes. She wanted time to get used to the different Mike; to have assimilated the first shock without Ruth's eyes watching her.

Suddenly she saw him.

He was alone, sitting in a wheelchair, looking down at something in his hand. He looked so unchanged that she heard herself gasp. The floppy fair hair was shorter and he was thinner and paler than she remembered but it was unmistakably Mike. He was wearing a shabby grey corduroy velvet jacket and there was a rug over his knees. He was laughing quietly in little bursts, watching the thing he held.

'Mike!'

He didn't respond, fascinated by his hand. She touched his shoulder. He didn't look up. Gently, she uncurled his hand and released a tiny butterfly, quivering and shaking

498

its wings, one of the last of summer. She raised his head, turning him to her. 'Mike? It's me – Polly.'

The unfocused eyes slid over her, quite blank.

The butterfly was lying on the grass. She picked it up and put it back in his hand. He didn't look at it but began to laugh again in small ripples.

She felt icy cold and her throat was dry and painful with feeling. Kneeling on the dry autumnal grass she put her arms round him and held him silently against her. Mike was no longer there. A tiny child lived inside the man's body. And all because of a piece of metal lodged near his brain. The war had taken Mike Wynne and ruthlessly destroyed the part of him that mattered, sending back to his wife this child who would need to be watched and nursed for the rest of his life. The one saving grace was that he was unaware of the great loss; he didn't remember that he had ever attained adulthood and marriage.

She stood up, carefully wiping her eyes. Useless to cry. The thing was done and she must learn to live with it as no doubt thousands of other women were learning to do. For them all, the war was not over and never would be.

CHAPTER TWENTY-SIX

The Last Enemy

In the first week in October Archie came up to Cambridge to begin his second year and Polly went to the station to meet him. It was four o'clock and the London train was due in ten minutes. The platform was crowded with soldiers waiting to board the train that would carry them on to the military camps dotted about the fens and on the Suffolk coast.

Threading her way through them, Polly found a seat on a bench between a soldier and a fat woman with a little girl on her lap. She was excited at the thought of seeing her twin again. More than a year had passed since she had been home to the rectory. That leave was very clear in her mind: she and David had become lovers for the first time. Tears sprang to her eyes and she hurriedly stared down at her shabby shoes. It was stupid to hark back. It could do no good. The trouble was she was so tired all the time. She and Walter Wynne nursed Mike between them. It was Walter who rose early and bathed and shaved his son and prepared him for the day. Polly looked after him at nights, the door of her room open to catch every sound. Sometimes she would be startled out of an uneasy sleep by the sudden unearthly noises Mike made and she would run in to find him aimlessly thrashing his arms about. The doctor had told her that these were involuntary actions, caused by the brain damage. Yet, every time, she hoped they were the signs of returning life to the passive figure who was as surely cut off from the world as if he had been enclosed inside a brick wall. She wondered if he ever slept. Each time she drew near him with a lamp he was awake, his eyes empty and staring.

She would go back to her room and lie awake with tears pouring down her cheeks. This living death was so cruel! Walter had again suggested putting him in a home for incurable soldiers but Ruth Wynne refused to consider it. She did little for her son that was practical and always saw signs of improvement where there were none. Polly's heart quailed too at the thought of sending him to live out his life among strangers. She agreed with Ruth: Mike was quieter, as if he knew he was back in his own home. During the day, he sat in his wheelchair being fed and washed and tidied like a docile child. The only sign of his head wound was the silver plate behind his left ear and Polly was allowing his hair to grow longer to hide it.

She emerged from her thoughts as people surged forward to meet the train that was arriving in a cloud of steam and grit. Standing well back, she scanned the faces of passengers for a sight of her twin.

Archie spotted her first and was shocked. To his eyes, Polly had changed very much. Gone was the pink and white colouring, the sparkling blue eyes and the long dimple in a rounded cheek. The woman who had suddenly sighted him looked pale, thin and careworn. Dark rings encircled her eyes and her warm smile went to his heart.

'Poll!' He hugged her with his one arm. 'My poor old girl, you look awful!'

'Oh, Archie – oh – ' She was choking suddenly, her head on his chest. 'Oh, I'm so glad to see someone from home at last. Tell me all the news. I'm starved for it. Here, let me carry that. There's a bus in the station yard – '

'Bustling me as usual, madam? We're not taking a bus with the luggage I've got. We'll take a cab.'

They chatted eagerly as they drove through the town

up Hills Road and past the Roman Catholic church, down Tenison Avenue, past the Fitzwilliam Museum, King's Parade and Trinity Street to Magdalene Street. 'You're not still in college?' Polly asked. The cab had stopped outside the main gate.

Archie winked. 'There are advantages to being a crock, you know! Cripples and scholars are in college. I'm delighted as I've a pretty good set of rooms, as you will see. How much?' he asked the cabby, reaching into his pocket.

Polly watched him covertly. A year at Cambridge had developed Archie. His left sleeve was still empty but he had evidently – except for his joke about being a crock – accepted his disability. His room was a pleasant one in the first court and as they unpacked she told him about Mike.

Although he said very little he was secretly appalled. Mike was a living dead man and his poor little sister was tied to him for life: her prospect of happiness was nil. Being Polly, he knew she would stick it out but what a destiny!

'Let's have some tea,' he said. 'I'll see if my gip's about. If not, I'll go across to the buttery for something. You lay the cups out and wait until I tell you about my evening with Aunt Nora – you'll never guess what she's been up to now!' He grinned at her and was about to open the door when it opened in his face and a girl came in like a whirlwind.

'Archie, you hound! You said you were coming up yesterday and I wriggled out of my first aid class and came over here but the porters said – ' She stopped and stared at Polly. Her arms that had been flung round Archie's neck dropped to her side and she looked helplessly at him.

'Polly, meet Miss Edith Templeton. My tutor's daugh-

Elaine was silent, afraid of saying the wrong thing. Ever since Sam Murray's death at Ste Mihiel in September, Anna had been a frozen image of her former self. She had retreated into herself, spoke little, spent most of her time in the convalescent hospital, working herself into an exhausted stupor most days. Elaine could find no route to reach the stony-faced young woman Anna had become. Now she watched her fold the solicitors' letter from Boston and place it neatly on top of the other unanswered ones.

'Why not write and tell them so, darling? Then Carl will stop bothering you and arrange a divorce.'

'Perhaps I will some day,' Anna said in a tired voice. She stood at the library window, her hands clasped in front of her. 'It's nearly two months,' she said, 'and I've got the rest of my life to get through.'

Tears sprang to Elaine's eyes; they were never far from the surface nowadays. She felt tired and defeated, filled with sadness for them all: for Anna; for Reggie; for Edward and for herself. To look back to the time before the war was like looking back at an upland meadow ... sunlight from a valley filled with dark fog. They ... that upland meadow again.

... her shoulders, Elaine went out ... raining and was now ... time of year. In the ... seemed

the grass grew rankly and the damp soles of her light shoes. She walked ... slippery, moss-grown steps to the ... the first time. ... ngland was a depressing ... like the stillness and ... gloomy as if it ... here and

505

on, not caring, across the damp grass to the beginning of the ploughed land at the end of the park. Leaning on a gate she stared unseeingly before her, her mind busy with worries as was usual now. If only David survives this war, she thought, her hands gripping the wooden gate.

And then she heard it. Suddenly, shivering through the mist, came the sound of a bell. Tentatively at first and then with a great joyous sound the bells of Northesk Church were ringing out the victory over these still fields. In the distance she could hear more bells: Eskton's. From the convalescent home came the sound of spontaneous cheering.

She felt her heart leap up in her breast, pounding, almost choking her. Putting her head down on the gate she drew in long breaths.

So it was over. The war was finished at last.

She stood quite still, great gulping sobs shaking out of her. *The nightmare is over. The nightmare is over.* Like a lesson learned by heart the words were repeating in her head. Yes, it was over and she was a changed woman; her hair was greying, there were lines in her face – and she didn't care! That was the strangest thing of all, surely? Now if only David came back to them, life could be rebuilt. A different sort of life but a life in which they were all together again at last.

The convalescent officers had come out on to the terrace and were calling to her to come and celebrate victory.

Polly heard

in a joyful

the flat fenlands

She felt too

shouting like the

she went towards them smilingly.

garden. They had been waiting for this moment and had made a guy like the Kaiser, determined not to have their Guy Fawkes bonfire until victory was declared. For a week they had pestered their elders with eager questions: 'Has the old Kaiser gone? Can we light it now?' Standing at the window she watched them running about collecting dry twigs, kicking dead leaves into great heaps. Tonight they would light the fire and cheer. She couldn't cheer. There was nothing to cheer about. The war was over and somewhere along the years she had left behind the light-hearted girl called Polly Paget and now inhabited the body of a careworn woman called Polly Wynne. But she prayed briefly that David had survived and would come home again.

The door behind her opened and Walter Wynne came in. 'Where is he?' he asked looking round.

'He's in the glass porch. I think he likes watching the boys out in the garden.'

For two months Walter Wynne had shared with her the task of caring for Mike. Ruth, although critical of their efforts, took no part herself. She behaved as if Mike were eight years old and recovering from measles. She chided him, chivvied him and encouraged him as if he understood every word she spoke. When she was alone with him they would hear her voice running on steadily. She asked questions and answered them herself. Polly heard nurse-maids on the Backs doing just this with their charges who were too young to speak yet. Ruth insisted that he understood what she said and would gradually respond.

Remembering David's stepfather, Reggie Ransom, Polly wondered. Mr Ransom had had a stroke, David explained, and couldn't speak. He was also paralysed on one side. 'But of course he understands what we say,' he had added, 'so come and meet him.' They had gone out on to the terrace and David had introduced them . . . But it was quite a different case! she told herself now. Mr Ransom's eyes, full of intelligence, had met hers. He had tried to speak and instead had conveyed his pleasure at meeting her with his eyes. Yes, his eyes had spoken for him. Mike's eyes were dead.

In her heart Polly knew that the war had destroyed Mike as thoroughly as a bullet through the heart. The body was there but the man inside the body had gone.

'You know, Ruth,' Walter ventured one day. 'Reed doesn't believe there can be any improvement in Mike's condition.'

'That quack! No one really knows. Remarkable things are being done nowadays – you've only to read the papers. Medical knowledge has advanced in leaps and bounds since 1914. Doctor Reed is obviously of the old school. I for one shall go on believing in his recovery however faint-hearted you two are.'

Polly heard her father-in-law sigh.

'It's over two years since it happened – '

'Those Huns did nothing to help him.'

'That's not true. Reed says – the Eastern General says he had a first-class surgeon who saved his life. The shell splinter is lodged in an awkward place. It could move – '

He stopped but Polly knew what he meant. That splinter could move and kill Mike any day. 'The boy is a cabbage. Are we to condemn Polly to years of looking after a husband who doesn't know her? Doesn't know any of us? I think we should let him go to a home – somewhere near where we can visit him.'

Polly's heart quailed. *Years*. Years with no hope, just waiting for Mike to die. She swallowed tears. Thank God, none of them knew about David and no one would for she had forced herself to stop thinking about him. He was the past. She couldn't think of the future. She must live in the present.

Sometimes, like her mother-in-law, she had the uncanny feeling that Mike knew she was there. Had his eyes really looked at her or was it a trick of the light? Had he turned his head or had it just fallen back against the cushion? She would brush his fair hair gently and he seemed to like it – yes, she could swear he liked it! One day she started up the gramophone, playing all the records they had danced to in 1916. He sat staring ahead, completely unresponsive. They meant nothing to him.

On fine mornings she wheeled him out in a Bath chair. He could walk but so erratically, weaving from side to side, that the chair was the only answer. They went up the road nearly as far as the university observatory and friends would stop to ask how he was, assuring Polly that he looked better for being home. 'But it will take time,' they always ended before smiling brightly and hurrying on.

Polly's wan appearance, her face diminishing a little every day, worried Walter Wynne. When term ended on 14 December, he came to her with a railway ticket to Whitby in his hands.

'We think you must have a holiday, Polly,' he said, putting it down on the table at her elbow. In reality, he had not discussed it with his wife but had taken the decision himself. 'You're to go home for Christmas. Archie told me that your sister and her husband are going to be there – you haven't seen their baby for two years, have you?'

'Oh, it would be – ' She stopped. 'No, it would be too much for you.'

'But I've arranged for extra help! Do you remember Miss Graham? She became a VAD and she's going to come in every day. She was always fond of Mike. She'll look after him.'

Amy Graham. Poor flat-chested Amy whose eyes had

509

doggily followed Mike. Polly drew a deep breath. Oh, to go home and see the family again! To see Alix and Kit and little Christine! Kit was recovering at last, able to walk unaided now. And Archie had asked Edith Templeton for the New Year, she knew. She might get news of David, hear at last that he had come through safely . . .

'The first Christmas of peace,' Walter said encouragingly. 'You must spend it with your family. You need a rest.' He took her hand and patted it, smiling at her. 'You're a good girl, Polly, and I wish with all my heart things had been different.'

She put her hand over his. 'It hurts just as much for you. I wish for you – and Mrs Wynne – this hadn't happened. Mike loved you, you know.' She put a gentle emphasis on the 'you' and she saw the expression on his face.

'Yes, I know he did,' was all he said.

She sent a telegram to tell them to expect her next day. Archie would meet her train, she knew. She packed the few clothes she had with her, realizing for the first time that there were many things at Eskton she badly needed down here. This would be the opportunity to bring them back with her.

When the taxi came to the door, she went into Mike's room. Walter had got him up and had finished shaving him. She put her arms round him. 'I'll be back soon,' she whispered. 'Goodbye, darling Mike.' His chin was sunk on his chest and he stared unblinkingly ahead. She ran her hand lightly over his fair head as a last farewell and went downstairs. There was no sign of Ruth so she kissed Walter and got into the taxi. 'Send for me if there's any change, *please*. I'll be back the first week in January.' As she drove away she saw again in her mind's eye Mike's good-looking profile etched against the light as she said goodbye. He wouldn't even know she had gone, wrapped as he was in the cloud of darkness that was now his life.

He had been frightened of death, of going out into the darkness, she thought, staring unseeingly at the familiar Cambridge streets, but how much worse to be alive with a mind that was dead. Perhaps he lived in dreams. They had no means of knowing. It was a cruel fate for a young man but all over the world there were other young men in the same condition being cared for by helpless relatives. There might be relief that the war was over but there couldn't be joy.

The trains were packed with demobilized soldiers or those who were going on leave. There was standing room only in the train after she changed at Peterborough but a young soldier gave up his seat to her while he sat on his pack at her feet. The noise and the fug from cigarettes made the journey uncomfortable but she dozed most of the way, a comfortable excitement in her heart at the thought of the rectory and her family.

It was a day that never got really light and gusts of sleet slid down the windows as the train rattled northwards. The soldiers began to sing softly all the old wartime favourites they had marched to in France and she slid in and out of sleep to the refrain of *Keep the home fires burning While your heart is yearning* . . .

Yearning. That was the word that summed up her hidden feelings for David. She yearned for him. It was disturbing that as they travelled north her thoughts left Cambridge and Mike and were almost wholly of David. Would he be home for Christmas leave or was he still in France? And if he were home, dare they see each other? She knew that though she had stifled her feelings, they were there and as lively as ever.

It was night when they pulled slowly into York and she felt bleary-eyed from the heat of the train. She pulled her case on to the platform and looked round for a porter

511

who could tell her when there would be a train to Whitby. She hoped very much she wouldn't have long to wait for the cold was intense and the waiting room seemed to be packed. People swarmed round her, everyone except herself seeming to know exactly where to find the next train, others being greeted by relatives.

She turned to pick up her case and saw a tall officer in a battle-stained uniform leaning against a truck piled high with luggage. His gaunt face was turned away but she would have known him anywhere. If she were strong, she told herself tremulously, she would turn round and run away into the shadows under the stairs. But she hadn't that sort of strength – she hadn't. She said aloud: 'David!' and he jerked round, his expression intent.

He said disbelievingly: 'Polly . . .'

'Yes.'

They stared into each other's eyes. The last time they had seen each other had also been on a station: Paris in February.

'David – oh, David!' She hurled herself towards him, all the barriers down as soon as she felt his arms closing round her. 'You're safe! I often wondered – oh, thank God for that!'

His rough cold cheek was pressed against hers. 'Oh, darling, I can't believe it! Where did you spring from?'

'Do you mind moving, sir?' A grinning porter was waiting to wheel the truck away. With arms round each other, they moved dazedly, coming to rest at last in the shadow of the stairs.

'I'm going home for Christmas.'

'Me too. I'm not out of the army yet. Your – your husband?'

'He's in Cambridge.' She forced herself to say the word. 'Incurable. He's incurable.'

'My God, how awful.' He held her close.

512

'He knows no one. He'll be like that until the day he dies.' Her voice caught in her throat. 'Except for the disc sewn into his skull, he looks the same but permanently asleep with his eyes open. Sometimes his arm waves about and he makes strange sounds. His mother thinks it's a sign he's waking up again, but it's simply a result of damage to the brain. A sort of child lives in his body, a helpless little child.'

David could find nothing to say, sensing the tragedy that was now her life. He could see how thin and worn she looked; even the redness of her hair had faded. Remembering the sparkling, happy girl in Paris he could only hold her mutely, helpless to take the burden off her shoulders. 'Do you mean to stay and look after him?' he asked at last. 'He could go on for years.'

'I must. His parents are old to be his parents and if they die, he'll have no one. He's been destroyed by this hideous war and I can't abandon him.'

In the midst of the noisy station filled with steam and screaming whistles they were both silent, deriving comfort from being close to each other again. He longed to take her across to the station hotel so that they could spend a night together; she needed warmth and love, he thought angrily. But he knew he couldn't ask it of her. It would only prolong the agony of the inevitable parting.

'Come on, our train's in.' He took her case with his own and led the way over the bridge. 'I only sent a telegram this morning so I hope they'll muster the petrol to meet me. We'll run you home first.'

They sat close, her hand in his, all the way to Whitby, talking in low tones of the future. He expected to be part of the occupying army in Germany after his leave; they were discharging married men first.

'Will you go back to the States afterwards?'

'No. I've decided to stay here and farm Northesk. M·

513

partner's been killed so the firm is wound up. My family are going as soon as they can get cabins.'

They were silent, both thinking that if things had been different, if she hadn't married Mike, they would have been planning their marriage now. How her mother would have enjoyed having a daughter settled near her! Northesk, that lovely house, needed a woman in it, a family of children. She looked out of the window, blinking tears away: someday he must marry someone and she must endure the sadness of seeing him with another woman, with his children playing on the lawns, with – with –

'Don't,' he whispered, squeezing her hand, knowing what she was thinking. He always knew what she was thinking.

At Whitby, he spotted Elliot's long red face looking for him but Polly could see no sign of Archie. It was dark and snow was falling, driven in from the sea in flurries.

'Look, darling, there's no point in hanging about waiting for Archie. We'll take you home. Take Mrs Wynne's luggage, Elliot.'

'Perhaps they didn't get my telegram,' she said, stepping thankfully into the Northesk motor, a huge Packard. 'On the other hand, Archie will flay me if he arrives to find I've gone.'

'You leave Archie to me. It would kill you to wait in this cold.' He was busy wrapping a fur rug round her. Under the rug he held her hand tightly all the way as they drove through darkness, the car lamps lighting up the snow-covered road before them. 'All well at home, Elliot?'

'Yes, sir. We only got your telegram an hour ago. The post office can't cope – there's that many telegraphing about coming home, the papers say.'

David turned to the girl beside him and slipped an arm round her slim body, drawing her close. With his lips

514

against her temples they sat in silence for the rest of the journey, each deeply moved by the closeness of each other. Then suddenly they were running over the narrow packhorse bridge and turning in at the rectory gates. Light was falling from the dining-room window on to the covering of snow on the lawn. Evidently the family was having supper quite unaware that the youngest member was arriving home; her telegram must have gone astray.

Jumping down she peeped in and saw them all: her father carving something at the sideboard, her mother sitting in the chair she hadn't occupied for years, Alix and Kit sitting together, Archie handing round the plates . . . they were all there except Dick and Imogen. The family was together again for the first time since 1914.

'Everyone's home except Imogen!' She turned a radiant face in David's direction. 'It's going to be a real Christmas!'

No longer caring that Elliot was an interested spectator, he took her in his arms. 'I'll be over tomorrow, darling. And every day until I go back!'

'But David – '

'No, Polly, I'm not going to listen to you,' he said against her ear. 'We love each other – how can we pretend otherwise?'

Elliot, grinning broadly, was tugging at the bell. A nice young lady. He'd always thought so. Lizzie said she was a widow. Well, there was widows *and* widows. He rather thought Mrs Wynne was the right sort.

Walter Wynne was settling his son for the night, chatting to him as if Mike understood. 'Shall I brush your hair? It won't be like Polly does it, I'm afraid. But I'll be careful of your wound – there! How's that? Now, sit up like a good chap. Polly's gone for a little holiday. She deserves one, doesn't she?'

Mike, propped against the pillows, stared straight ahead. His father stood looking down at him. It was no use pretending any more but there had been a definite deterioration lately as Reed had warned them. Walter sighed, putting the hairbrush back on the oak chest. Nothing seemed to reach the boy any more despite all they did to rouse him. He could go on for years, imprisoned in his young and healthy body. Just being nobody. A husk.

Shielding the lamp, he drew up a chair to the bed and took one of his son's hands in his and began to stroke it, humming a nursery tune as he did so. As a little chap, Mike had liked this sort of treatment and instinctively Walter had returned to it. His love for his son swelled in his breast until it hurt. What had it all been for? Oliver, even better-looking than Mike and good at every sort of game, killed in Gallipoli and Mike returned to them living but dead. All the striving to bring them up, all the loving – had it been wasted? He would never know.

He had pulled back the curtains and a white radiance from the outside filled the room where only one lamp glowed. He saw that the boy's eyes had closed at last. Walter looked long at the face on the pillow: so handsome, so untouched with one lock of fair hair flopping forward as always. 'Sleep now,' he said softly.

Releasing his son's hand he went across to a chair and picked up the big down cushion. It had roses embroidered on it, he saw. Unhurriedly he went across to the bed and pressed it down on the sleeping face. There was no struggle. The shallow rise and fall of Mike's chest rose and fell for the last time. He was dead.

Removing the cushion, Walter looked down at his son. *I gave you life and now I've released you from its torment. You'll be glad, I know.*

He replaced the cushion, looking round, leaving everything neat. He would come in to see the boy in the morning and then he would break it to Ruth.

It was better this way.

CHAPTER TWENTY-SEVEN
The Long Nightmare Is Over

So it was over.

Yes, the war was over but where were all one's friends? Great gaps had been blown into the fabric of society and a deep sense of loss bled like a wound that couldn't be staunched. People were tired, a deep weariness that would take a long time to lift. This war would remain like a dark stain on the inward spirit. Some would never shake free of the torpor that descended on them at the armistice. They had lost too much.

In Paris, this first summer after the war, the Peace Conference was about to close: Germany had at last signed the treaty of peace at Versailles. The Kaiser had gone for good and was now living in Holland, a broken old man whose dream of world domination had destroyed so many and so much. A war in Europe, everyone said, must never happen again . . .

Now every town and village in Britain was putting up memorials to their dead. In Eskton, it was a tall cairn of rocks and stones. Each stone and each rock had been borne to this spot by every man, woman and child in the village. Even Little Dick Paget had manfully carried his stone to the slowly rising cairn that was the village's memorial to their seven dead sons. It had been a game to him as the procession of people wound up the hill to the spot chosen on the moor above the little grey houses. Here two masons built the granite rocks into a moving memorial stone. Eight feet tall, its simple message read:

*To the Glory of God
and
In Grateful Memory of
the Men of Eskton who
Gave their lives in the Great War
1914–1918*

The name of Little Dick's father would be carved on that stone for all time but his child had never known him and Wilfred Filey, leading the procession with his mother, was the only father he knew. So he hopped and skipped with his stone and wondered a little at this new game everyone was playing.

It was a perfect June morning, promising to be a perfect day for a country wedding.

Polly, dressed and waiting to go across to the church, stood at her bedroom window watching the gay new hats of the women guests bobbing about under the green leaves of the trees. Throwing off war restrictions with their old clothes, people were dressing up again. She smiled to herself as she recognized Cass Byrne in pink from head to foot walking up to the church door with her father who was in a black top hat, carrying a large black umbrella. There was Doctor Mallory chatting to a group of young people – and Katy in her favourite corn colour taking Little Dick by the hand: he was very aware of his new white sailor suit.

She turned away, anticipation and happiness filtering through her veins. She was excited too at the new life opening before her, a life to be shared with David for – please God – the next forty or fifty years. How lucky she was to have found such love at last! She put her hands to her face and said: 'David . . . David . . .' like a prayer.

Walking across to the long mirror on the wall she looked at herself critically. Well, she'd filled out at la and her face was a healthy pink again. Or was it the peach-coloured rose under the brim of her hat that was reflecting on her skin? The cream dress of heavy silk had been made for her by a London dressmaker and had been Aunt Nora's present. The heavy rope of pearls round her neck had come from her new parents-in-law. Her father had given her the white leather prayer-book, her mother the gold brooch holding three peach-coloured roses in the lace of the wide bertha collar. She wore blue garters and had borrowed Katy's best petticoat. Well, she had everything a bride needed, she thought, even the return of her prodigal sister! For last night Imogen had come home; a thin, pale Imogen with secretive eyes whom perhaps they would never really know again. But she was home and the shadows had lifted from her parents' faces. Alix had been home for a week with Christine and the new baby, a boy called Timothy, and Kit had joined her two days ago. He was still walking with a stick and probably always would but he would be called to the Bar in a year or two and then he and Alix could look for a home of their own.

Tonight, she thought, I will be David's wife and we'll be going up to Scotland for a blissful fortnight together before he goes back to Germany to the army of occupation.

She sighed as she remembered this parting that lay ahead. She would be making her home at Northesk House from now on and when her parents-in-law returned to the States in the autumn she would have a lot to do. The convalescent hospital would be open until then but by November, David hoped to be home for good and they planned to reorganize the whole house. It was going to be fun. The smile faded suddenly. Would she ever get used to feeling happy and did she have to feel this sense of guilt? It was wrong. Not fair on David. Going across to her little desk she opened a drawer and withdrew a letter.

It was from Walter Wynne. 'Be happy, my dear child. You deserve to be. But I hope that my boy's memory will always occupy a small corner in your heart.'

Very deliberately she tore the letter into two or three pieces and threw them into the wastepaper basket. Mike. A long time ago. Another world almost. A tall, slim, fair boy with a tentative smile, a boy who was afraid and clung to her strength. She had mistaken pity for love then because she had been young and inexperienced. She hadn't even suspected at the tough, enduring quality of real love, the love she felt for David. Mike was her past. Her future with David beckoned brightly and she was going forward to meet it with a firm, sure step.

Where was Archie? It must be time to go across to the church. Through the open window she could hear the organ music drifting across the garden.

This time last year, she thought, Compiègne was being bombarded. I thought we all must be killed, that there was no future for us. For a brief moment, she smelled the peculiar smell of picric mingling with burnt flesh under the hot canvas of the marquees, could hear again the cries of 'Mes yeux! Mes yeux!' A shiver ran over her. Yes, it was over, but would they ever forget?

'Ready, madam?' Archie, wearing the frock coat that had been his father's, was standing in the doorway grinning cheerfully. 'I say, buck up, old girl! That's not the face of a bride!'

She stared at him and suddenly joy ran through her like a flame and she laughed aloud. 'Is it time to go?'

'Of course. The expectancy in church will be at bursting point.'

'Are you sure David's arrived? It would be frightful if in your hurry to marry me off you got me there before him!'

'Saw him arrive with my own eyes.' Archie was lead

521

her firmly downstairs. 'Under the best man's escort – a huge chap. No one could escape from *him*!'

'That's good,' Polly said placidly, refusing to rise to this. 'Better be sure than sorry,' she added quoting Mrs Linsey.

As they reached the hall the grandfather clock struck eleven-thirty. 'Perfect timing,' Archie pointed out.

A knot of well-wishers who hadn't been able to get in to the church were clustered at the porch.

'Good luck, Miss Polly! All t'best!' they whispered, urging her forward with beams of goodwill. One small child, thinking the time was ripe, began to toss confetti and got slapped for his pains by his over-excited mother. 'Give over, Jimmy!'

'Eh, she do look lovely!'

'Can't beat silk, can you?'

'Miss Polly! Grandad sent you this!' A girl burst through the little crowd. 'Herbert Lazenby, you know. He said to be sure to give Miss Polly his lucky penny and here it is, miss. Saved Grandad's life in Crimea it did.'

'Thank him very much, Mary – I'll come and see him when I get back. What would Father say?' she whispered to Archie. 'You know how he feels about *pagan luck*!' They went up the steps and suddenly her breath was caught in her throat and her heart began to hammer as a wave of warmth and a murmur of many voices reached her. People's heads were turning to stare at her and she felt sick at the thought of walking through them. All those people – half of them strangers – had come to see her married. Tightening her grip on Archie's arm she moved forward as the organ music swelled.

In the dimness of the church, she found it difficult to ee anything for a moment. Then a tall khaki–clad figure nding waiting for her turned and his eyes met hers.

There was a half-smile on his face and the mark of his wound folded in a laughter line.

They smiled at each other, forgetting the wedding guests, realizing at last that the long nightmare was over and their life together was about to begin.